THE CHANCE

By

DALE E. VAUGHN

Elias and the men of the 1st Kansas were ready, willing and very able to earn their freedom. All they wanted was the chance!

Island Mound • Sherwood • Cabin Creek
Honey Springs • Baxter Springs • Horsehead Creek
Roseville • Prairie D'Anne • Poison Springs
Jenkins Ferry • Flat Rock • Pryor Creek
1862-1865

Cover picture of unidentified Civil War soldier, believed to have served in a USCT regiment organized in Kentucky. *Courtesy Hasker Nelson, Jr., Cincinnati, Ohio.*

For information:
Dale E. Vaughn
3907 SE 30th Terr., Topeka, KS 66605-2107

nandale@networksplus.net

ISBN: 1-58597-243-6

Library of Congress Control Number: 2003116101

1. Historical novel — Kansas — Fiction
2. Kansas — Indian Territory — Arkansas
3. Civil War
4. Black Union Troops
5. Historical fact and fiction

A division of Squire Publishers, Inc.
4500 College Blvd.
Leawood, KS 66211
1/888/888/7696
www.leatherspublishing.com

Acknowledgments and Appreciation

I would like to express my appreciation to the many persons who have helped make this novel possible. The members of and many speakers at the Civil War Round Table of Eastern Kansas have given me the opportunity to feed my desire for knowledge and understanding of the most devastating period in our nation's history.

I would especially like to thank Tom Goodrich, author of *Bloody Dawn, War to the Knife* and other books covering the American Civil War period, and his wife, Deb, for their encouragement and support.

My good friend, Joe Poplin of Oklahoma, walked me over the battlefields of Cabin Creek and Pryor Creek, explaining the battles and circumstances the men of the 1st KCVI endured during their fight for freedom.

And a special thanks to my high school classmate, Sergeant Major Jack Elliott, for his prodding to get this book in print and to get started on Elias' search for his missing brother.

Many members of the Kansas Author's Club, Dist. #1, including Max Yoho, author of *The Revival,* and Sam Pierson, author of *She's Called Willie,* have given their advice and support to my writing efforts, for which I am very grateful.

Most surprising and appreciated was the great amount of assistance I received from the many museums, libraries, military forts and historical organizations I visited. As soon as I would explain my mission, I was immediately given access to files, maps, old newspapers and many delicate documents that provided facts and accounts of battles and attitudes of the people during this trying time.

Most of all, I want to thank my wife, Nancy, for her love, support and faith in me and my work.

Thank you all for helping to make this a very rewarding experience.

— *Dale E. Vaughn*

Chapter 1

April 1854, Virginia

"Elias, get up, right now!"

"Huh? Mama … wha…?"

"Hush! Get up and grab that bundle. Put your shoes on and get your father's shirt from back of the door. Do it now! And be quiet."

Nine-year-old Elias pushed back the thin muslin sheet and the hooked rug that served as a blanket. It was dark and he could barely make out his mother's shadow as she moved across the cabin. Even though it was dark outside, he could see she had on her broad-brimmed straw hat. Elias could tell it was the middle of the night because there was no light coming through the greased cloth that served as a cover for the one window in their small home.

Elias groped for his shoes and his pants. He slept in his long-tailed shirt because there was no heat and the cabin was cold. He dressed and pulled the bigger shirt from the peg on the door. As he bent over to pick up the bundle he had placed next to his cot the night before, he hit his knee on the edge of the bed frame and cried out.

"Hush, Boy!" his mother whispered. "You mustn't wake up the whole place. If anyone finds out we're leavin', we'll both be whipped."

"Leavin'?" thought Elias. "Where we goin?" He didn't dare voice his question. He had been told to be quiet and quiet he would be. His mother didn't give orders unless she was serious.

He crouched next to his mother as she opened the door and

looked out into the yard. It was a cool, dark-of-the-moon night, but being so familiar with their surroundings the pair had no trouble finding their way around to the back of their cabin and on to the side of the stable. After crawling under the fence, they made their way to the grove of trees that ran along the side of the small pond next to the closest cotton field. The unpicked cotton shown white even in the darkness and gave them direction away from the main house and slave shacks.

Quietly the mother and son crept along in the shadows and made their way toward the riverbank. Young Elias and his friends had been made to pick berries along the river, and the path was well known to both he and his mother. An early morning chill began to move over the fields, and Elias shivered as he followed his mother through the darkness along the riverbank.

After going about two miles Elias' mother turned to him. "We have to cross here now. You take off your shoes and don't you drop them or your bundle, you hear?"

Elias nodded. His shoes weren't much, they were too big and most worn out, but he would hate to lose them. He was sure he shouldn't speak for fear of being heard by someone. He hadn't been told that they were leaving, although in the past he heard both his father and mother discuss it when they thought he had gone to sleep. And he hadn't been told why his father wasn't with them. His father had been gone for several days now, but Elias figured they would meet up with him soon.

After wading knee deep in the dark cold water, Elias' mother led them through a small gully, up through a rail fence to another field. This was also white with cotton almost half way to the pike road. They followed the last row of unpicked cotton until they got to the trees that lined the road.

"We can follow the road for a couple of hours," Elias' mother whispered, "But as soon as it begins to get light we will have to find us someplace to hide."

"When do we meet up with Daddy?" asked Elias.

"You never mind about that now, you just be quiet and follow close behind me."

Elias shifted his bundle to his other shoulder and moved along in the shadows. He knew he must be quiet because he knew now *they were running away.* The thought made him tremble. He had heard the stories of other slaves that tried to run away and had been brought back. In fact, he never heard of any of them getting away. If anyone had made it, the overseer kept it to himself so no one else would think they had any chance at all to get to freedom.

"Freedom," Elias said under his breath.

"What's that, Boy?"

"Uh, nothin'," he whispered. Elias had heard the grownups talk about *"it,"* but he wasn't sure just what all *"it"* meant. They said that if they had *"it"* they wouldn't have to work any more in the fields. But if'n they didn't work in the fields, how would they live? How would they eat? As far as he knew, the whole world was made up of cotton and tobacco fields and a few places that grew horses. He just figured that it was his kind of folks that kept all that going. Who would do all the work if they just up and left? He was sure Massa John or even Jason the overseer wouldn't know how to do the work even if they were willing to do it.

It was hard work. And the worst part to Elias was that no one ever seemed to appreciate the fact that his mother and father were two of the best workers on the farm. When Elias did his best, his daddy would at least smile or pat him on his shoulder. He heard the overseer say that the slaves should be glad to get fed and given a place to sleep, but Elias thought there should be more than that. He was proud of the way his father worked and how he would be at the end of his cotton row well ahead of every other picker, with Elias' mother right behind him. They set the pace for the rest of the workers and were sometimes criticized by other slaves for working so fast. You could look back at their row and see practically no fluffs of white left on the brown stalks. He missed his father and could hardly wait until they met up with him.

Chapter 2

As the eastern sky began to show a gray haze, Elias' mother led them away from the road and toward a line of small hills. Trees covered the edge of a steep rise and gave way to an outcropping of rock. A large deadfall almost hid the opening of a cave that lay on the north side of a brush-covered knoll. Elias' mother led him into the darkness and pushed back about ten feet to the back wall. She had been told of this cave as one that had been used in the past by other slaves making a break for freedom.

Inside the mouth of the cave there was a bundle of sticks, branches and dead bushes. "You push this here stuff into the opening so no one can see in," Elias' mother told him.

"This where we gonna meet Daddy?" asked the boy when he finished. "How's he gonna find us with us all hid like this?"

"Come here, Elias," said his mother. Elias had a notion that he was about to hear something he wasn't going to like. His mother always used that tone of voice and called him by name when there was something serious she was about to tell him.

"We aren't going to be meeting your father … at least not right now."

"He's comin' later? He *is* comin' later, isn't he, Mama? We can't just go off and leave …"

"We aren't going off and leaving him, Elias. He just can't come with us right now. But he wants us to go ahead and try hard to be safe and get to freedom."

There was that word again. He wished he understood it more, but it had to be very important for so many of their friends to talk about it the way they did and risk the trouble and beatings he had seen and heard about.

"We runnin' away? That what we doin', Mama?"

"Yes, Elias, that's what we're doing. We're heading for freedom. We're going north. If we can get up around Wheeling, we may be able to find some of the folks that can get us out of the slave country."

Elias could just barely see his mother's face in the dim light in the cave. She was serious and he could see that determined look that told him their effort was necessary and the goal was well worth whatever it might cost them.

"Yes, Mama, I'll do whatever you say."

Elias' mother felt now was not the time to tell him he probably would never see his father again. Her husband had been sold three days ago. She had no idea where he had been taken or if he would ever have a chance to find them in the future. She knew if it were humanly possible, given the chance, he would search until he found his family. She knew he would always wonder if the child she was carrying was another son or the daughter he knew she wanted. In fact, it would soon be her time. Her pregnancy made it doubly hard for her to travel, but it also gave her more incentive to make it to freedom so her new child would not be born a slave.

Elias and his mother spent the day sleeping and staying toward the rear of the cave. They ate a small amount of the cornbread and a few bites of salt pork they had packed away. They had little food to get by on and must make it last as long as possible. Traveling at night would make it hard to find berries or nuts, so their only hope was that at dawn or dusk they could find a few eggs to steal from someone's hen house or maybe locate a fruit tree or a garden along the way.

After walking what seemed like weeks to Elias, he and his mother began to cross the Alleghenny Mountains just south of Staunton. Traveling by night and hiding by day, they proceeded north until reaching the Staunton Turnpike. Keeping back in the trees and still trying to keep the pike in sight, the pair moved through the darkness over the Allegheny Mountain Pass and across the Greenbrier River, hoping to follow the road to Huttonsville.

Elias' mother had been told of a route north and memorized the names of places they must reach. One of the slaves that drove a supply wagon to town was told that help just might be found up around Wheeling. It had been whispered that folks on the west side of the mountains weren't all that in favor of slavery and either never heard of nor cared about the fugitive slave law. She could only hope to find help soon for her condition was making it more difficult each day to travel very far. She had no idea it would be so hard to try to keep sight of the big dipper at night through all the trees. Finally finding the pike had been a big help, so now she could concentrate on making more distance. Each morning they would keep moving just a little longer the farther north they got.

It had been hard to find food, and a couple of times Elias managed to feed them by catching several fish. Neither had ever eaten raw fish before, but since they had no way to make a fire and wouldn't dare anyway, they made do with what they had.

Very early one morning as they neared the Cheat River, Elias' mother suddenly grabbed his shoulder and shoved him toward a large fallen tree. She placed her finger to her lips and motioned for Elias to lie down. Placing her bundle of belongings next to the tree trunk, she moved toward a clump of bushes and then across a small draw. She had smelled smoke before and now could faintly hear voices. As she straightened up just enough to see, she made out several horses that were cross-hobbled in a small clearing about twenty yards ahead.

"I tell ya, they is money to be made and we're just about to get right in the middle of it."

She could understand the words now, and she could smell coffee cooking.

"Yeah, I been hearin' that for days now and I'm just as pocket poor as I was when I started out."

"I believe Toady is right. Why I heard of a fella that came back with over four hunert dollars just for catching two bucks and it on'y took 'im six days."

"Did jew see that there money or jes hear about it? We been gone more'n six days and all I got is lots of talk and a sore butt."

Elias' mother pulled back down into the gully and made her way back to where Elias was crouched in the shadows.

"There are four men up ahead and I'm sure they are slave hunters. We must hide right now and be very…uh…uh…." Elias' mother dropped to her knees and doubled over. Elias started to cry out but caught himself just as his mother looked up at him and shook her head.

"It's all right. I just got a pain for a minute. Get your things. We have to move back the way we came for a ways and hide until night time."

The following night Elias and his mother turned north and followed the Cheat River for several miles. The next few days they made their way past Beverly and a couple of miles past Corricks Ford.

It was still dark when Elias' mother stopped to rest. Laying her bundle down in the leaves, she moved to a slab of rock that protruded from the forest floor at an angle. She rested her back against the rock and tried to pull her knees up next to her stomach.

"We stoppin' so soon, Mama?" asked Elias. "It won't be light for another hour or so."

"I know, Son. Mama's going to have to rest for awhile. I'm not sure I can go on right now." Her voice had a slight tremble, and she kept looking toward the sky, clamping her lips tightly together. Elias could hear her moaning ever so softly and saw her hands digging into the earth, grasping hands full of leaves.

"Elias, you have to find us a place to spend the daytime. You're going to have to do it alone and do it now."

"Mama, you all right? Can I …?"

"Just find us a place, son. And hurry, but you must be quiet."

Elias moved off up the river bank into the waning darkness.

Soon he returned and knelt next to his mother.

"I found just the place, Mama, and it isn't far. It's a cave and it's pretty good size near as I can tell. The mouth of the cave faces toward where the morning sun will come in just as soon as it clears the mountain."

Elias helped his mother to her feet, picked up both bundles and led their way through the trees and into the cave he had found. The cave was rather narrow at the mouth but widened as they went further inside. The roof was about as tall as a large man, and it was evident that bats had lived there at one time.

Elias' mother lay down toward the rear of the cave and asked Elias to bring her some water. They managed to keep from breaking a small fruit jar they brought along so Elias filled it with water and took it to his mother. He found a spot in the river where the water was fast running over some rocks and was only about six inches deep next to the bank. "I bet I can get us a fish down there, Mother."

Elias' mother smiled at the boy and then seemed to double up and grit her teeth.

"Mama?"

"It's all right, Elias. I think … I think it's time. You must stay close now and ... uh … do just as … uhhhhhh … just as Mama says."

Chapter 3

"I tell ya I know'd what I heard. They's somebody down there. If'n that warn't a giggle, then I ain't a foot high." Vern Wallace, the sixteen-year-old adopted son of Tom Wallace, grabbed his younger brother by the shoulder and pointed toward the riverbank. "Whoever it is, is down there next to them willa's."

As the two boys crept around a large rock near the banks of the Cheat River, they could see Elias tying a fish to a cord that also held a smaller fish. The black boy was gathering in his fishing line and winding it around his open left hand. Elias looked up for a second, but then returned his attention to his catch and proceeded up the bank toward the cave where his mother and new brother lay.

"You sure?" asked Tom Wallace as he took Vern by both shoulders. ""'Just who did you see?"

"How'm I supposed to know? We jes saw'm. I was gonna catch that nigger boy, but George here said we better jes git back here and tell you. I could a' handled it but George said …"

"George, you did right. You better let me look into this. I think I know what is going on," said Mr. Wallace.

Vern pulled away and looked at George with a hateful stare. Vern felt he had never been given the credit for being so much smarter than Mr. Wallace's two natural sons. Vern was convinced that he might even be smarter than Mr. Wallace for that matter. Vern had gotten along on his own for two years after his father left his mother. About the same time the Jenson girl ran off, it was. Seems odd how those two disappeared within a couple of days of each other and neither one had been seen since. Anyhow,

Vern knew how to take care of himself, but the county sheriff decided he needed a guardian, and the Wallaces took Vern in.

"George," said Tom Wallace, "you go on to the house with Vern and I'll look into this matter."

"Ain't you gonna need me to show ya just where them niggers is at?" questioned Vern.

"I know the spot you were talking about. You go on and tell your mother. I'll be back in a little while."

"She ain't really *my* mother," Vern said under his breath. George looked over at him, and Vern wondered if his remark had been heard. The two boys headed for the house while Tom Wallace started across the garden making his way toward the river.

"Oh, Tom," Mrs. Wallace cried as she held the kitchen door open for her husband. She had been told of her son's sighting of a young colored boy, but had no idea there was most of a family hidden down by the river.

Mr. Wallace was carrying Elias' mother, with Elias following close behind, his new brother in his arms. The baby was wrapped in Elias' father's shirt and had been diapered with a section of his mother's petticoat.

"Put them in the boys' room, Tom. I'll look after them in there."

Tom Wallace pushed through the curtain that hung in the entrance to the bedroom shared by his own two boys. He gently laid Elias' mother on the only bed and pulled the quilt up around her shoulders. She had not spoken a word since she awakened in Mr. Wallace's arms. Her dark eyes looked around for her two sons and showed a mild look of relief when she saw Elias holding the baby.

"You put the child there next to your mother, Boy, and come back into the kitchen." Mr. Wallace spoke softly to Elias and motioned him toward the bed. "We'll see if we can find something besides raw fish for tonight's supper."

Elias placed his brother next to his mother and turned to see

Mr. Wallace holding the curtain back, nodding for Elias to go into the kitchen. “They’ll be just fine. Mrs. Wallace will tend to them. You just sit down there at the table and maybe you can get down a cup of Ma’s vegetable soup. It will be a couple of hours until dinner, but maybe that will hold you ’til then.”

March 1855, Virginia

“They’ll be going with us,” stated Tom Wallace to his wife.

“I know, Tom. I had no doubt, ever. They are good folks and it’s our job help them get away.”

Susan Wallace pulled at the apron that covered the front of her dress as she and her husband sat at the kitchen table. They didn’t usually stay up near this late, but they both felt like talking. The rest of the family had gone to bed. The boys were back in their room along with Vern. Vern had been asked to give up the loft to Elias, his mother and little Cheat. The new baby had been named for the river that had brought them to the Wallaces’ farm. It was a special name for a special baby. The way the baby smiled all the time, it was as if he knew he had already made it to freedom.

“Have you said anything to the boys?” asked Mrs. Wallace.

“Not a word to the boys or to anyone. The only one that knows is Jeff Lauder at the bank. He said he would do his best to sell the place and send us whatever it brings as soon as we get settled in Kansas.”

Susan Wallace looked around the home that she had known for the last sixteen years. It hadn’t been much when Tom first moved them in. It had been abandoned and stood empty for several years. The land wasn’t too good, but with hard work on both their parts the house and the farm had been transformed into a home. Tom knew it wouldn’t bring much when sold, but he had dreamed of a real farm for a long time, and they decided together that now was the time to head for the free and fertile land of the Kansas Territory.

Chapter 4

August, 1862   Lawrence, Kansas

"No Sir," Elias said with his hat in his hand. He hated it when he felt he must behave this way. He was more of a man than Vern Wallace would ever be. He could out-work, even out-think this man eight days a week. "All I want is a chance," Elias replied as he bent his knees ever so slightly and glanced toward the ground.

"So, 'alls you wants is a chance,' huh?"

"I said *all* I want is a chance." Elias straightened to his full height. He didn't care if he appeared insolent. He was going to make his point even if it meant that he would suffer the wrath of Vern or even Vern's father, Mr. Wallace.

Tom Wallace brought Elias' family with him when he left northern Virginia in 1855, but Elias never felt that they really "belonged" to Mr. Wallace. Most people in the area assumed that Elias, his mother, and his brother Cheat had been the property of the Wallace family since being found on their farm in 1854. It was never mentioned or clarified by the Wallaces. It was no one's business.

"You'll *gets* your chance to find yourself out in the field so far you won't be heard from for weeks if'n you don't show more respect for your betters," snarled Vern.

"Mr. Vern." Vern Wallace insisted that the blacks and even the white hired hand call him *Mister*. "Sir, my family has felt this was their home ever since your daddy brought us here. We have been treated well and have been taken care of. It is only right that we repay your parents for what they have done for us."

Vern sneered at Elias and twisted his kerchief in his hand as he looked past the young, well-built black man and toward the farmhouse. He hoped his foster father was watching him through the large window in the living room of their home here in Douglas County, Kansas. He wanted so for Mr. Wallace to think of him as capable of handling the work of the farm. Vern felt he had never been given credit for being able to do anything of any importance.

"You'll *gets* back to tendin' to the stock and then working the garden. And if'n I hear any more talk of you wantin' to join up anything besides the rest of the darkies in the fields, I'll talk to Pa about sendin' you over to Missouri with the cattle. That way you won't have to worry about what's gonna happen to *your home* here in Kansas."

Vern wrapped the kerchief around his neck, tied it in a knot and with a yellow toothy grin, turned and headed toward the house. If Dad had witnessed this encounter between his adopted son and the nigger hand, Vern wanted to be sure Dad knew just what it was about and how Vern had put the issue to rest.

"Ain't no nigger gonna tell me what he's a gonna do." Vern wasn't sure how to handle the feelings he had experienced since his conversation with Elias. "The idea," Vern said out loud as he slowly walked toward the house. "That nigger thinks he should be allowed to volunteer for the Union Army. Hell, even I'm smarter than to want to go get my fool head shot at or shot off." Vern smiled and then shook his head. "No wonder them niggers is so damn dumb."

Some of Vern's acquaintances had volunteered for the army and gone up to Fort Leavenworth to join. Vern said that he wanted to enlist along with the two Wallace boys but was needed by their father to help run the farm and produce goods for the army.

James Lane, Senator from Kansas, and a friend, or at least an acquaintance of President Lincoln's, had assumed a commission in the western Union Army even though it was illegal to hold both offices. Lane had been very vocal about recruiting troops and made up his mind to form a black regiment from

Kansas. He wired Secretary of War Stanton of his intentions, asking for approval and confirmation. When it wasn't immediately forthcoming *General* Lane assumed approval and issued a proclamation asking for the voluntary enlistment of all available young colored men.

"My gawd," Vern said out loud, "them niggers wouldn't know which end of a gun to point and which way to run when the gunnin' started." Vern laughed out loud at his reasoning and was convinced he was so much smarter than the folks around which he had to live. He was probably even smarter than his adopted father. At least he would know better than to leave the runnin' of his property to a bunch of niggers and a dumb white farm hand. He wondered why he had been brought into such a feeble-minded family. Why, he could have been adopted by one of the smarter and richer families of Virginia just as easily as this bunch.

"Vern, what was that all about? I saw you and Elias out there. You didn't cause any trouble, did you? Elias is one of the best workers we have, black or white, and I'll not have you getting our help upset. We are short-handed enough what with your brothers gone. It looks like we are going to have a decent year after all the bad weather we've had and I can't run the risk of any worker trouble."

"That's just what I was tellin that Elias out there, Dad. He wants to run off and leave us short-handed, and I told him that I wouldn't allow it. Don't worry, I put a stop to it. It's all taken care of." Vern tried to make it sound like he solved a major problem and that his father had been spared difficulty and trouble with the hands.

"What do you mean, he wanted to run off? Elias wouldn't do such a thing. Why, he and his mother have been our most loyal workers ever since we got to Kansas Territory. And if he was going to run off, why would he have said anything to you about it? That doesn't make sense."

Vern knew he was in trouble and he might not be able to

think fast enough to make his point seem like the most logical.

"Well, Dad," Vern swallowed and pulled up at his belt, "that Elias said he wanted to leave here and he pretended that he wanted to join the army. He knew I had been on to his conivin' to run off and he wanted it to appear that if'n he was suspected of anything he could use the joinin' of the army as an excuse."

"I don't understand. Why would he want to leave? He knows he is safe here and that his mother and brother are cared for. Besides, he's the best worker left on the farm now that the boys are gone and I'd hate to loose him."

"The best?" whined Vern. "What about me? I work just as hard as any one does."

Without comment Mr. Wallace kept looking in the direction he had last seen Elias.

"Dad, you don't know how them niggers think. I tried to tell ya that them folks don't reason like we do. They can't figure much past their next meal. Elias hears all this talk about his people bein' free and about that Underground Railroad business, and he thinks that since he is here he is better'n us and can do as he pleases."

"Vern, I'm afraid you are the one that doesn't understand. Elias and his mother have always been devoted to our family ever since we found them on the river in Virginia. They are as much a part of us as if they were related. Like the Bible says, when we came here *"we were strangers in a strange land,"* and they helped make this our home as much as any of us did.

"Are you sure you want to do this, Son?" asked Elias' mother. "You know they've never had any of our people in the army before."

"Yes, I'm sure, Mama. Why, down south around LeRoy, the Indians organized the First Indian Home Guard last May, and I was told that there are even some colored boys that joined up with them. Word is that a few of the Indians around here are going to try to get into Lane's regiment, too. You do understand, don't you, Mama?"

With a pause, then a smile, Elias' mother took her son's hand and pulled him to her. "You make me proud, Son. We have so much to be thankful for, I am pleased you want to give back as best you can. There is no better way to appreciate freedom than to be willing to fight for it."

"I just hope they keep us close around here, though," said Elias with a worried tone to his voice. "That Quantrill fella raided into Lyon County last June and wrecked both *'The Monitor'* and *'The Herald'* newspapers and killed several people. I'm afraid he'll try something here in Lawrence and I don't want to be too far away to help.

"Mama, you risked everything just to get us here, so it's the least I can do to keep us here. We have the best home we have ever had, and maybe someday, after I get back, we can have our own place. I can build us our own cabin with an extra room just for you, Mama; a place with a water pump inside the house and a fireplace and windows and a garden for flowers as well as vegetables. And … and a porch where you can sit and watch the sunset." Elias' eyes sparkled as he pleaded with his mother.

No one noticed little Cheat as he stood watching his brother. His hands went from his front to his back and then to the top of his head. He squirmed and kicked his foot at the dirt. A worried look on his face began to erase the almost perpetual smile and his forehead began to crease. Cheat turned away and then turned back to face his brother. His frown increased as a tear crept away from the corner of one eye. "What about me … a … us? What we suppose'n to do?" There was a slight crack in the small, firm voice. He threw an imaginary rock at the ground and stuffed his hands inside his shirt. He tried to hide the hurt on his face with an even deeper frown.

"I thought you would be proud, too, Cheat. I'm going for you, too, you know."

"It ain't right, you runnin' off. We got work to do here," then added, "you an' me."

"I know how much work there is to do, and I'm counting on you to see it gets done. You'll have to work and look after Mama, but I know you can do it."

"Whose gonna be lookin' after you, Elias? Mama knows how to look after herself, but who's gonna be lookin' after you if'n you're off by yourself?" Cheat's voice began to rise. "You never know who's gonna sneak up after you and you can't be a watchin' ever where. Supposin' that … and if'n you can't see … how you gonna know …?" Cheat stood with the frown twisting at his brown face. His eyes wet with tears. "You just can't … it ain't right." Cheat turned and raced across the yard to the barn. "It ain't right," his voice came loudly through the scarlet and orange glow of the sunset.

Chapter 5

September 1862   Lawrence, KS

"Okay, Boy, I need a name." The private seated at the enlistment table glowered up at Elias. "Ya gotta have a name, what do they call you besides *Ilisha?"*

"It's not Elisha, its Elias."

"Okay, how do ya spell it? Can ya spell it?"

Elias pulled the paper from under the hand of the soldier, picked up a stub of a pencil and clearly printed out his name, shoving the paper back to the man and laying the pencil down slowly and deliberately. Straightening to his full height, he looked the soldier steadily in the eye.

"Fine, so ya can print your name. I still need to know what your last name is. Ya got one? Hell, everyone's gotta have a last name. Even you nig … you fellas." The private did not look up at Elias. He knew they had all been told they were never to use the word *nigger* or *Boy.* These men were to be called *men,* and later *soldiers.*

"Well, Sir," said Elias slowly, "I, well I …"

"You see how many *men,"* the private said, emphasizing the word, "I've got to get signed up here? I can't spend all day with just you. I need a last name of some kind. Who did you belong to? Don't you people take the name of who owned ya?"

"I'm my mother's! That's who owns me. I never …"

"Private, what's the hold-up? Can't you get these men processed any faster?"

A sergeant standing close to the sign-up table frowned down at the private. "Get these men moving!"

"But, Sergeant, I gotta have a last name from this fella and he don't seem to know what it is. What am I supposed to do?"

"What do you mean, he doesn't know his last name? Didn't I just hear him say he belonged to someone named Mothers? My gawd, private, write it down, let him make his mark and get on with it." The sergeant turned back to the other soldier to whom he had been talking and started to move away.

"All right then, that's it," said the private with exasperation, "Elias Mothers. Just finish puttin' your name down there and move along. You heard the Sergeant."

Elias stood looking at the paper upon which he had printed his name and then slowly began to print the name *Mothers.* "Elias Mothers," he thought to himself. His name was Elias Mothers. He had never had a real last name. He had always just been called Elias. His mother had refused to use the last name of the man who had owned them. It was a quiet defiance his mother had, and that was one of the ways she exhibited it.

As Elias moved away from the table and over to the group of men that had completed signing in, he wondered, "Does this mean that Cheat's name now is Cheat Mothers?" He had never heard that word being used for a last name, but that didn't matter. It was his now and his brother's, too. And it was different. They wouldn't be just ordinary black men that ran away from their past. They wouldn't be tagged by the name of someone that caused them fear and pain and caused his mother to run for her life and freedom for her son and her unborn child.

Elias had walked into Lawrence on a Tuesday morning, mid-August of 1862. He had been told Captain Henry C. Seaman was in charge of recruiting south of the Kansas River. Captain Seaman was in Lawrence talking with the colored men, explaining what General Lane was offering in the way of opportunities for the black man to serve what was becoming the Negro's country as well as the Indians and the whites.

"He told us we had an opportunity to show the entire country that we were real citizens," Elias told his mother later that evening. "We're no longer going to be just property, Mama."

Elias stood in the middle of their cabin and moved his arms in the air like a preacher. "We are men, Mama. We are real people, Captain Seaman said, and we are being given the chance to prove it. Mama, it's like you said, we could show everybody that we are able to do what we have to to earn our freedom. He told us that most of the white soldiers didn't realize that we were willing to fight hard for what they took for granted. When we fight, Mama, it's cause we need to and are willing to. They said I was to come back in two weeks with whatever I could bring with me."

Elias' mother rose from her chair and stood next to her son, looking up into his eyes. "I don't know when I have been so proud, Elias." Her eyes filled with tears as she held her son's face in her hands.

"Mama, don't ..."

"I'm happy, Son, not sad or worried. I know my son. I know what kind of a soldier you will be. When you come back to Cheat and me, we will be so happy and pleased. You will make it possible for us to be just like other folks. You will have helped earn our place here in free Kansas and we will be able to be as much a part of this country as the Wallaces or anyone."

Elias grinned at his mother as tears ran down both their cheeks.

Little Cheat stood watching his mother and brother. He knew he should be as happy as they seemed to be, but he couldn't help feeling that he was about to be cast into a situation he couldn't understand. He was losing his brother, and somehow he felt he should do something about it. His young mind didn't know just how he was to react, but there was something he had to do!

What?

Chapter 6

Captain James M. Williams moved across the much trodden field at the temporary camp of the newly recruited First Kansas Volunteer Colored Infantry of the Union Army of the United States. The camp of the Northern District, "Camp Jim Lane," had been laid out in the vicinity of Fort Leavenworth, Kansas. Situated just across the Missouri River from those of mostly Confederate bent, the camp consisted of over five hundred men being readied for duty by constant drilling and instruction in discipline. Supplies had been requisitioned from the Quartermaster, Ordinance and the Commissary departments. Senator James Lane, sometimes referred to as the "Grim Chieftain," had again telegraphed the Secretary of War that he would soon have enough black soldiers for two regiments. Now officially a General, Lane was anxious to resume his raids into western Missouri. In the fall of 1861 he had raided Bates County and on into St. Claire County, culminating in the total destruction of Oceola. In December of that year he and his "Kansans" had fired the towns of Butler and Papinsville, supposedly in retaliation for raids led into Linn County Kansas by Missourian John Clem, the Sheriff of Bates County. Time was 'a-wastin'. Lane wanted to move!

"Hey, fella, where ya'll from?"

"Name's Elias; I'm from just west of Lawrence. We live on the Wallaces' farm," replied Elias.

"Jes how'd you git there?"

"Mr. Wallace brought us along with his family from Virginia."

"Oh, you belonged to them folks? How's come they brung you instead of sellin' you off fo' the money?"

"We didn't belong to them. They helped us when me and my mama ran away from our place in southern Virginia. They took us in right after my brother was born, and we stayed until they decided to come to Kansas. Then we all came together."

"Yeah, I'm sho tha's right. The, jes brung you along 'cause they is neighborly."

"An' cause you is so purty," laughed a lanky black man sporting a small beard in the center of his chin. This remark brought a roar of laughter from all those lying around the campfire.

"Jes how long did your daddy have to sign on to Mr. Wallace fer?"

"No one signed on for anything. And my daddy didn't come with us. He was sold a few days before we left," replied Elias in a low voice. He looked down at his last scrap of biscuit and crushed it in his hand.

"You mean them folks jes brung you and you didn't have to pay 'em or work it off?"

"Oh, we worked all right. And my mother and little brother Cheat are still at home working, but not because they are made to. We are all grateful for what the Wallaces have done for us, and we try to repay as best we can. They gave us a room for our own for awhile, and then we built a room onto the barn. Now we are away from the house and can be by ourselves at night. I worked in the fields along with the Wallace boys and even get a dollar or two, when the crops grow good. We share in the garden and my mother raises chickens to share with the Wallaces and to sell in town."

"You got all that, how's come you here?" asked the bearded man. "Mosten' of us are here so's we can eat better."

"Yeah, and so's you can git yo butt shot off, the way you moves." Tom pointed at the man and laid back on the ground laughing. "Dat's why we calls you 'Slows' on a'count a how you moves."

"Dat's all right, I ain't so slow that I don't eat jes as good as you big man," replied Slows.

"But, Elias," said a young boy named Matthew, "why didn't you stay home and work for your own place like you said? That makes more sense to me."

Elias didn't reply. He didn't want to sound like a goody-goody, and he wasn't sure the others would understand.

"Ya'll didn't git in a scrape and have t' leave now, didja, 'Lias?" asked Matthew.

"No, it wasn't like that, although I didn't get along too good with one of the Wallace boys," said Elias, trying to change the subject. "He got kind of pushy and had an ornery streak. It's just as well I'm here. I can't bear to think what would happen to you brush hounds if I wasn't here to save your hides from the bad southeys."

"Don't seem right. Hell, you can even read 'n write I heard tell."

"I know he kin. I seed it for a fact. He read us some from a newspaper tuther day. An' I's there and heard it," testified Slows.

"How'd jew know what that there paper said? He could'a tol' you anything and you would'a jes nodded yo wooly head like you was agree'n with all of it," chided Tom.

"How'd jew learn, 'Lias?" asked Matthew.

"My mother could read," Elias replied. "She learned in church. We had a couple of Bibles hidden and folks would look up verses that they knew by heart and figure out the letters and words like that. Then she would scratch out letters in the dirt behind our shack and teach them to me. Mother and some of the others could have been whipped or sold if the overseer or master had found out. After we got to Kansas, we didn't have to hide it anymore. The Wallaces even helped Mother and gave us books to practice on. Little Cheat will go to school soon, we hope." Elias looked off into the deepening shadows. "That little guy, he'll be the smart one when he gets big, you can bet on that."

"Dat's all right, but I still think it's wrong that we don' git us pay like them white boys do. My shot-off butt is a gonna bleed jes like theirs will," complained Slows.

"Thought you was here just for the food," said Matthew with a grin. Matthew looked around at the rest of the men but found that he was about the only one smiling.

"No, it ain't right," came a low voice from back in the darkness, "but it all takes time. It took time for me to heal, but I can still see." As the man leaned forward, the others could see a long scar running across the man's face. The ex-slave explained that while being whipped, the lash had made a bad cut across his face and over his eyes. When it healed, it left the scar and made his eyes, especially the left one, look slanted like that of an Oriental. After that he had been known as "China Bill." "It took time to get here from Kentucky," he continued, "but I made it, and it's gonna take time to work up to the pay and the rank, but it's a comin'. Elias is right for doin' whut he is and so are we."

"Yeah, like 'Lias says, this here is our chance and we gonna make the most of it," put in Tom. "Now, ya'll go on to bed. I'm tired of hearin' you flap your mouths about not doin' better when ya'll had nuthin' but worse up till now."

"I hate to hear about you having trouble, Henry." Captain Williams strode to the window in his office, re-lit his cigar and rubbed the small of his back with his right hand. "It has already happened here on several occasions, but I was in hopes … oh, well. It's bound to happen. We're going to have to face it probably every place we go with these troops."

"I didn't come here to bring you a lot of headaches, Jim." Captain Seaman sat in a wooden rocking chair across from Williams' battered desk. "I know it's harder here due to your proximity to the pro-slavers just across the river."

"Across the river, hell," shot back Williams. "I've had to send men into Leavenworth to get some of our recruits out of the local jail. They have been accused of everything from accosting white women to stealing beer from saloon wagons. And it's all a bunch of bull. The only men that have been allowed to go to town are those with exemplary records. Several of them I know personally." The Captain sat in his chair and slumped over his desk. "Oh, I know we have a few of our black men that have gotten too big for their Union britches, but we spot them right off and don't dare let them near any of the townspeople."

"It's that same with us," replied Seaman. "We even had some of our own white soldiers try to keep the black recruits from drinking from our spring."

"How did you solve that?"

"Simple. I just put a guard around it and wouldn't let anyone get to it, black or white, until those boys got their heads straightened out. I'm afraid many of our white soldiers don't have much faith in the fighting ability of the coloreds."

"Dammit, Henry, I'm as convinced as General Lane that these men are every bit as good as most any we can put in the field, and I hope I have a chance soon to prove it. We even have a few half-breeds and a full-blood Cherokee. And I'll bet my life they will never let us down!"

"That's exactly what you're doing, Jim, and so are the rest of us. We're betting our lives on this venture of the Generals', and I hope to hell he's right."

"He is, Henry, and so are we by getting them ready as best we can. You'll see." Captain Williams reached into his desk drawer and took out several sheets of paper. "This is what I asked you here for," he said, handing the papers to Captain Seaman. "These orders direct Colonel Adams to take the 12th Kansas Regiment to Paola, and you and I are taking the 1st Kansas Colored to Fort Lincoln."

"You don't mean it. That's great, Jim, things are beginning to really warm up down there. General Blunt has had to move on toward Arkansas and the Cherokee Nation, and that has stretched our troops pretty thin along the Missouri border."

"Yep, we will have two companies at Barnesville and one at

Fish Creek. That should hold the area just fine with us at Fort Lincoln. I plan to continue to train the men there, and we have been assigned to help guard the Bushswhackers and Confederate prisoners. Our troops will get their first job of soldiering real soon."

Captain Williams had no idea how right his words were.

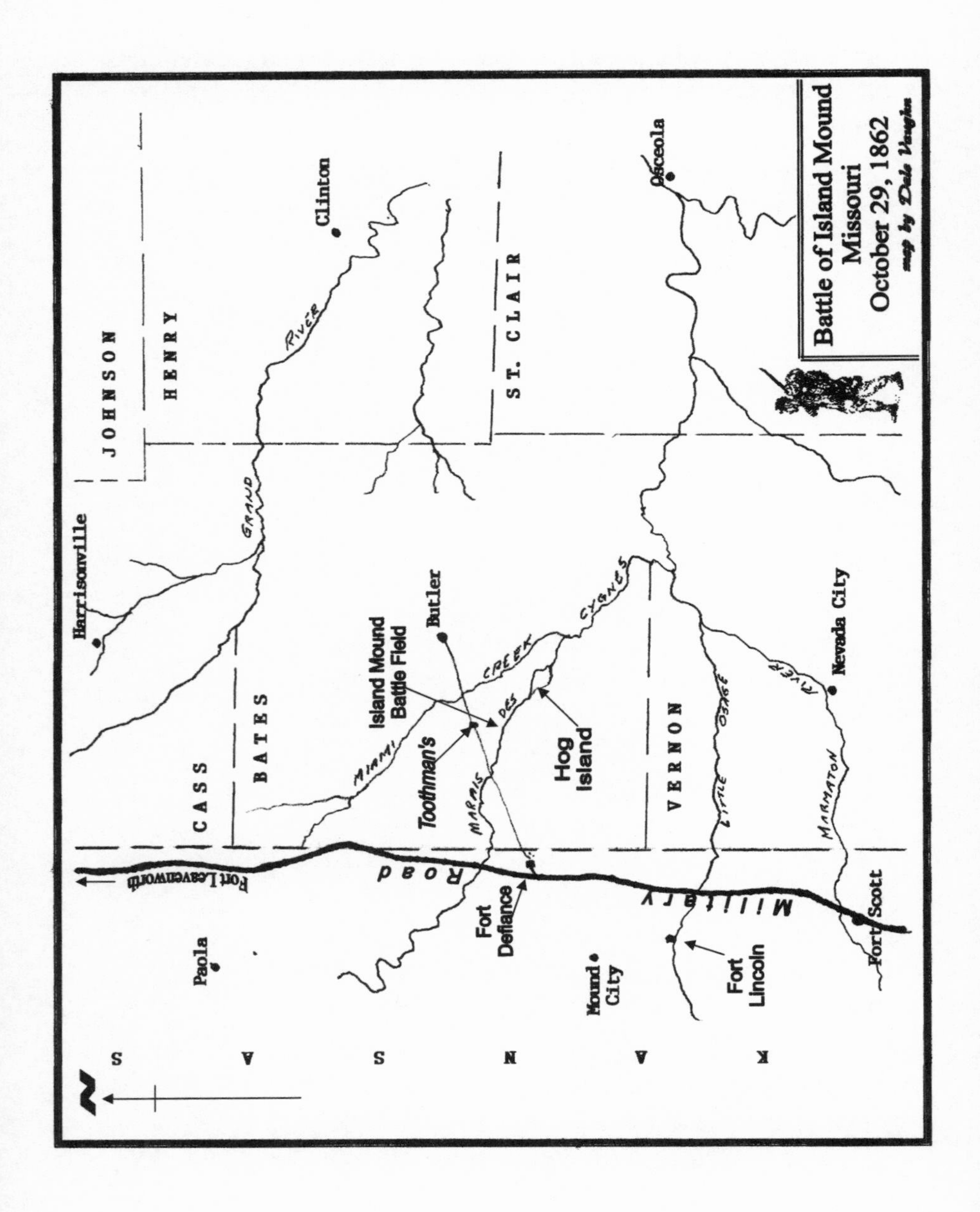

Battle of Island Mound
Missouri
October 29, 1862
map by Dale Vaughn
JOHNSON
HENRY
ST. CLAIR
CASS
BATES
VERNON
KANSAS
Clinton
Osceola
Harrisonville
GRAND RIVER
Butler
Island Mound Battle Field
Toothman's
Hog Island
MIAMI CREEK
MARAIS DES CYGNES
LITTLE OSAGE
MARMATON RIVER
Nevada City
Fort Leavenworth
Military Road
Fort Defiance
Paola
Mound City
Fort Lincoln
Fort Scott

Chapter 7

Sunday, October 26, 1862   Fort Lincoln, KS

Elias crawled from his tent early Sunday morning just in time to see and hear Corporal Elliott Johnson, of Co. A, yell at the bugler to get his horn and blow "assembly."

"What's up, Corporal?"

"Looks like we are about to get our chance for some real soldiering, Elias. Major Henning has ordered Captain Seaman to take part of us over into Missouri to clean up a bunch of Bushwhackers. You'll hear about it at assembly."

"Hot damn, we finally gets our chance," yelled Toby.

Elias didn't bother to correct Toby's speech this time. In the past, Elias had tried to help some of the men to speak better English. He knew this would help their image among the white soldiers and their self-image also. But right now he too was anxious to hear just exactly what they were going to do and if his company was going to get to go.

"Men," spoke Captain Seaman, "I want detachments from the following companies to prepare three days' rations and be ready to move in two hours. We are to meet Major Ward and proceed north up the Fort Scott Road through Mound City to Fort Defiance where we will camp for the night. Tomorrow we head east along the Butler Road. We will be searching for a band of renegades that have been operating from Hog Island. We don't know just how many there are, but I have confidence that we will be able to make short work of them."

After designating the companies that would be affected by the order, a cheer went up from the men as they began to slap each other on the back.

"We'll have none of that now," demanded Captain Seaman in a stern voice. "These will be real bullets and bayonets. There will be discipline and no unnecessary chances taken. Now prepare yourselves. Dismissed!"

" 'Lias, he says bayonets! Dat mean they is gonna be sogers, too? They gonna be Rebs?" asked George Brothers. George, an ex-slave called Joe by most of the men, had run away from southern Missouri and joined the 1st Kansas Colored Volunteers in Lawrence the same time as Elias. Because his last name was Brothers and Elias' was Mothers, they were known as the *family boys.*

"I can't say, George. There might be, I suppose. Maybe this will turn out to be a real fight, and not just a clean-up job we'll be doing for the local folks."

The command left at mid-morning and began marching up the Fort Scott Road. The drummer kept the beat as the men stepped out smartly in their gray uniforms, Union blue not yet available. Each man shouldered his Belgian musket equipped with a sabre-like bayonet. Officers and scouts from the 5th Kansas Cavalry rode at the front of the column, while skirmishers were sent on ahead. The men presented quite a sight for the people of Mound City as they paraded past the town. It was no doubt that the civilians had never seen a company of colored troops. Each man seemed to take pride in the stares of the folks along the road. They had been spotted by those leaving church after the morning service. Some of the women seemed to want to wave their kerchiefs but hesitated, wondering if it would be proper. Reaction to colored soldiers was still varied, and many Kansas people didn't know just how to accept them. However, the men of the 1st Kansas Colored knew what type of welcome they could expect from any Missourians they might meet.

After spending Sunday night at Fort Defiance, the men moved east toward Butler. Crossing the Marais des Cygnes River caused some delay. The soldiers milled around on both sides waiting for the "pull-rope" ferry to transport men and animals across. Once out of the timber and tall grass on the north side, a number of horsemen were spotted atop one of the mounds to the southeast. Cavalry scouts immediately started to investigate, but the riders disappeared over the mounds and south into the dense undergrowth.

Captain Seaman continued on until reaching a double log cabin that was identified as the Enoch Toothman farm.

"You're the one holding my son as a hostage," cried out Christiana Toothman, as Captain Seaman tried to question her. "You and them there damn niggers!"

"Ma'am, your son John was captured while with a raiding party in Kansas. He is being held at Fort Lincoln pending charges."

"I suppose now you're after my husband and other son. Do you aim to take me and my daughters, too?"

"We have no intention of taking you or any members of your family unless we are presented with just cause. We are here investigating the possibility of other raiders or Confederate troops in the area. We saw some horsemen just south of here, do you have any idea who they are?" asked the Captain.

"I don't know nothin'about nobody. My men are gone and I ain't seen nobody all day." Both of her daughters stood back inside the cabin staring at the black troops moving around the yard. The men were busy pulling down heavy rail fences and building a barricade south of the cabin.

"With your permission, we intend to camp here and scout the area."

"My permission, my foot, you'll do as you please," replied Mrs. Toothman as she turned, went back into the cabin and slammed and bolted the door.

That evening several horsemen were seen around the mounds south of "Ft. Africa," as the troops had named their encampment. The following day, numerous small skirmishes developed with no real effect on either side. The ever-present wind and the distance between the opposing riflemen kept the actual danger to a minimum.

"Captain, we believe those are the men of Colonel Cockrell's Rebel soldiers. And they have a bunch of Bushwhackers with 'em."

"Very good, Corporal, have three runners mount up and report to me immediately."

"I jes' hear'd they is sendin' for mo' men,'Lias."

"You *just heard* they are sending for more men, Tom," corrected Elias. "I know. I saw them ride off. How are you doing?"

"Ol 'One Shoe' is doin' fine, 'Lias," spoke up Toby. "That sandal thin' that the blacksmith made up for 'im sho seems to work, don't it, 'One Shoe'?"

The big black soldier smiled and looked down at his feet. When he joined the army, there were no shoes near large enough for his feet. He had walked into Lawrence barefooted and was ready to remain that way, when finally one shoe was found by the quartermaster that Tom Carter could wear. A week or so later the farrier found some thick leather and gave it to the blacksmith who riveted a broad flat hinge to the bottom. Straps were added, and a makeshift sandal was place on Tom's big right foot.

"I'm fine, 'Lias. Dis … *this* here works just okay," he said, pointing to the sandal. "I reckon it's gonna outlast the regular shoe. Won't that be sumpin'?" Tom laughed and leaned back against the wall of the cabin.

The Toothman girls could be seen looking through the window at the men milling around the yard. "Ain't they ever leavin', Mama?"

Wednesday morning a foraging party was sent out in search of food. Soon after they had gone, Rebel troops rode up from the mounds and began firing. The 1st Kansas Colored riflemen returned the fire, which resulted in several riderless horses galloping across the fields of tall grass.

"Come on, men, we're goin' after 'em." Elias and several other men grabbed their muskets and followed through the tall grass. They could see two of their officers, Captains Armstrong and Crew, on horseback ahead. Firing came from in front of them, but it was hard to see just how many Rebels there were. Shouts of "Come on, you niggers" could be heard over the gun fire. Steadily Elias plunged through the grass toward the noise ahead. "You jes wait, you Reb cowards," Elias heard someone shout back. "We on foot, but we comin'."

Suddenly smoke could be seen. "They fired the field," shouted Captain Crew. The wind out of the south was causing the Rebel-set fire to rapidly move north toward the Union troops and Fort Africa. Elias could see mounted Rebels and civilians riding through the smoke firing on the infantrymen. Captain Crew was off his horse and helping to build a backfire to clear a spot for his men to form-up as the Rebels charged. Two Union lieutenants, Huddleston and Gardner, had joined Captain Crew after riding south to the edge of the woods and being chased back by a large number of Rebel cavalry.

"Get down, Toby," yelled Elias, "here they come." Dozens of riders charged the detachment of black troops. A full volley of fire emptied saddles of the oncoming Rebs; still more rode through the small group of colored and Indian soldiers. With no time to reload, Elias and others stood up and began to swing their muskets as clubs. One Rebel dove from his saddle, intending to land on Private Curtis who had just been shot in the back. The Rebel was caught in mid-air by the bayonet of Elias' musket. With a surprised look, the soldier grabbed at his belly and died with his knees tight against his chest. Elias had braced himself on his knees as he drove his musket into the man. Now he sat motionless, staring at the first man he had ever killed.

Suddenly he heard a familiar voice. "Hep me, hep me! Oh God, I'm burnin'! I'm burnin!" It was Toby. Elias looked around through the smoke and horse's legs racing around him. As he sprang to his feet, another Rebel rider charged toward him with his rifle held in one hand aiming at Elias. Before the man could fire, Elias grabbed the rifle muzzle with one hand and the horse's rein with the other and jerked down hard. The horse turned and the rider slid down the animal's side. Elias let go of the rein and smashed his elbow into the nose of the rider. As the Rebel hit the ground, Elias shot the man full in the face with his own gun.

Dropping the rifle, Elias ran toward the spot he thought the cry for help had come. The flames were racing though the waist-high grass. Elias covered his face and ran as hard as he could. Again he heard Toby's yell.

"I'm comin', Toby!" yelled Elias. The noise from Elias' throat came out as a garbled cough. Again Elias tried to call out. Suddenly he spotted Toby. Toby's pants were smoldering, and there was blood on his side just above his belt.

"Oh God! Elias, that you? I'm burnin' … I been shot an' …"

Elias rubbed at the smoldering cloth and reached for Toby's outstretched hand just as a bullet struck the ground next to his foot. As he turned, he saw two riders headed his way. The Rebel raised his pistol, aimed at Elias and then screamed, twisted in his saddle and pitched backward. The rider just behind him was one of Sixkiller's scouts who had placed one of his own bullets in the Rebel's back. With a war-whoop the Indian raced on, heading for more of the enemy.

Elias dragged Toby along the blackened ground toward what was left of their group. He heard the voice of a Rebel somewhere close yell, "Surrender, you black devil." The reply came, "Nevah," as the black soldier plunged his bayonet into the neck of the white confederate.

On came the Rebels, firing and attacking, sometimes riding, sometimes hand to hand. As Elias neared the other Union troops, he saw Captain Crew on foot, walking backward toward his men while firing his pistol at the oncoming Rebels.

Captain Crew slowly moved his men backward as they continued to fight. Elias had managed to work his way through the grass and was heading north toward the camp. He saw Captain Armstrong of Co. H ride to the crest of one of the mounds and direct his men toward the group of combatants. As they charged down the slope, Captain Crew went down, fatally wounded. One of the Rebels stood over him and fired again.

"Hold on, Toby, we're gonna make it okay. We've got some help coming, too." Elias continued to drag Toby through the grass, pausing every once in awhile to catch his breath and wipe his eyes. Toby had not uttered a word since he felt Elias take hold of him. He kept his eyes closed, hoping to shut out the pain and the noise of battle.

"It's not that bad," said Dr. Macy, the surgeon. "The wound in his side tore up skin and muscle more than anything, and his leg burns will heal in a few weeks."

"Elias, you … you know you done saved …" began Toby.

"Hush," broke in Elias. "You were just the excuse I needed to get myself out of there. You lay still. I'm going to get me something to eat. You want anything?"

"I sho … *sure* could use a drink," smiled Toby.

"Right away," replied Elias as he got to his feet. "Be right back."

The following day troops were sent out to bring in the bodies of the slain Union soldiers. Some of the bodies were burned so badly that identification was difficult. The Rebels had requested, under a flag of truce, that they might also be allowed to recover their dead and wounded. After doing so, another fire was started by a few remaining Rebels who then attempted to rush Thrasher's company, but with no success. Finally all but three of the Union forces were accounted for. The following day those three bodies were found, mutilated and scalped.

"They say we lost ten men killed and twelve wounded, 'Lias. You figure tha's right?'

"I'm not sure," replied Elias. "I just got back and I haven't heard much about what happened."

"Where you went off to?" asked Toby as he pulled himself up onto a blanket he was using for a pillow.

"They called us out this morning to chase after the Rebs

down at the island. All we found was a cold camp." Elias' face sported a large grin. "And we brought back about a hundred head of cattle and a couple dozen horses. Those boys left in a hurry, I can tell you."

"I betcha they don' want no mo' of us, that right, 'Lias?" said One Shoe.

"You're right, Tom," replied Elias with pride in his voice. "I am so proud of all of you men … of our people. They'll think twice before they figure us as easy again."

" 'Lias, soon they gonna be talkin' about our very first battle and they gonna say we fought da battle of 'Hog Island.' Now that don' seem like much of a name for our first fight," complained Matthew Smith.

"Don't worry about it," replied Elias. "To begin with, I can't see why they call it an island. It is a piece of ground three or four miles long and about a mile across in the widest part, with the Marais de Cygne River running along the northeast and a little slough running along the southwest. Most folks would never know it was any kind of an island. It's more of a swamp than anything. Besides, we fought a mile and a half north of it. The Rebs and Bushwhackers just used it as a hide-out. I hear some folks refer to the area as Island Mound, too. Maybe that will sound better to your grandkids when you tell them."

Elias' smile faded as he got to his feet. "They're digging graves for seven of our boys and are going to bury them up there," he said, pointing north of the cabin. "They got Tommy Land, Marion Barber, and a fella named Rhodes from Company F, and one of Seaman's battalion named John Sixkiller. I believe he's the one that saved my neck." Elias shook his head and moved away. "I'll be back in a little bit."

The Fort Scott Weekly Democrat

Vol. IV No. 5 E. K. Smith Publisher Monday, November 3, 1862 2 Cents

1ST KANSAS COLORED VICTORIOUS

First Major Battle a Success Says Col. J. Williams

Enemy Routed at Island Mound

On Wednesday last the men of the 1st Kansas Colored Infantry showed their fellow Kansans their determination and courage in the face of battle at the Toothman farm near Butler, Missouri.

The setting, called by some 'Hog Island', became the battle field of the confrontation of the first Colored Union unit to fight Confederate troops in the current rebellion.

Assisted by Missouri guerillas, the Rebel troops were confronted and sent running by the outnumbered Black

(Cont'd on page 2)

Our Finest Hour Says Gen. Lane

Lane Told President 'Now The Time For Colored Troops!'

Gen. James. Lane, former Senator of Kansas, said today that his faith in the Black Kansas men has been reinforced since the victory over the Rebel forces/ in south western Missouri, last Tuesday.

"I had to hound Washington City until they finally listened," Lane told a Topeka reporter, after hearing of the victory of the Colored Union troops from Kansas.

Actually, the units were formed prior to receiving authority from the Secretary of War, but Lane seemed convinced he would

(Cont'd on page 3)

Congress Slow To Approve Funding For Union Army

President Lincoln Assures That Soldiers Will Not Suffer

Washington City

"Our boys will have whatever they require in the way of food, clothing and necessary supplies," stated President Lincoln in articles printed in eastern newspapers. It was reported that families of some of the soldiers expressed concern for their sons and husbands in the Army.

"We will do what ever we can to see that our brave men do not go wanting in the months to come," said a spokesman for the War Department on Monday.

"The President is deeply concerned and is pressuring the Congress daily for any appropriations

(Cont'd on page 4)

Emancipation Proclamation Still Causing Controversy

Many Still Claim War Not About Southern Slavery!

Washington City

Despite the complaints from many citizens, the President's Emancipation Proclamation has been published in northern newspapers. The full text was published Sept. 23rd last to mixed acceptance.

"I didn't send my boy to fight for the niggers," said a woman in New York. Her sentiments were echoed by many in the East, despite the assurance from the President that he sees no other way at the present time of causing the terrible conflict to come to an end.

President Lincoln has stated many times, "If I could reunite the Union by not freeing any of the slaves

(Cont'd on page 2)

Rumors Say McClellan To Be Replaced

Gen. Burnside to be In Charge of Army

Washington City

It has been said, by highly stationed men at the War Department, that General McClellan, known to his men as 'Little Mac', is soon to be relieved of command of the Union Army of the Potomac.

"Lack of action" is said to be the reason for the change to be made by the President. "I fear he (McClellan) has the 'slows'," stated President Lincoln. General Ambrose E. Burnside is said to be in line for the command.

A spokesman for the War Department says that some recent battles could have had a much more favorable outcome for the Union if there had not

(Cont'd on page 2)

Created by Dale Vaughn©

Chapter 8

Monday, November 10, 1862

"You're looking good, Toby, how do you feel?" Elias stood next to Toby's pallet along with several members of their regiment.

"I'm doing fine, Elias, but I sho … *sure* would like to get out'n this here place for awhile."

"What about it, Doc?" asked Elias as he turned to Dr. Tenney.

"It would probably do him good, but I haven't the people or time to move any of these men. If you can be careful and get him back later this afternoon, go ahead and take him out for a few hours."

"We lucky to be here all together," commented Toby as they sat around under a large oak tree.

"I have been hearing stories of some of the things that happened back there," said Elias. "I had no idea so much was going on. All I could see was the smoke from the grass fire and what some of those Rebs were doing right around us. A bunch of our boys were really having a tough time of it."

"You know," said Mathew, "I was just over a ways from Captain Crew when he was killed. I heard him tell them three Rebs that he wasn't gonna give up and if'n they was to shoot him they best go ahead and do it," Mathew paused, "And they did. Then they started goin' through his pockets and takin' stuff."

"Yeah, but I heard that they found one of them Rebs with Captain Crew's watch in his pocket. So's he didn' git no where's. He got his just doin's."

Elias got to his feet, walked a short way from the tree and turned. "They say these Rebs and Bushwhackers were aiming to raid Mound City because it is the home of Montgomery and Jennison. They figured if they could wipe out the town they could get back for some of the things that had been done to them." Elias turned his back on the men as they looked up at him. "It seems that everyone just wants to get one better than the other fella." Elias shook his head. "When will it stop? What will be enough?"

"All's I knows, Elias, is that I figure we'ns ain't alone no mo'," spoke up One Shoe. "I was right there when Lieutenant Huddleston jumped right in when Cap'n. Crew was killed. He was the only white man left, and he kept right on fightin' and killin' like he was protectin' his own. He aimed slow and right on th' mark ever' time. So I figure's that was jes whut he was thinkin'. He was fightin'n for us as well as his self." One Shoe lowered his voice; then with a slight quaver said, "I be next to him any time! Yas, sir, any time a'tall."

All was quiet as the men looked at the ground and off into the trees, each pondering their own feelings.

"Dis gonna be … sorry … this going to be a long way, 'Lias?" asked Toby. He was trying to stay on his feet after refusing to ride in an ambulance.

"Toby, I can't see why you are walking when anyone in the regiment would give almost anything to be able to ride," replied Elias.

"Yeah, but I ain't … *I'm not* that special. I didn't get hurt near as bad as some …"

"Boy," interrupted Slows, "you tryin' to make a fool o' yo'sef?"

"But," stammered Toby, "I'm just as much …"

"You just as much of a dummy as some others I could mention," put in China Bill. "You won't be of any use to the rest of us if you don't get yourself healed and back ready to help out.

You ain't doing anyone a favor by makin' things worse trying to show off."

"Bill," interrupted Elias, "I think you're being a little hard …"

"Never mind, 'Lias," said Toby in a low voice. "I know what he means. I guess I was tryin' to show off a bit. But y'all done … *did* so much for me that I wanted ya to know …"

"Jes shut up and git in the wagon, little man." One Shoe had Toby in his massive arms and was walking back to one of the ambulances toward the rear of the train. It was quite a sight, the big man walking with one hinge-shoe flapping and young Toby in his arms. They could be heard laughing as they moved toward the rear.

The march to Fort Scott was made in a day and a half. The journey could have been made much quicker had there been any real reason to hurry. The terrain was fairly level and not difficult. As the men passed along the Military Road, they could see burned farm buildings and fields. Not a single live person was encountered. At night the coyotes and an occasional bobcat could be heard. There were no livestock, practically no deer nor buffalo. The predators were having as rough of a time as the folks that had inhabited the area.

As the group approached Fort Scott from the north, they began to speculate as to their accommodations in their new home.

"I hear that they are the biggest supply fort in this part of the country," said Elias, as he and China Bill marched along together. "And they have the finest hospital you could ever want."

"Hope I don't want none of it, thank you very much," replied Bill.

"They gonna have inside beds fer us, ya reckon?" asked One Shoe.

"It's a large fort, but I doubt that they have empty barracks just waiting for us, Tom," said Elias.

"But I heerd it's gonna be a hard winter, 'Lias. Sho would be good to sleep inside."

The large stone buildings made quite an impression on the

men as they entered the gates to Fort Scott. The fort had been built under the direction of quartermaster Captain Thomas Swords, using material that was close at hand. Walnut, ash and oak trees grew in abundance in the area, and stone lay just a few inches under the surrounding soil. It took several years for all the buildings to be completed. After the barracks, officer housing, hospital, stables, magazine and various building were finished, the building program halted completely in 1850 when the money ran out.

After leaving, the Union returned some of its troops in 1857 and again in 1858 to try to quiet some of the unrest among the town's people and recognized the importance of this location at the beginning of the war.

Friday, January 16, 1863 Fort Scott, KS

"Well, 'Lias, does you feel *O'ficial* now?"

"It's *do you* feel official," replied Elias as he looked up at Toby.

"Ya know, they is … will soon be a callin' you P'fessor the way you are always correctin' us when we tell you things."

"Never mind that; what do you mean, 'I'm official'?" questioned Elias. He had opened his bed roll so he could place his extra pair of pants inside and roll them up with his blanket and rubber sheet. He learned that the white soldiers had a rubber sheet to be placed under their blanket when they slept on the ground and managed to get one from a private in a passing cavalry regiment.

"Didn't you hear? They say that we are now in the real army. Some lieutenant by the name of Sabin said we wa … were mustered in to the regular army and now we are official."

"I don't feel a bit different. Captain Seaman told all of us that we were in the Union Army no matter what anyone said. If General Lane said we were, that's good enough for me." Elias went back to arranging his clothing and bedroll.

"Yeah, but that ain't all. They wouldn't let Lieutenant Minor or Captain Matthews be *o'fficialed* 'long with the rest of us. They said that they couldn't have no … *any* black officers." Toby shook his head. "Dat ain't right, 'Lias. They fought hard as us."

"I know, Toby. But it's like Bill said. It will all come in time," replied Elias.

"But they is … *are* leavin' the army, 'Lias. I heard they going back to Leavenworth."

"It's too bad, they are good men. But I can't imagine them staying out for good."

Friday, May 1, 1863

A battalion of six companies had been formed in January by the consolidation of Colonel Williams' recruits with those of Captain Seaman and another four since then. This completed the regimental organization and it was ready to be sent wherever it was needed. The call would be coming sooner than anyone thought.

"Well, Henry, you can roll your socks and underwear, we're getting ready to move."

"You wouldn't kid me, would you, Jim? Oh, I aaaaam sorry. I mean you wouldn't kid me, would you, *Colonel.*"

"Never mind that," said the now Colonel J. M. Williams, as he talked with Captain Seaman. "General Blunt has decided that we need to establish a post down near Baxter Springs. He is sending us and a section of the Second Kansas Battery under the command of Lieutenant Knowles. We will be leaving in less than a week."

The aroma of baking bread drifted past the quartermaster house, the officers quarters, Blair house and through the walls of the headquarters building, located just east of the dragoon barracks. Though the bakery was located at the opposite end of the fort, the southerly winds carried the mouth-watering vapors all across the compound. It would be hard to leave the comfort of an established post and go into an undeveloped area.

"I guess that's good news, Jim, but I have one question."

Captain Seaman pushed back his hat and scratched at his dark wavy hair. He was a fine looking officer and had a better than average relationship with his men. He was well respected because they knew he was the type of officer that led and not just commanded his men. "Well, you just tell me," continued Seaman, "how this war is getting so damn far out of hand?"

Colonel Williams placed a small chunk of wood through the door of the short sheet stove that was used to break the chill of the morning and keep the coffee warm. He retrieved his half-filled coffee cup from the top of the stove and drank.

"Secession is nothing really new, Henry. The folks up in New England talked about it when they wanted nothing to do with the war of 1812 and even before. They claimed there was nothing in the Constitution that clearly forbids it. Now the South feels the same way. They are out-numbered and they feel threatened. Texas becoming Confederate helped some, but …"

"And that's another thing. How can they make Texas and all that other territory we got from Mexico into slave country?" asked Seaman. "Hell, most of the soldiers that fought in Mexico were northerners and the Federal Government paid all the bills."

"I know, Henry, that's what Sam Houston said when they kicked him out as governor of Texas. He said it would cost millions of dollars, thousands of lives and probably come to nothing. And before he became Confederate Vice President, Congressman Stephens of Georgia tried to talk his state out of seceding. I agree it isn't right, that's why we're here doing what we are."

"You can't just up and quit the Union, I don't care what anybody says. You remember, Jim, how President Andy Jackson threatened to send troops into South Carolina back in '32 when they were going to do away with the tariff laws the Government set up? The Union is a whole thing made up by and for everyone. One group of people shouldn't be able to mess it up for the rest of us."

"Yes, Henry, don't get so steamed up. We'll fix it."

"And the fugitive slave act; you think I'm going to be a party to sending those poor folks back to a life like that? Not by a damn site, I won't!"

"Have you read what the South has said about our troops?" asked Colonel Williams.

"Now what?" replied Seaman.

"They say that any colored troops captured will be either killed or returned to slavery and not be treated as prisoners of war. And on top of that, any white officers leading them will be treated as criminals and possibly executed." Smiling, Colonel Williams pointed his coffee cup at Captain Seaman and said, "You're the same as a wanted man, Henry. Better watch it."

Chapter 9

Monday, May 18, 1863   Baxter Springs, KS

What finally became Baxter Springs started out as a stopping place on the Military Road intended to protect several small forts and the local population from hostile Indians. In 1842 the Government tried to establish a post at Spring River, close by, but the Indians would have none of it and demanded an outrageous price for the land, causing the military post to be built at Fort Scott instead.

After the war began, supply trains heading south from Fort Scott would use Baxter Springs for an overnight camp area. In 1862 several field camps were built in Baxter Springs to supply troops to escort the trains on south into Indian Territory, to chase Missouri raiders back eastward, and to fight Confederate Indian troops and Texas Cavalry. The springs, and later the town, was named for an early settler by the name of John Baxter.

Baxter and his family had moved here in the spring of 1849 and built a general store and an inn in order to give travelers a place to spend the night and to eat. The feisty preacher, and father of eight, was always seen carrying a pistol and spouting Bible verses to the folks passing through.

The formal name of the fort was Fort Blair, but was usually referred to as Fort Baxter. During May and June of 1863, two more field camps, Camp Joe Hooker and Camp Ben Butler, were built by Colonel Williams' 1st Kansas Colored.

"Colonel Williams, the foraging party from over toward Sherwood is back."

"Oh, good!"

"At least what s left of 'em."

"What do you mean, Sergeant, what's left of them?" asked Colonel Williams as he jumped from his cot and reached for his hat. "What's happened? Where is Major Ward?"

"I'm right here, Colonel." Major Ward was walking toward the Colonel's tent, leading his horse. He dropped the reins and slowly saluted. "I'm afraid we ran into trouble, a lot of it. We were caught right in the open by some Rebs and a bunch of civilians. I think the soldiers belonged to that Confederate Major Livingston. We lost almost half of our men killed, wounded or taken prisoner." Major Ward removed his hat and wiped his forehead with the back of his arm.

"Come into my tent, Major, and give me the whole story. Corporal, take the Major's horse and bring us some coffee."

As the two officers settled themselves in the colonel's tent, Major Ward explained just what had happened. Early that morning Colonel Williams had sent out a foraging detail of about forty or so white and colored soldiers with five or six mule teams and a number of artillerymen. They were headed some ten to twelve miles east of Baxter Springs toward the vicinity of Sherwood, Missouri, just across the Kansas-Missouri border into Jasper County.

The black troops stopped at a farm occupied by a Mrs. Rader to load supplies, while the artillery troops continued on east. Soon the artillerymen spotted a large number of mounted men riding in a northerly direction. A scout, Hugh Thompson, was sent back to Major Ward advising him of the presence of the Bushwhackers. Just as Thompson arrived, the Rebels attacked.

About twenty of the colored troops had stacked their rifles and had climbed up into the loft of the barn to throw down corn. Three-fourths of those troops were killed immediately. The scout, Thompson, had been shot but managed to reach the shelter of the woods where he met two men of the 1st.

"I don't know, Colonel, all of a sudden they were on top of us. I still don't know how as many of us got away as did. Near as

I could tell, we left fifteen or sixteen men dead or wounded and they got five of our men as prisoners."

"Who did they get, Dick?'

"Three of the Second Kansas and two of our boys."

"All right, first thing in the morning I'll send a runner to see if we can exchange prisoners. In fact, we have several of theirs that we brought in a few days ago. That ought to make it easy, if Livingston is willing to negotiate."

The following morning, under a flag of truce, a party of three mounted Union soldiers located Confederated Major Livingston. Returning about mid-morning and followed by three Confederate cavalrymen, the party pulled up in front of Colonel William's tent.

"They say they will only give us these three, Colonel," said one of the Union riders, pointing to the three white soldiers of the 2nd Kansas Battery. "They wouldn't give us either of the colored boys."

"What's the meaning of this, Sergeant?" stormed Colonel Williams as he faced one of the Confederates.

"I'm sorry, Sir," said the young Rebel soldier as he saluted the colonel. "We have our orders, Sir. We are not to turn over any nigg … Colored troops. That's why I was sent, Sir. I have a copy of our orders, and I have been instructed to read it to you, Sir." The young sergeant was evidently very nervous as he held up the paper he had removed from inside his jacket. His hand shook as he began to read.

> *"Section 7, All negroes and mulattos who shall engage in war, or be taken in arms against the Confederate States, shall, when captured in the Confederate States, be delivered to the authorities of the State or States in which they shall be captured, to be dealt with according to the present or future laws of such State or States."*

"Major Livingston sends his compliments and says that he is certain you as an officer will understand that he must obey his orders just as you obey yours … ah … Sir."

"Well, you can just tell your Major Livingston, that Colonel Williams does not recognize any damn 'Section 7' or any other such crap as that! And you can tell him that Colonel Williams intends to have his other two soldiers back and I want them now! Today! Do you understand, Sergeant?"

"But Sir, I can't tell …"

"They ain't two to get back, Colonel," a voice came, from a few yards off. "They done kilt Private Mitchell of Co. F, I seen it myself." One of the men from the 2nd Kansas Battery moved toward the cluster of men. "Cpl. Carter of Co. E. is still alive, but Mitchell's dead. They said he was a mouthy nigger and wasn't worth keepin' and feedin'."

Colonel Williams turned toward the three Confederate soldiers, his face blood red. "Is that true?" he yelled. "Well, is it?"

"I … I couldn't say, Sir," stammered the sergeant. "You see, I …"

"He was there, Colonel. He saw it, same as me," said the Union soldier as he shook his finger at the nervous Rebel.

Turning to his three mounted men, the colonel gave the order for all six men to return to Major Livingston's camp and bring back not only the remaining colored member of the previous day's detail, but the Confederate soldier responsible for the killing of the black Union soldier.

"But, Sir, I'm afraid Major Liv …" stuttered one of the Confederates.

"Just get it done! Now!" The colonel turned and marched away without another word.

"What's you figure gonna happ'n now, 'Lias?" asked One Shoe, as several of the men stood off to one side.

"I'm not sure, Tom, but I wouldn't want to be in that Major Livingston's boots if he doesn't do what the colonel asked."

"I wouldn't wanna be in any of them there Rebs boots right about now," spoke up Slows.

" 'Lias, didja see jes whut they did to some of our men yestidy?" asked Joe Brothers. "I saw some of them Rebs just up'n club a couple of them wounded black boys, when they couldn't do nuthin' but lay there. They got Riley Young, Pete White, Greene, Booth, Aggleson, and I don' know who all else. How could they do that, 'Lias?"

"I could do that if it was other way 'round, by God," said China Bill.

"Then that makes us no better than they are, Bill. Is that what you want? Is that the kind of free men you want us to be?" Elias turned to walk away and then paused. "I know it's hard. It was hard when Mama told me that Daddy was never coming back and that we were on our own. And it was hard to go off and leave Mama and Cheat, but if we don't learn how to be honest and fair, what's the good of being free?"

"You think all the free white folks is fair and honest, 'Lias? You think that just 'cause we is up north and fightin' with them, that everone is gonna be good and treat us like they do they own? You really believe that?" asked Toby, as he stared at his scarred ankle sticking down from his short trouser leg. "You dreamin'," he finished almost under his breath.

"All I know is what Mama taught me it meant to be a man, and that doesn't include beating or killing a man when he's not able to defend himself. I hope I never get to a place where that's the only choice I have." With that, Elias moved into the shadows and slowly walked toward his tent. Thoughts of his mother flooded his mind, and he tried to remember exactly how she looked. The image in his mind was nothing but a blur and he couldn't bring a clear picture into focus. Why couldn't he remember how his mother looked? For the first time he felt really alone.

"I didn't think he would, Colonel," said Colonel Williams' sergeant as he returned with the others that had been sent to

Livingston's camp.

"You see, Sir," said the same Confederate sergeant that had delivered the earlier dispatch, "the Major could not give up one of his men until it had been determined just what had actually happened. There could have been any number of circumstances that caused the unfortunate incident. You do understand, don't you, Sir?"

"Yes, Sergeant, I understand! I understand exactly! And I believe I understand just what it takes to get your Major's attention!" Colonel Williams turned back to his own sergeant and ordered him to bring one of the Confederate prisoners to him immediately.

As the Rebel soldier stood next to the Union sergeant, Colonel Williams gave the order for him to be taken out and shot. This order was carried out within minutes.

"You take that back to your Major Livingston," declared Williams, through clenched teeth. "And you can tell him that he has not seen the last of me and that I had better never see a sight such as I saw this morning when I was at that battlefield. I saw my men with their heads beaten in. I saw where wounded men were mutilated and bayoneted where they lay. I saw some of those men lying naked in the sun after their clothes were stripped from them. You tell that to your Major. And you tell him for me that I will never forget this day, and I can assure him that, by God, neither will he!"

"Sergeant, bring me Major Ward. I'll be in my tent." Colonel Williams stood looking at the three Confederate soldiers and then deliberately turned and quickly walked away.

Shortly after the Colonel had entered his tent, a call came from outside.

"Come in, Major."

"It ain't the major, Sir, its Sergeant Wills. I have something here you need to see."

The colonel placed his hat on his head and walked toward the unseen voice. Out side his tent stood a sergeant, two privates and a man the colonel didn't recognize.

"Just who is this, Sergeant, and why do you bring him to me?"

"Name's Bishop, Colonel. Found him on our way back to the Post."

"So?" exclaimed the colonel with a bit of impatience in his voice.

"Well, Sir, take a look at his boots and that there shirt he's a wearin'," replied the sergeant. "Them's Army boots, and new ones at that, and that there is blood on that shirt. I think I know where that all comes from, Sir. This here fella is one of the Rebs that was released from Fort Lincoln. They was all supposed to go home and not fight no more, but that there is fresh blood. I'll just bet he was in on that there fight we just had."

"Well, Bishop, what do you have to say for yourself? Can you explain where these clothes came from? Were you at Fort Lincoln?" asked the colonel.

"I'm a civilian and I don't have to tell you …" stammered Bishop.

"I recognized him, too, Colonel," spoke up one of the privates. "He played cards with some of us before they paroled him."

The colonel turned back to the sergeant, "You know the penalty, Sergeant."

"Just you look here, you can't up and shoot …" yelled Bishop.

"Sergeant!" With that the colonel turned and went back into his tent. He had hardly seated himself when several shots rang out.

Justice!

"Richard," the colonel's voice was thick with anger as he spoke to Major Ward. "I want everything that is growing or standing within a five-mile radius burned or destroyed. I want every field, farmhouse and barn burned. I want every animal destroyed. I want no killing of civilians, even though some of them are probably the ones in yesterday's fight, but everything else is to go. Do you understand, Major Ward?"

"Yes, Sir," replied Ward without further comment.

"When that is accomplished, we're taking a few scouts and some cavalry, and we are going to even up the score for yesterday." The colonel's eyes narrowed as he continued in a low voice. "We may even get us a few extra, just for good measure." And that was exactly what happened.

Chapter 10

Tuesday, June 2, 1863

"Jes where does ..." Toby stopped in mid-sentence as Elias cast a quick glance in his direction. "Just where do you think we are goin', 'Lias?" he continued.

"The sergeant said they were sending us down to Fort Gibson with a wagon load of something. I don't know yet just what it is, but we are to make it fast and get back. They want to know something about another supply train that's going to be sent soon. Don't know when or where." Elias continued to wrap his clothing into a roll and then cover it with his blankets.

"You means ... *mean* ... they are sending us on this here trip? How come's we ... *we're* goin?"

"I wasn't told everything, but I think they need everyone else to stay here so they can finish the forts."

"We been workin' hard as any of 'em," said One Shoe. "Then they make us do drillin' and cleanin' up stuff."

"Yeah," said China Bill, "but just think. We get to ride all the way." Smiling, Bill began to take his tent down and pack it with his other gear.

"The sergeant said we only have one week to make the trip," said Elias. "That means we have to make at least thirty-five miles per day, with one day to stay over before we start back. I guess that's why they are sending extra horses and the four of us."

"Anyway," said Toby, "the weather is good and all we has ... *have* to do is ride, sittin' down. I approve of that, fer shore ... *sure."* Toby glanced at Elias, and Elias returned his big grin.

"Keep this under your hat, Sergeant," Colonel Williams was addressing the sergeant of the supply wagon that was to leave early the next morning. "The rest of your men don't have to know this, but Lieutenant Colonel Dodd, of the 2nd Colorado Infantry, will soon be bringing a supply train from Fort Scott on to Fort Gibson, and we think there is a chance he could be attacked by some of the Rebels trying to free General Cooper's Confederates that are being held south of the Arkansas River by Colonel Phillips. Our people need supplied down there, but we aren't certain just who Colonel Dodd might run into. In fact, I'm seriously considering an offer of some of our troops to help Dodd get there." Colonel Williams looked up from the map of the Cherokee Nation he had been studying. "Phillips' people will know more about this situation than we do, so I need to find out fast. I would send just a courier, but there are some items in your wagon they need right away. You get there and give this envelope to Colonel Phillips. Send his reply back by your man with the fastest horse. The rest of you can get back with the wagon as quickly as you can." Colonel Williams rolled up his map and returned the salute given by the young sergeant.

"Yes, Sir. We'll be leaving just before first light in the morning, Sir." The sergeant turned and moved quickly out of the colonel's tent and headed for his men who were gathered under a tree next to the drill field.

"Rations for three days, men, and be ready before dawn tomorrow." The sergeant moved away under the stares of the gathered men.

"We still don' know nuttin', but I guess that's whut we's suppos'n to know." Toby rubbed his scarred ankle and pulled up his sock.

"May not be big enough wagon if we have to carry three days' grub for us and One Shoe both," snickered China Bill.

"You jes watch yo' mouth there, furriner," jibed Bill with an ever so slight smile in his eyes. "You probably just takin' a sack o' rice and that's all with you."

"Okay, boys, just be sure you have everything you're going to need for the next week," instructed Elias good naturedly. "I don't want to hear any griping about not having socks or a blanket if the weather gets cold."

"Don't got no socks anyway, 'Lias," grinned Slows.

"Borrow some from Tom, Amos."

"Them ain't socks," Slows replied, "them big things is gunny sacks."

The breeze was cool and the men had to brush the dew from their blankets as they moved about in the dark gray of Wednesday morning. Tent halves had to be packed the previous day, so the men slept under wagons or trees. Elias had slept in the stable but was the first up and stood over his men, rousing them from their deep sleep. The sergeant in charge had the team harnessed to the wagon and the two men from his unit almost ready to mount when Elias and his three friends piled their gear on top of the canvas-covered rig.

"We got lots of miles to cover, men," called the sergeant from atop his horse, "let's get at it."

Elias climbed up next to the wagon driver, while One Shoe and Toby got atop the wagon. When it was learned that China Bill was an experienced horseman, he was given a large chestnut gelding to ride.

Saturday, June 6, 1863 Fort Gibson, Indian Territory

"They got in late last night, Colonel. We are unloading the wagon now." The lieutenant saluted Colonel Phillips as he handed the colonel the large envelope that had been sent from Colonel Williams. Since the Military Road they traversed was mostly level ground southward, the trip was an easy one, though hurried.

"Bring back some coffee, Lieutenant, and we'll go over this together."

Elias and the rest of the detachment had been awakened, fed and were helping to unload the supply wagon. It was going to be another hot day, just as the days had been on their journey south from Baxter Springs. They had made good time, but had to ride past sundown two of the three days in order to keep their schedule. Today they could rest up and get ready for the return trip on Sunday.

Fort Gibson was first established in the 1820s as an outpost to help whites settle the surrounding area. The Indians resented the intrusion, but after the Indian Removal Act of 1830 the horse troops were aided by the arrival of Mounted Rangers. Soon the post was the designated Headquarters of the Southwestern Frontier. Being a stop on the water part of the Trail of Tears, the fort was kept busy trying to aid in the re-settlement of various Indian tribes.

The post remained fairly active until 1857, when the troops were withdrawn and the buildings and land were turned over to the Cherokees.

At the start of the war, after occupying the once Union fort for a short time, the Confederate forces established Fort Davis, about five miles to the southwest on the southern bank of the Arkansas River, only to have it destroyed by Union forces in December of 1862.

Five rather ominous looking Indians were squatting together next to the well just outside the bakery, watching the proceedings down the hill and muttering in low voices. They would make a statement and then nod toward Elias and his men. As a sergeant, with the look of many years of service, left the hospital and walked northwest, one of the Indians slowly arose and blocked the sergeant's path.

"Who?" said the Indian nodding toward Elias' troops.

"What cha' mean, 'who,' Chief?" the soldier smiled slightly, and knowing what was coming, feigned ignorance.

"Them niggers?"

"You mean them fellers down at the wagon?"

"Uh," came the Indian's reply.

"Nope, don't think so."

"Looks like niggers."

"Them there boys are some of the finest Union soldiers you will ever see. Don't get them confused with the darkies ya see mosyin' round here. Them's fightin' men!"

With that, the Indian muttered something and moved back to his group, shaking his head.

Elias had started up the hill to the powder magazine and overheard a part of the conversation. The sergeant turned and followed Elias. After picking up additional ammunition for his men, Elias and the sergeant walked over to the bakers to pick up some rolls.

"What was that all about?" asked Elias, glancing back toward the still crouching Indians. "And who are they? They certainly don't look like the Cherokees or Creeks around here?"

"They're not," replied the sergeant. "Them there boys are Comanche. They're up here from down south wantin' to join up. They are hopin' they'll get a chance to fight some of the Texans. Bad blood between them, so's I heard."

"I guess they have never seen black soldiers before," said Elias.

"Nope, and they think it is pretty strange."

"What was that the fella said just as he walked away?" asked Elias.

"Posah-tai-vo," replied the sergeant, with a grin on his face.

"What's it mean?"

"That's Comanche for 'crazy white man.' " A bigger grin spread across the sergeant's face at which Elias too broke out in a chuckle.

"Maybe he's right. The white man is crazy for having us in his army and we are just as crazy for being here." Elias paused and then said, "Well, I hope they get their chance, whatever their reason."

"Oh, they will," stated the sergeant. "We're up to usin' everyone we can get." Then, looking straight at Elias, said, "And we shore are grateful for your help."

Colonel Phillips had been advised that the Confederates knew there would be a supply train before long. In his reply to Baxter

Springs, the colonel included this information along with what else his pickets and local spies had learned about General Cooper's movements and what possible reinforcements he could expect.

"Think you can do it?" asked the lieutenant as he reached up and handed China Bill a leather pouch.

"There is no doubt about it, Lieutenant," smiled Bill. "And it will be there a lot faster than it took us to get down here. I've spent lots of time in the saddle and I know how to travel. Ya' see, I've had to make it my business to move around fast and without being seen much."

"I have every confidence, Soldier. We have heard good things about your regiment, and we're glad to have your help." After returning Bill's salute, the lieutenant watched China Bill's horse trot away from the tents and head for the tree line running next to the Grand River to the north of Fort Gibson. Elias and the others waved as Bill rode through the gate and assured him that they would soon be back also.

Many of the buildings at Fort Gibson were constructed of native stone, and it was said that the workers had been Cherokees and their slaves.

"Had no idea them fellas was slaves, 'Lias, much less belongin' to th' Indians," remarked Toby under his breath, pointing to a group of black laborers. "Seems we ought t' try t' do sumpthin' fer 'em."

"We will, Toby, but now isn't the time. It will come, you'll see."

When Elias and his group returned to Baxter Springs, he found a letter from his mother waiting for him. It was only the second one he had received from home, and he read and reread the letter several times. He even read parts of it to his friends. "She says that things are fine there and that it is starting to get hot and there was not much rain during the spring. She says that they haven't had any trouble to speak of from Border Ruffians or the Redlegs. She said that they heard from one of the Wallace boys, but not the other one, and they don't know what to think. The boys thought they were going to stay together, but something must have happened and they don't know what."

And yet there was no word of Cheat. He guessed that she was so concerned about her boy that was away from home that she didn't think to mention the one still with her. Yet that wasn't like his mama. She knew how close he and Cheat had been. He had made sure to mention Cheat in his letter home so the little fella would know that Elias was thinking a lot about him. He would ask her the next time he was able to send a letter back home. He sure missed that little guy with his big grin and happy carrying-on, and the other fellas had also asked about his brother with each of the two letters he had received.

"They say we might be movin' south sometime soon, Elias. What you think gonna happen?" asked George Brothers, as the men sat around a camp fire. It was just about sundown, but not time yet to get to bed. The men were smoking and watching the fire. It was peaceful and quiet, which made the war seem far away or maybe even just a tale that had been told to pass the time.

"Don't know, George," replied Elias. "I just hope we will be as lucky as we have been up till now."

"When we was down to Gibson, didn't seem to me that them Rebs much wanted any fight," said Toby, rubbing his scarred leg. "They warn't … *weren't* nowhere's in sight."

"Maybe they done heard o' us a'ready," said young Matthew Smith. At that everyone laughed and pushed at each other, shouting "Yeah" and "tha's right."

"Why, I betcha the whole Reb army done heard o' us by now," put in Slows.

"Probably da whole South." The comment started more cheers and laughs.

"No, Sir. You don't mess with any o' us from the 1st," chimed in Bill.

With that, all fell silent. The men continued to stare into the fire and let their minds wander back to thoughts of happier times. And yet Elias thought about not only his home and family, but his friends around him. He looked from one to another.

Big old Tom Carter, "One Shoe." There was not a man that could match him for strength. Elias doubted that there was anything that this man couldn't move if he could get his massive arms around it. Yet, he had seen him show the gentleness of a child when around animals. He saw Tom gaze at wild flowers and smile. He was surely a gentle giant unless riled.

As he watched Toby Washington staring at the fire, Elias remembered all the smoke and then the fire that had caused the smoldering material of Toby's pants to leave scars on his legs, the scars that Toby would constantly rub. Elias wondered if Toby was unconsciously trying to rub them away. Toby was a proud young man. He had told Elias, in a very private way, about a girl. A girl at home that he hoped he had impressed by joining the army and hoped he would return to marry some day. Elias wondered if Toby thought that now he was damaged goods and that pretty young girl at home wouldn't want him. Would she think of him as a hero or just a scarred boy that was no longer handsome and desirable?

George Brothers, the light-skinned young man that, because of his name, had been linked to Elias as one of the *Family* boys, Brothers and Mothers. Joe, as he was called, was one quarter white and had come from western Missouri. He had worked on a tobacco farm and had hidden away in a wagon laden with tobacco that was headed for Rolla, Missouri. Joe had slipped out of the wagon and into a ditch late one evening and had managed to escape to the Kansas border. He then found sympathetic Indians that helped him get to Mound City, where he worked at a saw mill until he enlisted in Captain Seaman's Union Army.

Elias didn't know much about Matthew Smith. He was young, as were most of them, but a lot more quiet. He had joined at the same time as Elias, and it was said that he came from Missouri as did Joe. Always ready to help, but hesitant to say much about himself. A mystery, thought Elias.

Then there was "China Bill" Foster. Bill had made his way north from somewhere in the deep South, Elias thought. Elias knew he was the oldest of the group and certainly the most knowledgeable and worldly. He was also quiet and yet not distant. He was always ready with help or advice, but you had to ask first.

"Bill," asked Elias, "you said you went north from somewhere in the south. How did you manage?"

"We originally come from Kentucky back in 1856," Bill began. "We crossed over the Ohio River when it was froze over and got to Cincinnati, my older brother 'n me. Then we met up with some others from Kentucky name of Garners. There was a whole family of 'em. There was four kids and then the grand folks too. Me an' my brother got sent to Canada by the Underground Railroad, but the Garners had to wait. I was told later that the slave catchers came to get them and Mrs. Garner killed her own baby girl to keep it from bein' brought up a slave. She said she would a' done the other kids, too, if she'd had the time." Bill shook his head as he looked around at the other men.

"It was later on that we met up with some people from Kansas that Old Cap'n Brown had helped get away. They told us about the farm land in Kansas and how they was black folks, Indians and white folks all just goin' 'bout their own business and livin' and never mind. That's when my brother and me started out for Kansas. I didn't want to live in another country anyhow, even though they were good to us. I just didn't feel like I belonged, ya know?

"And wouldn't ya know those were the same folks that 'Lias helped, weren't they, 'Lias?" Bill grinned and poked his finger at Elias. "You knew Ole Cap'n Brown, didn't ya?"

Elias looked up and nodded. He sat quiet for a few minutes while the other men waited for the story of the fabled Brown;

hero to many, villain to some. "Yes, I met the man; reddish brown hair, beardless during his stay in Kansas. They say he grew a beard after he left Kansas, sort of a disguise. He was a scarecrow of a man, tall and thin, with deep wrinkled lines all over his face. He had sky-blue eyes that could crackle like lightning or turn soft as a baby's. I once saw him make a man shrink back and almost wither with one of his looks. The man had been beating a mule when Brown turned on him. Brown didn't say a word, and yet the man dropped the reins and stood by absolutely quiet as Captain Brown, with the tenderness of an angel, lifted a small brown child up on the mule's back and led the animal away."

"How'd you come to know him, 'Lias? Whut was ya doin?" asked Matthew.

"I only met him once," replied Elias. "I was fourteen at the time. We had been in Kansas territory almost four years." Elias removed his blanket roll from beneath his arm and sat up with his legs crossed. "I had heard about him and read about him. Mr. Wallace would have a newspaper sent to him once in awhile. He liked to read *Frank Leslies Illustrated Newspaper.* It was printed in New York and had all the latest news about politics. Mr. Wallace liked politics and always wanted to know what was going on back where he grew up. We even read about the very first campaign speech Lincoln gave right after he decided to run for President. Did you know that it was given right up there by Atchison, Kansas?" Elias paused and looked into the campfire. "Mr. Lincoln gave that speech the same day that Old John Brown was hung, December second, 1859.

"There was a story in one of the papers about that. It seems there was this actor that got himself an army uniform and went to the hangin'. They wouldn't let any civilians near the place, but this fella got to be there and talk to the other marines. Then he told his story to the newspaper reporter. They printed his story because he was famous and they believed him. Name of Booth he was, John Booth. His family are actors, too, I heard

Mr. Wallace say." All was quiet as Elias and the others sat motionless.

"But what about you and Cap'n Brown?" asked Matthew.

"Yeah, go on and tell 'em," urged China Bill.

"Well, it was in January of '59, a little over four years ago. Earlier, in December, he led a raid on a couple of pro-slavery homesteads just across the border into Missouri. He brought back eleven slaves and he intended to get them to Canada. A man had been killed in that raid, and Captain Brown was a wanted man after that. Even President Buchanan offered a $250 reward for him." Elias smiled as he recalled, "Would you believe it, Old Brown turned around and offered a $2.50 reward for the capture of good old President Buchanan."

All the men burst into laughter and pushed at each other as they waggled their heads and slapped their legs with their hands.

"Mr. Brown set out with his slaves from down around Osawatomie and headed north," continued Elias. "It was bitter cold but he was afraid the Missourians would come after him and try to get their slaves back. Mr. Wallace had some friends that knew Captain Brown was coming and would need help. He asked me if I would drive a wagon for a friend of his that lived in Lawrence. He didn't want me to know the man's name in case something went wrong. That's when I met Mr. Brown … both of them."

"Whut you mean, bof' of 'em?" asked Toby as he squirmed and inched closer to the fire.

"We were to have a wagon ready and supplies for about twenty people. Mr. Brown had horses and a couple of wagons for his people, but that was all. Mr. Wallace told me that I was to go with his friend and the caravan as far as the Iowa border." Elias stared into the dying campfire, reliving a fond memory of his home and family.

"It was late in the evening when Mr. Brown came to our farm," continued Elias. "Mr. Wallace brought him to our place next to the barn and my mama asked him in. He bowed and called mama 'Ma'am.' " Elias paused and then said "And I'll never forget how he picked up little Cheat and held him so tight I thought he would squeeze the life out of him. When he finally put Cheat down, he looked over at Mama and I could see tears in Mr. Brown's eyes."

"That Cheat boy, he is sumpin' all right," said China Bill.

"Yes, but I also met the Captain Brown that sat his horse and watched his people hack to death five men for being pro-slavery," stated Elias as his face turned grim.

"I thought that happened cause them men was in on the raid on Lawrence, 'Lias."

"As far as Brown knew, that was just a rumor. Anyway, we loaded up and left that night. We moved along, mostly at night, until we got up through Nebraska Territory and over into Iowa. The 5th of February we drove into Tabor, Iowa. Captain Brown had friends there that helped him and his people go on to Grinnell and then to Chicago and finally to Canada."

"And those are the folks I met up with," stated Bill. "So you might say, I wouldn't even be here if it wasn't for Elias!"

"Can't say as I believe that, Bill. You would have found some way of getting where you wanted to go," said Elias. "I bet you could go anywhere and get just about anything you wanted to."

"Well, let's hope so, Elias. Maybe I can come in handy some day, too. You just give me the chance."

Again there was quiet. Each man looked around at those lounging around the fire and then wandered back into the comfort of his own thoughts, feeling the security of his comrades, knowing that now he was no longer alone. Most had the feeling of belonging for the very first time. Elias knew that as much as he missed his mother and brother, he would hate to be parted from these men that had become so much a part of his adult life. Had he finally grown up to become a mature adult? He wanted to be such, and yet he didn't want to give up the feelings and attitude of the young man he had finally enjoyed becoming since coming to the freedom of Kansas.

Two officers were standing off to one side listening to Elias tell about John Brown. "You know, Captain, those easterners are the ones that had the money, but it was Old John Brown ..., Old Captain Brown that had the nerve."

Both men stood silent for a few moments. "But it was odd," one finally spoke, "Old Brown never did try to leave Harper's Ferry. He probably could have. You know two of his people got away across the river, before the rest of them was either killed or captured. And yet Old Brown stayed. Maybe it had something to do with the fact that the very first one of his men that was killed that day was a freed black man named Dangerfield Newby. He was trying to get his wife brought out of slavery. In fact, when he died he had a letter in his pocket saying that she was about to be sold."

"I think maybe I know why," replied the other man. "With all the smoke and the screams and men yelling orders back and forth at each other trying to make some order out of the chaos, it was the very first time in his life Brown had been in control of his own destiny. All those years of owin' folks and not being a success; for a few hours anyway, he was in charge. He had control of what was going to happen at Harper's Ferry." After a pause the man continued. "He won, you know."

"What you mean he won?" questioned the other. "He got a bayonet in him and then they hung him."

"That's all right, he still won. Everybody up and down the East Coast heard about Old John Brown and what he did and why he did it. No, Old Captain Brown won all right."

Chapter 11

Wednesday, June 24, 1863 Baxter Springs, KS

"You always hearin' 'bout sumpin', Big Ears," said One Shoe.

"Yeah, well when was the las' time I was wrong, 'Big Feet'?" replied Toby. "I said that Corporal Johnson of Company A said we was … *were* going to Sherwood, didn't I, and we went, did'n we? Now I's … *I'm* tellin' ya that we's going to sommer's down south and you just wait n' see!"

"Now what are you two carrying on about?" asked Elias as he pulled off his hat and sat beneath the tree with the others. "You guys are always after each other. What's it about this time?"

"Well, I'm sure glad you got here in time to hear the latest general order from Commander Washington, here," said One Shoe as he threw a mock salute towards Toby. "He doesn't bother to have his orders printed up, he just runs around yellin' 'em out to all of us so's we can pass 'em on."

"You just wait …," said Toby in a more subdued tone, "you'll see."

"What?" demanded Elias with an exasperated tone in his voice.

"The Commander here says we are gonna be movin' out of here and headin' south," reported One Shoe. "Says we might as well get packin' cause he says so."

"I didn't say it's cause I say so, ya big dumb private, I said it's on account of what Corporal Miller says, and he knows, 'cause he works for Captain Earle."

"Toby may be right, Tom," said Elias. "I heard the same thing less than an hour ago. It looks like the colonel knew what he was talking about. There is supposed to be a very large supply train coming along near here headed for Fort Gibson."

Toby didn't say a word, he just pushed himself up to a sitting position and arched his eyebrows high into his forehead. His blank gaze was all the "I told you so" that was needed to make his point.

"We're moving the regiment Friday morning," said Colonel Williams to his lieutenant. "I've been in touch with Colonel Dodd, who's in command of the supply train's escort, and we will probably be needed before the train gets to Gibson. We should meet up with them before nightfall Friday."

"Yes, Sir," replied Lieutenant E. A. Coleman of Company A. "I'll advise the company commanders right away, Sir."

"We should be joined by Major Foreman with his Indian Home Guard somewhere along the way also," said Colonel Williams. "Colonel Dodd already has some of the 2nd Colorado, 3rd Wisconsin, 9th and 14th Kansas Cavalry and they've sent some of the 2nd Kansas Battery along for fire power."

"Sounds like a hell of a train … a … begging your pardon Colonel," replied the lieutenant.

"You're right, Lieutenant, it is a hell of a train. That's why General Blunt needs it and why General Cooper and Stand Watie want to get it away from us."

"Yes, Sir," replied the lieutenant. "I understand."

"And tell the men to take all of their belongings. This will probably be a permanent move. At least, a temporary-permanent move."

The lieutenant returned the smile as he saluted, turned and left the colonel's office. "It's going be a long ride," he thought to himself.

"Man, that's gonna be a long walk," muttered One Shoe.

"We might as well be going somewhere when we's walkin'," said George Brothers, "instead'a just walkin' back and forth, and up and down 'round this here place. That's all we been doing since we got the forts all done."

It was a deceivingly cool June morning, that Friday the 27th.

The men gathered all their gear and wrapped it in their tent halves and blankets. At least most of the personal belongings could be carried by the baggage wagons. It was sure to get a lot warmer later in the day, and Elias was certain that July in the Cherokee Nation would be just as hot and miserable as it was in Kansas. No doubt by ten o'clock this morning, the men's shirts would be soaked with sweat.

The next few days were just as Elias and his friends expected, long, dusty and hot. The officers and cavalrymen would walk their horses as much as they would ride. Breaks were too short and too few. At noon more time was spent trying to find a cool spot in which to sit than eating. Sunday and Monday the train started at dawn, took long noons, and kept going until well after sundown, in order to avoid the heavy humidity and pressing heat of the daytime.

Elias wondered if the Confederate generals would dare try anything with as large a guard as the supply train had. He estimated that there must be well over a thousand men moving along with the train.

"It's hard to figure out just how they keep all this here train going, 'Lias," said Toby, late Monday evening. "How do they know when everybody is supposed to git up and start walkin' and when they supposed to stop?"

"Ya watch the fella in front of ya," said One Shoe. "That part's easy."

"Well, I'm sure glad that I'm not the first guy. He's gonna be the first one to see the trouble, up there," said Toby, pointing south down the road they would travel the next day.

"What makes you think there will be trouble, Toby?" asked Elias as he squirmed around for a comfortable place to go to sleep.

"You think them … *those* Rebs are gonna let all this here stuff just walk on down the road? No, Suh. They gonna try for it, you just wait and see."

"Mo word from the gen'ral," mumbled One Shoe.

"Quiet down," a voice came from off in the shadows.

"Are you thinking what I am, Jim?" asked Lieutenant Colonel Dodd, as he rode next to Colonel Williams. It was mid-morning on the 1st day of July, 1863. The movement of the supply train had gone without a hitch.

"Don't even mention it, Ted," replied Williams. "I know very well what you're thinking. I've had the same feeling since this time yesterday."

"I'm certain we have been seen by the Reb scouts, Jim, and I just hope they think we are too big a force to attack. If I know McIntosh's Cherokee scouts, they have a better headcount of our people than we do."

"If that's the case, Ted, maybe they will realize that with all the white, Indian and colored troops we have, along with the artillery and cavalry, they wouldn't stand a chance."

"Then why are you jumpy, Jim?" asked Colonel Dodd, with a smile.

"Because I happen to think that the Rebs might just be foolish enough to try to take us. I once heard a southern senator brag that it would take four Union soldiers to equal one Confederate."

"I'm sure they have found out differently by now, Jim." Slowly, the officer reined in his horse and trotted back toward the center of the train.

"Ain't we gonna be stoppin' for noon, 'Lias?" asked George Brothers? "I think it is hotter today then it was yesterday."

"That's cause it's July today," replied One Shoe.

"I think you're probably right, George," said Elias. "But there are some trees up ahead. Looks like it's a river or something. Maybe we will stop there."

"If they's … *there's* water in it, I just might fall in and get all wet," laughed Toby. "Who wants to push me in?"

"Who wants to hold 'im under?" laughed One Shoe.

"The scouts tell me that's Cabin Creek up ahead, Colonel," said Captain Ethan Earle. "And I have been advised that one of Major Foreman's Indian Guards is certain he spotted some of

Stand Watie's Cherokees. I'd bet anything we are in for an ambush at the creek."

"You're probably right," replied Colonel Williams. "I was hoping to avoid this, but if I were in their shoes, that's probably what I would do."

Colonel Williams rode back to where Colonel Dodd was standing next to a wagon. After relaying the information, orders were issued to move out slowly and be prepared for a sudden attack at or near the distant creek or village.

The ford at Cabin Creek actually amounted to much more than a place to cross the creek. The area was part of a plantation belonging to a Cherokee man named Martin. He had, it was rumored, over one hundred-thousand acres, all southwest of the Grand River, that included not only two homes he had built, but out-buildings and slave quarters for his more than one hundred slaves. In those days land could be *rented* from the Cherokee Nation and the land upon which homes were built could be owned outright. In 1861, Martin and his two sons had joined the Confederate forces of Colonel Stand Watie, after sending their families south, and told the slaves to look after the place until their return.

The ford was a favorite stopping place for settlers heading south and included a trading post, a blacksmith shop, a stage station and several other homes. Once a buffalo path, then Indian trail, wagon trail and now a Military Road, it was said that over a thousand wagons had passed in a six-month period.

"It's gunfire, Elias," said China Bill. "And it's close."

"It's right up ahead, Bill," replied Elias.

"That's Major Foreman's Indian Guards," spoke up One Shoe.

"That's right. They's leadin' and they's done run into trouble, sho nuff," said George Brothers, excitedly. "Hear it comes,'Lias. We's in fer it now."

"We ran into their pickets, Sir," reported Major Foreman to Colonel's Williams and Dodd. "We killed three of them, but we also brought back three of them as prisoners." Foreman pointed to three Cherokees standing nearby under guard. "My scouts were right. They're Stand Watie's men. I guess he and McIntosh joined up with General Cooper. That's what we are facing, Sir. The main body is lined up on the south side of Cabin Creek, and they have the ford completely controlled."

"All right, Major, this is what I want," stated Colonel Dodd, as he outlined his plan.

The wagon train was brought together and parked in the open prairie so all sides could be watched. Three companies of the 2nd Colorado and a detachment of one hundred men of the 1st Colored were placed as guards around the wagons and stock.

"Now, let's take a look at that creek." Major Foreman, Colonel's Williams and Dodd along with Major J. N. Smith of the 2nd Colorado Mounted Infantry rode south toward the main ford of Cabin Creek.

Being posted near the ford, Elias was one of several men standing close to where the officers were looking over the creek. They had moved west of the main ford and were trying to determine if the creek could be crossed at any other point. The shadows of the trees along the bank offered some cover since it was almost eight o'clock in the evening.

"Water's running pretty fast and it looks like it's higher than normal," said one of the officers. "I can't tell if we could make it like this or not."

"Let me find out, Colonel, that's easy," said one of the soldiers standing close by. With that, he dropped his rifle, pushed off his shoes and jumped feet first into the water. He had no sooner surfaced in the swirling cascade of muddy water, than a shot rang out and the man jerked and then went under. A Rebel sharpshooter's bullet had found its mark.

Without hesitation, Elias was at the edge of the creek and plunging into the water. His powerful arms pulled him toward the spot in the water that the wounded man's back could barely be seen. As another shot rang out, water erupted close to Elias. Then there was firing from the north side of the creek. Union riflemen were returning the Rebel's fire trying to cover Elias' attempt to save the wounded man.

Grabbing the limp body by its belt, Elias struggled his way back to the north bank. Big One Shoe was waist deep in water, one arm wrapped around a tree root at the edge of the bank, the other stretched out for Elias to grab. The connection made, the unconscious soldier was pulled from the water and Elias crawled up the slick, grassy creek bank, gasping and spitting out muddy water.

Back at one of the small campfires, it was found that the wounded Union soldier had been knocked unconscious by the Rebel's bullet as it creased the back of the soldier's head. He would have a headache for a day or two, a nasty scar below his hat line, but probably little else. Preparing to change into dry clothing, Elias stood nearby.

"I suppose you want me to feel obligated just cause your captain made you go after me? Well, maybe I do owe you sumpthin', but I'm here to tell you that if it wasn't for you niggers I wouldn't have to be here in the first place." The soldier began to cough and spit. "And if they think I am going to risk my neck for a bunch of niggers and redskins again, they got another think comin'. Hell, them Indians will be the first to run. You can't depend on anyone but a white man, if you ask me."

"I didn't ask you, *white man,* but I can tell you two things." Elias spit out the words through clenched teeth. "First, my captain nor anybody else sent me in the water after you. I made that mistake on my own. And second, you owe your life to an Indian and a black man!" said Elias.

"Just how the hell do you figure that?"

"A black man just pulled your sorry ass out of the creek when you were shot and about to drown. And this nigger that pulled you out of that water had his neck saved by an Indian when a Reb was just about to shoot me in the face at Island Mound, Missouri! Now if that is too much for you to take, I can sure as hell throw you back and you can crawl out of the creek bottom by yourself!"

None of the men had ever seen Elias so mad or heard him talk this way. Nor was there any doubt that they were glad they were not the object of his anger.

As the men were preparing for bed that evening, Elias was very quiet. Not knowing for sure if they should say anything after Elias' outburst, not a word was spoken. Finally, Elias arose from his bed and walked away into the darkness. He skirted the wagon train and searched out the area where the 2nd Colorado was camped. Finally he made his way to a small tent where the wounded soldier had been placed.

"Just stopped in to see how you are doing," said Elias in a quiet voice.

"Huh? Oh, it's you," said the soldier. As he lay on his side, his bandage showed white against the blanket that had been rolled up for a pillow. "I'm doin' fine, I guess. I suppose I could'a been hit somewheres else that would'a done more damage."

Elias smiled and then knelt down next to the man. "I'm sorry I yelled at you today. I'm sure you were probably hurting pretty bad and I should have known better. I'm sorry."

"Well," the soldier hesitated and avoided Elias' eyes, "I should'a kept my mouth shut. Ya did save my sorry ass like ya said."

"Forget it," replied Elias, "someone would probably have done the same for me."

"But you're sayin' that it wouldn't a' been me."

"No I didn't say that. I didn't even mean that. I have been thinking, and I may understand what you meant this afternoon. I suppose it is hard for you to understand just why you are risking your neck when it really isn't your freedom or your country that is in real danger."

"Maybe I don't know what you're getting' at, Fella."

"My name's Elias. Elias Mothers. I'm from up around Lawrence, Kansas. Well, I'm really from Virginia, but we have been in Kansas for about eight years now. We were slaves in Virginia and ran away. We got some help and made it to Kansas."

"Well, hell, if'n you're free, why'd ya join up?"

"It's because I finally know what it's like to be free, that's why I joined. I don't ever want me or my family to lose what we have now. Now I have a chance to do something that might help hold on to my freedom, so … here I am."

The young soldier finally looked up at Elias, stretched out one leg trying to get to a comfortable position and moaned slightly.

"You know?" continued Elias, "I guess what you fellas don't seem to understand is that we black folks have a lot in common with the Confederates that most of the northern white people don't have. We are both fighting for *our country.* I'm not saying I agree with what they are doing, I just think maybe I understand. The southerners are fighting for the way they want their country to be able to live. You might say they are fighting for their independence just like America did in the Revolutionary War. We colored are fighting for our independence so we can have a country to live in, the way we would like to live. You white northerners already have what you want, so it is harder for you to understand why you have to go off and get shot at."

"I don't know much about that," replied the soldier. "We didn't talk about it, a bunch of us just up and volunteered one day. I guess we thought it would be a lot of fun, goin' out and killin' Rebs. I don't suppose we thought much about getting' shot at our own selves. Now two of the bunch have been killed already and I almost was. That sort of thing kinda gets to ya'. Guess I shouldn't have mouthed off like I did," with a somewhat lower voice he continued, "sorry."

"It's okay," replied Elias, "and I'm sure glad you guys are around. I have a notion it's going to take every one of us tomorrow. You really did do your part, you know. You proved we are going to have to wait until at least morning before the creek goes down enough for us to get across. Thanks for your help."

Elias arose and left the tent.

"Damned if I ever will understand them there folks," said the soldier as he turned and drifted into a troubled sleep.

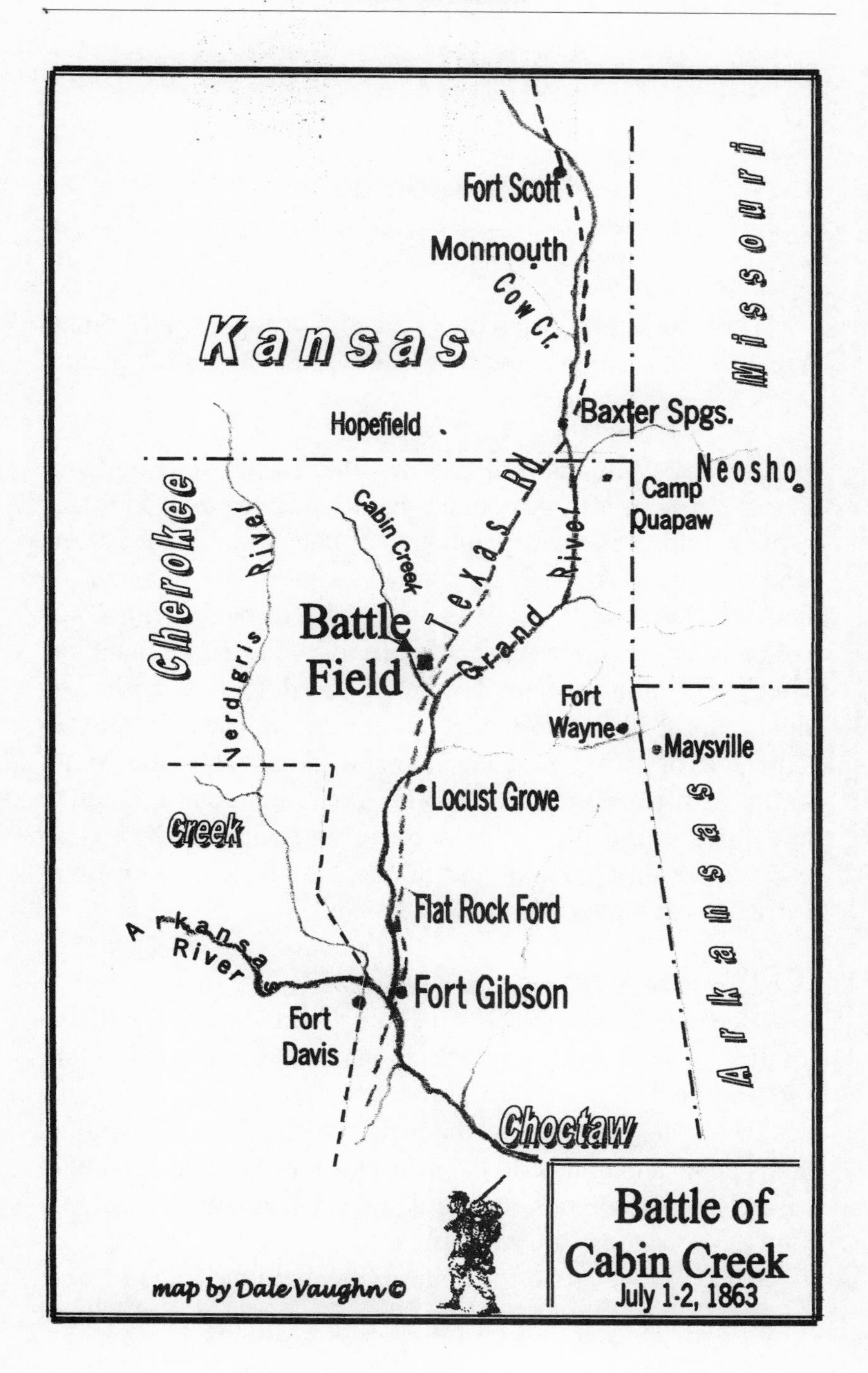
Fort Scott
Monmouth
Cow Cr.
Kansas
Missouri
Baxter Spgs.
Hopefield
Neosho
Camp
Quapaw
Cherokee
Cabin Creek
Texas Rd.
Grand River
Verdigris River
Battle
Field
Fort
Wayne
Maysville
Locust Grove
Creek
Flat Rock Ford
Arkansas
River
Fort Gibson
Fort
Davis
Arkansas
Choctaw
Battle of
Cabin Creek
July 1-2, 1863
map by Dale Vaughn ©

Chapter 12

"Have the bugler sound officers call, Corporal," said Colonel Williams, late that evening. It was time to map out the plan of attack.

"Yes, Sir, right away, Sir."

Colonel Williams outlined his plan to his staff and line officers. "I want two six-pound cannons located on the left flank up on that ridge," he said, pointing to a hill overlooking the creek, "and one twelve-pound howitzer and a mountain howitzer on the right. These will lay down cover fire to begin with. They will be accompanied by detached portions of the Indian Battalion. After the shelling, Major Foreman, you'll be first with your Indian Home Guard followed by Colonel Bowles and his ten companies of the 1st Kansas. Following them will be you, Major Smith, with your 2nd Colorado Infantry Regiment. I intend to hold three companies of Wisconsin and Kansas Cavalry in reserve. Get this fixed in your minds, Gentlemen, and we will confirm at dawn tomorrow. That'll be all."

Thursday July 2, 1863 Cabin Creek, I.T.

"Better grab a mouthful of whatever ya got t' eat while ya got the chance. I'm afraid we're gonna be in fer toss and ketch-it fer awhile."

"And you keep your head down," replied Elias as he pulled on his boots and hunted in the near dawn for his canteen. There was an almost coolness to the damp air that would surely be gone as soon as the sun was up.

"They say we are to form up right behind the Indian Home Guards. I heard the colonel say that the Colorado boys were going to be right behind us."

"I guess that means that them Rebs is … *are* going to get red, black and white for breakfast, 'Lias," said Toby.

"They'll know they been in a scrap," chimed in One Shoe.

"Fo' sho'." Slows nodded and showed a large grin.

"I'm sure they will, still you guys watch yourselves," warned Elias. "We have a long way to go before we're done with this and I want every one of us to show up when it's time to muster out."

"All right, men," said Colonel Williams to a group of officers gathered in his tent. "Remember, I want our flanks secured by detached portions of the Indian Battalion. The artillery will commence firing approximately thirty to forty minutes before we begin our attack. Major Foreman, you're to lead the attack, the 1st Colored right behind you and a battalion of the 2nd Colorado Infantry behind them."

The officers nodded and peered down at the rough sketch of the area that had been laid out on the colonel's field table.

"Any questions?" asked Colonel Williams.

"My men are all ready, Colonel," spoke up Major Foreman.

"All right, Major. So far we have not detected any major build-up of troops close to the south side of the creek. We believe that if there is, the artillery will move them back and you can safely cross before you run into much resistance." Colonel Williams straightened up and looked at his watch. "The artillery will begin firing at eight o'clock sharp. You men be ready to cross the creek when you hear the bugler. And Lieutenant, you make sure the guards around the train are on their toes. I don't want someone penetrating our rear and getting to those supplies."

Everyone nodded and headed toward their respective units to prepare for the attack.

"Well, I suppose'n it won't be long now, 'Lias," said George.

"I suppose not," replied Elias. He could hear the anxious tone in George Brothers' voice. This was George's first taste of combat. At Island Mound and Sherwood, he had been ordered to remain behind and be ready for a second attack if one was necessary. George, just like everyone else, was worried about being hurt or killed, but was just as concerned about performing bravely and not letting his friends down. That was probably the biggest fear of all of the men. Even Elias was nervous. The men seemed to look up to him, and even though he had not chosen the role of their leader, it just seemed to fall to him.

"Oh, God!" cried Toby, "there they go!"

The artillery opened up with a roar as clouds of smoke drifted along the creek banks. The noise was deafening even though Elias and his men were some distance away. From both their flanks the cannons roared. Whistling and whirring could be heard as the solid shot sailed across the creek and landed in the trees on the south bank. Mud, limbs and water shot into the air as round after round was directed at the supposed enemy positions. The men gripped their weapons and checked to be sure they were loaded. Without an early morning breeze, the smoke hung along the creek.

"When do you think we will be going?" shouted One Shoe, as he crouched close to Elias.

"They said we would go when the artillery stopped and the bugler sounded the charge," replied Elias. "Stick close to me, I may need you."

"I'm stickin' close to ever' body," said One Shoe.

Suddenly all was still. The quiet was almost louder than the shelling had been. The men held their breath waiting for the sound that would send them into the water and on to the confrontation that was their mission. Prayers were said, glances between friends and comrades, weak smiles were traded. There were determined looks on the faces of some of the men that seemed to say they could hardly wait to meet their foe and wipe them out.

The sound! The stillness was pierced by the shrill sound made by Little Max the bugler. Max stood five foot one, was sixteen years old and could blow his horn louder and with more gusto than Gabriel himself. And you could bet that as soon as the charge was sounded, Max would be running forward as fast as his short legs could carry him. He always managed to stay close to the flag bearer, just in case. Should the flag begin to fall, Max had vowed to himself that it would never touch the ground nor fall into enemy hands.

Major Foreman could be seen at the edge of the creek, waving his sword as he moved his horse toward the water. Although the water level had lowered during the night, the Indian troops still had to hold their weapons and ammunition high above their heads as they plunged into the creek. The yells and whoops of the Home Guard could be heard back among the men of the 1st, as they began to move south. Elias could see One Shoe just to his right, George next to him, Toby a step ahead to his left. China Bill was on Elias' heels, tightening his belt and pulling his hat down over the scar above his eyes.

"Hell, I still can't see a damn thing," said China Bill as he almost tripped over Elias.

"How we supposed to know where we's goin'?" asked Toby.

"Ya jes folla the man …"

"Yeah, I know, One Shoe, I just folla' the guy in front of me," replied Toby. "An' how come you ain't the man in front of me?"

"Cause I tol' 'Lias I'd look out after yo' butt, so's I'm doin' it from right here where's I can see it!"

The smile on Elias' face quickly disappeared. As they neared the creek, suddenly the south bank opened up with merciless fire. The Rebel soldiers had hidden themselves and waited until the Indians were just about to climb the creek bank. Major Foreman could be seen on his horse, thrashing around in the water. His horse had been struck several times by musket balls, but was still on its feet. Confusion caused the surprised Indians to falter and stumble over one another. Men screamed, tried to return fire, only to trip and stumble in the muddy creek bottom.

Major Foreman twisted in his saddle and sagged to one side. A musket ball had found its mark. As the major struggled to stay on his horse, he was struck by a second ball which threw him into the water. As the Indian troops saw their leader fall, all heart for combat was lost and they began to withdraw back across the creek.

Elias and his men rushed to the creek bank and began to fire into the enemy on the far side. Colonel Williams ordered three more companies of the 1st Colored to the right of the Union center to lay down a blanket of covering fire. The artillery opened up, tearing away at the Southern forces in order to force them to retreat from the creek's edge.

"Look," Elias yelled in order to be heard over the sound of rifle fire. "See those two cuts in the bank, head for them." Those closest to him looked and then nodded.

Even before the artillery had ceased firing, the black troops charged the creek and were in the water. Struggling in the mud and swirling water, they made their way to the south bank. Grabbing for tree roots, hands full of grass, anything to help them up the bank, the men clawed their way on to dry land. The artillery was still firing. Flying mud, tree limbs and rocks were competing with enemy musket balls for space along the water's edge.

A swishing sound, then an explosion, followed by flying debris completely surrounded Elias. A scream sounded almost at his right shoulder. Smoke and falling leaves obscured his vision as he tried to locate the horrible sound.

"Elias, oh God, Elias, I done been killed … I been killed in the leg … hep me, 'Lias … don' let em git me." Then a gurgling sound cut off the voice. It was George. Elias could just make out the form of his friend hanging by one leg with his body head down in the water. The artillery shell had unearthed a large cottonwood tree and caused it to fall across George's leg, throwing him back into the creek. The leg was shattered to the point that it might even tear away from its body.

Elias dropped his musket and plunged back into the creek. He grabbed for George's shirt front and pulled his face up above the water. Suddenly Toby was next to Elias, trying to steady the now limp body of their friend. George began to sputter and then let out another scream as pressure from the moving current, plus the efforts of his comrades caused horrible pain in his leg still caught under the large tree.

Elias heard a grunt and groan as George's leg came free. He looked up to see big One Shoe bent over the cottonwood. His arms were wrapped around the trunk and he had lifted the massive tree enough for George's leg to slide free.

"It's out, Tom," shouted Elias.

One Shoe sagged and dropped the heavy burden. One of his arms was caught beneath the tree, but due to the softness of the mud he was able to pull free.

Elias and Toby pulled George up to the water's edge and with Tom's help got him on to the bank. George's leg was badly mangled just above the knee. George moaned and grabbed at Elias' arm. Elias couldn't make out anything George was saying, but grabbed his hand and held tight.

"Come on, George," said Elias as he leaned over close to George's ear. "Big Tom got you free and you're out of the water. It's going to be all right. We'll get you taken care of. Don't worry."

George looked at Elias with a glassy stare. "Don't let 'em git me, 'Lias. Ya know whut they do to us if'n they …"

"No one's gonna get you, George. We aren't going to leave you. You hold on, ya hear? Remember, George, family. You remember? We're the family boys, you and me. Mothers and Brothers, that's us. No one's going to get either one of us. Remember, George, nobody dies! Nobody dies!"

Toby looked at Elias, then to George's almost severed leg and then back to Elias, and slowly shook his head.

"You heard what I said, Toby," said Elias as he gritted his teeth. "Find someone to help tie up George's leg and get him back across to Doctor Harrington or Ensor. Do it now!"

George passed out as Elias gently laid him back onto the grassy creek bank. "Come on, Tom," said Elias as he spotted a muddy musket, "we've got work to do."

As Elias, One Shoe, and China Bill began to move away

from the south bank of Cabin Creek, they could hear cavalry crossing the creek A mounted unit, commanded by Lieutenant Philbrick, moved through the infantry to protect the flanks of the Union line.

"Stay together and watch out for each other," yelled Elias. "You know what'll happen if they take any of us." Thoughts of torturous treatment, submission to slavery and even instant death flooded the minds of the men of the 1st Kansas. And yet, the discipline of the troops was superb. The main body of the enemy was less than a quarter of a mile away. The Union line formed perfectly. Then the center portions of the line fell back, allowing Captain John E. Sturart to bring two companies of his cavalry to the front to form a single line of horsemen.

Sabers flashed in the morning sun as yells and cheers were heard from the Union troops as they charged the Confederate secondary entrenchment. Across the open prairie the Union soldiers ran, pistols firing and infantry bayonets pointing the way.

Side by side, Elias and his men raced toward the Rebel line. Soon they could see some of the soldiers in gray rising up to fire. Elias saw one young boy drop forward after taking Elias' musket ball in the upper chest. Another started to aim when One Shoe's shot took away the man's jaw.

Closer now, one Confederate was trampled under a Union cavalryman's horse and raised from the ground just in time to catch a saber swipe across his shoulder and back. Elias stumbled and fell onto the body of a wounded Rebel soldier. The soldier grunted and tried to hit Elias in the face with a pistol. Elias, without thinking, drove his elbow into the man's groin and buried his bayonet in the soldier's stomach. The man's blood soaked Elias' pant leg as he struggled back to his feet. Screams of pain and yells of exuberance could be heard mixing over the prairie. It seemed as though everyone, Confederate and Union alike, were running southward as if in a foot race toward a rich prize. The prize was life itself; the future, any future. Everyone wanted some kind of future, regardless of what it might hold.

Firing, loading, running a few yards and firing again, the black troops forced the Rebels to abandon their fortifications. The Confederate line fell apart, and the men in gray ran for their lives, ignoring the commands of their officers to stand and fight.

"They're on the run," cried Colonel Williams. "Have the infantry return to the creek." With that, Colonel Williams ordered the cavalry reserves to give chase. After about five miles the cavalry returned to camp and prepared to resume their march to Fort Gibson.

"The cavalry's back, Colonel. They chased 'em and killed a few more, but finally let 'em go. According to the prisoners, we were right. It was Stand Watie's Indians, McIntosh's Cherokee and Creeks and detachments from two different Texas regiments. That means they outnumbered us over two to one."

Colonel Williams nodded in approval with a smile on his face. "I knew our men would stand! I just knew it!"

"I figure about fifty Rebs killed and fifty more wounded, Colonel," reported Lieutenant Philbrick. "We have one killed and about twenty wounded. Captain Earle of Company F was wounded, but he's going to make it okay. I can't say the same for Major Foreman. He was hit twice, bad."

"Damn!"

"Don't know why we has to miss all the fun," spoke a member of the wagon guard. "Hell, I could hear all the shootin' and all we got to do was stand around."

"Yeah, I heard some of them guys tellin' 'bout how they had them Rebs a runnin' and crappin' they pants."

Laughter rang out as the men slapped at each other and made scared looking faces, mocking the enemy.

"Why, I heard one of the fellas tellin' 'bout how he got two Rebs with one ball. He found one sojer hiddin' ahind tother'n and got'em both with one shot."

"Dat's da way. Not so much loadin'," laughed another.

"Did you hear the screams, too?"

All of a sudden the laughter stopped. The men looked up at

Elias standing over them with both fists clenched, knuckles bulging like rocks. "You want to help wash some of the blood out of my pants? You want to go over and tell George Brothers how much fun he had?"

"Hell, we didn't mean …"

"No, you didn't mean … you didn't think …" Elias lowered his voice to just above a whisper. "You didn't see Major Foreman's body floating face down in the muddy water. You didn't hear George's screams when they took off what was left of his leg this afternoon, did you?"

The men stared silently at Elias.

"You want to go out there and help find all the body pieces and fit them together with the dead?" Pointing southward, Elias continued, "You want to go out there and tell some of those kids that are dying that you're sorry you missed out on the fun?"

Elias turned and walked away. "You make me sick."

"Now, what the hell is wrong with him?" spoke one of the men standing next to the campfire.

Just then Toby let go with a hard right cross that sent the man to the ground. "Don't you say another word, ya hear?" said Toby leaning over him. "Not one more goddamn word!"

"I have never been so proud of any group of men in my whole life." Colonel Williams rode next to one of his line officers. The dust rose around them and the heat managed to work its way through the blue uniform jackets of both men.

Earlier that morning Colonel Williams had ended his engagement report on Cabin Creek by stating; *"I cannot close this communication without referring to the chivalrous and soldierly conduct of the entire command during the engagement; the whole command crossing this difficult ford and forming in the face of the enemy, with as much ease and little confusion as if on parade. Had there been no train to guard, so that the whole force could have been employed against the enemy, I don't know but I should have been able to capture the whole Confederate force."*

" 'Lias, you suppose we gonna walk all the way to Mississippi? I don't think I've ever put my feet down and up so much in all my days," said young Matthew Smith. "How come I didn't join up in the ridin' army?"

"You ever been on a horse?" asked China Bill.

"Well, I been behind lots 'a mules. And I rode a cow in from the field couple 'a times."

"It ain't the same, Matt. I'm not sure you got legs long enough to reach down the side of a good-size horse."

"But I do got legs long enough to walk all the way to Jeff Davis, is 'at it?"

Elias smiled as he listened to the banter among his friends. They were actually more than friends now, they were certainly family. He could remember thinking about that back in Baxter Springs. They had had their first battle, been to Fort Gibson and back and now headed that way again after their second real battle. The bond between them would last a lifetime. Long after they left the army, when a future July heat would bake into their bodies, they would think about the July they ducked the minni balls that were being thrown at them by the men they were racing to catch up with. They would think about the men they trusted to be at their side when lives depended upon someone watching all directions. They would value the opportunities they had had to show they were worthy of the trust placed in them. Elias was certain he would miss these men. He would never miss the war, but he would carry thoughts of the warriors with him forever.

"I heard Tom Mitchell got killed, 'Lias," said China Bill.

"Who dat … *who's that?"* questioned Toby.

"He was from Company F," replied Elias. "Remember? His brother George was killed at Sherwood."

"What they gonna tell them boys' mama? She done lost two now," said One Shoe.

"Better yet, who's gonna tell her? I'm sure glad I don't have to be the one. How long do you think it'll be before she's gonna know?" asked Toby.

"An' how she gonna get along with both her boys gone?"

"It's going to be rough for a lot of families," said Elias as he looked toward the ground and slowly shook his head.

"Ya know, we just done … *did* pretty good back there at the Creek, didn't we, 'Lias?" asked Toby. "We didn't run like them Indians did, and we showed the white boys they would have to step out smart to keep up with us." Toby looked around with a grin on his face.

"It would have been easy to get rattled," said Elias. "That water was pretty swift, and when the Indians saw Major Foreman go down, well, I'm not sure what I would have done. They weren't expecting the Rebs to be hidden along the bank. I guess things all happened so fast, they weren't sure just what to do."

"Well, you seemed to know just what to do when George got hit with that big ole tree. You didn't expect nothin' like that and yet you got right to 'im."

"That was just a reaction. He yelled for me and I was lucky enough to get to him in time."

"Yeah, he would'a drowned if'n you hadn't done whut ya did, 'Lias," said One Shoe.

"You were the hero, Tom. How in the world did you manage to lift that tree?" asked Elias.

"That weren't nuthin'. It wasn't hooked down and I could get my arms around it. No different than liftin' a barrel of flour or like that."

Elias shook his head and felt a warm glow inside that had nothing to do with the July sun. He was glad he was a member of this group. In a way, he had never felt so safe in his entire life. He loved these men and he knew they felt the same about him. He was free, he had real friends, and he was able to do what he felt was necessary to keep him and his friends free. He had his chance. He would make the most of it.

Chapter 13

Saturday, July 11, 1863 Fort Gibson, I.T.

"That fella sho' in one hell of a hurry, 'Lias," exclaimed Matthew. "Where you figure he comin' from?"

"I don't know, Matthew, but it must be something important. He headed right for the colonel's tent."

"Guess it ain't no letter for me then," said One Shoe with a sly grin.

"Who do you know that kin write?" chimed in China Bill?

"I'll have you know I knows several people that kin write, smart ass!"

"Yeah, who?"

"Well, 'Lias kin write and so's can Ole Sarah, back at Fort Scott."

"Okay, Elias is right cheer, so's he ain't gonna write, special see'in how he knows you cain't read, and Ole Sarah wouldn't write cause she ain't got nuthin' to say to the likes of you," said one of the men as he pulled on his boot.

"Sides, I heard she's a witch-woman," put in Matthew. "Most a' what she says is conjure stuff. That's scary, t' me."

"That ain't so. Most a' what she says is Bible stuff. That there mammy can read real good, too. And she don't mind folks knowin' now that she ain't in the south no more," said One Shoe.

"Isn't in the south *anymore,"* corrected Elias

"Okay, but she said plenty to me when we was in Scott, and it warn't no conjure nuthin'," replied One Shoe with a defiant tone to his voice. "She tol' me that we had lots to be proud of cause the white folks was jealous of us colored!"

"You out yo' ... *your* mind?" Toby pulled at his pant leg and scratched the scars on his ankle. "Why in the world would the white folks be jealous a' us?"

"She says they is jealous cause we got sumpthin' that they don't. She says that we got *skin-pig-ment* and they don't and that's why they jealous."

"What kind a' pigs is that and who you know what has some of 'em?"

"I think what she meant was that we have a color to our skin and the white people don't," broke in Elias. "So it is true we have something that they don't, but I'm not so sure they envy us for it."

"But we stand out, Elias," said Matthew, "we look different. Those white folks, they just all look alike. Ain't you noticed that?"

Elias smiled. "I believe I have heard them say the same about us, Matthew."

"Aw, come on,'Lias," Toby began, pointing to One Shoe, "I sho … *sure* don't look nuthin' like that big old …"

"Watch yo' mouth, little fella."

"Come on, guys, let's see if we can find out what kind of news that fella took to the colonel. It must be something important, that horse looks like it was rode mighty hard."

"Colonel," panted the rider as he entered Colonel William's tent, "General Blunt is about fifteen minutes away with about five or six hundred cavalry and a dozen wagons."

"What? Why in hell didn't I know he was coming?" stormed Williams.

"I couldn't say, Sir. All I know is that we saw him and his advance scouts told us he was headed for Fort Blunt. I got here as fast as I could, Sir."

"Fort Blunt, where the hell is that?"

The soldier lowered his voice slightly and looked around. "That's here, Sir. Someone has re-named Gibson. It's now Fort Blunt. That's what the scout told me … Sir."

"I'll bet I know just how that happened," said Colonel

Williams. "All right, have the bugler sound officer's call, immediately."

"Gentlemen," Major General James G. Blunt looked around at the company and staff officers that had been assembled. "We are about to begin a new campaign that will take us south of the Arkansas River and directly into the Confederate forces massed there. I have word that they are planning an offensive campaign, and I intend to beat them to the punch. Our possession of Fort Blunt clearly puts us in a position to take the offensive ourselves, and I want us to gain complete control of this portion of the Indian Territory."

The officers looked around at each other, quietly evaluating the proposed plan. It was well known that the Confederates had a large compliment of close to 6,000 troops just to the south around Elk Creek. The Union strength, even with the Kansas and Wisconsin cavalry that had just arrived, amounted to about half that.

"You will find, in some of the wagons, new 1861 Springfield rifle-muskets. Some of the men were issued Springfields before they left Baxter Springs. Now we have enough for the rest."

"I have organized our mounted troops and infantry companies into two brigades," continued the general. "The First Brigade, commanded by Colonel Judson, will be made up of the 1st Kansas Colored, the 2nd Indian regiment, dismounted as infantry, and various sections of artillery. The Second Brigade will be commanded by Colonel Phillips and will be comprised of most of the rest of the infantry companies. I will use my cavalry as scouts and reconnaissance as well as leading charges as I see necessary."

"How much time do we have to prepare, General?" asked Colonel Williams.

"I intend to move immediately, Colonel. I don't want news of our offensive to leak or be guessed by Confederate observers."

"Sir, the Arkansas is quite swollen and would be impossible to ford. We will have to wait until it goes down."

"Colonel, I have no time to wait! If we can't ford, we will cross by boat and raft. Set your men to building those rafts at once. We have no time to waste!" The general looked from one officer to the next. "Well, do I hear any other objections?"

"What happens after we get across, General?" asked one of the men.

"We will form on each side of the Texas Road and proceed south until we engage the enemy. After the rout we will return and retain command of the entire area."

"Sounds easy to me," muttered one of the officers to the man next to him.

"Shouldn't take more'n a couple of hours," the man replied under his breath.

The sound of axes echoed throughout the fort the next three days. Logs were lashed together into rafts and piled three and four to a wagon. The evening of July 15th, scouts reported that they had found a place to cross just south of the fort. At midnight, General Blunt had assembled 250 cavalry, along with some supporting artillery, all taken from the First Brigade. "We will be the first to cross," stated the general. "We will set up a defensive post that will allow the remainder of the force to cross and assemble."

"Golly, guess he really means business if'n he's gonna be the first over, huh, 'Lias," said One Shoe.

"Most men don't get to be a general unless they have that kind of determination, Tom. He sees himself as a leader, so he is leading," replied Elias. "We better get ready. We are supposed to move out to the ford and wait until the general says it's safe to cross. That could be any time now."

The remainder of the First Brigade left Fort Blunt and made their way in the dark to the edge of the Arkansas, to await their turn to cross. In the distance scattered shots could be heard. The rest of the night the men tried to catch naps and what rest their nerves would allow.

"It sho' ... *sure* doesn't help for it to be dark whilst we just waitin'," whispered Toby. "Wish I knew who was doing the shootin'. How them boys know what they shootin' at, 'Lias?"

"It's probably the Rebs shooting at noises," replied Elias. "Our troops have scattered out and fire back once in awhile to make them think they are just pickets here and there, I think. Try to get some sleep. We will have a long walk once we get started."

"When you figure them gray-backs will know we on our way?" asked One Shoe.

"By the time we are across, the Confederates will know what we're up to and how many of us there are," said Elias. "Their scouts are just as good as ours."

"I don't like to hear that, Elias," said China Bill.

"Get some sleep," repeated Elias. "That's what I'm going to do." Elias turned onto his side, but failed to sleep. His thoughts went back to their last battle. He could still see the surprised look on the face of the young Rebel soldier as Elias' ball tore through the boy's chest. And that was exactly what he was, a young boy. Elias doubted the boy had been even Elias' age. A farm boy, no doubt, just waiting to get back to a tobacco farm or maybe a Missouri cotton field. What a waste.

On the march to Fort Gibson, a ... Ft. Blunt, they had seen dead horses in the fields south of Cabin Creek. There was also equipment and soldier's gear scattered along the way. Scared boys dropping whatever hampered them from escaping death or capture. Elias wondered if the white soldiers of the Confederacy knew what difference capture would be for them as opposed to capture of black soldiers? The Rebs could expect either parole or at least a prison camp somewhere. Did these boys know that Elias would probably be shot on the spot? Or if he was lucky, yeah, lucky, he would be sent south to be a slave for the rest of his life.

"Is that what the fight is about?" wondered Elias. "Are we fighting because they want to send us all back to work for them until we die? Is that their purpose?"

"All's we want is our rights," he remembered one of the captured Confederates saying. "Ya'll come to our homes and try to take away the way we live. Hell, I ain't never been twenty miles away from our farm before, and I ain't never told none of ya'll how ta' git by." The young soldier looked around in bewilderment. Elias mentally shook his head, wondering if he really understood both sides of this terrible conflict that had been thrust upon so many confused young men. "I know why I'm here———— I'm pretty sure————but I ————" Sleep without rest took Elias into the night.

Thursday, July 16, 1863

Dawn, more scattered shots and yells from across the Arkansas brought the men of the First Brigade to the edge of the river. The barges and rafts were brought to the water's edge, and men and equipment began to be poled across. Trip after trip was made. Still a few scattered shots could be heard, although they seemed farther away. General Blunt's men had set up a defensive perimeter that allowed the rest of the force to cross the river in relative safety. All day and into the late evening, men, horses, twelve pieces of artillery, ammunition chests and wagons were ferried across the muddy Arkansas River. By ten o'clock the last trip across the water had been made. After being issued new rifles, the rest of the day was spent by the men cleaning and inspecting their new weapons.

"I see we have gone back to the metal caps," observed China Bill.

"What did they use to use?" asked Matthew.

"They had what they called a Maynard primer," said Elias. "They were stuck on a piece of tape and were fed onto the nipple when you cocked the rifle. It was the right idea, but on a damp day, it got wet and wouldn't work."

"And they say we's gonna git rain tomorrow," said One Shoe. "I don't need no more trouble than what them Rebs is ready to give, that's for sure."

"Wonder how far we'll have to walk tomorrow before we get in the middle of them … *those* Rebs, anyone know?"

"I heard someone tell that the Rebs are 'bout twenty mile on south, down the Texas Road."

"They are just across Elk Creek, they said, this side of a place called Honey Springs."

"Damn, all we do is cross creeks. Ever'thing I got has been wet half a dozen times."

"'Lias, didja' hear that Colonel Schaurte lost three of his Indians when they were crossin' the river last night?" asked China Bill.

"No, Bill, I didn't," said Elias.

"I knew one of them," went on Bill. "I met Huston Mayfield just before Cabin Creek. He was in the water that first day when all hell broke loose just when the crossin' started. He told me he didn't know which way to go, so he followed the rest of the Indians back to the north bank and crawled out."

"I guess everyone was scared or confused about then, Bill," said Elias.

"Yeah, but he didn't run. He jumped back in and got himself across and took after them Rebs right along with the rest of us. Now he got himself drown in the middle of the night just trying to get across the damn river."

"I tell ya," said One Shoe, "I seen more water in this here army than most a' the guys in the navy, I betcha."

"We still have twenty miles to go, so we better get some sleep," said Elias.

"That's for me," said Toby. "I took a nap today and yet I'm still tired just from sittin' around."

"You ought to be good at that," snickered One Shoe. "That's what you does best."

"That's what I *do* best," corrected Toby, "and it ain't what I do best. What I do best is try to look out after your big ole' dumb …"

"Boys, I think we may have to put off that sleep," broke in Elias. "That's Little Max blowing assembly."

"Huh? Now?" moaned Matthew. "It's bed time."

"General Blunt says we are to form up and be ready to move immediately."

"That fella mean us, 'Lias?" asked One Shoe.

"I believe so, Tom. All right, you fellas, we've been laying around all day, now it's time to head south."

"Would you look at that?" said Matthew, "General Blunt is goin', too."

"That's right," agreed China Bill. "He's right in front of those other mounted fellas. What'cha know?"

The 1st Kansas Colored formed a column on the Texas Road and began to march south. Just behind them came the Indian Brigade of Lieutenant Colonel Schuarte. On through the night the troops marched. The stars shown briefly in the late sky only to be obscured by clouds, which produced showers off and on during the night. Occasionally the men would stop long enough to refill their canteens from a ditch or depression in the road. Dawn was hard to recognize since the clouds still covered the sky by seven o'clock in the morning of the 17th.

"It's the Confederate's advance guard," shouted General Blunt as musket fire broke the stillness of the early morning. "I want the cavalry up here and charging immediately."

"Yes, Sir."

One of the mounted scouts turned and was lost in the haze of the cloudy morning. Soon the cavalry was rushing down the Texas Road and firing into the Rebels. The confederates vanished as quickly as they had appeared and apparently moved back toward their main force.

"They're in that timber next to the creek, General," was the report given by a cavalry officer.

"Very well," replied General Blunt, "I want to see for myself what fortifications we are going to be up against. How far ahead are they, Lieutenant?"

"About five or six miles, Sir. They are just on the south side of the creek"

"All right, you come with me." The general motioned to several of his mounted party. "We're going on to see what they have waiting for us."

"General, don't you think it would be better if we sent a scouting party? You are needed here with the men."

"Colonel," stated General Blunt in a stern voice. "It's because of my men that I should go ahead and see what I must send them into. Do you understand?"

"Yes, Sir. Very well, Sir. You heard the General," said the colonel. "Prepare to move ahead." With a cautious sound in his voice, the colonel added, "Quietly as possible."

"While we are gone," General Blunt instructed, "have the men close up ranks. We scattered a bit during the night and I want everyone in close touch with their commanders."

General Blunt moved his horse south down the Texas Road toward the spot where he thought the enemy had formed their line. He was certain he would find them spread out just ahead of their main entrenchment. This was, and had been for some time, Confederate territory. They had had time to dig trenches and build buildings and other fortifications. Here they would make their stand. They would be confident that they could repulse any attack. And no doubt they were certain they would have superior numbers. Blunt knew the Rebels were right on that score at least.

"We've got to get closer," said the General. "I can't tell where they have their artillery. Can you see anything?" He directed his question to the cavalry captain just to his right.

"I'm not sure, General," was the hesitant answer.

"Well, damn it, we have to know." The general moved his horse forward and off to the left of the road. His horse's left hind hoof slid off the road and into the ditch, causing the general to grab at his saddle and pitch forward.

A shot rang out and then another. The general reined his horse back up onto the road as a third shot found its mark. The captain he had just questioned slumped in his saddle and slid to the ground.

"We need to be out of here, General," said an aide as he grabbed the bridle of the general's horse and turned it back north. In a rush, the small group raced back to the main body of Union troops.

"I want that man's body back here," said General Blunt. "Do you understand?"

"Yes, Sir," said his aide. "I'll see to it."

"You'd better!" The general paced the ground next to his group of officers.

"We're about half a mile from their line. Have the men rest and eat whatever they have in their haversacks. We'll wait here behind this ridge and move out at 10 o'clock."

"'Lias, I don't know 'bout that there General Blunt," said One Shoe as he gnawed on a piece of hardtack. "I heard that he was hard to git along with and had a big head, but I can't see why he went off and did what he did. He's a gener'l and spose'n to have someone doin' things for 'im. Not going off and getting' his self shot at."

"I told you he was a leader, Tom," replied Elias.

"He still has a big head, if you ask me," spoke up China Bill. "He figures those stars on his shoulders are supposed to make him special."

"I hope's he's right," said One Shoe. "Long as he looks out fer us, maybe we got's a chance."

"We always have a chance, Tom," said Elias. "As long as we have each other, and do the best we can, we always have a chance. I wouldn't be here if I didn't think that this chance was given us so we could show how we deserve what we have."

"I guess you're right, 'Lias, but I would just as soon sweat behind that mule I used to foller, than to get all shaky waitin' around for them Rebs to make me prove I'm supposin' to be free." Matthew pulled his arms up around his shoulders and shivered slightly.

"Some chance. Heard Henry Peppins o' Company C drown crossin' th' Grand yestidy," spoke up one of the men. "Joined up when we did, went through all them there shootin' times, got through okay just to drown wadin' a river. I git skeered wonderin' if'n I'll ever see home agin."

"We all gets nervous," said Slows. "Hell, we all gets so scared sometimes we can hardly move."

"You get to feelin' that way, too, 'Lias?" asked Matt.

"Nobody with any sense can keep from being scared and I'm no different." Elias paused, "I guess I just remember why I volunteered. I guess I just remember why I care enough for my friends that I will do everything I can to help keep them safe and to save my own brown skin. Ya' see, I got's me a heap o' funnin' to do when I get's home too." With that, all the men began to laugh.

Pointing to Elias, Toby said, "Thats zackly how I'd a' said it."

Chapter 14

Little Max's officer's call had assembled the company commanders around General Blunt. "Gentlemen, the First Brigade will form up on the west side of the road and the Second Brigade will position itself on the east side. Each column will have its infantry formed by company, the cavalry in platoons and artillery stationed by sections. I want everyone to keep a tight and close formation so the Confederates will get the impression we have more strength than we actually do." After a few questions were asked and answered, the officers went to their posts and prepared their men to begin the march.

Colonel Williams was advised that his men would occupy the right and support Captain Smith's battery when they were sent into a skirmish line. "Men, I want you all to keep cool, and not to fire until you receive the command; in all cases aim deliberately and below the waist. I want every man to do his whole duty and obey strictly the orders of his officers."

As the men moved to the right side of the Texas Road, Matthew asked, "Elias, why did the colonel say to aim below the waist?"

"I'm sorry to say, Matt, that the army feels that a wounded enemy is harder to care for than a dead one. If there are wounded men, someone has to go out and look out for them, which takes those men away from the actual fighting. And the wounded require a lot of care and supplies."

"Anythin' t' make life mo' harder for the Rebs," said One Shoe.

"I believe I'd rather be just killed than to be all hurtin' and just lay there," said Matthew.

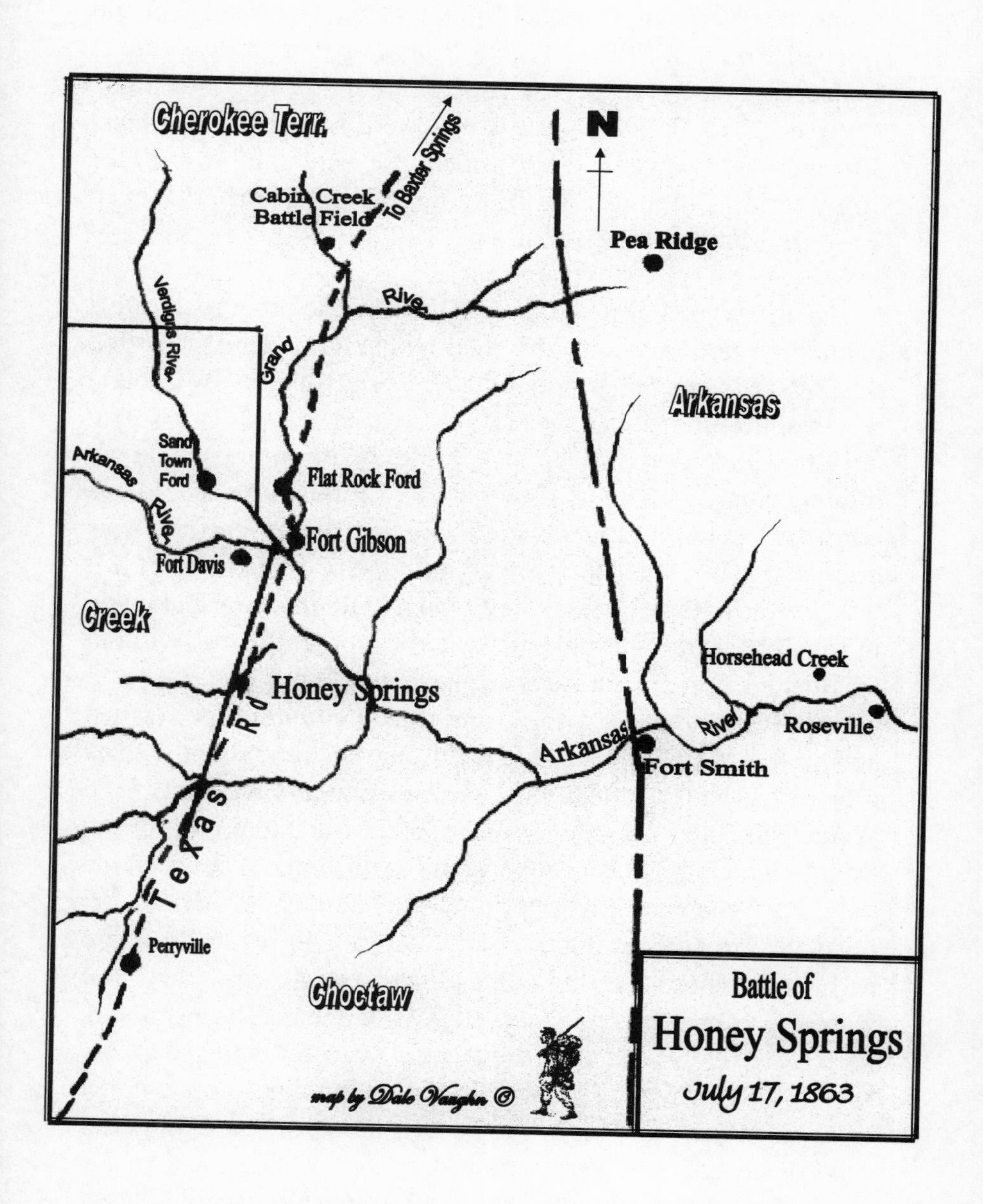
Cherokee Terr.
To Baxter Springs
N
Cabin Creek
Battle Field
Pea Ridge
Verdigris River
River
Grand
Arkansas
Sand
Town
Ford
Arkansas
River
Flat Rock Ford
Fort Gibson
Fort Davis
Creek
Horsehead Creek
Honey Springs
Texas Rd
River
Roseville
Arkansas
Fort Smith
Perryville
Choctaw
map by Dale Vaughn ©
Battle of
Honey Springs
July 17, 1863

"No you wouldn't, fella. I can swear to that," spoke up Toby. "I may be headin' into another fight, and maybe I'll get shot and maybe I won't, but I'm still glad 'Lias was there to save me at Island Mound. I sho' … *sure* enough am glad I'm not dead!"

"And if'n you was, what would we do for gitin' the latest information? We would all be blind in the ears if'n it warn't for Toby," chimed in Slows. There was a grin in his voice that even Toby couldn't take exception with.

Near the head of the column Elias and the other men of his company marched along the road heading south. Just behind them was Colonel Schaurte's Indian brigade, followed by Captain Smith and four artillery pieces.

Elias looked across the road at the white infantry soldiers moving smartly along as if on parade. By this time, a soldier's color was seldom considered. The color of the uniform was uppermost. If it was blue, you could depend on it for help. If it was gray, kill it! Of course, the problem with that was that many of the Rebs were wearing confiscated Union uniforms. Without adequate supplies both sides wore whatever they could get.

The white men had seen how well the colored performed and were confident they would do their share and sometimes more. Elias had become friends with a number of the fellas from Wisconsin. Talks about home life, farm work and hopes for the future seemed to wipe away most of the differences between the men. Each man was just as proud of his unit as the other.

A healthy competition even showed itself occasionally. There had been a sharpshooting contest held several weeks ago, but when the winners had been asked to volunteer as sharpshooters for a forward unit, to a man they would not offer to take that job. Killing an enemy face to face was one thing, but to draw down on an unsuspecting man while he was eating or standing guard was considered little short of murder.

As the morning drew on, the sky became almost completely covered with dark gray clouds. It was still warm and the wind blew in gusts. It caused the tall prairie grass to wave and undulate much as an ocean would. Small islands of trees showed themselves dotting the open fields, and further ahead a thick line of trees could be seen. Everywhere carpets of yellow daisies, with dark brown centers, patch-worked the hills. It was a peaceful and gay contrast to the ominous feeling of danger that was felt in the breasts of each of the men as they stared into the green line of cottonwood, walnut and pecan.

"Must be the next creek I gots to wade through," spoke up One Shoe.

The advanced guard began to receive Rebel musket fire when they had come within a quarter of a mile from Elk Creek. A halt was sounded, and then the order was given to deploy into battle formation. Each column began to swing out from the road like spokes of a huge wagon wheel. In less than five minutes the whole force was spread out covering the enemy's entire front. Skirmishers were sent out to draw fire, and the artillery was positioned among the ranks.

As was hoped, the Confederate artillery opened fire, disclosing their position. The union forces slowly worked its way forward. Cavalry units on both flanks dismounted and fired as they moved along on foot with the infantry. As the Union artillery returned fire, the infantry drew closer and closer to the heavy tree line. Suddenly, a large explosion gave evidence that the Rebels had lost one of their howitzers.

"Our position is right here in the center, men," shouted Colonel Williams. "Keep an eye out for any soft spot in the Reb's line." The colonel moved across the line of the Kansas 1st and gave the order to fix bayonets.

After what seemed like an eternity of heavy shelling, smoke and deafening noise, Colonel Bowles rode his horse out in front of the black troops and ordered them forward. The entire regiment moved out and marched in a perfect line toward the still concealed enemy forces. Elias and his men seemed to form a slight point as they moved several steps ahead. Almost like a spearhead the men slowly made their way through the tall prairie grass and toward the woods. Smoke from Rebel muskets could be seen erupting from the trees ahead. Screams of men and occasionally a horse could be heard over the noise of grape and canister being thrown from both sides. Hundreds or maybe thousands of musket balls could be heard whizzing and whining through the air.

Two of Smith's 12-pounders had taken a position within three hundred yards of the enemy line and were trying to search out the exact location of the confederate canons that were tearing holes in the line of black Union troops. Still the 1st Kansas continued to move forward. Inspired by the courage of the black troops, members of the 2nd Colorado Cavalry dismounted and joined the colored soldiers in their relentless battle with their still mostly unseen counterparts. The 2nd Indian Home Guards fell in just behind and reinforced the attack.

Colonel Williams gave the command to halt and prepare for a volley. Kneeling in the damp grass, each of the men checked their rifles; then the command. "Ready ... aim ... fire!" Hundreds of rifles spouted fire, smoke and balls. Almost at the same instant a like volley poured from the trees. It was almost as if the Confederates were also obeying the command of Colonel Williams. Loading, firing, loading, firing, each man tried to concentrate on one objective, killing his share of the enemy. Each man fixed his gaze directly ahead so he would not be so aware of the men on either side of him falling with blood spurting from torn arms and legs. Pieces of flesh and bone would shower a rifleman as he tried to drive another shot into his rifle. The noise would graciously drown out the sounds of the hurt and dying. A small fire tried to gain life in the now wet grass only to sputter and give forth nothing but smoke.

It began to rain lightly. Still the smoke clouded over the battlefield, making it difficult for Elias to see just where the line was on either side of him. A gust of wind suddenly cleared a small area, and he could see Colonel Williams, still on his horse, waving his sword and shouting encouragement to his men and those that had joined them.

He was just about to give the command to "charge," when Elias saw the colonel almost thrown from his horse. His hat flew several yards away and, as he fell, blood could be seen covering part of his face and across his chest. Even one hand was awash with the red substance of life. Several men rushed to where the colonel had fallen, but Elias could not see through the threefoot-high grass exactly what was being done.

Swearing to himself, Elias continued to load and fire toward the dense cover hiding hundreds of the Rebel force. Then he could hear shouting and the firing on his right seem to slacken. He could see Colonel Bowles franticly waving his sword and motioning for someone to move back toward the rear. Elias couldn't hear what was being said, but it seemed to be causing some confusion.

"It's them Indians," shouted One Shoe. "They done got themselv's right out in front of our line."

Elias saw two of the Indian Guard fall, apparently by fire from the Union line. Colonel Bowles managed to get the artillery to cease and most of the infantry to pause until the Guard could return to safety.

Seeing the Union troops fall back and becoming aware that most of the fire had stopped, the Confederates thought that the Union soldiers were beginning a retreat. Rushing from the woods, dozens of Rebel infantry advanced upon the Union line, which stood fast. Running and yelling, on came the Confederates.

Elias and the others immediately realized what was happening and deliberately held their fire. Closer and closer the enemy moved through the prairie grass. Over a slight rise to within 25 paces trotted the Rebels, almost shoulder to shoulder. Suddenly a solid wall of smoke blotted out the whole scene. A volley of muskets roared and Union shot decimated the Rebel line. Screams and yells competed with the noise of more rifles discharging death into the southern ranks. Complete surprise and confusion took hold of a Texas regiment as they desperately tried to race back to cover.

The charge was sounded and Elias and his comrades began to follow their enemy toward the creek. Just ahead, a Texas color-bearer faltered and threw out his arms as a musket ball tore through his back. Within the time it took to move three steps, little Max had grabbed the falling enemy battle flag. Tearing it from its standard and stuffing it in his shirt, the little bugler proudly raced on, his horn bouncing against his side.

Yelling and cheering, the men of the 1st trotted on, occasionally stopping to load and fire and then trot closer to the tree line. The enemy could now be seen wading through the water and struggling up the southern bank of Elk Creek. Many barely cleared the water when brought down by Union fire.

Just to the left, a group of Confederate soldiers paused and formed, trying to hold a small bridge spanning the creek. Twice, as one Rebel group would fall away from the bridge, another would take their place. Finally the effort was totally abandoned and the bridge was secured by Union troops.

Still moving forward after crossing the creek, smoke could be seen in the distance. Horses pulling the cannons strained and slowed after their trek across the prairie and through the creek. Still occasionally shots would be directed toward the retreating enemy. Through the area where the Confederates had been camped, men of the 1st Kansas moved still further south. More small skirmishes were caused by groups of Rebel soldiers firing from hills and bluffs in front and off to the right of the Union troops.

Showing the same determination they exhibited during the main battle, the black troops made short work of any token resistance. It was discovered that the buildings that had been set afire had been Confederate commissary buildings. The enemy had successfully destroyed most of their supplies and would be hard-pressed to survive in the immediate area for very long. A detachment was dropped off to guard the Southern supply depot while the remainder of the force continued to chase the Confederate troops.

Both animals and men were near exhaustion when they were halted almost three miles south of Elk Creek, at what was called Honey Springs. In the far distance the Confederate cavalry could be seen, but further pursuit was impractical.

"I believe that's General Cabell's cavalry, Colonel Moonlight," said General Blunt, as he sat his horse and looked southward. The clouds caused the late afternoon to appear closer to dusk than the clock showed. "We knew he was on his way from Fort Smith, but I hoped we would have this affair finished before he could be of help to Cooper."

"Do you think he will attack, General?" asked Lieutenant Colonel Moonlight, General Blunt's chief of staff.

"I hope to God he doesn't. We're about out of ammunition, and our men are dog tired after walking all night and fighting all day. But I'm not going to give him the impression we are the least bit worn out. I want our men to bivouac here on the field. We'll let him know we are not the least bit intimidated."

"He's brought close to 3,000 more cavalry with him, General. That's almost equal to our whole force, infantry and cavalry."

"He doesn't know that, Colonel. Anyway … let's hope not."

Colonel Moonlight nodded. "I'll have Colonel Schaurte take his Indian Guards back to Elk Creek and camp there until tomorrow, General. Then they can head back to Fort Blunt."

"After they've eaten and rested a bit, have Colonel Bowles camp his colored troops just south of Schaurte's. I want them to be in full view. Also, just in case the Confederates decide to attack, we will be ready for them. Better check on the ammunition and be sure it's distributed the best we can." General Blunt took one last look to the south and turned his horse back toward Elk Creek. "Any word about Colonel Williams?"

"Best we can tell, General, is that it wasn't quite as bad as we first thought. I checked with Dr. Harrington just before I came here. Colonel Williams will be out of commission for awhile, but I'm certain he will recover."

"Did you ever see a unit perform the way his colored's did?" asked General Blunt.

"I swear, General, I never saw anything like it. There they were. That Private Mothers, you know the tall, good-looking black fella? He was the one kneeling two, three feet out in front of the others. Then there was Washington, Foster and big ole Carter on one side of 'em and Smith and Miller and the rest all lined up. They all kind'a stuck out a bit from the others, each of them watching the other out of the corner of their eye. They loaded and waited just as calm as you please, with the others in the company sorta going by what these fellas were doing. Colonel Williams had said that some of these men could load and fire three times a minute but I never believed it until now, and I saw it first hand. Damn!

"Then those Rebs started getting' closer and closer. Well, Mothers knelt there and the others did, too. I figured they thought they could stare those Rebs to death. I don't know, General, it was the strangest thing I ever did see.

"About the time I thought those boys were frozen, Mothers took aim and dropped the lead officer and began to reload as if he was takin' practice. The others opened up all at the same time and then reloaded, dropped another gray coat and reloaded; you would think they had all day.

"Finally Mothers stood up and started trottin' toward the Rebs. He fired and then shoved a bayonet into one of the Reb's cavalryman's horse and caught the rider with his musket butt on his way down. He stood next to the horse, loaded up again and took another Reb right in the belly. Colonel, all them boys just did the same thing. I don't think there was a wasted shot amongst the lot of them. And you would'a thought they were wearin' armor or something. Not a one of them was even scratched. The whole regiment just followed along, and in no time them Rebs had all they wanted and turned tail."

"I know, Colonel, and I'm going to make mention of them in my report," stated General Blunt. "Damn fine soldiers, damn fine!"

"General," the sergeant saluted and stepped up next to General Blunt as the general dismounted. "Colonel Williams would like to see you, Sir, if you have a few minutes to spare."

"Naturally, Sergeant, I'm anxious to see how the colonel is doing."

General Blunt made his way to the field hospital where Colonel Williams had been treated for his wounds.

"Glad you're awake, Jim, how do you feel?"

"Just one thing, General, how'd my men do?"

"Excellent! I never saw such discipline and courage. You can be proud. I know I am."

"Then if I die, I can go happy, General. I have had to listen to all the talk about how my men wouldn't fight. Now they have proved themselves again." Colonel Williams breathed heavily and sank back onto his cot. The bandages showed the red stains of his injuries.

"Nonsense, Jim. You'll be back with your men in no time. And I'm certain they are anxious to have you back. But for now, you relax and heal. Your men will be well looked after. I'll see to that."

"Thank you, General. They deserve the best we can do for them."

"They've all gone, General." Captain H. G. Loring stood with a smile on his face.

"Who's gone, Captain? What are you talking about?" General Blunt looked up from his breakfast while taking a drink of hot coffee.

"General Cooper, Sir, and it seems he took General Cabell and his cavalry with him. You've done it, Sir; looks like most of the Indian Territory is in Union hands. Our scouts say that the Confederates are at least south of the Canadian river."

“Very good, Captain. Now let’s see if we can keep them there.”

“Come on, fellas, we’re supposed to look through the ruins and see if we can find anything the Rebs didn’t destroy.” Elias was feeling good after the night’s rest. The evening before, shortly after eating and washing off in Elk Creek, he had crawled into his blankets and was asleep before he finished his evening prayers. He didn’t dream and wasn’t sure he even changed positions during the night. As soon as he awoke, he went to see how Colonel Williams was doing. The colonel was still sleeping, but Eliab Macy, one of the assistant surgeons, assured Elias that Williams would recover and probably be back in command before many weeks.

“I shore am glad of that,” smiled One Shoe. “He’s one of the bravest officers I know of.”

“You betcha,” agreed China Bill. “That man just did his work without paying those Rebs no never mind.”

“You guys did pretty well yourselves,” said Elias. “I didn’t have to come drag any of you out of a jam.”

“What? I’ll have you know I was too busy lookin’ …”

“Come on, Toby. We have a job, remember?”

“ ’Lias,” said Toby, as they walked toward one of the burned buildings, “how come some of them Rebs was wearing blue coats? And then there was those Union belts they wear upside down?”

“They wear what they can find, Toby,” replied Elias. “They have to do without a lot more than we do. They probably got them from some prisoners or …”

“Yeah, from some of the fellas they killed, I supposed, but what about the belts?”

“They wear them upside down so the *u s* looks like *s n*. They claim that stands for Southern Nation. That way they can use the belts, too.”

“Guess they have to make do jes … just like we do, huh?”

Toby was silent for a short time and then said, "I found me a harmonica over in that draw. It was pokin' out of the pocket of one of them dead young Reb boys."

"Does it work?" asked Elias.

"I put it back … it was his."

Elias looked at Toby, placed his hand on his shoulder and nodded his understanding.

The men pushed away burned timbers and moved rocks that had been a part of the building's foundation looking for anything salvageable in the ruins of the Confederate commissary buildings. Most all of the edibles had been totally ruined, and only a few barrels of salt, sugar and flour was of any use. Some bits of charred meat were gobbled down by the men fortunate enough to find them. Several slabs of bacon, a few hams and four boxes of dried fruit were hauled to the cook.

"Colonel Bowles, the men have found something you might want to see." Second Lieutenant Ezekiel Coleman led the colonel to some rusty iron that had been piled next to the ruins of one of the buildings.

"They're shackles, Sir," said Elias. "We found them in that building. I remember seeing some just like these back in Virginia when I was a boy. Any time one of the slaves would be caught after running away, they would be put in these and kept chained to a stake in the yard. I've seen legs rubbed raw and bleed from these thing, Sir."

"I checked with some of the prisoners, Colonel," said Lieutenant Coleman. "They told me they were kept in case they captured any of our colored troops, Sir. Any black soldiers were to be taken back down south and sold."

"One of the prisoners said they brought so many of these things 'cause they were told by their officers that the blacks wouldn't fight. All they would have to do was just walk up, take 'em prisoner, put them in chains and take 'em away."

"At least it wasn't taken for granted they would be instantly shot," replied the colonel. "Get these things out of here. Take them off and bury them. You might even throw them in one of the Rebel graves; good place for them."

"Yes, Sir."

"You men don't deserve that sort of thing." The colonel looked at Elias and then at the others. "You did this army proud yesterday. And the army won't forget."

Elias came to attention and started to salute when the colonel reached out and took Elias' hand and shook it. The colonel then turned and headed back to his tent. As all of the men stood looking at each other, Lieutenant Coleman smiled and nodded toward Colonel Bowes. "Special."

As Elias turned to go back to his area, he noticed several men of the 2nd Colorado standing off to one side watching. One of them, still wearing a bandage around his head, was the man Elias had pulled from the creek after being wounded. The man looked down at the pile of shackles and then at Elias. As the two stared at each other, the young soldier's eyes filled with tears. Just before he turned to leave, he said in almost a whisper, "I'm so sorry."

In General Blunt's battle report, dated July 26, 1863, he included the following:

"The 1st Kansas (Colored) particularly distinguished itself; they fought like veterans and preserved their line unbroken throughout the engagement. Their coolness and bravery I have never seen surpassed; they were in the hottest of the fight, and opposed to Texas troops twice their number, whom they completely routed. One Texas regiment (the Twentieth Cavalry) that fought against them went into the fight with 300 men and came out with only 60."

(End of report.)

Chapter 15

"Mistah Corporal, Suh!"

"Umm, umm. What'cha know 'bout that?"

"All right, that's enough," stated Elias.

"I know'd … *knew* it was bound to happen," said Toby. "And we are proud certain, 'Lias."

"You betcha," chimed in One Shoe.

Elias was too embarrassed to reply. He sat next to his tent in the early evening, obeying the sergeant's order to sew his new corporal stripes on his jacket. His actions during the recent battle had been noted by several of the officers in the field, and the way he led his men into the face of the enemy with determination and valor had made an impression on the company commanders. Elias had been noticed by his superiors in the past, and it was inevitable that he should rise in the ranks. "He's officer material, if they would only allow us," one captain had remarked.

"Mama would be proud," thought Elias. "And so would Cheat. I wonder why mama hadn't mentioned Cheat." He had two letters in three months and not a one had said a word about Elias' little brother. "Well, no news, good news, and like that."

"So, what you got to say now?'

"I still say I didn't join up to fight for no nigg … blacks."

"Yeah, but you said you didn't think they would be worth anything when the real fightin' started. You said that little scrap at Cabin Creek didn't prove nuthin' and you didn't like dependin' on no darky to save your skin. Now whatcha think?"

"Okay, I got to admit that they did a fair job …"

"Fair? Come on, you saw what they did. I'm sure glad they

were on our side in this here fight. Boy, they were right in the center where all the Reb strength was and they just headed right on."

"Okay, okay, they did good. But I'd use a mule to fight if he could fire a rifle gun. And I guess they can stop a musket ball same as me, but I still didn't volunteer for them!"

The Wisconsin cavalry sat cleaning their Springfields and eating hardtack. There had been an ongoing discussion between several of the men since they had joined up with the force that included the 1st Kansas Colored Infantry. They had heard about the colored troops, but had not seen any, much less been in battle with them.

"People's people, far's I can tell."

"Maybe you wouldn't think so if they were comin' into your part of the country and going to take away your job."

"Now who says they're gonna do that?"

"Just where do you expect them to go if they find themselves free to take off and move to anywhere they see fit?"

"Hell, I dunno. Maybe I didn't give it any thought. Maybe I don't rightly care just as long as I get back to our place. I doubt if any of them are going to wind up in Wisconsin anyway. What do they know about cows?"

The men all chuckled and busied themselves with their chores.

Elias moved away from the trees and on into the shadows. "Is that what most of the white men thought about him and his fellow black soldiers?" he wondered. The feeling of pride for himself and his friends for their part in the fight was suddenly dampened. They had done their job and more. Even General Blunt said so. Elias had watched men from the 1st fall with terrible wounds, several of them killed. "What in the hell do they want from us?" Elias felt a rage he had never experienced. "We're doing what we want to do! We volunteered, we weren't forced to join and fight. If they don't want to fight with us, let them go home. We can do it by ourselves and alone if we have to!"

"S'matter, 'Lias?" asked Toby.

"Just leave me alone!"

Toby looked over at One Shoe and then at China Bill.

"Let me talk to 'im." China Bill put down his tin cup half filled with lukewarm coffee and swallowed his last of a piece of cold ham. He gathered up a handful of dried fruit and reached for his hat. Moving away from the group of men he had been talking with, Bill followed several yards behind Elias toward the ruins of one of the Confederate buildings.

"Elias, you had anything to eat?" asked China Bill as he sat down next to the pile of burned timbers.

"Not hungry."

"Better have something. I brought over some of those dried apples I found. Here, have a mouthful." Bill pointed to a large handful of the dark yellowed chunks he had wrapped in a piece of paper. He hadn't told anyone of the fruit he had found earlier. Elias looked at Bill and then at the fruit.

"You upset about something?" asked Bill.

"I'm fine."

"I don't think so," said Bill, moving from a squatting position to stretch out his legs. "I've never heard you talk to Toby the way you did. I think you might have hurt his feelings a little bit."

"That right? Maybe he shouldn't be so touchy. Maybe he should grow up. Maybe I didn't take him raise."

China Bill stared at Elias. He had never seen him act this way. Bill knew that something had happened to greatly upset Elias, and he wasn't sure how to find out what it was. "Well," thought Bill, "only one way. Just plow right in."

"You gonna take it out on Toby?"

"What?"

"Whatever it is that got up your butt! You had no call to get on to him that way. That boy loves you more'n anything. You saved his life and he would give his for you in a minute. Now! You gonna treat him like he was some field hand that you had no need for right now?"

"You don't understand. You didn't … no one really …"

"I guess maybe I don't. But if I don't it's because you haven't bothered to tell any of us what happened and why you're takin' it out on us."

Elias looked at China Bill, sighed and reached for the apples. Nothing was said for some time. Elias chewed on the rubbery fruit while China Bill sat and watched.

"I don't have to … why should …"

"Because we are family, remember? Not just you and George, but all of us. We all started together and we have no one else to look to for help. And I don't mean just when the balls start flyin'."

The two sat in silence for several more minutes. Elias chewed on the apples, and China Bill just looked aimlessly around waiting for Elias to explain his attitude.

"Why are you here, Bill?" asked Elias, first looking at Bill and then casting his gaze off into the distance. "Why did you volunteer? You made it to freedom. You could have gone on to Colorado or even stayed in Canada. Why did you come back here and join the army?"

"Hell, I just didn't have any place else to go, 'Lias," said Bill with a grin.

"I won't swallow that, Bill. You went through a lot more than me and my mother. You are older than almost anyone in the outfit, and you've probably seen and been through more than anyone I know." Elias paused and seemed to drift to a place far away. "As a boy, I saw some of the things that happened to slaves who made the overseer mad and how some were treated after they had run away and been brought back. You had that happen to you." Elias looked at Bill. There was anger in his eyes and also a feeling of sorrow in his voice. "You know just what it's like to be beaten and whipped. You got away and made it to freedom. You didn't have to fight any more."

"Yeah, I guess I did *get* my freedom, but I didn't *earn* it. Elias, what about those that didn't have a chance to get away like I did? What about those kids and those women that couldn't stand up to the lash the way I was able to? Who earns them their freedom? How they gonna make it?" Bill raised and looked straight at Elias. "Why are you here?"

Elias returned Bill's gaze and then sagged back and dropped his head. Tears welled up in Elias' eyes. "I wish I was as wise as you, Bill. I wish I could understand the feelings I have inside. You know I didn't mean to make Toby feel bad. I know we are the only family he really has. Yet, I just wish some of …"

"You want the white folks, the white soldiers, to understand what you and the rest of us are fightin' for, don'cha?" Bill slowly shook his head. "You expect them to know how we feel? It ain't gonna happen, Elias. They'll never understand. They've never had to worry about being separated from their mamas or their daddies. They've never had to worry about whether they were gonna have enough to eat or not." Bill hesitated for a minute, "Well, maybe some of them have gone through that, but not for the same reason as us. They don't understand what it's like not to be able to stop if they're sick. They don't know how it feels to have to ask for a drink of water or if'n they can go pee."

Elias looked up and saw China Bill with a half smile on his face.

"They're never gonna know for sure, Elias. They will never understand how we feel. I once knew a Mormon kid, when I was making my way through Missouri. Name was Jeremy Potter, it was. He was just about as close to understanding our troubles as anyone I ever met. People wouldn't let him and his family live in peace. They had to try to change the way them folks wanted to live. They didn't take time to listen to what the Mormons were sayin'." Bill paused. "Folks just seemed to know their own way and don't like things to change it."

Elias stared into Bill's face.

"Don't ask these young white boys to understand our ways, Elias," continued Bill. "Maybe we can hope they'll just go along with what's happening until they get to go back home and so do we. Just getting' along for right now will be a big step. But we got to help 'em. We have to do what we can to make it easy for them to accept. It's stranger for them than it is for us."

"I wish I hadn't … you know, you're the one who should be wearing these stripes, Bill. You're a lot smarter than I am."

"Hell, Elias, everyone knows that privates are smarter than most everyone else. Why would I want to go and give that up?"

Private Lester Ames of the 29th Texas Regiment sat huddled next to a tree. He and his fellow prisoners had been herded to a remote area just south of where they had been camped less than a day ago awaiting battle. Barely nineteen years old, Lester left a small ranch in Texas along with several other boys that decided one Saturday night to "join up and kick hell out'n them damn Yankees."

"You better listen to what Governor Houston said before they kicked him out, Boy," his father had told him. "This is stupid. There is no way the South is gonna whip the Union. They have more of ever'thing than we do, and I'll bet even old Jeff Davis knows it by now.

"We're cattle men around here, not soldiers. You belong here on the ranch. We've done pretty well and we've got all those new horses to take care of. So, I don't want to hear any more about it."

"But Daddy," Lester pleaded, "I gotta go. All the others are goin' and I can't back out now. Besides I promised, and anyway they ain't no Yanks that can whip a Texan. Never did and never will!"

"Damn, I wished t' hell I'd a' listened to Daddy," muttered Lester.

"What you belly-achin' about, Kid?" asked Charlie Miles in a disgusted voice.

"Leave 'im alone Charlie," said old Bill Johnson. Then turning, he continued, "Don't worry, Les, it's gonna be all right." Bill was the oldest man in the unit. He had been in and out of the army for over twenty years. He had fought in Mexico beginning in 1846, got out and then back in the army several times. He had joined the 29th Texas just after the war started, mainly because he had no place else to go. The war came along and offered him a home again. "If you had any sense, you'd be worried, too, Charlie."

"Hell, what I got to be worried about? My fightin' days is over, Old Man. Yours, too, probably. And I don't need to listen to some snot-nosed kid whimperin' about being caught by no Union army."

"Bill, what's gonna happen to us?" Les asked quietly. "Ya' know what we was told to do with any black prisoners we got, what'll they do now that they done caught us?"

"It's gonna' be okay, I told ya, nothin's gonna happen."

"But, Bill, don't you think that them blacks know we was supposed to kill 'em or send 'em back to bein' slaves agin? They gonna take it out on us, I betcha. Wouldn't you if'n you was in their shoes?" Young Lester had a sob in his voice as he looked into the eyes of the old veteran. "Bill, I don't wanna die like this. I never wanted to be no hero, but I don't want my daddy to find out that I got myself captured and killed by some no-account nigger."

"You ain't gonna be killed, Lester. They don't do that sort a' thing," reassured Bill.

"You don't think so, Old Man?" said Charlie. "Hell, they just been waitin' for a chance like this. I betcha we don't even get another meal before we're piled in a hole and covered up." Turning to Lester, he said with a dry smirk on his face, "You don't need to worry 'bout your daddy, Boy. He ain't gonna know what happened to you. You're just another dead Reb along with the rest of us."

Lester broke into quiet sobs. He turned away from Bill and the others and tried to hide his fear. Old Bill put an arm around the shuddering shoulders and then looked over at Miles. "You shut your mouth, you sorry excuse for a soldier. Just one more word from you and I'll shove your worthless ass in a hole before they get a chance to shoot you."

Charlie Miles came off the ground and threw his body at the

old soldier. Bill twisted to his right, and Charlie slid across the old man's shoulder. Bill grabbed the back of Charlie's pants by the belt and jerked him over on to his back. Arms wrapped around each other, the two men wrestled and swung fists, each trying to free himself from the other. Charlie threw a wild right that Bill dodged. Bill's brawling skill, honed over many years of rough and tumble scraps from Louisiana to California, showed itself as he landed a jarring left that split the young soldier's ear. Blood spurted across Charlie's face as another blow tore a gash over his right eye. By this time the old veteran was up on one knee powering two callused fists into Charlie's face and stomach.

"Here now, stop that." A yell came from one of the Union guards as he and several other blue-clad soldiers rushed into the midst of the fight. "Get off him, get away." The guard grabbed the back of Bill's shirt and pulled him to one side, allowing Charlie to get to his feet.

Just then one of the other prisoners grabbed an old musket from an unsuspecting guard and pointed it at the Union sergeant that had just arrived at the commotion.

"Git back or shore as hell, I'll kill 'im. I mean it. I got nothin' ta' lose. I'll do it. Ain't no bunch of niggers gonna kill me."

"James!" Old Bill Johnson had gotten to his feet and taken two steps toward the young Texan holding the rifle. His voice was firm and steady. There was a low commanding tone that caused immediate silence through out the whole area. "You ain't gonna shoot nobody. Now give me that there rifle."

"Get away from me, Old Man!" There was fear in his voice as he pointed the rifle at Bill. The boy's hands shook, and there was a wild look in his eyes as he glanced from side to side. "I'll kill you, too, if'n you try to keep me from gettin' away. I'm gettin' me a horse and I'm headin' away from here and I'll kill any man that tries to stop me, blue or gray."

"Tell ya' what, James, you go ahead and pull that there trigger. Ya' know ya' only got one shot anyway. Then what ya' gonna do. You just gonna keep clubbin' on the rest of us until you go get that horse, get him saddled and get up on 'im?"

"You heard what I said, get me a horse or that there sergeant is a dead man."

"Wouldn't you rather kill a nigger than that white man?"

James turned his head while keeping the rifle leveled at the sergeant. "Huh? What'd ya' mean? Who said that?"

"I did. Don't you want your friends see you cut down a black man with your last attempt to get free? And it will be your last try, you know." Elias stepped away from the trees and walked slowly forward toward the soldier holding the rifle. "How do you feel being surrounded by people that won't let you *go? Not very nice, is it? Make you mad enough to want to kill someone?"*

"I don't know what you're talkin' about. I ain't gonna be cooped up behind no fence by a bunch of Yankees, and I sure as hell ain't gonna be kept prisoner by no niggers."

Elias took several steps toward the man. "Not much fun feeling like you may never be free again, is it?"

"Don't give me that freedom stuff. I'm white and you're the one that is supposed to be the slave. Ya' been slaves and you always will be. That's just the way it is, now git!" The man raised his rifle as the sergeant pushed Elias to one side and walked toward the frightened soldier. As the Rebel aimed and pulled the trigger, there was a sharp click.

"You Rebs are dumber than I thought. You think I'm gonna have a primer on that there gun I carry around all day. Boy, how stupid kin ya' be?"

"Sorry about the lad's behavior," said Bill as he stood next to the sergeant. "You can understand how it is with the young people. They're scared, Sergeant. Young Lester there has heard some terrible stories about what happens between the whites and the blacks. I'll bet this might even be the first time he has ever seen one. There's lots of Indians and Mexicans where he comes from, but I doubt there are any colored."

"You better keep these fellas in line or they may be in a lot more trouble than they already are." The sergeant directed the guards back to their posts and walked away.

"You tell Lester, we all aren't set on killing white men just to get back at them," said Elias. "Tell him he will probably be exchanged and paroled if he swears not to go back to fighting."

"I can just about guarantee that none of these men would go back to fighting if they didn't have to," replied Bill. "Not that they are cowards, mind you. I don't think there is a one of them I didn't trust comin' into this battle, it's just that they can't see any use to fight for something that isn't going to benefit them any." The old veteran paused. "You know what I'm sayin'?"

"I'm not sure," replied Elias.

"These here young fellas are a lot like those from Arkansas. General Cabell's loosin' men by the dozen. Lots of 'em are actually northerners in their hearts. They had no slaves and never wanted any."

"Then why are they in the army?" asked Elias rather bewilderedly.

"Would you believe most of 'em was forced into the army? Lots of 'em ran away when the Confederates began their conscription program. They ran and hid in the mountains and woods of Arkansas until they were caught. They were hunted like criminals or runaway slaves, and then arrested and put in the army. Naturally this made 'em madder'n hell and they went about tryin' harder to run off. You can't blame 'em for feelin' that way, espically when they hear that if'n a man has twenty or more slaves, he gets to stay home."

"You mean they are really deserting?" asked Elias.

"Yep, leavin' and headin' home."

"I hope they all make it, Sir. And thank you. I had no idea. I guess it's a little easier for me to understand now."

"Thank you, Corporal," said Bill, eyeing the stripes on Elias' sleeve. "And I appreciate how you handled James. He's as scared as the rest, you know, he just has to sound big to hide it."

Elias nodded, looked away and replied softly, "We're all scared."

Chapter 16

Saturday, August 22, 1863 Honey Springs, I.T.

"It's going to be early, so prepare your men, Corporal." The sergeant moved away in the gathering darkness of what was left of a very hot summer's day. Elias turned and went to his tent to call the men together and gather his belongings.

"What's gonna be early, 'Lias?" questioned Toby. "What we gonna do now?"

"We're leaving first thing in the morning, Toby," said Elias. "Get the others together and I'll explain."

After Elias' men had answered the call to assemble around Elias' tent, Toby continued his questioning. "What's that mean that we got to get our stuff together and be ready early, ready for what?"

"Ready for another long walk, Skinny Legs," spoke up One Shoe.

"Tom's right. We leave at first light tomorrow. It's said that Confederate General William Steele and General Cabell are forming up about sixty miles south of here. General Blunt is set on giving them another good beating, destroying whatever we can and running them out of the territory. Get your stuff together along with four days rations that you can eat on the move."

"We gonna be walkin' for fo' … *four* days?" quizzed Toby.

"Probably not," replied Elias, "but you never know when we will be able to get a decent meal again. We better be ready for almost anything. General Blunt is very determined to whip these Rebs."

"Yeah," said China Bill, "you mean he's anxious for us to march our butts off and then make him look good."

"Now, Bill. The General has taken good care of us, and if we can do this bunch in this time, what with their not being able to get reinforcements, we may never have to fight them again."

"I heard from some of the prisoners that the Rebs are havin' a hell of a time with the folks that live around here and over in Arkansas," spoke up Matthew. "They are mostly all for the Union and they run off the foragers when they can get away with it."

The men gathered together what they intended to take with them and then turned in for the night. No one was sleeping in tents because of the heat. Even at night, it hardly seemed to cool off. The bugs buzzed and the night noises didn't help dispel the anticipation of a long hard march ending in another battle.

"Spos'n it'll be a bad fight, 'Lias?" Toby spoke into the darkness as he lay a few feet from Elias.

"Don't know, Toby," was the reply. "Whatever happens, they'll know they been up against the 1st again, you can bet on that."

"We been doin' good, ain't we?" Toby didn't bother to correct himself.

"You bet you have, and I'm proud of every one of you boys."

"Hey, who you callin' 'Boy'?" there was a slight chuckle in Toby's voice. Then, after a few minutes, " 'Lias, what you thinks happening to ole' George?"

"I bet he's doing fine, Toby." Elias tried to speak with confidence in his voice. The surgeon had taken off the leg of George Brothers after the fight at Cabin Creek, and then George had been sent up to Fort Scott. The fort had the best hospital in the entire area. "You know George," Elias continued, "he has the strength of two men and he's young. Besides, we have seen lots of men lose legs and arms and come right back almost good as new."

"I sure hope so. I miss the big fella."

"Me, too, now get some sleep. I don't want to have to carry you tomorrow."

There was surprisingly little noise from the men, horses and wagons as they made their way down the Texas Road in the gray of the dawn. They were told that the distance would have to be covered in no more than two days. It was expected that One Shoe would sure enough have another river to cross when they got to the south branch of the Canadian. Confederate Generals Steele and Cabell would certainly have their troops fortified on the south side of the river and probably concealed in the trees just like at Honey Springs. Another head-first battle was sure to erupt.

"There isn't a sign of them, General," stated Colonel Judson. "We sent out scouts and they verified that everyone is gone."

"Gone, what do you mean gone?" stormed General Blunt. "Do you mean to tell me that after we came all this way our original information was all wrong? How could that be?"

"No, Sir, our information was correct. They were here. We found indication that there must have been six or seven thousand men, but they left before we arrived. We did bring back several prisoners, though." The colonel paused and then said, "Well, not exactly prisoners. I guess they are actually deserters. They sneaked away when the main force was pulling out and hid in the trees until they saw us coming. That's where we got most of our information, Sir."

General Blunt had the Rebel deserters brought to him and, along with several other officers, questioned them as to what they knew about Steele's plans. It was learned that General Steele had split his forces and sent General Cabell with his brigade in the direction of Fort Smith. General Steele, along with Cooper's command of about five thousand men, was heading south on the Texas Road in the direction of Perryville, a distance of about twenty more miles.

"All right," stated General Blunt, "have the men rest on their arms until three o'clock. That will give them about five hours rest. Then we march south. I will, by God, have Steele before he gets out of our reach!"

Dog tired, the men dropped almost where they stood and

were soon sound asleep. They had been marching most of two days, eating sometimes while they walked. The weather had remained hot and water was in short supply.

It had been determined that there was a supply depot at Perryville and another at Northfork. If these could be captured before Steele could move or destroy them, Blunt could strike a severe blow to the Confederate forces in Indian Territory and western Arkansas. Without his own supplies and with no help from the locals, Steele would have no alternative but to run.

Tuesday, August 25, 1863 Perryville, I.T.

"He's Choctaw, 'Lias. Least that's what that there other Indian says. That's the same as them what was killed," One Shoe prodded the stoic Indian towards the colonel's tent. It was ten o'clock in the morning when the advance men stumbled onto a company of the southern Indians that had been detached to watch for the Federals. The short skirmish produced four of the enemy killed and several taken prisoner, which included the captain of the Indian force.

"We have them now," determined General Blunt. "Tell our scouts and advance men to keep going, and to report to me every time they learn something. I'll be at the head of the column. Now, let's move!"

Just before dusk, a cavalry scout reined up next to the general's party. "They've opened up with canister, General. They have two howitzers posted in the woods."

Elias and Matthew lay next to a large cottonwood. It was nearly dark, but they could still see the puffs of smoke from the Rebel rifles. Each time smoke was seen, both Elias and Matthew would fire into it. The Union cannon had been answering Rebel shelling with balls of their own for twenty minutes.

"They thinnin' out, 'Lias," shouted Matthew.

"I do believe you're right." Elias placed another cap on the rifle's nipple and fired. A silhouette slowly staggered away from a bush across the river and slid down the bank, into the water.

Elias swallowed and then reloaded.

Suddenly the Confederate cannons opened with a continuous fire. The iron from the concealed cannons was flying so thick it almost formed a cloud over the battle area. The men of the 1st had never seen so much smoke and heard so much noise from only two or three guns. Elias was huddled next to Toby, with Matthew just a few feet away in a small grove of trees as the shot caused branches and leaves to rain down around them.

Out of the corner of his eye Elias saw one of his men raise to his knees and lunge toward another tree for cover. Just then another burst of canister roared through their line. With the intention of pulling the soldier to the safety of their position, Elias reached out to grab him. Just then he felt a sting and thought he had accidentally run his hand into the tree trunk. He stared into the dim light to see what had happened and then began to feel a burning sensation. As he focused on his right hand, he could see that his thumb was missing.

"Damn."

"What, 'Lias?" yelled Toby.

"Never mind," replied Elias, "keep your head down." Elias pulled his large blue kerchief from his pocket and wrapped his hand, trying to stop the flow of blood as his hand began to throb.

"Here come the Sixth Kansas," someone shouted. The cavalry unit had been dismounted and was proceeding up both sides of the road. Elias and his men slowly moved forward as the darkness gave way to moonlight. The Confederate firing had ceased as quickly as it had started, and the smoke began to slowly dissipate as darkness covered the countryside.

"I think that does it." Elias stopped and knelt down on one knee and tightened the bandage around his hand. He could feel the warm sogginess and knew he had to get his hand cared for as soon as possible. He hurt, was very tired and yet concerned about his men. It was too dark to see all of them, so he got up and made his way along the line to the west of the road. Elias had been moving south along the ditch during the skirmish, with his men deployed to his right. The order had been given to cease fire and assemble forward at the small cluster of buildings that was known as Perryville. It was here that Elias gathered his men, and determined that everyone else in their company was uninjured.

Elias found the surgeon, the bleeding was stopped and his hand given a proper bandage. Even with the throbbing, soon, sleep was sweet.

"They've spread out all over everywhere, I heard, 'Lias." Corporal Miller of Co. F, rested against the side of one of the storehouses that was about to be burned. "They say them Creeks have gone north with McIntosh and the Cherokees have headed west to God-knows-where. We're told to get you fellas to help us burn everything in sight and get ready to move again."

"We hit the jackpot here, Orin. We should have enough supplies to get to anywhere the general wants us to go. But I sure hate to see what's left burned. I keep thinking about the folks that are doing without. Some of the people up and down the Kansas-Missouri border are starving and going without most everything." Elias raised his elbow to his knee to get his hand elevated so the throbbing would ease a bit.

"That where your mama's at?" asked Orin.

"No, we're lucky. She is on a farm outside of Lawrence, up in Kansas. I doubt that she has seen much trouble."

"You mean you didn't hear?" said Orin. He hesitated at first to go on, but Elias broke in immediately.

"Hear what? Did something happen up there? What do you know?" pleaded Elias.

"We heard by telegraph that Lawrence was raided last Friday by a bunch of Rebs and outlaws led by that Quantrill fella." Orin paused, wondering how much information he should give.

"Well, go on! What happened? Was there people killed? Did they just get food and horses or what? Dammit, Orin, tell me!"

"Look, Elias. I don't know a lot of the details. I just heard the officers talking about it just before we left. Seems that fer some reason we sent some men from Company I up there and they got caught up in the fight." Orin looked at the ground and lowered his voice. "They had one man killed. Private Pope, I believe. Did ya know …?"

"Dammit, are you going to tell me or do I …?" Elias was on his feet glaring down at the corporal.

"Hold on, Elias, all I know is the fellas said that this bunch hit Lawrence early in the morning. They were looking for General Lane and some of the top town's people. Quantrill said somethin' about getting back for the killin' of his brother and that jail that collapsed over in Missouri that had them women prisoners in it."

"So, what did he do?"

"Well, I guess they pretty well burned down the whole town," Orin said in a subdued tone.

"What about the people?" Elias leaned close to Orin and glared into his eyes.

"They say there was about a hundred and fifty people killed." Orin shoved himself backward with his hands and quickly added, "But they didn't say anything about them raiders going out in the country for nothin'. Didn't you say your mama lived on a farm somewhere's? They didn't go out there, least not that I know. Our guys said it was hot fightin' for a spell and then Quantrill up and left."

Elias crumpled to his knees and then sat back leaning against the log building. "Why the hell didn't I just stay home? Why did I go off and leave Mama and Cheat? Why am I here anyway? Dammit, I wish …"

"I thought we'd been all through that." A voice came from out of the morning sun as Elias looked up trying to see who had spoken. "There is nothin' you can do now except the job you asked for, remember?" It was China Bill.

Corporal Miller took that opportunity to get to his feet and move away toward a group of his own men preparing to fire one of the other buildings.

"Why do you do that?" Elias looked at Bill. "You always

have to remind me …"

"Hey. You asked for this job and you pulled us all together. You're the one lookin' out for us." Bill placed his hand on Elias' shoulder. "Don't you think that while you are keepin' us under your wing, that Mr. Wallace is lookin' out for your mama and Cheat? You've told me about him. He sure seems to be the kind of fella that would do all he could to protect his people. And your mama … well, I bet she is smarter than the whole lot up there in Lawrence. She ain't gonna let anything happen to her or any of her own, the Wallaces, too!" Bill took a breath and continued in a strong yet gentle voice. "She must be some lady to send us a fella like her son to help us do what we gotta do." Bill's forehead furrowed and his damaged eyes bore into Elias'. "And you know what we gotta do." Bill leaned back and pushed his hat back on his head. "We gotta burn this here place and go on and chase us some Rebs, just like we gittin' paid to. Ya' hear?"

"Colonel," Elias looked around, staring into the surrounding area with mock inquiry, "Would you please give this man your rank straps and make him the regimental councilor?"

"I won't take the job if'n I don't get the pay that goes with it!" stated China Bill.

Chapter 17

Thursday, August 27, 1863

"I can't believe that we have missed them again." General Blunt's rage caused his horse to rear and prance almost uncontrollably. "I'll not have Cabell and Steele getting away!"

"But, General," offered Captain Rogers, "we've captured and destroyed all of their supplies and what with the desertions we have heard about, I can't help but think you can clearly count your mission as a grand success."

"I'll count my success' when I see white flags or wood crosses in the ground with their names on them and not before!" With that, General Blunt galloped back to the main group of officers and dismounted.

"Colonel Cloud," General Blunt began, "I want you to take your brigade at once and head for Fort Smith. I'm convinced that General Cabell is headed for the fort and plans to make a stand there."

"Begging the General's pardon, but my men have been on the march and then fighting for several weeks, and what you're asking is another march of a hundred miles, Sir."

"If your men are not up to it, Colonel, maybe we can get them relieved and find some soldiers that are ready to do their work."

"That will not be necessary, Sir. My men are up to anything I ask of them. You can be assured that we can complete any orders given us." Colonel Cloud made no attempt to hide the indignation he felt.

"Very well, then," continued General Blunt. "Now, Colonel Judson, I want you to take your troops and battery and head northwest and find those Indians that McIntosh has. Find them and either wipe them out or discourage them from ever attempting to engage Union troops again. Do I make myself clear?"

"Very clear, Sir," replied Colonel Judson. He made certain he did not make the same mistake Cloud had made by even insinuating he would have difficulty carrying out his orders.

"That's what I want to hear," stated Blunt, glancing at Colonel Cloud. "Now, let's get at it."

"That means us, fellas." Elias had made it a policy to be as close to the officers as he could when they were planning strategy, hoping to overhear what was to transpire. "We go with Colonel Judson."

The next morning Elias and most of the 1st Kansas Colored was moving north along the Texas Road. As the somewhat pleasant morning began to work its way into the normal heat of the day, they marched past McAllister and Reams. Then just north of the village of South Canadian they forded the Canadian River and headed in a northwesterly direction. Within a few miles they crossed the north fork of the Canadian, sometimes referred to as Rabbit Ear Creek, and marched to Council Ground after fording Deep Fork Creek.

"All's I do is wade rivers," complained One Shoe. "Wouldn't be so bad if'n I had fittin' shoes."

"They aint … *aren't* shoes to fit feet like yours," said Toby.

"Well, if'n they want real men in this here army, they ought to get real clothes. Ever time I get's my feet wet, these here shoes just shrivel up and I can hardly walk."

"Maybe you ought to be wearing socks, Tom," offered Elias. "It would be more comfortable, I'm sure."

"Ain't got no socks, 'Lias. 'Sides, they ain't room for all my toes in there much less them wool socks, too. I was better off when I had my hinge sandal. At least one foot could breathe and stretch out."

The scouts had ridden out at intervals, covering from Deep

Fork and Warfields south to Greenleef's Store and back west toward the Sac and Fox country. Then they reported back to the colonel as to what they had found.

It was determined that as the movements of McIntosh's Indians were tracked, it appeared that there were fewer and fewer troops. After several days, they began to be approached by groups of from three to ten Indians, claiming to be deserters from the Confederate forces. It wasn't long before all but around one hundred fifty Southern Indians were accounted for.

"Colonel, we can't take this many prisoners. What're we gonna do with 'em?"

Colonel Judson was forced to try and hide a smile. "I guess we're just running them out of ambition, Corporal."

"They keep sayin' that they was lied to, Colonel. They say that the Confederates told them they could keep out the Union troops, save their lands for 'em and even get back some more, if they just help in the war. So far, they've got nuthin' but shot at and killed. And they don't get fed worth a da ... worth nuthin', Sir."

"All right, Corporal," said Colonel Judson, allowing his smile to show. "Tell them that if they want to get even they can go to Fort Gibson and enlist in a real army. That should give them a chance to fight if that's what they want."

The march back to Fort Davis was a more leisurely one, except for One Shoe. He was positive he would have to wade all the streams and rivers over again.

"Tom, just think how clean your feet will be by the time we get back," offered Elias.

"Go ahead on, Corporal, make fun of ol' Tom."

"I wouldn't do that, Tom." Elias smiled and then assured Tom that they would make their way east until they reached the Texas Road and probably wouldn't have to wade more than four or five rivers. At that the rest of the men broke out in good-natured laughter.

"Das all right. My turn'll be a'comin some day." Then in a

quiet tone he asked, "Hows that there thumb? I mean … where it was … er … well …"

"It's going to be fine, Tom. It still throbs some when I let it just hang, but I'll manage."

"You gonna git you a commendation, 'Lias? Fer gittin' wounded, I mean?" asked Matthew.

"Wonder just what kind'a letter you git fer a thumb?" questioned One Shoe.

"You don't get letters or commendations for thumbs. Toby is the one that deserves the honors. He's the one that has all the scars," replied Elias. "And I know those legs hurt at times, too, don't they, Toby?"

"Well, they does … *do* some when the sun gets to 'em, but they's nothin' now. I'm fine, 'Lias, and 'least I still got m' legs, thanks to you."

The men of the 1st continued for three more days heading back through the heat and dust, bunch grass and bluejoint. Twice they saw small herds of buffalo. When possible they had followed streams and creeks and, at times, were able to take advantage of the shade offered by the large cottonwood and walnut trees that covered the banks. One evening several of the men caught and fried catfish. Some wild onions were found and added to the 'home' cooking. The men felt good. They had conquered the enemy, when they were able to find them, and those that were left were on the run. They had loaded down their haversacks with dried fruits, smoked meats and even a few canned peaches before they destroyed Perryville and were eating well even while being on the march. Then, crossing Pecan Creek and a small branch of Elk Creek, they reached the Texas Road heading back north to Fort Davis. Soon they would be back where they had left their belongings and would at least be able to change clothing.

"It looks like it's coming along fine, Corporal. Just try to keep it clean." Dr. Harrington, the regimental surgeon, had inspected Elias' hand as one of the nurses was applying a fresh bandage. "Guess you'll have to use your left hand to thumb your nose now," he said with a chuckle.

"If I ever find the Reb that did this, I won't be thumbing my nose at him," replied Elias, with a sly grin. "I'll be spreading his nose all over his head." Then with a nod he said, "Thanks a lot, Sir. I appreciate the help."

The doctor patted Elias' shoulder and then said, "You heard what happened while you boys were out west chasing Indians?"

"About what?" questioned Elias?

"Why, General Blunt is sitting in the office of the post commander at Fort Smith. Has complete control of the fort and the town; ran the Rebels south into the mountains."

"You mean that Fort Smith is ours now?"

"It certainly is, Corporal, and I wouldn't be surprised if we wouldn't be headed that way very soon."

"Looks like Colonel Cloud managed to get himself ambushed by Cabell's rear guard at the foot of Backbone Mountain and then fought it out for over three hours." Elias retold the story he heard at the surgeon's tent earlier that afternoon. "That's a place south and east of Fort Smith," he continued. "After that a whole bunch of Cabell's men turned and ran back through their own lines and even took a bunch of Union prisoners with them."

"Boy, 'Lias," said Matthew, "they sure must'a been scared of our fellas."

"It wasn't that. These fellas were men that had been made to join up and were really Union men from Arkansas."

"I remember hearing about those guys," said China Bill. "They probably didn't want to be firing on some of their own."

"But that's not all. Only two of Cloud's men were killed." Elias then lowered his voice some. "One of them was Captain Lines of the Second Kansas Cavalry." Several of the men had known E.C., as he was called, and were saddened to hear of his death.

"Colonel Cloud had twelve wounded and captured thirty

prisoners. And listen to this. That evening dozens of Rebs walked into Cloud's camp and volunteered to join up. They call them "mountain Feds," on account of where they came from. Now that's something."

All the men began talking at once, giving their opinion as to what the results of the victory would mean. It seemed to many that it would mean an end to much of their fighting. To some, the whole war amounted to just what was happening around their part of the country. To others, success was obvious. "If we can win where we are," some thought, "the rest of the Union must be doing the same thing."

Corporal Miller, of Co. F, had walked up during Elias' report and offered, "And guess who's in charge at Fort Smith now? It's Colonel Cloud."

"I don't understand," said Elias.

"General Blunt got sick and went to Fort Scott and left Cloud in charge."

September of 1863 was spent by the 1st Kansas Colored Volunteer Infantry, drilling, marching and with inspections even in their remote camp of Fort Davis, as primitive as it was. Supplies were received from Fort Gibson just up the river, and even a clothing ration was delivered around the middle of the month.

"Wonder just what they got up their sleeve," commented China Bill. "Wonder why we need new clothes?"

"Now jes when do you mostly git new clothes?" asked One Shoe. "When you goin' somer's, that's when. We probably gonna be travelin'."

"You get you some more shoes yet?"

"Shut yo' mouth."

"Man, it sho is hot 'round here," declared Matthew.

"Fella, wha'chu mean, you hot? You cain't be hot."

"Wha'chu mean? Sho I'm hot. I never been so hot as when

I gotta wear these here wool shirts and them there heavy pants in the middle o' summer."

"I say you can't be hot cause I heard some of the white boys complainin' 'bout the heat and one o' them said that it weren't as hard on us colored cause we came from Africa where it's hot all da time."

"Oh yeah? Jes how long it been since you been t' Africa?"

Elias smiled at the good-natured bickering between Tom and Matthew. He loved these men just as he loved his mother and brother at home. He had gotten word from his mother relating her experience during Quantrill's raid, August 21st of this year, and settling himself at the base of a tree, he began to re-read the letter.

She had gone to town on Thursday with Mrs. Wallace to do some shopping and stayed with some friends that night. Mrs. Wallace had an evening church meeting, and Elias' mother said she would get a ride back to the farm with some friends the following day, being the 21st.

She was awakened by the shouting and shooting early Friday morning and fled with her friend and the children while her friend's husband remained behind trying to organize a resistance. The women and children had fled east past Massachusetts Street just as the Eldridge Hotel was being burned. It was said that General Lane was in town and was the object of a desperate search on the part of Quantrill's men, but if that was true, apparently the general had made good his escape.

Elias' mother and her friends tried to make their way southeast toward Mount Oread to where there was a fortification, but the raid was over before they could reach it. The rest of the day was spent trying to aid the hurt and dying and restoring some order to the devastated town.

Elias had heard about the outrage of the citizens at not being better protected and also about the infamous *Order Number Eleven* issued immediately after the raid by Union General Ewing. It stated that all of the Missouri counties along the

Kansas-Missouri border south of the Lawrence and all the way to the middle of Vernon County was to be depopulated and all the property confiscated or burned. Those loyal to the Union could move into Kansas, but others were on their own.

Elias' mother assured him that she was well and that everyone at home was well also. She said she would write again soon and that she was praying for her sons.

Sons? It sounded strange to Elias for her to word her letter just that way. And again, no specific word of Cheat. What had happened? He had made it a point to ask about his younger brother in his letters home, but had not received any definite answer.

Elias spent two evenings writing a long letter to his mother. He told her of his adventures, the battles and his promotion. He did not mention he was missing a thumb and hoped that it was not apparent in his writing. It had been difficult at first holding a pencil, but he soon got on to it. For now his bandage helped hold the pencil in place. He wasn't sure how it would be later.

How fortunate he was. It was only a thumb. It was almost embarrassing to acknowledge that he had been wounded and hold up a hand missing one thumb.

"Look at it this way," China Bill had rationalized. "You only had two and you gave one for your country. Man, that's half of what you got. Who else can say that they were willing to give up half of what they had in defense of their Union?"

Elias had to smile as he recalled the remark. Then the more he thought, the more he chuckled and finally began to laugh out loud. A soldier strolling by glanced over at Elias, looked wonderingly and then quickened his pace as Elias looked up at his curious glance and began to convulse with laughter.

By this time it seemed that the Union was finally getting a break. During the summer, Union General Grant had renewed his effort to split the Confederacy by controlling the Mississippi. After the fall of Vicksburg the Union had more troops to concentrate on other areas, one of which was the Arkansas campaign. Confederate General Price had replaced the ailing General Holmes and prepared to defend Little Rock from what he was certain was to be an attack from the north by Union General Frederic Steele. After defensive works were built and a number of rifle pits were dug on the north bank of the Arkansas River, Price finally determined that he had been mistaken and that the attack must surely come from the south. Price's attack on the Union garrison at Helena had resulted in an embarrassing defeat with heavy casualties. Fort Smith was in Union hands, and the lack of coordination among the Confederate forces caused the future to look very bleak for the Rebel army.

Steele approached Little Rock from Helena and after a skirmish with Colonel Archibald S. Dobbins' troops at Ashley's Mills, crossed the Arkansas and met Marmaduke at Fourche Bayou. Flanking fire from Union artillery on the north bank of the Arkansas quickly dispersed the Confederates, and Price began pulling out, destroying everything he could as he moved his troops toward Arkadelphia and the new and temporary Arkansas capitol at Washington.

The loss of Little Rock had caused morale of the Confederates to drop to an all-time low. This was their third major defeat in 1863. Arkansas Governor Flanagin complained that desertions were decimating their army, and looting by disheartened soldiers was widespread.

"We must be doing something right," said Colonel Williams to himself with a smile.

Chapter 18

Wednesday, September 23, 1863   Fort Davis, I.T.

"I told'ja," said One Shoe, "I told'ja we was movin."

"It's *'I told you,'* you big old darkie," said Toby with an air of superiority. "When are you going to learn to speak in a civilized manner?"

"Huh?" replied One Shoe. "I done tol' you what I meant. Wassa matter? Don' you unerstand nuthin', Boy?"

"Boy? Now look'a here, you big dumb…."

"Attention!"

The boys jerked upward and became rigid.

"I don't want to hear that, understand? Now just what is all the commotion about?"

One Shoe, relaxing, slumped slightly and looked around to see Elias standing with a smile on his face.

"I'm just trying to tell this here little fella that we was movin' and he don' seem to understand nuthin' I'm a sayin."

"How could anyone understand such common and uneducated talk, Elias?" stated Toby. "The man is a word type disaster."

"He don' even know what that there means, 'Lias. Sometimes the little fella has got brain numb, I bettcha. It don' show 'cept when his mouth drops open. Y'ever notice that?"

Toby scratched at the scars on one ankle, trying to appear distracted and uninterested.

"Okay," said Elias, "what are you two going on about? You want to let me in on it?"

"I jes heard that we are movin' and I was warnin' young Toby here that he better git his self ready." One Shoe lowered his voice and leaned toward Elias. "Him bein' a little slow, it takes him longer than some to get caught of things, ya know."

"Now you jes look'a here, ya big ol' …" Toby reverted to his old self and drove into One Shoe with both verbal barrels. "You ain't never seen the day that I couldn't scorch yo' black …"

"I said I didn't want to hear this! You both understand?" Elias shouted, straightened up and pointed first to one and then to the other, trying hard to keep a straight face.

"Toby, I don't want to hear another word until I ask. Understand?"

"Yas … *yes,* Sir."

"Tom, try to tell me exactly what you are saying." Elias hesitated and then, as sternly as he could, added, "And I don't want to hear about Toby or anything other than what you have heard. What do you know that I don't?"

"Corporal Miller, ya know, the fella that all'ys knows everthin'? Well, he says that we is … okay, we are movin', and we are goin' to Fort Smith. Now, how hard is that to understand, for a normal fella, that is?" One Shoe looked over at Toby and then back to Elias.

"Well," Elias hesitated and then continued, "I've heard the same rumor, and I must say it figures. We can't stay here in a temporary camp, and it seems to me that we should follow the Rebs if we intend to run them back to where they came from."

One Shoe straightened to his full height and glanced quickly to Toby and then concentrated his attention toward Elias.

"I thought you would like to know, Sir." One Shoe deliberately turned away from Toby and clasped his hands behind his back. "If you wish, Sir, I'll alert da others. Wif yo permission, a'corse."

"Let me verify this, Tom, and then I'll let you know."

Toby grunted and appeared to concentrate on the scars on his ankles.

"That's right, Corporal, and it will be a permanent move.

The main force will proceed to Fort Smith in about a week or so and see what orders they have for us there. However," … 2nd Lieutenant Wm. R. Smith paused and then continued. "They're sending part of a company up north to Fort Blair. That will be us."

"Fort Blair, Sir, you mean Baxter Springs? You mean Camp Hooker again?"

"I'm afraid there is no more Camp Hooker, Corporal. They are tearing it down so we can use the material to help build a regular fort. You and your men are part of our group. We are to leave on Sunday. I'm sure we'll all be together again in Fort Smith before long."

"Yes, Sir; thank you, Sir. I'll see to it that my men are alerted," replied Elias, rather downhearted. The lieutenant returned Elias' salute and started off toward the shack the men had constructed for Colonel Williams under the trees next to the river.

Several days before, word had been received from Fort Scott that Colonel Blair, commanding the District of Southern Kansas and the post at Fort Scott, was having a fort built at Baxter Springs. Since the 1st Kansas Colored had left in June, there had been little or no troops stationed there at all.

"There just isn't any real protection for supply trains, troops or anything else all along the border south from Scott," said Colonel Williams. "Blair and Blunt both are very concerned. The 3rd Wisconsin Cavalry at Dry Wood, twelve miles south of Fort Scott, is all there is, and they have been busy all summer chasing guerillas. It's said that Hunter and Coffee may have upwards of a thousand men roaming around western Missouri." Williams shook his head. "They've been hitting supply trains headed for Fort Smith and making things difficult in general. And there's no one to spot any movements up and down the border since *Order 11* cleaned out all the people."

"So now they build a fort and supply men for escorts," said the lieutenant "is that it?"

"Looks that way. Colonel Blair has sent Lieutenants Crites

and Cook to Baxter to start construction. Now they want us to send some help, too. But as soon as our men are finished with what they can do, they are to join us at Fort Smith."

"They will be glad of that. But you know we should have done something more than just make encampments when we were there earlier, Sir."

"Well, we had no idea we wouldn't have the Military Road protected then."

"Guess you're right, Sir. Hope this works."

"So do I. They say Quantrill is still roaming around western Missouri, and we don't need any more trouble from that bunch."

"Weren't they supposed to be heading for Texas?"

"You can't tell about people like that. The Confederates don't even formally recognize him as one of their own even though they are glad for his help. That rank of Colonel is self-awarded, but he still sends in reports just as if he was an actual part of the Confederate force."

"We've got until Sunday, fellas. Get all your belongings ready to be loaded on the wagons. We are going to Fort Smith, a … by way of Fort Blair." Elias hesitated and then continued. "They say that Smith is much better than anything we have been in since leaving Fort Scott. So we better …"

"Jes one minute," interrupted One Shoe, "ya say Fort Blair? Ain't that back up north agin'? That there's Baxter Springs. Ain't that the long way 'round? Seems t' me a fur piece out'n the way."

"We're just going to be there long enough to help get a regular fort built. Won't be much. It will just amount to a little more time and a longer walk, that's all."

"Huh," replied One Shoe, "yeah, dats all."

"Hey, we're still going to end up at Fort Smith. Remember, Fort Smith, with the permanent buildings and a town and civilized people?"

"You mean we ain't … *aren't* going to have to live in tents no … *any* more, 'Lias?" questioned Toby.

"Well, I don't know how many buildings they have there,

but maybe we will be inside," replied Elias. "That would be nice for a change."

"Hardly remember when I had a roof over m'head," said One Shoe.

"Wouldn't be surprised, if it won't be the first time," muttered China Bill, with a wink to Elias.

"Now look'a here. I'll have you know that I's born under a roof," stated One Shoe.

"Yeah, they hatch lots o' weird things in them coops down south," offered Toby, as he dodged a nearly worn-out boot thrown by One Shoe.

Elias grinned and shook his head. He felt really good. He was among the dearest friends he had ever had, he was healthy and there was no battle in sight. Maybe they would be able to spend the coming winter at Fort Smith. It would beat holing up in some shack or trudging through two-feet-deep snow on the way to being shot at. Yet, that is why they were all there. To get the shooting out of the way and get everyone home again, Confederates as well as Union.

Elias had met some really likeable rebel soldiers and was having a hard time reconciling his mixed feelings. Most of the southerners seemed to as anxious to get the war over as he was, and kept saying that all they wanted was to be left alone. Well, if that is the case, why did they start this whole thing? He had learned that the slavery question was not necessarily the main thing that caused the shooting to start. He knew that what had been referred to as *states rights* had more to do with it than most anything. So why not go about it the way most arguments should be settled? Why not sit down and figure out what would be best for everyone and get on with making a living?

For many in the south, making a living was accomplished on the backs of the colored and they certainly weren't going to give that up. Yet, most of the Reb fellas he had met didn't come from a farm that had slaves. Some even told him of free colored that had their own business. Now, how could some be slaves in the south and other free colored ignore the situation and go on just as if it didn't exist? Elias began to see the complexity of this war question, and decided it was easier to do his duty and take his orders from others that, he hoped, were smart enough to make sense of what was happening and know the right thing to do to bring it to a stop.

"Elias," he said to him self, "you're thinking too much. You're going to give yourself a headache." Smiling, Elias gathered up his dirty clothing and headed off to the wash tubs.

After Chaplain George W. Hutchinson had finished church services Sunday morning and the men had had their noon meal, everyone began to pack their belongings and stack them on the wagons that would follow them on their way to Baxter Springs. It was a disappointment to most of the men, not going straight to Fort Smith with the rest of the group, but they knew their help was needed to secure the travel up and down the Military Road. Still, they were ultimately heading for a place better than their primitive camp here.

Many stories had been heard about Fort Smith. There were real stone buildings, walls surrounding the fort, guarded gates and a town in which the men could find rest and recreation.

"I know jes 'bout the recreation we gonna find," stated One Shoe. "They gonna be right happy to see us black sojers, I bet."

"Tom," began Elias, "I have heard that there are many colored that are volunteering for the army just like we did at home. We may find that things are different there."

"You put yo' pennies on that, 'Lias, and I'll have mine to spend later. This here is th' only place I ever been welcome, and probably the only'st one they is." The big man shook his head and continued packing his few belongings.

"Our day will come, Tom," said Elias to himself. "We have our chance to show we are real people and folks will recognize it when we're done with this war. How can they help but see what we're doing? Up until now, we have only been considered three-fifths of a person, and here we are fighting and stopping musket balls just the same as the white boys, and we *volunteered* to do it." Elias was convinced that their efforts would not go unnoticed nor fail to be appreciated. It made him feel proud for his men and himself.

Chapter 19

Sunday, September 27, 1863

They had traveled seven hours and about fifteen miles when the group of which Elias and his men were a part stopped to camp for the night. Along the way they would occasionally recognize the countryside they had traveled earlier this year on their way to Fort Gibson. Many remembered that it seemed to take forever. It was just as hot and it didn't seem that they were making much headway. Moving along mile after mile gave each of them a lot of time to think. It was hard to realize they would soon be passing the spot of their first real test of battle when they encountered the Confederates at Cabin Creek. They had done some fighting before that, but not such all-out combat.

Elias wondered how George Brothers was doing. He had not heard anything for several months. Perhaps when they got to Baxter Springs someone might come down from Fort Scott who would know or he could send a message.

Cabin Creek, Honey Springs, an occasional skirmish with renegades … the short summer had been a lifetime. Friends had been maimed, some had died, and boys had been forced into manhood in a matter of minutes.

"'Lias." Elias jumped as if he had been hit. He had been deep in thought when Toby spoke.

"'Lias, how kin ya … *can you* tell the difference between some of these wild flowers and some of them there weeds that has pretty blossoms?"

Elias smiled at the serious look on the young man's face. "Well, Toby, I suppose you might sort of have to wait a bit to know for sure. I guess the flowers and the weeds are kind'a like people. The flowers, like good people, just try to fit in and make things look and seem better. The weeds, like some of the ornery folks, try to move in and take over."

"Hummm," nodded Toby as he watch two scissor-tail swallows dart through the evening sky. The nights were cooler and more comfortable now that it was the beginning of fall. The smell of coffee was in the air, and the men seemed content to just sit and watch the blue-black sky begin to show tiny holes of twinkling light through the trees. There was little chance of the enemy being anywhere close to them here, and the work of building that lay ahead of them was not an unpleasant thought.

The reddish glow from a pipe could be seen sometimes swinging back and forth as Lieutenant Smith sat at his camp table and talked with two other men. He was looking forward to seeing his old friend, Lieutenant R. E. Cook, with the 2nd Kansas Colored Infantry. They had each been assigned to a colored unit when the 1st and the 2nd were mustered in, and had served together at Fort Leavenworth, been separated for a time and would now get to catch up on old times as soon as his part of the 1st got to Baxter Springs.

"Them there p'simmons soon gonna be ripe," said One Shoe as they walked along the road. "Need a good frost first tho, I reckon. Sho don' wanna get 'em too soon."

"Yeah," agreed Toby, "they ... *they're* best when you can pick 'em up off the ground. I generally go up and give the tree a little shake and watch to see what falls. If you can find 'em, then they are sure good."

"Once't in awhile ya kin see little piles of them seeds and then ya know there are some good ones around that the groundhogs or armadillos have found."

"Da' army-whats?" asked Toby, forgetting to correct himself.

"You know, them little aminals with the pointy nose and the foldin'up shell all over 'em," explained One Shoe. "Ain't you seen any a' them?"

"No, but I seen ... *saw* a couple of those big things that

scampers along and looks like a great big brush."

"Those are the groundhogs Tom was talking about," said Elias. "If you ever see one of them in the rain, you'll see that they aren't nearly as big as they look when their fur is all fluffed up."

"They have some weird lookin' varmints around this part of the country," said Toby with a shake of his head.

"Jes like yo' folks did at home," added One Shoe, moving just out of Toby's reach.

Sunday October 4, 1863

Elias, his men and the rest of the group arrived at Baxter Springs a little after noon. The encampment was located east of the Military Road and less than a quarter of a mile west of Spring River on the edge of the woods. A blockhouse had been placed on a slight slope just north of Spring Branch which emptied into Spring River. The blockhouse was surrounded on the north, east and south by a series of breastworks. Just to the east of the blockhouse was another building which was used by Dr. W. H. Warner of Gerard, Kansas as a residence and a hospital of sorts.

Lt. Smith reported in to Lieutenant Crites and was told to have his men set up their tents inside the line of breastworks if there was enough room. The breastworks consisted of logs and earth about four feet high. The plan was to construct an adequate, even though perhaps primitive, fort in which enough troops could be stationed that would provide escorts for trains to and from Fort Scott to Fort Smith and Fort Gibson. The fort would be needed only as long as the threat of enemy attacks existed, which might even be the duration of the war. It was fairly certain there would no longer be any danger to the town's people from hostile Indians, so a military presence would not be needed.

Elias and his men had not stopped for their noon meal since they were so close to Baxter Springs. A sergeant of the 3rd Wisconsin Cavalry directed the men to the cook's area, which was a large tarpaulin roof open on all sides and fastened to poles which had been set in the ground and anchored with guy-ropes.

"After we eat," said Lieutenant Smith, "store your belongings and report to the sergeant here," motioning to a stocky, cigar-chewing black man about five feet two inches tall. "He will tell you what your duties will be."

Finishing a short but loud indoctrination, the feisty sergeant directed the new arrivals, "… and be sure your sleeves are rolled up. We're burning daylight whilst we're standin' here gabbin!"

"But today's Sunday and we jes' got here," muttered one of the men.

"You wanna complain?" glared the sergeant, "ya see me after supper. That is if'n ya earn any 'tween now 'n then!"

"Welcome to Fort Baxter," said Elias under his breath.

China Bill smiled, nodded and replied, "My kind'a soldier."

After Elias and the others had found a place for their bundles and tents, just at the west edge of the breastworks, they gathered by the blockhouse to receive instructions.

"We're gonna be extendin' this here breastworks to the west far enough to git ever' one inside. That means ya'll be cuttin' down them there trees over there," he said, pointing to the woods to the east, "an' haulin' them over here and settin' 'em just like we been a' doin." The sergeant removed his cigar, spat, and placed it back between his teeth in the center of his mouth. The cigar lost its shape when placed in the sergeant's teeth and became just a gray-black spot between his lips. His jaw remained stationary as he spoke with the words managing to find their way around the cigar butt and through the sergeant's teeth.

"I swear, that's the same cigar he had when he got here over a month ago," whispered a private from the 2nd Kansas to a newly made friend of the 1st. "I ain't never seen him without it and I ain't never seen him with a new one or that one lit."

The sergeant had the men fall in and then went up and down the line picking men with wide shoulders and big arms. "I want you men, if'n that's what'cha call yer selves, to grab on t' one of them there double-bladed axes and take the man next to ya and head fer them woods. First, ya look at the logs we been a bringin' over here and be damn sure you get some jes like 'em. The rest o' you foller along and after ya got the limbs trimmed off, drag them logs over here and I'll show ya how to stack and chink 'em.

"We're gonna extend this here breastworks to the west, and when we git it to our likin' we're gonna close it in. I'll tell ya when that'll be."

There was a pause and then suddenly the men began to move about hurrying to their assigned tasks.

"I don't wanna git on the south side o' him," muttered one soldier.

"Keep busy and don' look up," replied another, "thas th' secret."

"Where'd them guys come from?" asked China Bill, pointing toward a group of soldiers.

"I heard they came in early this morning," replied Elias. "They are the 3rd Wisconsin."

"I thought they were at Dry Wood."

"They were, but Colonel Blair had reports of a lot of activity in southern Missouri and northern Arkansas, so he sent Lieutenant Pond and his men here to help." Elias finished his cup of coffee and motioned to a corporal next to the mess table. "He was up getting breakfast started and told me who they were."

Lieutenant James B. Pond, now the ranking officer on site, was directing placement of his twelve-pound mountain howitzer, the only artillery at Baxter Springs. Placing the cannon just outside the north breastworks, Pond directed the men as to how the ammunition was to be stored and how much was to be kept close to the piece.

"Seems to know what he's doin'," said China Bill.

"We better hope so," replied Elias. "I haven't heard if anyone's coming right away, but I'd just as soon get this piece of work done and head for the walls of Fort Smith."

"You'n me both!"

Chapter 20

Saturday, October 3, 1863

"Messengers just arrived from Fort Smith, General."

"Very good, send them in." General Blunt took one last swallow of tepid coffee and moved a stack of papers from the center of his desk to a wicker basket at the left edge.

"Give me a quick synopsis of what is going on and then I'll read the dispatches."

"Well, Sir," began the corporal, not used to addressing such a high-ranking officer. "A course, I haven't read the dispatches, Sir, but …"

"I know that, Corporal, but you men always seem to know what's happening, much of the time before the commanders do. What is it?"

"Well, Sir, it seems that Colonel Shelby ran into some of the 1st Arkansas Union Infantry and gave 'em what fer. We lost several killed and captured and everyone figures that Shelby, Cooper and Cabell are fixin' to raise hell … ah … beggin' your pardon, Sir …"

"Yes, yes, go on," said General Blunt in an anxious tone.

"Well, Sir, since Price got his butt kicked at Little Rock, he's probably on the prod and wants to get back some of his dignity. The best way to do that is maybe get back Fort Smith or something else out in western Arkansas. He may be formin' up all he can get his hands on over at Arkadelphia and getting' ready to lambaste someone."

"Very good," said General Blunt, his hands forming a tent with his fingertips. "I like the concise way you put things, Corporal. I'll prepare a message to be wired to Fort Smith right away. And just so you will continue to be in on things," he said with a slight smile, "I'll be moving my headquarters back to Fort Smith immediately. You men can return along with me. We'll be leaving tomorrow afternoon."

"Yes, Sir. It will be a pleasure to accompany you, Sir, although it will probably be a pretty dull trip. We've had men movin' up and down the border without so much as a potshot taken. I figure most o' the Bushwhackers are hidin', afraid they will be taken for some of that bunch that hit Lawrence. If we ever get our hands on any ..."

"Yes, I'm sure, Corporal. That'll be all." General Blunt waved a hand in an impatient gesture as he had already begun to contemplate what must be done in a short time.

The rest of the afternoon General Blunt studied the dispatches and reports from Fort Smith. Telegraph reports from the north had advised him of some of the military movements in lower Missouri and northern Arkansas, so he was not surprised at the request for reinforcements for Fort Smith. It was up to him personally, he felt, to see it was done properly.

"So I says to th' Gen'ral, 'maybe you better hightail it down to Fort Smith and get everyone ready for a big ta'do,' I says," the corporal related to several soldiers standing outside the headquarters building. "'Corporal,' says th' Gen'ral, 'I believe you're right. We'll leave tomorrow and I be obliged if'n you' ride along with us.' 'Be glad to,' I says. So ya'll better be gittin' yer gear together. We're movin' out." As the corporal finished, two young lieutenants looked at each other, smiled and walked toward their barracks.

"Thing is," commented one of the lieutenants, "he's right. I've just been told we are moving."

"And I thought it was the sergeants that made all the decisions," laughed the other officer.

The brigade band struck up another stirring march, as they waited on the plaza in front of the headquarters. Part of the 3rd

Wisconsin Cavalry, under Lieutenant J. G. Cavert, part of a company of the 14th Kansas Cavalry, under Lieutenant R. H. Pierce, along with clerks and orderlies, were ready to head south to shift General Blunt's headquarters of his district to Fort Smith. On this sunny, pleasant afternoon, it was remarked that the band had never sounded so good nor looked so fine in their new uniforms.

Accompanying the General among his staff was Provost Marshal Major Henning, Major H. Z. Curtis, Assistant-Adjutant General, who was the son of Major General Curtis, and other aides and scouts. Among the civilians were not only the teamsters, but Mrs. Lydia Stevens Thomas, wife of the gravely ill Captain Chester Thomas, who was being treated at Fort Gibson, and a war correspondent and artist, James O'Neal, writing for *Frank Leslie's Illustrated Newspaper.*

Stepping out smartly, the train and escort began to move south, the band still playing as their shiny wagon caught the glint of the Sunday afternoon sun. Waves from the many civilians and salutes from attending soldiers marked the route for several blocks toward the edge of town. It was four o'clock as the last of the train disappeared down the Military Road, on a happy and yet fateful journey that would be the last march for many.

Camping about six miles south of Fort Scott and resuming the journey very early the next day, the troops covered about thirty-five miles, ending a very long day's march at Cow Creek. On Tuesday the train covered the remaining distance in quick order. The fairly level terrain allowed steady movement, and the freshness of the men and animals caused the miles to disappear under their feet.

The General, riding in his new ambulance, was at the head of the column, one of his aides leading his horse. Right around noon the head of the train arrived to within about a quarter of a mile of Lieutenant Pond's encampment, although it was unseen by the General due to the rolling hills just in front of him. There he changed into his dress uniform, positioned the band directly behind him and waited for the regimental medical detachment and the supply wagons to catch up.

"Riders approaching, General," reported Captain W. S. Tough, General Blunt's chief of scouts.

"Ride out to meet them, Captain. It's probably a welcoming committee from Lieutenant Pond."

There appeared to be about 150 mounted soldiers in the group, rather large for a reception committee, but could be men on a training exercise or a large scouting party. They had just emerged from the timber along the Spring River and had formed a line as if to mount a charge. "Just showing off for the general," thought General Blunt as he readied himself for the greeting.

Lt. Pond sat in his tent at noon wondering how long it would take his foraging party to return. He had sent sixty men along with wagons and teams out to gather what supplies they could find. And with a larger than normal number of men reporting sick, he found himself short of workers. All that were left in camp were a couple dozen cavalry and sixty or seventy of the colored troops. "Well, that will just have to do for now," thought the Lieutenant. At least he had the new troops from Fort Davis, for a short time anyway.

Most of the men were south of the breastworks milling around a cooking fire waiting for their noon meal. A commotion which seemed to come from over beyond the breastworks caused Elias and China Bill to look up and see First Sergeant W.L. McKenzie rushing toward Lieutenant Pond's tent. In a minute Pond and McKenzie appeared at the opening of the tent and began looking toward the east.

"Looks like we got here just in time, 'Lias," said China Bill as he hungrily spotted some food and watched the cook preparing the last of the meal.

"Any later and we'd missed out all together," replied Elias. "And I wouldn't want to miss this. I tell ya, this fall weather sure brings out the appetite. I bet I could ea …"

Suddenly the thunder of horses and the startling sound of gunfire filled the air. Men dropped their plates, filled or empty, and looked up to see mounted men charging and firing right into their midst. Some men dropped to the ground, others made a dash through the smoke, horses and other soldiers heading for the breastworks. Most all of the weapons were stacked beside tents, left inside the breastworks or racked in the block house.

"Elias …!" Toby yelled and shoved at the same time, causing Elias to fall to the ground just as a yelling, shooting rider crashed through the cooking fire and shot one of the cooks through the hand. The large ladle flew through the air, causing hot soup to splash across the flank of the rider's horse. The horse screamed, twisting away and almost spilling his rider.

Lt. Pond and four of his men raced across the opening trying to reach their weapons. Only the Lieutenant made it.

Elias half crawled, half ran through the crowd of men until he could see his rifle stacked next to the tent he would be sharing with China Bill. Without slowing down, he grabbed the weapon, dove for the ground and landed on his back at the west end of the breastworks. Forcing a load into the barrel of his rifle, he rolled onto his stomach and up on his knees just in time to see an enemy rider rushing toward him. With a spontaneous aim, he blasted the rider from his horse and into the path of another of the enemy cavalry. If the ball from Elias' rifle hadn't killed the man, the slashing hooves of the horse charging over him certainly did.

A pistol bullet hit the log nearest Elias' face, showering his cheek with splinters. He could see out the west end of their meager fortifications that the attack was coming from there as well as from the east. Many of the Union troops were caught out in the open between the cooking area and the uncompleted fort. Some lay apparently dead, while others either clutched at a wound or attempted to crawl away trying to find some sort of protection from the circling and shooting enemy force.

"Their comin' 'round agin', 'Lias," shouted One Shoe. He

had just reloaded and had an enemy rider in his sights when a figure in blue dashed in front of him and raced toward the howitzer just in front of the north breastworks.

"It's Pond," shouted someone, "he's making for the cannon. Try to keep the Rebs off'n him."

More rifle and pistol shots rang out as the young lieutenant feverishly worked at getting a charge and canister down the throat of the howitzer. None of the on lookers were very familiar with artillery, so the best they could do was to try to keep the rebels away from their courageous leader.

"I tried to tell ya', dammit," came a cry from the hospital building, as an older man who was known as 'Fatty' leaned through a window.

The second attack came charging in from the northwest and the northeast. Firing and reloading, the Union forces kept the enemy on the move. Just to the east of the breastworks the dependents' camp was in shambles. Several civilians could be seen either dead or wounded. Further toward the woods lay several bodies of Union troopers that had not made it back to the fort area.

Yells and screams from both the riders and the men inside firing out could be heard through the sometimes blinding smoke. The howitzer exploded its shot out toward the enemy, but it went over their heads. The shot had missed its mark due to the fuse not being trimmed properly, but its existence was enough to make the enemy pause for an instant and reconsider.

The soldier next to Elias jerked as Elias felt the man's blood spurt across his hand. The man slumped to the ground making a gurgling sound. A few quivers and the body lay still.

"Damn you …" Elias' rifle took another rider from his horse and spilled the man across the dark brown grass about thirty yards out to his right.

"Good for you, 'Lias, you … ow," hollered Toby. A large chunk of chinking flew from the breastwork and hit him in the mouth.

"Now yo' really got a fat lip," yelled One Shoe with a loud laugh.

Racing out of range, the riders, which unbeknown to the Union troops at that time belonged to the infamous William Quantrill, sought shelter in the range of trees next to the river.

"They may be forming for another attack," shouted Lieutenant Pond. "Stand ready."

As the quiet seemed suddenly very loud, two riders could be seen coming toward the rifle-pits. Several Union soldiers trained their rifles on the pair until Lieutenant Pond shouted for them to let the riders come in.

Major Henning and Captain Tough slid their horses to a stop as both dismounted and tried to explain while catching their breath.

"It's Quantrill and his men. They're attacking General Blunt's train just over the hill!

"Well, what is it, Captain," questioned General Blunt in an irritated voice. "Just what are those men doing up there?" General Blunt had moved forward just far enough to make out the noise of gunfire at Lieutenant Pond's camp.

"It's a bunch of Rebels, General, and they've already attacked the fort."

As Quantrill's men began to move toward the train, General Blunt's escort began to move toward the advancing enemy. Hardly any orders could be heard, and the confusion kept any sort of effective formation from being made. The General quickly mounted his horse that had been held by his aide just behind his ambulance. The supply wagons that were just catching up with the front of the train began to turn and move off to the west. The gaudy wagon carrying the band also turned off the road and headed in the same direction as fast as the driver could make his horses run.

Most of the raiders that had been attacking the fort had now been called to join Quantrill's main force. Moving toward the badly assembled escort troops, Quantrill could see his forces would outnumber the Union troops about four or five to one. After they had approached within rifle range, the Union troops realized the same thing. One volley was all the escort could manage before panic overcame them and they began to scatter.

General Blunt shouted to Major Curtis to try to rally the men, but his orders were lost in the chaos. Attackers drove into the fleeing soldiers, shooting and trampling as fast as they could pick out a target. Many of the raiders would circle back and shoot wounded men as they lay on the ground. Union soldiers would throw down their weapons, thinking they were being attacked by Confederates, and hoping they would be taken as prisoners. Those same men would sometimes even be shot with their own weapon. Wholesale slaughter of the Union detachment was carried out as the bandits whooped and shot their way over the prairie.

General Blunt caught the attention of Major Curtis, pointed toward an opening in the enemy line, and they both raced their horses toward it. Union troops could be seen running in most all directions with General Blunt shouting for them to stop and reform. He could just as well have been shouting at the prairie dogs. In his report the following day, General Blunt gave his version as to what transpired next.

It seemed that he, the General, had followed a group of about fifteen men for a mile and a half before managing to get them to stop and form into an orderly attack force. He had lost track of Major Curtis when they had both jumped their horses over a small ravine. It was later learned that the Major's horse had been burned by a bullet and had thrown the Major over its head. The Major's body in its bloodstained new dress uniform was later found, apparently having been shot after being captured by Quantrill's men.

General Blunt and his men managed to keep a small group of the enemy at bay and even turned on them once, causing them to rejoin Quantrill's main force. General Blunt then ordered Lieutenant Tappan and several others to ride to Fort Scott and get help.

"I haven't enough men to defend our position here if that bunch returns, much less give you any," stated Lieutenant Pond to Major Henning.

"Dammit, that's the General out there. I've got to get him some help," demanded Henning. "Give me something!

Henning and Tough rode toward the north with half a dozen cavalrymen and topped a rise just in time to see Quantrill's men finishing off wounded Union soldiers and the members of the band. The Reb raiders were stripping the dead of their belongings and plundering the wagons that had stopped. Many of the Union soldiers could be seen having been shot through the head after being wounded or having tried to surrender.

As the bandwagon driver had tried to get away, the rough terrain caused one wheel to come off, bringing the wagon to a sliding halt and spilling some of the band members to the ground. All aboard had been brutally murdered, piled on or under the wagon and the wagon fired. Among the dead was O'Neal the newspaper correspondent. Several yards away from the blaze the body of a young drummer boy was found with all of his clothes burned away save that which was between him and the ground.

Quantrill stopped and formed his men on a rise just to the west of the fort. Sending Captain Todd with a white flag of truce, it was demanded that the fort surrender. Lieutenant Pond stated that it was out of the question. When he was asked for an exchange of prisoners, Pond said they had taken no prisoners and that it appeared that Quantrill's men had been able to take their wounded with them.

"I don't know so much about hittin' 'em agin, Colonel," said Todd as he reined his horse next to Quantrill. "They got that there cannon and they can fort up pretty well in them there rifle pits."

Quantrill muttered, turned his horse and headed in a southerly direction with his raiders whooping and yelling after him.

Easing wounded soldiers and civilians on to make-shift litters, Elias and his men helped bring survivors into the breastworks. Moans and cries could be heard throughout the compound. Men could be seen retching and bleeding onto the ground outside the small, already crowded hospital building. Dr. Warner hovered over a wounded soldier as a civilian woman, with her foot bandaged, sat holding her badly wounded child and sobbing. Her husband, the father of the child, had been murdered in cold blood as he struggled to save his family. Now she desperately clung to the hope of her child's recovery.

Sergeant Jack Splane, Co. I, 3rd Wisconsin Cavalry, had been brought in with five bullet wounds, including one in the head. In excruciating pain but still conscious, Splane recounted his ordeal. "The sunofabitch that shot me in the head stood over me and told me to 'Tell old God that the last man you saw on earth was Quantrill'."

"I heard Cap'n Campbell of th' 14th Kansas tell o' hearing Quantrill brag about never taking prisoners and never intendin' to," spoke one of the doctor's aides. "Campbell had been a prisoner at Fort Smith before the Union got it back. He was gladder'n hell Bill Quantrill wasn't in charge o' them then."

"I tried to tell ya, dammit, didn't I? Huh, didn't I? But no one would believe Ol' Fatty."

"Wha'chu mean, Ol' Man?" asked One Shoe as he put down his end of a litter.

"Jes what I said now and b'fore! I told that there young lieutenant, but no, they warn't about to listen to Ol' Fatty. No Sir!"

"Told him what?" asked Elias as he wiped blood from his hands on to a piece of a shirt.

"I told 'em, and they wouldn't listen."

"What," demanded Elias?

"It was like this here," began the old man. "Coupl'a weeks ago me and this here other mail carrier got ourselves shot up and caught by that there Quantrill fella's men. On'y thin' that saved our hides was that I knowd one of 'em. Cy Gordon was a leading this bunch and I knowed Cy back in Leavenworth. We used to run around, drink and even one night me 'n Cy went over to this girly house and …"

"Never mind, what happened?"

"Oh, yeah, well, me and Cy got to jawin' and he was a wantin' to know all about back in Leavenworth and what had been a hap'nin' and such. So's after we jabbered awhile he got old Bill to turn us loose. Hell, they took ever'thin' we had, horses, mail, the whole shootin' match, but they let us go. We weren't hurt all that bad but what we weren't sure ready to hightail it out'n there.

"Well, anyways, afore we left, Ol' Cy said he'd probably be a seein' us soon, on account they was low on kettles 'n blankets 'n such and would probably be takin' supper with the garrison here pretty soon. And now they done it!

"You think that there young lieutenant would listen to Ol' Fatty? Hell, no! He knowed better'n me. Yeah, well, I guess he knows now what's what. An' I betcha he ain't no smarter fer it nuther."

Later that afternoon, the body of Corporal Bedford Green, Co. A of the 1st Kansas, was found just outside the west end of the breastworks.

"Sho' do seem a waste, huh, 'Lias?" said One Shoe.

"This part of the world had better belong to us again after this," stated China Bill.

"What'cha … *what do you* mean, Bill?" questioned Toby.

"I heard a couple of the fellas back at Fort Davis say that the Rebs actually own this corner of Kansas. They said that in June of '61 th' Cherokees sold a bunch of land to the Confederate States right after the war started and part of that land was right where Baxter Springs is."

"Could they do that?" asked Toby.

"To the tune of half a million dollars, they could."

"Where'd the South get that much money?" questioned Toby.

"Maybe they done give 'em a sack full o' beads and tol' 'em it was worth that much," said One Shoe with a grin.

"You can bet the Cherokees are a lot smarter than that," replied Elias.

"Well, most of 'em weren't smart enough to pick the right side when it come to the war," said China Bill.

About that time, several horses and voices could be heard just outside the breastworks. General Blunt rode up with Major Henning.

"Ya see that there Major, there?' said a wounded soldier named Heaton, of Co. C, 3rd Wisconsin Cavalry. "That man is one of the bravest I'd ever seen. If'n it weren't for him I be dead right this here minute. When all hell was breakin' loose, five of them raiders done had three of us and were draggin' us towards Quantrill's main bunch when here comes Major Henning ridin' right in to the middle of us. Well, sir, he had his pistol out and nailed one of 'em and scattered the rest and got all three of us back here.

"I tell ya, I was so fuddled that th' Major had to jab me in the ribs with his boot to get me headed in the right direction. Then, off he went tryin' t' foller them Rebs."

"All right, Gentlemen," spoke up General Blunt. "I have sent word to Fort Gibson and Fort Smith to be on the lookout for Quantrill and his murderers. I doubt if they will be seen soon, but at least we managed to save Fort Blair here. I hate to have lost our people and the train, but I'm glad we came along when we did. If that had not been the case, I'm sure the entire fort would have been lost."

"One of the men from the 2nd Kansas leaned over to the man next to him and whispered, "Ya know he really has it all figured out. He says that its *God's will,* whatever happens. That a' way if'n sump'in goes wrong, it ain't his fault."

"He must'a got that from McClelland," replied his friend.

Chapter 21

Sunday, October 25, 1863

Several weeks had passed since that fateful day when Elias and his friends had been suddenly thrown into a completely unsuspected battle with William Quantrill and his band of renegades. Elias had thought many times how his mother and little brother must have felt when this same horde thundered into Lawrence, shooting, killing and destroying the town. He hoped little Cheat hadn't been too frightened. He hated to think about the boy being exposed to such slaughter and destruction. That was the very thing Elias and his men were fighting for, a peaceful way of life for their families. Children should have the chance to grow and enjoy their younger years, regardless if they were black, red or white. For that matter, the adults too should be able to enjoy their lives by having a home, constructive and profitable work to do, and a future filled with hope for a better world for those to come. It would be that way, it must! Otherwise men like George Brothers, the Mitchell brothers, Henry Peppins, George Pope and Bedford Greene were hurt or dead for nothing. And that mustn't be!

Had little Cheat been … then he remembered. Elias' mother had still never mentioned Cheat. Again he wondered why. There had to be a reason. He hadn't been too concerned after the first letter or two, but now even after he had made a point of asking, there still had been no word. A strange feeling crept over him, like they say when someone steps on your grave. How could he find out? He had to know.

"That's where Blunt and Cloud put the run on Thompson and Cabell," said China Bill pointing to his left. Then with a laugh he continued, "That's 'Skunkyville,' least that's what the boys like to call it. Really it's Scullyville, but our fellas put the *skunk* on them Rebs and ran 'em south while we moved right into Fort Smith, just as pretty as you please."

"As I recall," said Elias, "Cloud's men were pretty beat and worn out and General Blunt came down sick just after they got to Fort Smith."

"Well, they took it and kept it, anyway. That's the mainest thing!"

It had been a long, weary walk, but Fort Smith would soon be in sight. Home at last. At least the men hoped that would be the case. Winter was coming on and it would be good to settle in for a few months.

Approaching from the southwest, the men crossed the Poteau River and were in sight of the fort.

"Man, would you look at that," said Slows.

"You reckon they have a place inside there for us, Amos?" asked Elias.

"It sho looks big enuff," said One Shoe.

The fort was surrounded by stone walls, three feet thick and twelve feet high, almost completely covered with dark green vines. Its walls were broken at intervals by gates, each of which was guarded by troops. The main gate was located on the northeast toward the town. Inside, a broad gravel roadway encircled the lush green parade ground. In the center stood a tall flagstaff from which a huge garrison flag was waving in the cool autumn breeze. The sight of the Stars and Stripes never failed to send chills of admiration down Elias' back. He considered his flag as one of the most beautiful sights he had ever seen.

Large porches ran the length of two-story brick buildings, which Elias was to learn later were officers' quarters. A white brick building at the north end of the grounds exhibited bars on the windows of the first floor indicating the guardhouse. A well stood in front of a building housing enlisted men and offices.

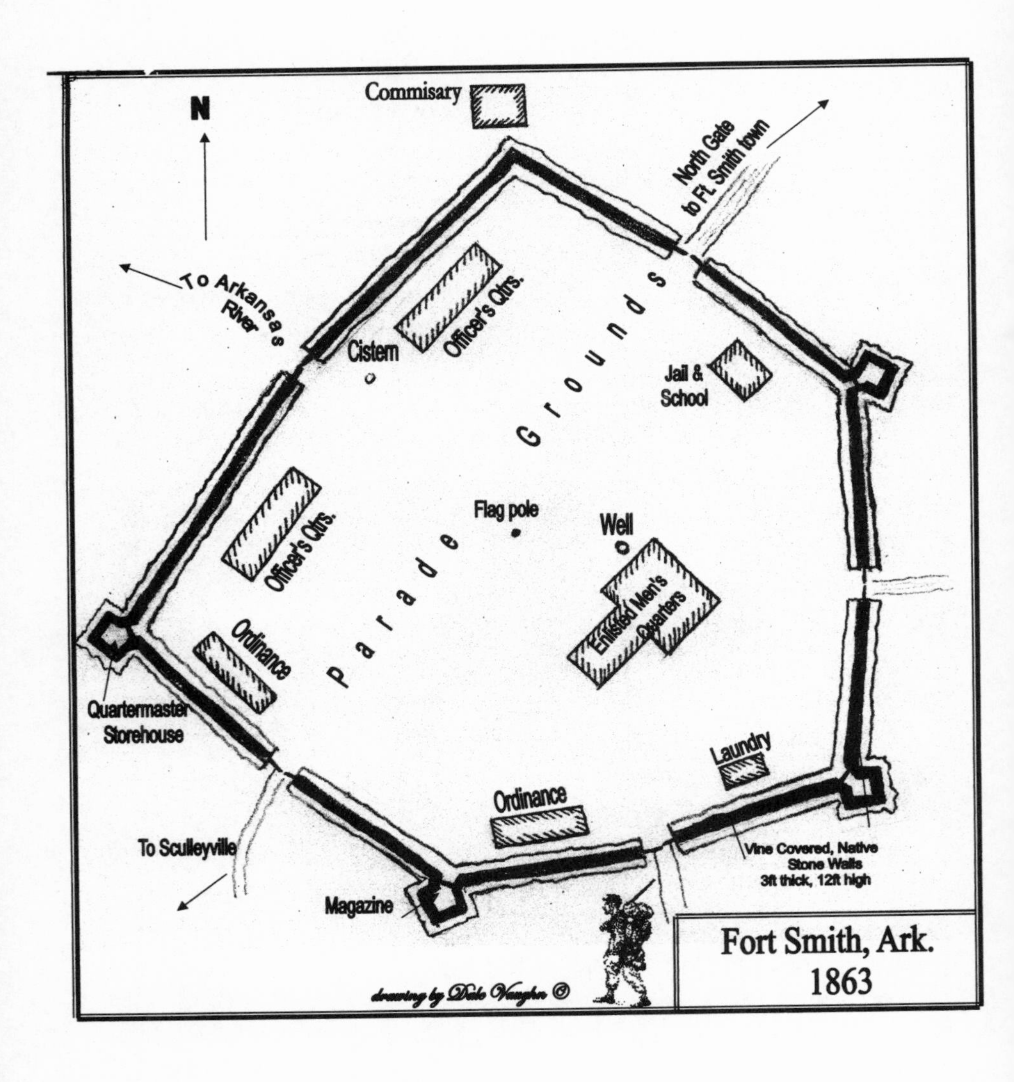
Commisary
N
North Gate
to Ft. Smith town
To Arkansas
River
Cistern
Officer's Qtrs.
Parade Grounds
Jail &
School
Flag pole
Well
Officer's Qtrs.
Enlisted Men's
Quarters
Ordinance
Quartermaster
Storehouse
Laundry
Ordinance
To Sculleyville
Vine Covered, Native
Stone Walls
3ft thick, 12ft high
Magazine
drawing by Dale Vaughn ©
Fort Smith, Ark.
1863

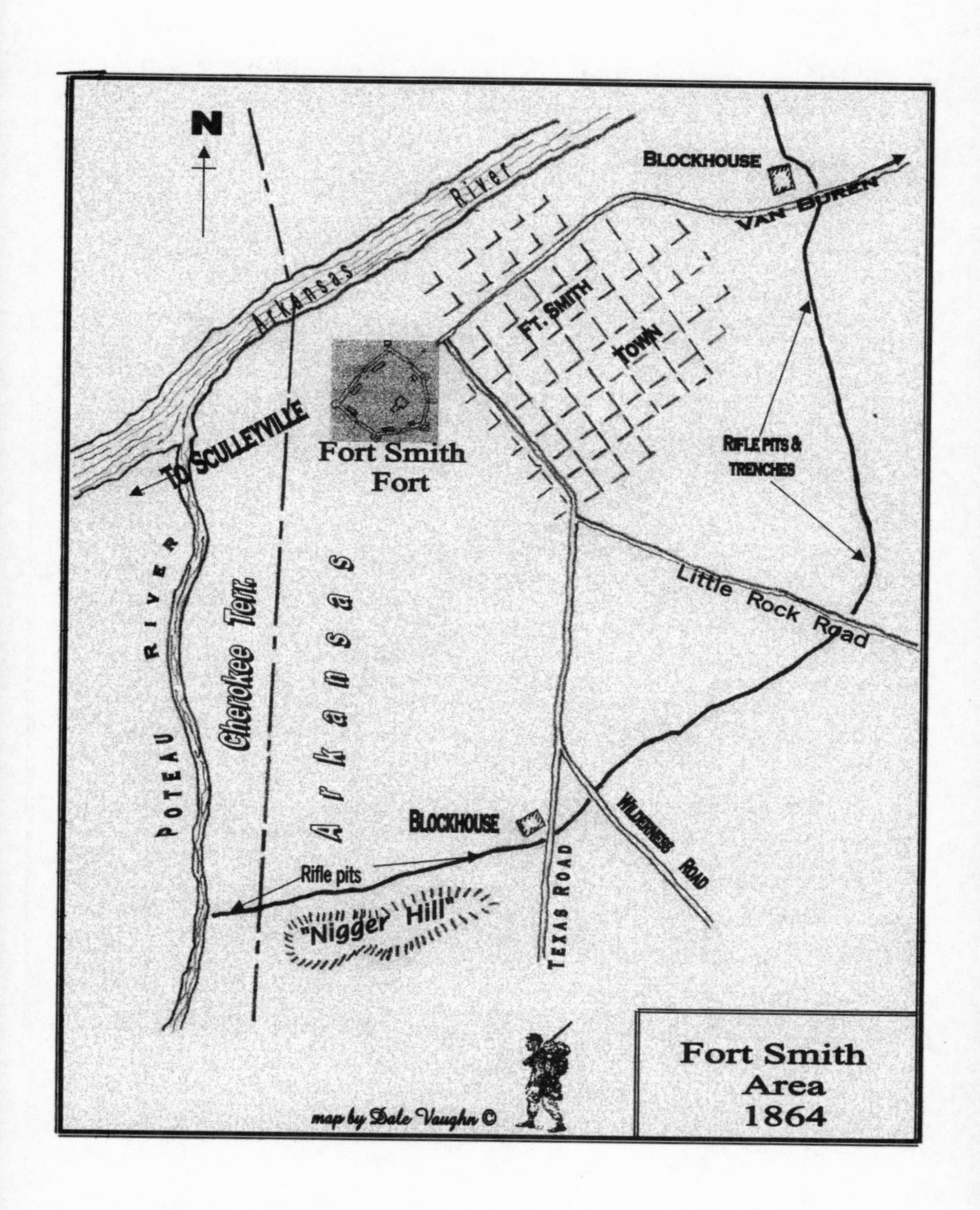
N
Arkansas River
BLOCKHOUSE
VAN BUREN
FT. SMITH
TOWN
TO SCULLEYVILLE
Fort Smith Fort
RIFLE PITS & TRENCHES
POTEAU RIVER
Cherokee Terr.
Arkansas
Little Rock Road
BLOCKHOUSE
WILDERNESS ROAD
TEXAS ROAD
Rifle pits
"Nigger Hill"
map by Dale Vaughn ©
Fort Smith Area 1864

"You suppose they is … *there is* room enough in there for us, Elias?" asked Toby.

"I would sooner imagine that the room for us will be more like those tents you see scattered around the grounds," replied Elias. Even at that he was to learn he was mistaken.

"Might as well send 'em on out to 'nigger hill,' I reckon," said a corporal.

"You know I don't like that name, Corporal," said his sergeant as he mentally counted Elias' men.

"I didn't name it, Sarge, that's just whut they call it."

"That's not what we call it, Corporal, and I don't want to hear it again. Understand?"

"Fine with me," said the corporal as he shrugged and started to walk off.

"Not so fast," said the sergeant. "Since you are so familiar with that post, you can escort these men there and turn them over to the sergeant in charge."

"Aw, but …" complained the corporal.

"Thank you very much, Corporal. Now would be just fine, I think." The sergeant turned to Elias and said, "Since there are just a few of you, you can go with the corporal here and either replace or add to the unit guarding our perimeter to the south. We have a line of fortifications, such as it is, to help guard the town. That's where you will be spending most of your time I would imagine."

"Yes, Sergeant," replied Elias. "We will get our belongings from the wagon and be right ready as soon as the corporal is."

"Yo don' have t' be so anxious," muttered One Shoe. "Nigger hill, is it?"

"Just like being home again," said China Bill with a grin on his face, "ain't that right, Slows?"

"Like we never been gone, sho 'nuff." Amos grinned back and shook his head. "Nuthin' changes."

"Sure it does," said Elias. "We don't have to clean up after someone or wash dishes. We're doing what we came here for. We're guarding the fort and the town."

"Sounds like 'Lias is right," declared Toby. "At least we're being treated like soldiers."

Children began to spill from the white building with bars on the windows.

"Why in the world do you suppose …?" said Matthew.

"They got 'em a school on the second floor," volunteered the corporal. "Guess it's over fer th' day."

After retrieving their tent halves and haversacks, Elias and the rest of the men gathered at the well just in front of the enlisted men's barracks.

"Cold and sweet," said Elias as he finished a cup of the water.

"Just as soon it had some coffee in it," said China Bill.

"We'll get some when we get to camp, I bet," said Elias. "If they don't have it made, we can do it."

"Coffee and a nice nap," said Slows, "that there's fer me. 'Specially the layin' down part."

The men headed east and then south on the Texas Road until they could see the perimeter that had been set up around the town. The timber had been cut and the area made as bare as possible so any enemy could be seen. They were positioned on top and just to the north of several hills. It would be their job to guard their part of the defensive line. To their right they could see the Poteau River bordering the Choctaw Nation, and to their left they could see the Wilderness Road heading southeast.

"Actually," said Elias, "this could be a real hot spot. I imagine the Rebs would be coming from the south if they decide to try to get the fort."

"I just hope they figure it's too late in the year to try anything big," said China Bill.

"Yeah," agreed Toby, "maybe they'll just go on down south and come back next spring."

"Like da ducks do," laughed One Shoe.

"Don't bet on it," said Elias. "They'll probably wait for a bit until we think that's what they're doing and then let us have it. Anyway, that's why we're here. To see it doesn't happen."

"By the way, 'Lias, I heard Private Pulham of Co. F died. 'Member that tall, skinny fella, that was wounded at Cabin Creek? Jes couldn't make it, I reckon." Toby shook his head and looked away.

Cold days and colder nights led on into the winter as Elias and a portion of the 1st took their turns watching and maintaining their line of defense. They were relieved at times and were able to spend some time at the fort. Taking turns at guard duty and unloading and storing weapons, ammunitions and powder in the two ordinance buildings and magazine at the south side of the parade ground were part of their duties. During their free time it was nice to be able to take advantage of some of the facilities they missed since leaving Fort Scott. It was good to be able to take their clothing to the laundry building that was located just to the east of the enlisted men's quarters, next to the fort's thick perimeter stone wall. The commissary, located just outside the wall to the north, was something the men had not been accustomed to for some time. Here they were able to replace personal item lost during various battles and on the long marches when packing and unpacking in the dark caused many items to be left behind. China Bill purchased a new deck of cards, Toby got a set of dominoes, and young Matthew bought a mouth harp.

Occasionally the men would go into town and were somewhat surprised at the reaction or rather lack of reaction of most of the people. They were not welcomed with open arms, but they were not treated as some of them had feared. As long as they behaved they were left alone. They could look in the stores and make purchases, even though they were not always treated like the white customers.

Part of their acceptance was probably due to the fact that Fort Smith was forming its own 11th Regiment, United States Colored Troops. Black men were recruited and volunteers had been accepted since early fall of 1863. They would soon have four full companies with the expectation of a fifth in the early spring of '64. Building and maintaining earthwork fortifications surrounding the city kept the new recruits busy, as well as drilling and performing guard duty. The most enjoyable duty for Elias and his men was formal dress parades. They were among the best on the fort at drilling and marching in perfect unison. So much so, that the fort and district commander, Brigadier General John McNeil, wrote in his report to Major General Schofield, commanding the Department of the Missouri, that *"the Negro regiment is a triumph of drill and discipline and reflects great honor on Colonel Williams in command. Few volunteer regiments that I have seen make a better appearance. I regard them as first-rate infantry."*

General McNeil had been directed to assume command of the District of the Frontier when General Blunt had been relieved of that command. In addition, in the same report the General stated, *"In prospect of open communication with Little Rock, and to protect our bread supplies, I deem it important to at once seize and hold Waldron, about 40 miles south of this place. I have directed Colonel Cloud, when he has driven Steele and Cooper, to occupy that place."*

When Blunt left Fort Smith earlier in the fall, he left Colonel Cloud in charge. Now Cloud would be under the direct command of General McNeil and be able to get back to chasing Confederates out of the Indian Territory and Arkansas, which was just what he was about to attempt. Confederate Generals William Steele and D. H. Cooper had been harassing Fort Smith and the surrounding area for some time and had even managed to get to within twelve miles of the fort. It was their purpose to control the foraging areas that General McNeil depended on for his troops.

Food wasn't General McNeil's only problem. *"We have salt and sugar, but are entirely out of hard bread, coffee, candles and soup. The service also requires all kinds of quartermaster's and ordinance stores. We need arms … ammunition … many recruits of the old regiments are without clothing. I have immediate and urgent need of assistance."*

"We goin' t'morra," announced Toby.

"Mo news from General Toby," said One Shoe.

"I'm gitt'n … *getting* tired of your know-nothing comments," declared Toby. "I'll have you know that 'Lias is the one who told me. Now, what you got to say about that, shoe brain?"

"He's right, I heard 'im," said Slows. "We headin' south."

"Just like ole Captin' Simmons said, 'we gonna march through the south with a Bible in one hand and a gun in th' other,' " said Toby.

"You fellas that anxious to head back south?" asked one of the white soldiers, jokingly. The men were gathered inside the enlisted men's barracks just after the church service and their noon meal. "I've never been down south and never talked to anyone that had lived there, but it sure sounds scary to me." He hesitated and then added, "Well, I mean … ya' know just …"

"That's all right," spoke up Elias, "I know what you mean and you're right. It's more than scary, it can be terrifying."

"Never made much sense to me," said the young soldier. "Of course, I've lived in Iowa all my life and never gave it much thought. Up north we don't have anything to do with slaves and like that, so …"

"Don't you believe it, soldier." Heads turned at the sound of a voice coming from the rear of the group. "I was brought up in New Jersey and I know all about this slavery business." The man speaking was a captain that appeared to be in his late forties. "Did you know that more slave ships have been built in New York than anyplace else? It's big business back there. Businessmen would commission the building of several ships, turn them over to a captain and send them toward the Caribbean or Africa. The captain would then hire a foreigner to sail with him, and if he got caught he would say that the ship belonged to the foreigner and he was the captain."

"Can they do that?" asked Elias.

"Sure, Corporal. And when the ship returned full of slaves, they would unload someplace along the coast and burn the ship to get rid of evidence."

"You mean they would destroy their own boat?" asked one of the men.

"That's right," replied the Captain. "The profits were great enough to make it worth it." The captain continued, leaning back against the wall. "If a captain got caught, he would merely say that the blacks were 'slaves when I got 'em. I'm just in the shipping business, not the slave business,' and sometimes he could get away with it.

"The business men rationalize like this. They argue that they can go to Georgia and buy a slave for $100 and take it to Alabama with no trouble. They say, 'Why then can't I go to Africa and buy one for $10 to sell in Alabama?' They claim the government is picking on them and inducing a hardship on free enterprise."

"Sounds like a bunch of politicians to me," said Elias.

"And some o' them people back there think that this here war is a gonna change all that," spoke up China Bill? "Capt'n, this here is nothin' but a killin' war. We fight, bleed and die and when it's shut down for a little bit, we mostly don't get to keep the ground we fought over. You really think we're gonna make a difference with those kind of men back there? How many young boys do we have to kill to change their minds?" Bill got up, stared at the officer and walked out into the cold Sunday afternoon.

All was still in the room for a few minutes, and then in a low voice, the Captain said, "I wish I knew, Soldier, I wish I knew."

Chapter 22

Monday, November 2, 1863

The men were thankful that the wind was at their backs on this cold November morning. As they headed south, all eyes were searching, hoping not to find a sign of the enemy yet. It was hoped that the advance patrol would be able to notify the main unit before any action began. Waldron was close to forty miles south and east of Fort Smith. The terrain was rolling and dotted with small patches of forest in land otherwise used for farming. The stubbles of corn could be seen where farmers had harvested a less than average crop this fall. Hopefully the granaries would be full anyway and their trip well worth what it might cost them. Men and animals must eat, and their job was to see that the Rebels didn't control this food and supply source.

"Boy, it sho is cold," exclaimed One Shoe.

"Before you were complainin' about how hot you were and how you were goin' back to Africa," said China Bill with a wink to Elias.

"I din't say nothin' 'bout goin' to Africa."

"Always gripin'. Hey, least your candles ain't gonna melt in your sack. That's what happened to me and I had to get that new deck of cards."

"Well, whut happin'd to that in between kind a' weather? I don't remember havin' any fall weather hardly at all."

The men continued their chatter off and on as they progressed on toward Waldron. They had passed Greenwood and Dalton, and if the gray sky hadn't been so low they might have been able to see Sugar Loaf Mountain off to the West. After crossing Black Jack Creek they knew they were getting close to their objective. Waldron couldn't be over two or three miles. Elias expected to see the forward scouts returning any minute with a warning to prepare for battle.

"I heard the colonel say that Steele and Cooper could have three, four thousand men," said Elias in a guarded tone, "so I want all you guys to keep sharp. I don't want to have to carry anyone all the way back to Fort Smith."

"If it's all the same to you," replied Matthew, "I'd just as soon walk back, too. I don't wanna be ridin' in no ambulance."

"Wonder what ya gotta … *you have* to do to get to drive one of them there wagons?" spoke up Toby. "I wouldn't mind that, getting to ride and all."

Just then a rider came over the small rise just ahead and stopped next to Colonel Cloud. "It's just ahead, Sir."

"All right, let's get everyone ready. How many …?"

"No need," spoke the scout. "The place's empty. It's been abandoned, Sir."

"Are you sure, Corporal?"

"Yes, Sir. They been here all right, but they must a' lit out when they knew we were comin'. Can't be gone more'n a few hours or last night at the best, the way it looks, Sir. There's still fresh horse sh… droppings scattered around."

"Have thirty men stay here, the rest follow me. I'll find them if I …" Colonel Cloud's voice was lost in the wind as he galloped off with the rest of the command close on his heels.

A few miles down the road, the soldiers ran into a small band of guerrillas that, after starting a skirmish, thought better when seeing the number of Union soldiers with which they would have to contend. Shots were exchanged and the enemy fled toward the trees topping a nearby hill.

"Never mind them," shouted Colonel Cloud. "We're after bigger fish."

Within a few miles a small wagon train and a herd of about thirty cattle were seen just ahead. At full charge the men headed right toward the group of Rebels, catching them by surprise. After a few random shots, seven of Bankhead's men and their leader, a lieutenant, were captured. The train was turned around, a dozen men put in charge of driving the cattle back north, and the army made its way back to Waldron. Upon determined interrogation by Colonel Cloud, it was learned that the Rebs were headed toward Doaksville with the intention of going on to the Red River.

In correspondence directed to Major General Schofield, on November 4th, General McNeil wrote, *"...........making this the last rebel army to leave this valley. This will enable us to garrison Dardanelle with the recruits of the Second Arkansas Infantry, and to move a regiment to Waldron."*

After arriving back at Fort Smith, the men in Elias' company returned to their duties of guarding, drilling and maintaining breastworks and fortifications around the city.

The men had passed several more weeks of duty at Fort Smith, when a portion of the 1st Kansas was sent back to Waldron on escort duty and was then ordered to proceed northeast to the post at Roseville which was located on the Arkansas River about forty miles east of Fort Smith. This was a fairly large outpost that, among other things, served as a distribution point from which Fort Smith could receive food and other supplies from boats coming north. During many occasions the water in the Arkansas would get so low that Roseville was as far as riverboats could get. In the winter, the upper Arkansas would freeze over, at times hard enough to support animals and loaded wagons, so that too would keep the supplies from reaching Fort Smith by boat.

In addition to service as a supply link, there were a number of cotton fields and mills in the area that the Union wanted kept out of the enemy's hands. A telegraph line, that had to be closely guarded, extended to Roseville and on to Fort Smith. This made the area around Roseville a likely target for almost continuous attacks from small Rebel forces and Bushwhackers alike.

"So much for our nice comfortable fort," said Elias as he looked around. The post was located on the west bank of the river with several docks available up to which boats could tie and be unloaded. In the center of the river was a small island that, in warm weather, the men would swim out to and lay in the shade of the trees. It seemed to give them a sense of being away from the war for an hour or two.

"We may be able to walk out there, if it gets much colder," said China Bill.

"At least we'll get ourselves first crack at the bread and beans," said Matthew.

"Whut makes yo think so, little fella?" said Slows.

"Hey, if'n I gots to unload all that there heavy stuff, you kin bet I'm gonna git my share," stated Matthew. "After all, I gots to keep up my strong."

The men were assigned in small groups that would patrol the telegraph lines, be sent out as scouts and take turns on picket posts. It being evident that tents would be less than adequate, the men began to build huts and even cabins. Several cabins had stone-lined wooden fireplaces located at one end of the structure. One such residence was built for the captain, and several existing buildings were built on to house the additional men of the 1st.

Brigadier-General Totten:
Ft. Smith, Jan.4, 1864

The Arkansas River is frozen over sufficiently to sustain horses. Six inches of snow on the ground. We must soon have navigation. Steam-boats loaded with supplies should be at the mouth of the river ready to ascend. We are now on half rations of bread, and in a week shall be destitute of bread supplies, except what a few country mills can afford over bad roads with scanty transportation. Our train had to go to Devall's Bluff (about fifty miles east of Little Rock) for supplies, there being none at Little Rock, and cannot be expected here before the 25th.

John McNeil
Brigadier-General

Headquarters Department of the Missouri, St. Louis
Jan 8, 1864

Respectfully referred to Co. T. J. Haines, chief commissary of subsistence, Department of the Missouri. By order of Major-General Schofield:

J. A. Campbell
Assistant Adjutant-General

Office Chief Com. Sub., Dept. of the Missouri, St. Louis
Jan. 12, 1864

Ample supplies have been sent to Devall's Bluff. The subsistence department cannot procure transportation beyond that point for what is required at Little Rock for Fort Smith. This should be referred to the quartermaster's department.

T. J Haines
Colonel and Chief Commissary of Subsistence

Headquarters Department of the Missouri, St. Louis
Jan. 8, 1864

Respectfully referred to Co. William Myers, chief quartermaster, Department of the Missouri, for his information and action should any seem to be required. By order of Major-General Schofield:

J. A. Campbell
Assistant Adjutant-General

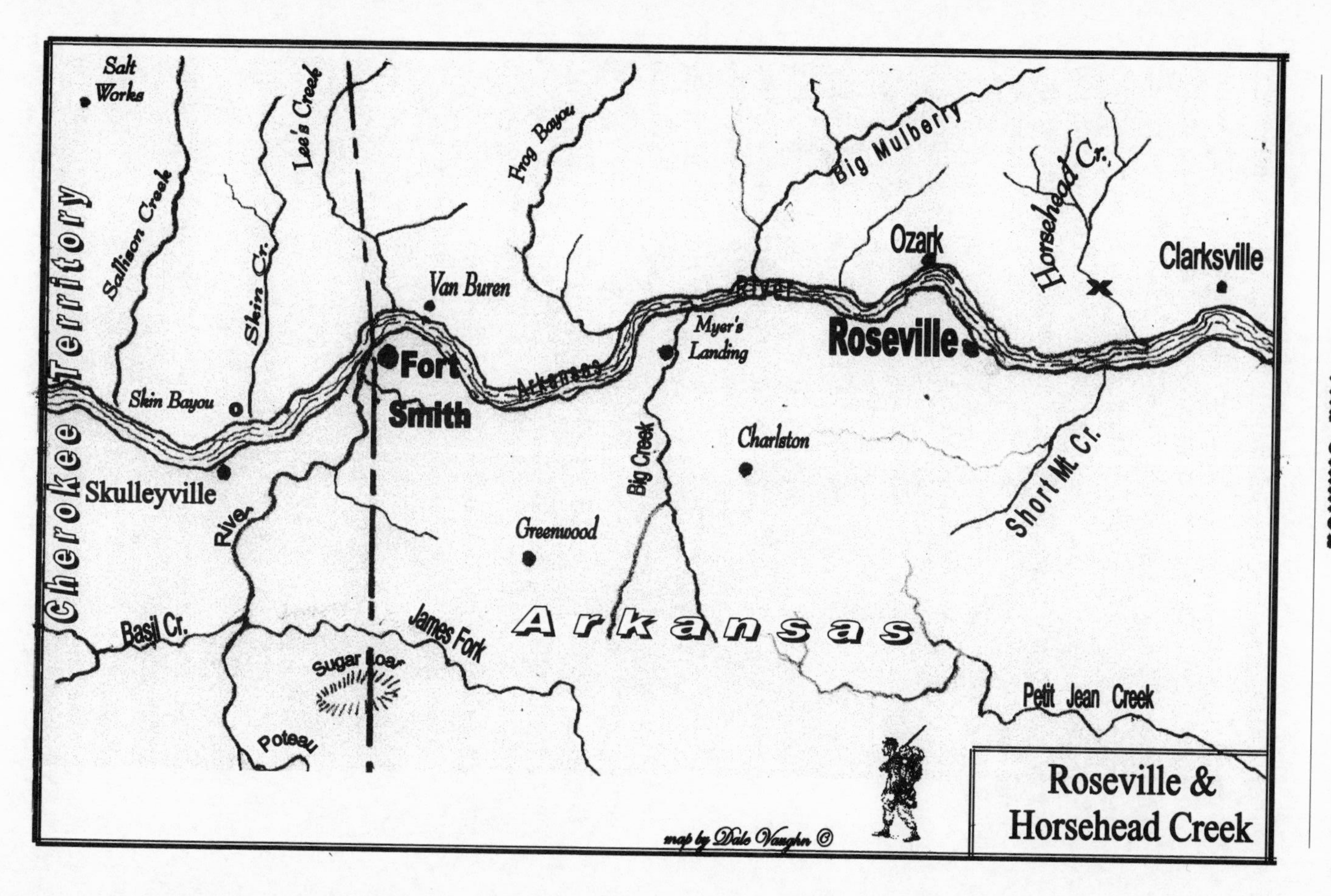
Roseville &
Horsehead Creek
Salt Works
Cherokee Territory
Sallison Creek
Skin Cr.
Lee's Creek
Frog Bayou
Big Mulberry
Horsehead Cr.
Ozark
Clarksville
Van Buren
River
Arkansas
Myer's Landing
Roseville
Fort Smith
Skin Bayou
Skulleyville
Charlston
Big Creek
Short Mt. Cr.
Greenwood
River
Basil Cr.
James Fork
Arkansas
Sugar Loar
Petit Jean Creek
Poteau
map by Dale Vaughn ©

"Wish I knew who dreamed up the system this goddamned army is supposed to run on. Hell, we could starve to death while people are sending letters back and forth trying to figure out whose job it is to get something done!" General McNeil smashed his coffee cup down so hard it shattered. "Clean that mess up," he shouted to a startled young lieutenant who had just entered his office. "Never mind, I'll do it. I'm sorry, Lieutenant. It's not your fault."

"Yes, Sir. I mean … no, Sir. I'll be glad to clean …"

"Never mind, I made it, I'll clean it up. Now! What did you want?"

Elias drove a small wagon pulled by a pair of mules along the path below the telegraph lines. It was a cold, dark day. The wind blew and the clouds hung what seemed to be about thirty feet off the hard, frozen ground. Tiny bits of ice crystals flew into the men's faces and held to their eyebrows and lashes. They had covered almost ten miles when they came upon a dark form hanging from one of the poles. The form looked like a bundle of rags suspended from near the top as it slowly swung and bounced away from the dark, weathered wooden shaft.

"What in hell is that, Elias?" asked Bill as he pointed toward the top of the pole. "Is that what I think it is?'

"Looks like it, Bill. Someone's been hung from the telegraph pole. Looks like the body's been there for several days."

"I heard they were doin' it, but I never knew of it happening for sure."

"I heard some of the men that have been here awhile talking about the order General McNeil had posted around Fort Smith. In fact, whoever did this nailed one on this post. A warning, I guess, with evidence to show how things are going to be around here, probably."

The notice was headlined "Bushwhackers Beware!" It went on to read that since the organized forces of the Confederacy had been driven out of their area, it was reasonable to assume that any resistance to the Union efforts would be done by guerrillas and Bushwhackers. And that being the case, those involved would not be treated as prisoners of war but as common belligerents. In each instance that they would be caught cutting telegraph wires, they would be hung from the nearest telegraph pole, *"and as many bush-whackers shall be so hung as there are places where the wire is cut. The nearest house to the place where the wire us cut, if the property of a disloyal man, and within ten miles, shall be burned." It was signed By Command of Brig. Gen'l John McNeil, Fort Smith, Ark., Nov. 17, 1863.*

"I guess the gen'rl wasn't kiddin', huh, 'Lias?" offered China Bill.

"He meant what he said, Bill," replied Elias, looking up. "You would think this body might be gone by now."

"Hell, in this cold, he'll be there till spring. Guess that's the idea. That way if'n some of those other raiders see what they're up against, it might help change their minds."

"Would it change yours, Bill?" asked Elias, as he pulled his coat up around his face.

"Reckon not. I'd just work faster and ride quicker."

Having covered their assigned route, the pair returned to Roseville and parked the wagon with its load of repair tools and line and headed for their dinner. Inside they could smell coffee and see beans being kept hot in a large vat. The hard bread could be softened if left in the bean juice long enough, and when an occasional weevil would float to the top it would be spooned out without comment. Any hot food was greatly appreciated at this point.

After their meal, Elias and Bill wandered over to a group of men nursing cups of coffee and telling stories.

"J'ever notice, that when your lucky 'nuff to git somethin' good'n hot to drink, all ya gots is these here tin cups what burns your mouth s'bad ya cain't drink?" asked Slows to no one in particular.

"Well, s'cuse us. I'll report right now to the Capt'n and he'll see that you git's china cups and saucers t'morra," said Matthew. "I can't imagine such hardships for our brave sojers, kin you, 'Lias?"

"I'll burn mor'n yo smart mouth, there, Boy," said Slows as he drew back a large black fist. His wink at Elias did not go unnoticed by anyone, and they all began to throw up their hands and shudder and moan in mock fright.

Christmas had come and gone along with the old year. A slightly better than average meal had marked the holiday along with the exchanging of small gifts among Elias and his men. A small pine tree had been set up in one of the buildings, decorated with pine cones, paper cut-outs and bits of cloth tied in bows. The highlight of the day was the singing of carols. Surprisingly rich and mellow voices were displayed from some of the most unlikely sources.

"Hey, whassa matter here? This here jug ain't got no cork," said One Shoe as the heavy brown crock was passed to him.

"Don' you know nuthin? That ain't supposin to last long enough to need no cork." With that all the men laughed and rolled around slapping at each other.

"Tha's right, it never did last that long befo'."

"And if'n it do, it ain't no good no how and should be gotten rid of."

"An' I'm jes the fella what kin take care of that chore, sho nuff!"

Then, it was back to work.

Small skirmishes were carried out every few days. At one time, several of the enemy had broken into one of the small supply buildings to find it bare except for a half-dozen empty flour and sugar barrels. One man was slightly wounded and carried off by his companions as they made their escape.

"Didn't you see them trying to break into that building, Amos?" asked Elias after hearing the rifle fire.

"Yep," replied Slows. "But I had nuthin' else t' do cept'n

watch and I knowed the buildin' was empty. At least they got in out'n the cold for a few minutes and the rest of us got a good laugh.

"He gonna be limpin' fo' awhile, too, 'Lias, my shot took off the heel of his boot, and I'm sho I got's part of the meat cause they's a red spot in the snow over yonder."

Elias shook his head and went back to his shack. Inside it was at least a bit warmer and they had until tomorrow before they had to make another patrol. As he entered, he realized he had walked in on a discussion about how they would be living after the war was over and the black folks were free.

"No, Suh! Da ain't no reason for da women to do no talkin' when da men folks is takin' care of b'iness," explained Slows. He was talking about being the head of his household. "I learned that from m' daddy fo' he was sold. Da hen got no b'iness crowin' and the tom supposed to do da gobblin'." Each man looked around at each other and then burst out laughing so hard they began to roll on the hard-packed floor in front of the fire holding their sides.

"Das awright, my daddy knowed whut he wuz talkin' 'bout. He said it, he did it, and I learned it. I learned lots from him an' das why I'm here watchin' out fo' yo' black butts and keepin' ya'll alive. Now den, laugh at dat."

"Amos," said Elias, after catching his breath and wiping his eyes to clear the tears of laughter, "I believe you and I do know you're right. And I'll never say anything to make you mad enough to quit watchin' out for me."

"Yeah, well, ya'll go ahead on and giggle at ol' Slows, but you be glad some day 'bout my daddy and 'bout me payin' 'tension."

"You must a' been lots better off 'n us, we was so po' we couldn' afford to pay attention," said One Shoe as he gasped for breath and held his sides, rolling over and burying his head in Toby's lap.

Each day the men would stand picket duty, ride the telegraph lines and patrol various areas when it was rumored either Confederate forces or guerillas had been seen. Small cavalry units and patrols on foot would cover the surrounding countryside close to Roseville. There were times the men were drilled and paraded even when there were several inches of snow covering the ground. Discipline had to be kept up even during the sometime idle times. Trees were felled and brush cut and cleared away in order to make it harder for the enemy to slip into the compound.

Elias, Toby and two other men were ordered to patrol south and west of Roseville and watch out for footprints in the snow of either men or horses. They had learned that the enemy was having even a harder time getting supplies of food and clothing than were the Union troops.

After passing Sub Rosa and crossing a small frozen creek, the men spied a partially fallen down barn next to what had been a farm house. "You guys go on," said Elias, "I want to look at that barn. Besides, nature is calling me over there."

"Don't go off and leave anythin' runnin'," said one of the men with a smile. "And don' freeze nuthin'."

Elias grinned, waved and started toward what was left of the old structure. Weeds and frozen knee-deep grass made the walking difficult as Elias made his way toward the south side of the barn. The roof had half collapsed over the front of the building, but the main door still managed to keep both halves attached to the structure. Elias slowed as he noticed where the lower part of the door had made a circular mark in the snow as it had been opened. Someone had been around the door, but not for some time. The wind had partially filled the tracks with blowing snow, making it hard to identify who had been there. Elias looked around to see if he could tell where the tracks came from, but they were lost in the grass.

Slowly he made his way around to the east side of the building and worked close to where a couple of boards were missing from the wall. The cloudiness of the day and the darkness of the interior of the barn made it impossible to make out anything or anyone inside. Slowly and carefully, he stuck his head in side just enough to see. To his right was the side of a horse stall. To his left was a small open area next to which was piled some hay or straw.

Keeping in a squatting position, Elias duck-walked into the near darkness and stopped as soon as he was inside. He slowly rose up until he could see over the side of the stall, finding it empty. After his eyes adjusted to the dim light, he cautiously moved ahead one quiet step at a time. Ducking some cobwebs and moving directly into some more, he jerked around wiping at his face.

Suddenly he saw a gun barrel pointing out from behind an old wooden trunk and heard the click of the gun's hammer. At the same time, he heard a whimper. Diving and grabbing the gun barrel, Elias' weight shoved the trunk back, pinning his assailant against the barn wall.

"Don't kill me, please, Nigger …" Sobs came from the small dark bundle huddling in the shadows. "Please … let me go …" more sobbing as the trembling hands were raised hoping to fend off an attack.

Elias saw the rusty old pistol in his hand had two shots left. He then looked in the direction of the voice. He could barely make out a pair of eyes and a dirty face.

"Come on out of there, youngster, nobody is gonna kill you," said Elias in a soft tone. "That is, unless you're General Price or maybe one of Cooper's men."

"I ain't them. I ain't never heard of 'em."

"Well, then, come on out and let's have a look at ya."

It was a young boy, about seven or eight years old. "Just about Cheat's size," thought Elias. Then he remembered it had been a year and a half since he had seen Cheat. "Who knows how big he …"

"What are you doing here, young fella? How long you been in here?"

"Been here a coupl'a days, I reckon." The boy was shivering. "Probably as much from fright as from the cold," thought Elias.

"You ain't gonna kill me like them others said you'd do, are ya Nigg … Soldier?"

"Course not. What's your name?"

"Name's Will. Will Taylor."

"How long since you've eaten, Will Taylor" asked Elias?

"Don't know, same coupl'a days probably."

"Where'd you come from? Where do you live?"

"Right close here in Charleston," the boy hesitated, "well, outside of Charleston. We had a farm until the soldiers came and took everything. Ma said they couldn't have it all, and when she grabbed a broom, they shoved her down off the porch. I think she broke her arm, but Daddy, he jumped in on 'em and they shot him." The boy began to sob, rubbed his nose with his sleeve and then looked up at Elias. "They said we had to leave, and then when Ma tried to get to Pa, one of the soldiers ran over her with his horse and I guess she died. I couldn't … she wouldn't get up … there's nothin' I could …" The boy broke out into fitful sobs and crying.

Elias gathered him up in his arms. At first the boy tried to push away and then suddenly threw his arms around Elias and broke down completely. Elias opened his heavy overcoat and pulled the boy in next to his warm body. Folding the coat over both of them, Elias sat slowly rocking back and forth, allowing the boy to let out his grief. Elias remembered how he felt comforted when his mother would do the same for him when they were back in Virginia. He patted the boy's head and pulled the scarf up around the boy's ears.

When young Will had quieted down, Elias said, "You know, if we get a move on, we can get back to camp in time to get somethin' t' eat, you'n me." Will looked up into the dark brown face, not knowing how to react. He was very hungry, and yet he had been warned he must fear these black people. He told Elias how the *soldiers* had said that all the blacks had to be killed or they would kill all the white folks and take their belongings.

"Just what soldiers did that to your folks, Will?" asked Elias as he helped the boy to his feet. "Were they north or south?"

"Well, I don't really know, because they weren't wearin' regular uniforms. They said you fellas were a'comin' and we better go along with what they were a'sayin' or we'd be killed."

"They were probably guerillas," thought Elias. "You don't have to worry none now, Will, we won't hurt you. We'll get you something to eat, get you warm and then figure out what to do."

"Just what in the hell ..." and then in a quiet voice, "what are we gonna do with this here kid, Elias? We can't keep 'em here." The lieutenant turned so he couldn't see Will's face. "We can hardly feed ... he doesn't belong in an army camp."

"What about some of the people around here, Lieutenant? Won't they take him?"

"Maybe, I guess, only we aren't the most popular people around here either, ya know. We just happen to be a little better than the Rebs, so most folks put up with us."

"I know we can find someone. I'll ask around. These folks won't let a little boy just run loose and starve."

"I ain't goin'! I ain't!" Will Taylor stood with his arms wrapped around his chest in a defiant stance. The wool shirt he was wearing was given him by Toby, and even though Toby was the smallest man in the outfit, his shirt was four times too large for the young boy.

"What do you mean you won't go?" asked Elias. "We have to find a home for you and someone that'll look out for you."

"I can look out for myself. And besides, you been doin' a good enough job helpin' me. That's all I need. And ... I ain't goin'!" With that, Will ran outside and slammed the door.

"See what you got yo'sef ... *yourself* into?" said Toby. "Now what you gonna do?"

"Yeah," thought Elias, "now what am I gonna do?"

Just then a commotion outside drew their attention. "What's

the noise about, Toby?" asked Elias.

The door opened and Matthew came in swinging his arms to gather in the warmth of the cabin. "Damn sneaky bunch, them are if'n y' ask me." Matthew slammed the door and shuddered as he pulled off his coat.

"Who's a sneaky bunch, Matthew?" asked Elias. "What's going on?"

"Another line patrol just came in. One of 'em has a busted leg." Matthew backed up to the fireplace and began to rub his backside. "Seems they saw a wire down and one of the fellas began to climb the pole to hook the wire back up. Just as he got to the top, the pole began to fall and the fella got caught up in the wire and the pole came down a'top of 'im. Had his leg doubled up behind himsef somehow and busted it just below the knee."

"I guess I don't understand," replied Elias. "What is so sneaky about that?"

"Cause, some one of them there Bushwhackers had chopped the bottom of the pole just about in two and then piled brush and weeds around it so's it couldn't be seen. That's what made it fall. They knew some one of us would have to climb up there and the man's weight would make that there damn thing fall takin' the guy with it."

"You right," someone muttered. "That's sneaky and snotty."

There were mutters about the cabin as Elias and Toby just shook their heads.

Young Will, scared by the commotion, had moved back into the cabin and huddled in a corner while Matthew was relating his story. Elias looked back at Will. The boy stood with his arms wrapped around himself, staring at the soldiers that had just returned.

"I'm sure sorry," he said as he looked up into Elias' face, not knowing what else to say.

Elias moved to him and patted Will's head. "I know."

Chapter 23

Wednesday, February 3, 1864

"They were bushwhackers or guerillas, Lieutenant," said Elias as he warmed himself in front of the fireplace. "Anyway, they weren't wearing uniforms, and if they had been regular Rebs they would have just killed them."

"You're probably right, Corporal. I have warned you men to be on special guard. I'm sorry it is the way it is, but there is nothing we can do about it. The colored units are invaluable to us, but we can't treat you any differently than we do the whites or the Indians. I think you realize that."

"We don't ask for any special favors, Lieutenant," replied Elias, "we all knew what could happen to us when we joined up and we're ready to look out after ourselves and each other."

Three of the pickets that had been posted that morning were from the 1st Kansas Colored. They had taken their posts and moved around their assigned area all day without incident, trying to keep warm and hoping it would be a peaceful watch. For days, there had been raids, small and large on Roseville, and reported skirmishes and raids on Clarksville and Dardanelle as well. It was one of the coldest winters any of the local folks could remember, and the foraging parties had long since gathered most of everything that was to be had. The Confederates, as well as the Union army, were desperate for food, clothing, ammunition and almost everything. The Arkansas River was frozen over and boats were not able to bring cargo north. Even wagon trains to Little Rock were returning half empty at best.

"They're worse off than we are, I betcha," said China Bill, referring to the Bushwhackers, "And these folks around here ain't gonna part with anything they can keep. They don't like most a' the Rebs no better'n they like us."

"If'n you hadn't come along," said one of the rescued pickets to Elias," we would'a been headed south fo' sho'."

"Yeah," added one of the others, "they said they could get a bounty on us or maybe sell us themsev's and git mo' money."

"One of 'em got my long coat afore we got ten yards away, even."

"Seems they had no mo' than we do, and meby less."

"You can count yourselves lucky," said China Bill. "Even around here blacks are treated pretty bad."

"I know that for a fact," said one of the black soldiers from the back of the room. "I grew up around Helena in the cotton patches as a kid, and I saw what happened to most of my folks.

"I've seen men stripped naked and told to hold their hands over their privates and then whipped until they couldn't stand. Then the overseer would have someone wash down the fella's back with water and salt. I seen men with six or seven hound dogs just sit on their horse whilst the dogs would nip and bite on a black man until the blood run, and them fellas wouldn't say nothin'. They jes kept they shotgun on they lap darin' you to kick out at the dogs or try to git away."

Silence filled the room. Occasionally one of the black men would nod in agreement as pictures of his own experiences filled his head.

"My daddy was buck and gagged for three days after trying to keep me from bein' whipped for sumpin' I didn' do. They whipped him with birch sprouts and then rubbed his back down with vinegar, salt and pepper. 'You gonna remember this ever time you feel them scars,' they tol' him. Then my mama took him and soaped the splinters that was left in his back so she could get 'em out."

"My family was free, even," said another man sitting on a cot against the wall. "We didn't think we was gonna have no trouble, but then Arkansas passed a law in '58 that all blacks had to leave the state or be sold into slavery. Hell, we didn' know nuthin' 'bout that law until they come and got us. Then it was too late. My daddy was whipped right there on the spot in front of my mother and us kids. After it was over, they rubbed him down with lard and red pepper. One of the white men yelled, 'Rub 'im good. We don' want 'em to spoil, now.' That was just their way of showin' off. They did it just cause they could."

"I've seen meanness just for meanness' sake, too," said China Bill. "When my little brother was just four, he would get tired in the middle of the afternoon, y'know, he was just a little guy, but they wouldn't let 'im take no nap or nuthin'. If they didn't have any regular chores for him to do, they would make him go out in the yard and pick up chicken and duck feathers just to keep him awake. Sons-a-bitches …"

"It's gonna be an awful thing up yonder," said a black man named Holloway, "when they hold a judgment over the way things was done down here."

"That'll be the damn day," muttered China Bill.

"Don' you talk that'a way, young fella," said the older man. "Don' you even pretend that God won't have His way. And He knows … you betcha … He knows and He cares. I know it's so."

Occasionally the cold would seep under the door or through a crack, causing some of the listeners to pull their jackets tighter around themselves. The fire crackled and some of the smoke drifted into the room. Elias saw Toby rubbing his tear-filled eyes.

"Chimney needs cleanin' out so's the smoke'll go up," said Toby as he looked away. "Gits in y' eyes."

Elias nodded and looked away, not wanting to embarrass his friend.

The lieutenant stood up, placed his coffee cup on the rough hewn table, headed for the door, then paused and looked back. "Be careful, ya hear? I don't want to lose a one of you."

"See," said Elias, "they're not all bad. We have more friends than we know."

"Hope I live to agree with you," said China Bill.

"You will," put in Elias. "Don't you know? We're all gonna live forever."

Wednesday, February 17, 1864

"There's cause to believe there are a group of renegades to the east and north of here. It's a place they call Horse Head Creek, and they may have it in mind to raid the camp looking for supplies." The lieutenant had called out Elias, China Bill and four others to go on a scouting mission. "Be careful, but it's up to you men to find them if they're there.

"Remember now, if there are too many, just report back. Don't try to take on a whole company alone. I can't spare anybody just now, so don't get yourselves killed." There was a slight smile on the lieutenant's face as he added, "Good luck."

"We'll try not to leave you short-handed, Lieutenant," said China Bill.

After a couple of hours of moving east and a little north, Elias and China Bill separated themselves from the others and eased through the dry brown grass next to a forest bordering what must be Horse Head Creek. The cold wind caused their faces to smart, and the snow was dampening their boots. They thought they had spied movement back in the underbrush and went to get a closer look at the area. Tracks had been seen, but it was difficult to make out just what had made the tracks in the tall, stiff grass.

Quietly the two moved through the brush and trees. It was close quarters and difficult to see more than twenty yards ahead. Trying to pick their footing, Elias and China Bill slowed and looked around.

"They gotta be here, 'Lias," whispered Bill, looking first at Elias and then around the forest that seemed to be closing in on them.

Elias nodded toward a large walnut tree and began to move in that direction. Bill followed on Elias' right about ten feet away and slightly ahead. He headed for the right hand side of the massive tree while Elias held back and to the left. A small gray squirrel leaped from the ground in front of Bill to a pine trunk and scampered skyward. Bill hesitated and then was about to take his next step when a figure swung around from the far side of the large walnut tree.

The young guerrilla fighter's eyes were as large as duck eggs as his musket came level with Bill's chest. "Oh, God," exclaimed the boy as his gun threw fire, lead and smoke.

Bill and the young man with the gray Rebel cap stood for an instant staring at each other. Elias started toward the two when his foot caught in a vine that twisted its way toward a pine tree. As he fell, he thought he saw Bill's knees bend and was certain he was going down, badly wounded. Instead, Elias heard the gurgling sound that came from the young Reb, and saw Bill's left hand gripping the boy's collar. At first Bill's right hand was hidden by the falling body, but then came into sight holding his bloody bayonet. Bill had reached into his right boot and pulled his knife just in time to catch the guerrilla fighter staring at the Yank he had just shot. The bayonet caught the enemy just below the heart, surged upward and caused instant death.

As Elias got to his feet, Bill was on his knees holding his stomach. He slowly sank to his right and came to rest in the snow with his back against the walnut tree.

"Bill … Bill," called Elias in a low voice. "Did he …?"

"'Believe he did, 'Lias." Bill rasped a quiet reply. "Hope nobody heard the shot. Maybe they…………" Bill grimaced andtried to stifle a cough.

"Don't talk, Bill, let me look. Where did …?" Elias saw the blood oozing from between the fingers of Bill's left hand as it clutched his stomach. "Don't worry, I'll get you back."

"Just let me rest for a minute, 'Lias." Bill's eyes were wide as he looked at Elias. Then his head seemed to flop backward and he squeezed his eyes shut and ground his teeth. After a moment or two he looked at Elias again. "Hand me my canteen."

"Bill, you know that you aren't supposed to have any water when you have a stom … a wound like yours."

"Just hand it to me. Ain't plain water, 'Lias." Bill's familiar grin tried to force its way across his pain-ridden face. "It's Arkansas mountain water. Them boys know you can't drink most of the water around here, that's why they make this here potion."

Bill gulped a large swallow, coughed and smiled at Elias. "Wouldn't ya know it? Getting shot here at Horse-ass Creek. And by a wild young kid … cough … that probably couldn't even get in the regular Reb army."

"Bill, I don't think you …" Then Elias realized the liquor would dull the awful pain Bill must be suffering, and he knew there was no help for a wound such as he had. Bill's hand could hardly hold his stomach together, and his voice sounded like possibly a lung had been punctured.

"Lias, you know what I always liked …(cough) … about you? You never called me 'China Bill' like the others. You always said just 'Bill.' " Bill's face showed the pain he was suffering, and Elias could see his hand tighten trying to cause the blood flow to slow down.

"Never mind that now, Bill, just let me …"

"You never called me Willie neither. Never could stand to be called … uh … owwww," Bill moaned and dipped his head so he could spit out the blood in his mouth. "Never could stand, Willie," Bill continued in a softer voice. "One of the overseers would call me that after he heard the master's missus call me that several times." Bill looked up at Elias, trying to smile. Elias watched the tears slowly run down Bill's cheeks. "She always called me 'Willie' when she was in her 'requiring' mood."

"Bill, you've got to let me get some help. I know I can get you …"

"You know what, 'Lias? Think I'm gonna retire." Bill paused to get his breath. "Yes, sir, that's it, retire. This here is my last battle. Ain't … ain't … gonna do no more fightin', 'Lias. I'm a goin' home."

"Sure, Bill, we are all going to make it home."

"And, 'Lias, you look after these here boys, ya hear? They look up to you, 'Lias, and they love you. We all do, 'Lias. You've done … uhhhhh … Oh God … I …"

"Bill, I'm going for help! I'll get you home!"

"Never mind, 'Lias, I gots all the help I need, and I can make it home all right." Bill had grabbed Elias' hand and was gripping it very tightly. His voice was so faint Elias could hardly make out the words he was saying.

"You've been a good man, 'Lias, I'm gonna miss … Oh …'Lias … I think … 'Lias, just … uhhhh … my … Our … Our … Fa … Father, who … art in heav …"

Elias felt Bill's hand release its grip and lay motionless on Elias' leg. The hissing sound from Bill's throat quit, and the blood that had been pumping from Bill's stomach slowed and then stopped.

Elias looked around but could see nothing through the tears that filled his eyes. He reached for Bill's limp hand to feel the warmth just once more. Suddenly Elias had never felt so alone. Bill had always been there as a base upon which Elias could rely. Bill's wisdom had helped Elias through many problems; now it was to be relied on no more. With shoulders shuddering and a voice hardly audible, Elias sobbed, "I'll look after the boys, Bill, I promise."

Trying to compose himself, Elias rose and moved away from the two bodies on the ground. Then he saw one of the other men trotting toward him and heard him call out, "You okay? I heard a shot. Where's Bill?"

Elias looked over at the panting soldier, paused for a moment then quietly replied, "Bill went home."

Chapter 24

Even with the skirmishes and the raids, the cold, dreary days seemed to drag by. A pall had fallen over the men of the 1st. The body of William 'China Bill' Foster, the only Union casualty of the skirmish at Horse Head Creek, had been brought back to Roseville.

"We gonna … *going* to leave him here, 'Lias?" asked Toby. "I mean … well … a … probably none of us will ever get back here again. He's just going to be here all alone."

"Don't worry, Toby," said Elias. "Bill will never be alone or lonely, ever again. And besides, all we're leaving here is a body. The real Bill is going along with each of us wherever we are."

Elias was right. Each of the men felt they wanted to say something about their friend, but the right words just wouldn't come. So a silent tribute was made by every man. Each person knew they were both richer, for having had Bill for a friend, and poorer, for having lost him much too soon.

"Greater love hath no man than this, that he give up his life for a friend."

"Goddamn war anyway," said one of the officers as they sat around after their evening meal. "There is just no sense in it, none at all. Why that damn Governor Pickens ever fired on Fort Sumter is beyond me. There was no reason for it. Even Beauregard advised against it."

"Don't talk to me about Fort Sumter, man. The war started up in Kansas nine, ten years ago." The voice was that of Hal Billings, now a lieutenant, who had been a teenage boy living in Illinois during the 1850s. "There was more killing and fighting going on up there between Kansas and Missouri than anywhere else back east."

"Why couldn't those politicians get this all settled without us havin' to go off and start killin'?" asked one of the men as he re-lit his pipe.

"Hell, they've been fighting among themselves for years. Slaves, no slaves, pro-slavery, abolitionists, free-staters. You wouldn't believe how they carry on." Billings stood up and began to gesture in the cold evening air.

"Honest to God, I saw all kinds of stuff happening. Before we moved to Kansas, I had a job as an aide to Stephen Douglas, you know the Senator, back in Illinois, and I worked on the Senate floor. You never saw such fighting, swearing and name calling. Kansas was first approved by the Senate as a slave state in '58, but the bill couldn't make it through the House. In fact, one night those old men got to battling so, there were fists flying and guys rolling around on the floor. It was only the lack of muscle and wind that kept anybody from getting hurt.

"Then Douglas up and took the other side and the Southern Democrats got madder'n hell and said he was a traitor.

"Did you know that Kansas had four territorial governors in just three years? First off, President Pierce wouldn't back anybody, and then after Buchanan got in he went first one way and then the other. He tried to get Douglas to go along with the Southerners and said he would get the Presidential nomination if he did."

"Gosh, why wouldn't he do it then? He sure as hell wanted to be President."

"Douglas said he couldn't put his name to a bill based on the Lecompton Constitution. Said he wouldn't push something like that down the throats of people who didn't want it."

"Don't make sense to me."

"Sure it does. If Douglas had gone along, he might have gotten the Presidential nomination, but he would have lost all the northern Democrats which meant he would have lost the election and been out all around. So that split the Democrats and got Lincoln elected."

Elias, who had stopped in to bring a message to one of the officers, had also gotten a cup of coffee and hung back to hear the conversation. Slavery, states rights, sovereignty, northerners fearful of losing their jobs to cheap labor, political equality, social cultures being abandoned, property rights … no one mentioned freedom. Elias wondered if anyone besides him and his fellow black soldiers really knew why they were here.

"I know why," thought Elias. "And I'm convinced that my family and me, and all the rest of us will have a better life when this is over. Maybe not right away, but even though we were brought here against our will, we will someday have a better life and more freedom than we would have had if we had been left in Africa."

Elias had heard the old ones talk about the way of life they had before they were caught and brought to America. Many lived in jungles, warring with other tribes, going hungry and dying with maladies that no one could understand. Some even told about being taken prisoner by other blacks and being taken to the coast and sold. Their own countrymen would betray them to the slavers just for money and many times for spite. If you get a chance to kill your enemy, do it. If not, capture him and sell him. That was even better. You would not only get money, but reduce the size of your enemy and take his land and property.

"Doesn't seem much different to me," thought Elias. "Most of it is the same, just happening in a different country. Only here, we're doing something about it. And we're going to make it stick!"

Elias smiled to himself as he put his cup in his pocket, and with a glance back at the officers, still arguing over the war, closed the door and made his way back to his own cabin. He knew why he was here. He knew why Bill was willing to leave the freedom of Canada and come back to die at *Horse-ass Creek.* They'd make it! "You damn right we will!"

Sunday, March 20, 1864

Gunfire in camp!

"Any idea who they are and how they got here?" yelled the lieutenant.

"I think they are Battle's brigade," answered the colonel as he swung his side arm around his waist. "And all they had to do is walk across the river. It's frozen solid, what little water there was to begin with."

Men were rushing every direction, hoping not to get in the way of incoming shot and shell. The enemy seemed to be pouring in from the north and trying to gain access to the main compound area. The rifle fire was sporadic, but well directed. Elias and his men were awakened by the cannon fire and then the bugler. They had been directed as to where they should form in the event of an attack and had gone through this procedure several times, but no one expected an attack on a Sunday morning. That was probably the best reason for the enemy to attempt one.

"Don't them fellas go t' church on a Sunday?" bellowed One Shoe as he struggled with his massive boots.

"If'n you'd been up fer church, you'd already been dressed, so what you talkin'?" came a reply from Slows. "Jes git out there and try to save my br'fast fer me and quit yer complainin'."

"We didn't even know they were in the area, Colonel," stated a sergeant as he brought his commander's horse.

"The lines have been down since yesterday, Sergeant. We fixed two breaks, but there must be more east of here."

"They've set fire to the cotton, 'Lias, what do we do?" shouted Toby.

"Never mind for now, just stay down and make every shot count."

Elias moved past a small hut used for storage of tack for the cavalry. He could make out several of the enemy scurrying away from the fires that had been set. He fired toward the fleeing enemy but didn't seem to hit a one of them. The still, cold air echoed with rifle fire, and the shouts of commanders trying to set up defenses.

A break in the defensive line around the main supply building allowed several Rebel soldiers to get beside the door on the west side. Elias and Toby both spotted the men at the same time and fired. Two rebel soldiers collapsed, causing the others to retreat.

"Should a' let 'em go on in," said Toby as he jammed home another ball. "The place is damn near empty any way."

Part of a fence rail split next to Elias' face and drove several splinters into his cheek causing his eye to water. Brushing away the tears, he continued to fire into the smoke in front of him, hoping his shot would find the guy that just shot at him. Smoke from the guns, along with that from the burning and smoldering cotton, filled the air to the point to where it was difficult if not impossible to see where to shoot. The enemy cannon had been silent for several minutes, which meant that it had been disabled or that they were pulling away. The Union cannon had finally been able to return several shots after having to be moved and redirected.

A Confederate officer on horseback, later found to be a major, charged across the open area between the officers' barracks and the kitchen, heading for only he knew where. Just as he neared the rail fence, he seemed to pause and then tumble from his saddle. A whoop went up from a black soldier off to Elias' right, along with a "Das da way," cry from a soldier nearby.

What seemed to be an hour was over in a fourth the time. The enemy was gone as quickly as it had appeared, leaving behind ten killed and fifteen wounded, including the major and a lieutenant. Eight Union wounded were brought to the hospital building, and four were laid next to it awaiting burial.

"We have to risk getting our telegraph line back in working order," said the colonel. "Send crews out east and west and make sure they have protection with them. We have to make contact with Fort Smith, but I don't want to lose men doing it. If we can't get that accomplished, I can always send a courier."

"Sho glad that's done with," said One Shoe.

"Maybe we should'a been in church, ya reckon? Maybe da' Lord would'a put this off for awhile."

"Maybe he kept us here so we could do this here part a' His work, what about dat?"

"Either way all of us are okay. That was some shooting, Toby," said Elias as he placed his hand on Toby's shoulder.

"You done pretty good yourself, One-thumb," replied Toby.

Elias took a backhanded swing at Toby as all the men within earshot of the remark burst out laughing. "That's all right, fella, you'll get yours. Just keep an eye out." It felt good to be able to joke now that the danger was over and everyone was safe.

Elias left their small cabin and started for the sergeant's hut to check on what damage had been done. It had been reported that two cotton gins had been destroyed and over a hundred bales of cotton burned.

As he came around the east end of a poorly constructed hut, he heard sobbing. A young private was huddled next to the building with his head buried between his arms as if afraid the world would collapse in on him.

"Are you hurt, Soldier?" said Elias as he bent to see what was wrong.

The boy looked up at Elias. He was shaking and sobbing and suddenly bent over and began to wretch. Elias placed one hand on the boy's shoulder and the other on his forehead.

"It's okay," said Elias, "you're gonna be okay. Just hold on for a minute and it'll be all right."

Soon the boy began to calm down and quit shaking so hard. He wiped at his mouth and then at the tears in his eyes. He averted Elias' eyes as he tried to compose himself and struggle to his knees in the snow. Reaching up toward a window sill, the boy pulled himself to his feet and without looking at Elias said, "I guess I'm okay now, I jes … I guess I …"

"I know, Soldier, I've been that way, too. It just hits you

sometime and then it goes away. Everybody goes through the same thing; sometimes, some of us more than once."

"Ya mean you … naw, I bet you weren't never scared. I jes got here two days ago and I never … I didn't think it would be like this. Everybody was shootin' and I couldn't even tell who was who half the time." The boy shuddered a couple of times and then settled down.

"Don't worry about it. You're a veteran now. You'll do just fine."

"But supposin' I shot the wrong guy? Who knows what I'll do next time, I don't know what'll …"

"I do," said Elias with both hands on the boy's shoulders. "You know what it's like now and by the time it happens again you'll be ready for it. You're a soldier and if you couldn't learn to handle it you would have run. Now, you didn't run, did you?"

"No, Sir, I didn't run, but I wasn't sure who I was shootin'."

"So see, just what I said. You are no coward. You stood your ground and did what every soldier is supposed to do. I'm glad we are going to be able to count on you from now on."

"Thanks, Corporal, and I'm gonna try. I'll try real hard. You can count on me. I guess I just got a little nervous there for a minute, huh, Corporal? I mean no need to tell any …"

"Tell anyone, why sure, I'll tell my friends all about how you stood there and did what you were supposed to. They'll be proud of you just like I am."

Elias turned and headed on across the hard-packed ground as the young soldier stooped to get a hand full of snow with which to wash his face.

"He'll do," thought Elias.

The cabin was warmer than the outside, but not so warm that Elias was ready to shed his uniform to get in bed. He threw another log into the fireplace and removed only his outer coat. Young Will Taylor was there to gather it up, and reaching high over his head managed to get the coat to hook on the wooden peg in the wall.

"I done what you said, Elias," said Will. "I stayed put and didn't get out from under the bed 'til the shootin' stopped."

"It's *I did* what you said, Will, and yes, you did just fine. But still we have to find you a decent home."

"Whut's th' matter with right here? I ain't complainin' and I got everthin' I need. I don't eat that much and I can do whutever chores ya …"

"It isn't that, Will. You ought to have a home, a real one with a mother and folks to do for you and watch out for you."

"But I don't need …"

"Will, you're just a boy. You are a good boy and you're smarter than most, I agree, but still you ought to be in school and going to church and all."

"I was a ready t' go t' church, but when all hell broke loose, I …"

"Now that's what I mean. You have no business talking like that and that's the kind of talk you are exposed to around here. You need a proper bringing up and we can't do it here."

Will turned away as his lower lip began to quiver.

"We are leaving early in the morning. The sergeant just told us and I have to get our things ready. We have to meet General Thayer. We will be heading south, for how long I don't know. You can't just follow us around until the war is over; you're smart enough to know that."

"I can earn my keep," said Will defiantly. "And I proved I could keep out of the way."

Elias shook his head and began to remove his boots. "Have you eaten anything this evening?" he asked. After receiving an affirmative answer, Elias had Will get ready to climb in bed with him. Prayers were said and the blankets pulled up around both their heads. "Better give me something," said Elias, silently adding to his prayers.

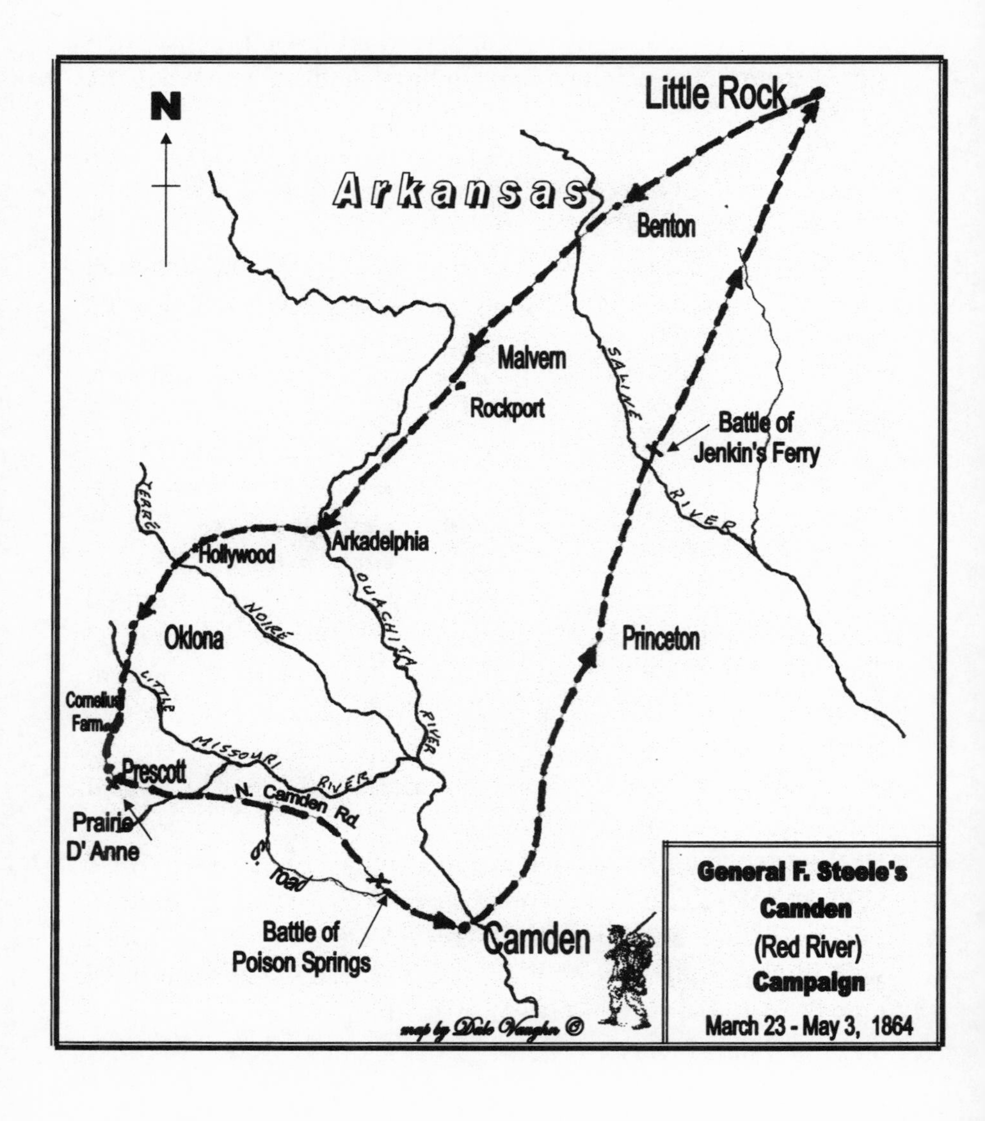
N
Little Rock
Arkansas
Benton
Malvern
Rockport
SALINE
Battle of
Jenkin's Ferry
RIVER
TERRE
Hollywood
Arkadelphia
OUACHITA
NOIRE
Oklona
Princeton
Cornelius
Farm
LITTLE
MISSOURI
RIVER
RIVER
Prescott
N. Camden Rd.
Prairie
D' Anne
road
Battle of
Poison Springs
Camden
General F. Steele's
Camden
(Red River)
Campaign
March 23 - May 3, 1864
map by Dale Vaughn ©

Chapter 25

Monday, March 21, 1864

For a change it was sunny and not so cold. The men of the 1st had begun to stow their personal baggage on the wagons, when an officer approached and ordered the men to leave all but their essential equipment behind. "I have no idea how you people manage to accumulate so much stuff. There is no way on earth the army can cart all that baggage all over the country."

With a disgusted look on his face, one of the men turned to Elias. "What we gonna do 'bout our stuff, Mr. Corporal, Suh? Nodding toward the lieutenant he went on, "Bet he gonna take his b'longin's. Bet he don' leave no letters or none of his books behind."

Elias told the men to do as the officer had said and gathered what few things he could carry in his haversack. It was still dark as the men headed west toward Charleston to meet up with General Thayer's forces that were leaving Fort Smith this same day. It was said that the men at Roseville were supposed to leave for Fort Smith several days ago, but the downed telegraph lines and the skirmish of the day before had cause a slight delay.

"Did ja hear whut we's gonna do, 'Lias?" asked Slows as they made their way along the road with the rising sun to their backs.

"I heard the colonel say that Thayer is meeting up with General Steele. We're heading south to try to push the Rebs away from this side of the Mississippi, I guess."

"Steele? I thought he was a Reb."

"That's William, this is Fred. He's one of ours."

Elias had not been privy to the entire plan which was to isolate the Confederate troops that held Texas, the western part of

Louisiana and the southwest part of Arkansas. What started out to be known as the Red River Campaign was halfheartedly approved by General Grant. Major General Banks, a politician from New England, was bringing 20,000 troops north from Alexandria to attack Shreveport. He was to be met and assisted by General Frederick Steele, leading 12,000 of his own force, including the 1st Kansas Colored. Hopefully this would bury Confederate General Kirby Smith and end the war west of the Mississippi.

Stopping for a short rest and a bit of lunch, Elias enjoyed the warmth of the sun and the colors of the first spring flowers that were showing their brilliant petals along the prairie. Seated by the side of the road close to some bushes and trees, Elias watched yellow finches dart around the bushes and along the ground searching for seeds that had dropped. The black feathers along the lower part of their wings looked like corporal stripes. With them were the gray and brown females and even the dark, dusty red-breasted variety. They gathered by the dozens, flitting with incredible speed through the trees that swayed gently as a slight breeze stirred. Skinny gray squirrels raced across the ground and before you knew it were twenty feet up the backside of a tree peering out with just an ear and one eye showing.

The birds flitted in and out of the blossoms dipping their bills into the nectar and pollen and then landed on the ground to find insects. A large streak of bright red indicated the sudden presence of a black masked cardinal. The area was alive with creatures completely oblivious of the tumult that brought human intruders into their world.

This was beautiful country. The wooded areas reminded Elias a little of the woods and mountains of their home in Virginia. He guessed he would always consider that place a home of sorts, even though most of those memories were of a harsh and difficult life. It caused him to wonder just what his mother …

The sound of the bugle abruptly reminded him that his job was to move on, find the enemy, kill him, and then think about the beauty of the land. Killing and beauty; how strange to think of those opposites in the same breath.

That evening, when camp was made and their evening meal been eaten, the men began to huddle around small fires. The evenings were still cool, sometimes to the point of being cold. This evening, clouds rolled in and indicated a storm might accompany them on their journey south.

Word had been passed that the total force would end up being over 30,000 Union troops, which meant more than just skirmishes. No doubt a big battle was soon to be fought, and the men thought long and hard about their future. Almost all of these men had been in enough hard fighting to qualify them as seasoned veterans. Pain and death would be no new companions.

Off in the distance a harmonica could be heard. Soon a young tenor voice took up the strains of *"Barbara Allen."*

'Twas in the merry month of May,
The green buds were a swelling,
Sweet William on his death bed lay
For the love of Barbara Allen.

The lyrics swept across the camp and caused the night to become even quieter. Each man had his own Barbara somewhere.

"Oh, Father, go and dig my grave.
Go dig it long and narrow.
Sweet William died for me for love,
I'll die for him for sorrow."

Elias listened to the words and wondered if someday, he too, would have a woman willing to die for his love. More than that, willing to live for that love and help it grow into a long and productive life. A life complete with their own children, a home … maybe and a good … farm … and …

Day dreams faded into night dreams, some more nightmares filled with shouting, shooting and killing.

The shouting seemed to go on and on, growing louder and louder. Suddenly he was being shaken.

"You goin' with us or you gonna wait and join up when we on our way back?"

One Shoe stood over Elias, shoving on Elias' shoulder trying to wake him.

"What? … Huh? Golly, I guess I must have really been out. Are we … is it time …?"

"You bet. You gonna eat, you better git to it. Sun be up soon and we sposin' to be movin'."

It was actually later than either One Shoe or Elias realized, and the sun was making its way across the Arkansas sky, but would be hidden from view. Dark clouds had continued to roll in throughout the night and rain was imminent.

"That's all we need," said Elias as large drops began to fall. The men were all scrambling to get their gear packed, and some pulled their ground sheets over their heads trying to keep their wool uniforms from getting soaked. Should the sun come out later, a wet wool uniform was one of the government's harshest punishments.

After meeting General Thayer's troops, the force headed southeast hoping to meet General Steele. Although they had not met any of the enemy thus far, it was generally conceded that their movement was known. It was difficult to conceal thousands of men when much of the terrain was open prairie. Occasionally hills and patches of trees would hide some of the group, but men, wagons and animals would make enough noise to call attention to their presence.

Day after day the rain made the roads difficult and at some spots impassable. Routes were changed, troops tried leaving the road and walking through fields and forests. At times trees would have to be felled to make way for supply wagons and artillery, causing additional delay.

"We will never reach Steele at the appointed time," complained General Thayer. "And to add to our difficulties, we are running out of provisions and forage. If Steele is having the same problems, and I bet to God he is, he is in worse shape than we are."

The General tried to control his horse as the animal pranced and blew, sensing the nervousness of its rider.

"We have no choice, General," stated a colonel riding alongside, "we are going to have to corduroy the road in order to get the wagons through."

"More time lost," complained Thayer. "Very well then, if there's no other way. It's fortunate there are trees near by. But be as quick as you can. Steele will eat us alive for being late."

Through the evening hours the men slogged their way southward. Mud clung to boots; grass clung to the mud, until the men's feet seemed three times their normal size. Uniforms were muddied up and down their fronts from heaving against mired wheels. Mules staggered and fell, then balked at being pulled to their feet.

More rain fell. Clouds darkened the sky by day and made it impossible to see three feet in front of a man during the night time. Meals, what few there were, consisted of part rain and part Arkansas earth. At least, the wet uniforms seemed to hold the body heat partway into the night.

"Don't ask me where he come from. All I know, he comes hanging 'round our camp every three or four days. Leaves, then comes back. Heard he's been doin' the same thing all up and down the train. The captain finally caught 'im and when he said he belonged to you, he said to git 'im here and the captain don' wanna see him hangin' 'round no more."

Elias looked first at the private and then down at Will Taylor. There were tears in the boy's eyes and then a slight smile crept across his dirty face. "I been stayin' out of your way, like you said, Elias."

"I'll handle this, Private," said Elias in a low voice. "I'll see he doesn't bother you again." Elias wanted to grab Will and shake him good and hard, but instead just looked at the thin, questioning face. The look on the boy's face seemed to shout, "If you don't take me, what will happen to me? I have no one." Elias knew the feeling. He and his family had felt the same way several times until the Wallaces befriended them.

"What will I do with you? You were supposed to stay at Roseville until someone could find you a home. I told you that you couldn't just follow …"

The boy threw his arms around Elias' waist. "Please …"

"Hell, it took over two weeks just to make 75 miles. I'm surprised you did as well as you did, John." General Steele stood in ankle-deep mud next to his horse talking with the newly arrived General Thayer. "I just hope to God Ol' Pap is having as much trouble as we are. I have over 800 wagons to try to move through this muddy mess and very little to feed the men and animals."

"We were in hopes you were better off than we are, General," said General Thayer. "We have been on half rations for several days now."

"I understand, John, but we'll make it somehow. We haven't been able to do much foraging because of the hit and run tactics of Price's men. They have been dogging us ever since we crossed the Ouachita River up by Rockport."

"The same thing happened to us, General." General Thayer bit off a piece of dried cracker, spitting it out after finding it too hard to chew. "We had to change our route several time because of the rain and mud, but that didn't seem to stop the guerillas from sniping at us. We couldn't even get our couriers through to you, and none of yours seemed to be able to find us. You had already gone through Rockport when we got there, so we tried to move along as fast as we could to catch up."

"I can appreciate your problems," replied General Steele. "We waited at Arkadelphia for two or three days hoping you would find us. It allowed the men and animals to rest a bit, but after we left Shelby found us and we had to fight him off. I hope this is all worth it."

The General tried to scrape some of the mud from his boots on several large tuffs of prairie grass as he went over the situation he faced. "I wouldn't be surprised, even if we get a break and manage to get to Shreveport, to find that something has happened to Banks and he turned back."

"That would leave us high and dry in Louisiana," stated General Thayer.

"Damn right it would," General Steele agreed. "And I haven't been able to establish communications with anyone who knows what is happening for sure."

The decision was made by General Steele to strike east and march on to Camden. He was certain that Kirby Smith had moved most of his Confederate troops south anticipating Banks' move, and that would allow the Union forces to easily occupy the post at Camden. It was reported that Camden was a rather large and well-fortified Confederate supply depot, but if not heavily guarded, Steele assumed much of the stores would have been destroyed before the Confederates left.

On the morning of April 10th, the Union troops began to move south from a place called the Cornelius farm. Elias and the 1st were placed in the rear of the train as reserves.

"Least we ain't got no ... *haven't got no* ... *any* dust to eat back here," said Toby.

Elias grinned and opened his shirt front to let out some of the steam that seemed to wrap around his body. It was somewhat warm though still cloudy. The column moved slowly through the grass next to the sodden road. Wagons and artillery pieces moved quietly through the damp countryside, only occasionally squeaking when straining to make progress.

A pine forest just ahead of the moving troops made it necessary for them to get back on the road. Several times shots could be heard from the guns of guerilla sharpshooters which caused the men to keep looking from side to side into the woods. The temperature began to drop and a cool breeze came out of the northeast.

A little before four o'clock gunfire could be heard toward the front of the column. Before long, artillery fire began, and it was easy to tell that the big guns were being fired from both

Confederate and Union batteries. The train had stopped and the men were put on alert but ordered to remain where they were.

"They's a couple 'a ridges up there," said one of the men that had been sent to the rear for ammunition. "Them Rebs got their riflemen behind the first one and the cannons behind the second. They got themselves a perfect place to hunker down in." With that, the men were headed back south with their ammunition.

The fighting kept up the rest of the afternoon and into the evening. Elias and his men had little information and could only guess what was happening by listening to bits of talk from men moving back and forth to the front. Elias was glad none of his men were at risk even though they would like to be closer to the action. They were real veterans now and understood that their job was to make the enemy retreat or die in the attempt. The only way to get back to their homes and have the freedom they all held so dear was to convince the Rebs they couldn't win.

Darkness crept over the prairie and into the woods where the Union forces were told to keep on the alert. Men were tired and cold. They had had scant to eat and prospects were none too good for the near future. Men stood or knelt peering into the darkness, when suddenly Confederate artillery belched fire and shot toward the Union lines. This continued for almost two hours. Men lay prone in the undergrowth and watched from behind trees as the ground in front of them erupted from artillery shells.

After the firing ceased, the stillness was almost as intimidating as was the shelling. Horses' hooves and yells of "Charge" broke the silence around eleven o'clock. Rifles were brought to shoulders and fired into the darkness toward the noise. The Twenty-seventh Wisconsin and Fortieth Iowa Infantry had opened up on the enemy. Seconds later Captain Vaughn's Battery A, Third Illinois Artillery, joined in by hurling grape and canister into the charging cavalry, sending them back to their earthworks and leaving the prairie littered with dead Confederates.

For the next two days, skirmishers continued to fire and artillery from both sides could be heard answering each other. On the morning of the 12th, General Steele ordered his three divisions to attack Price's works, with General Thayer's Frontier Division in reserve. Steadily the Union forces crossed Prairie D'Anne, driving the Confederates back to their fortifications. Price's left flank was turned, which caused him to abandon his works and head toward Washington, fully expecting Steele to pursue.

General Steele gave the appearance of pursuit by sending part of his cavalry after Price, while turning the bulk of his command toward Camden on the northern most road of three that headed east.

Elias and the 1st Kansas were still toward the rear of the train along with the rest of General Thayer's command and were put on guard just in case of an unexpected attack. The roads were worse than those they had been traveling on, and their movement was delayed once again by having to wait for the mud to be covered by logs and rails. By the 13th Captain Wheeler's pioneer corps had repaired bridges and made their way as passable as conditions would allow.

About one o'clock in the afternoon, Elias and Matthew Smith were standing next to a line of wagons that had their teams harnessed and men ready to move out.

"They gonna hit us agin, 'Lias, ya reckon?" asked Matthew.

"I certainly hope they are still heading west, Matthew. We need to get on to Camden. Maybe we can get some decent food and into some dry uni …"

A shot rang out followed by dozens of others. Matthew turned and went to his knees. Elias saw a darkening spot on Matthew's upper left shoulder. The boy fell to his right and rolled over onto his back. More shots were thudding into wagons and mules. Elias bent to help Matthew just as a rifle shot took his haversack from across his side. Elias hit the ground next to Matthew and looked into the boy's eyes.

"How you doin'," Elias shouted?

"Don't know, but I'm still alive, I guess. M' whole arm is numb."

Elias pulled his kerchief from his pocket and shoved it into Matthew's coat to cover the wound. More firing by rifle and then the artillery joined in. All twelve of Thayer's cannons threw grape and canister at the charging Rebel infantry and cavalry, finally causing them to retreat and regroup.

For more than four hours the assault continued. Elias pulled Matthew under a supply wagon and into a grove of trees. The bleeding finally stopped, and Elias managed to find a canteen from which Matthew drank. Elias could tell the boy was in much pain by the look on his face, but not once did Matthew cry out.

Elias left his friend several times to check on the rest of his men who had been heavily engaged trying to repel General Dockery's Rebel troops. Finally the enemy was driven from the field and forced back about three miles, giving the men of the 1st a breather.

Immediately they were ordered to move on east on the Camden road through the swamps and mud of Terre Rouge bottoms. Again at Cypress Bayou the pioneer corps had to repair rain-damaged bridges and roads. Wagons loaded with what supplies that were left, and those carrying wounded, including Matthew, were pulled and shoved through mud and water. Wheels would slip off the logs used to corduroy the road, and moans could be heard from the wounded. Darkness hampered the progress even more as Elias and his men slowly worked their way toward what they hoped would be rest and a chance to regroup in both body and spirit.

Elias managed, during the night, to heat some water and make a broth of a piece of dried ham and corn meal. "You're gonna be just fine, Matthew. This will warm your insides and get you back going again." The bullet had somehow missed all but Matthew's collar bone and would do little but disable the boy's arm until the bone knitted. If he could be careful, he would be fine in a few weeks.

"I thought I was gonna die, 'Lias," said Matthew as he sipped the broth. "I just knew I would, and I didn't know what to do." Through the darkness Elias could see the sparkle of tears in the boy's eyes. "I wanted to pray, but it happened so fast, and I … I couldn't remember how. Ya' know, 'Lias, I couldn't remember how?"

"I know, Matthew."

"But what would'a happened if it had been a real bad one, 'Lias? If'n I couldn't pray, what would'a happened to me?"

"Don't you ever worry, Matt. God knows what's going on and He won't let you down. He understands when things are happening so fast …"

Matthew interrupted, "But what's He know 'bout me? I never did do much religion stuff, I … I guess I was too scared."

"Oh Matthew, why should you be scared? He never wants you to be scared of Him."

"Well, the preachers always said He was a terrible God and we had to fear 'im. And that didn't seem too friendly t' me, so's I just kinda kept to myself."

"Don't ever do that again, Matthew. He's as much a Friend as I am and He'll look out for you and all the rest of us. He loves us all, Matthew, especially when we're scared."

"You mean you get scared, too, sometimes, 'Lias?" asked Matthew as he finished his broth.

"You bet I do, lots of times."

"Was you scared this afternoon, too?"

"Sure I was. I was scared you were gonna bleed all over my pants and these are the only ones I've got."

"You mean? … aw … go on, you're just …"

"Go to sleep. I'll be back to see you come daylight." Elias moved away, found a dry wagon and pulled an empty potato sack up around his shoulders. Sleep as dark and cold as the night finally shut out the thought of war from Elias' mind for a few brief hours at least.

Chapter 26

Friday, April 15, 1864   Camden, Arkansas

"We here, 'Lias, now whut?" One Shoe was trying to dry out his one and only pair of blue wool pants. Holes in one knee and the seat allowed his long underwear to show through, although being so dingy their color came close to that of the uniform.

"I hope we can rest a mite, Tom. All of us are dead tired and about to starve."

"That's another story," offered Toby. "They say they ain't … *there isn't* any more to eat here than we had before we got here."

"Dat's right," put in Slows. "They says they takin' some of the corn from the mules and givin' it to the men, but we gots to grind it oursev's. And 'em Grays done busted up most o' the mills 'round here."

"It's going to get better, fellas, I know it will. General Steele isn't going to let his men starve. He'll figure out something." Elias mentally crossed his fingers hoping he was right. They were in sad shape and could not be expected to continue fighting without being fed.

After another day of fighting the Arkansas mud, and occasionally the Confederates, they had finally reached Camden and the Confederate Fort. Someone had said that Rebel General Price had done more for the Union forces than most of Union generals by building up such good forts for the Union to occupy. So far they had captured Little Rock, Camden and soon would probably have Washington and Fulton. Camden alone had taken the biggest part of a year for the Confederates to construct and it showed the effort. Located on the Ouachita River, which was capable of navigation by supply boats, Camden was protected by seven different forts, guarding the town as well as each other. It would have been a real feather in Steele's cap under different circumstances.

"Sir, I think I finally have some good news for a change." General Steele's aide moved across the room and handed the General a note that told of the 1st Iowa Cavalry capturing the steamer *Homer* at Frenchport Landing, just fourteen miles below Camden. It was loaded with 2,000 bushels of corn and would be at Camden on the 16th.

"Good," stated the General. "Captain Henry had word from our spies and friends in this part of the country that there are stores that can be purchased and also more that we can commandeer west of here. Folks around here went to planting grain last year instead of so much cotton because they weren't certain where their market would come from, and much of that grain was hidden away from the Confederates."

"Yes, Sir," replied the aide, "You can eat corn, but you can't eat cotton."

"That's right. Do you realize we have over 10,000 animals to feed besides the men? And even though the Rebels destroyed much of the grain, last year was an exceptionally good year around this area, so there is still some available."

Saturday, April 16, 1864

"Captain Thrasher?"

The captain looked up and then jumped to his feet, saluting smartly as General Thayer entered his office early in the evening.

"I'm looking for Colonel Adams. Have you seen him?"

"Sir, I am afraid he is gone for the evening. May I be of assistance?"

"All right, what about Colonel Williams?"

"Yes, Sir. I believe he is in his room, Sir. Shall I go get him?"

"That's all right; I'll go if you will direct me."

"Sir, I'll be glad to accompany you, if you wish. His room is in the next building."

The two officers made their way to the building in which several of the officers had their quarters. Colonel Williams' room was on the second floor facing the evening sun. After receiving General Thayer and Captain Thrasher, the three took seats around a small table as Thayer addressed Colonel Williams.

"General Steele came to me last evening and requested me to select an exceptional officer to take charge of a foraging train. You can appreciate the situation we are in, and while I mean no disrespect to our brigade commanders, I would like for you to command this very important endeavor. Our men and animals are bordering on starvation in the near future and we have been advised there is forage to be had if we make a concerted effort."

The general arose and walked to the window, peering out at the setting sun. "We have been fortunate thus far, but if we ever intend to make this campaign effective, we must be able to supply ourselves. Our trains from Pine Bluff have not been able to get through, and we cannot depend on help for over a week or so. I know your diligence and that of your men. You are the man I want for this job."

"Yes, Sir. I will be honored to be of service. My men have not had a lot of rest, but under the circumstances we will do our best."

"I'm counting on you to do just that. Now, I know it's late but I want you to advise your men and be ready to leave as early as possible in the morning. I'm not asking you to do this alone, of course. I will be sending the forage-master with you to direct your search, and I'm notifying Rabb to send a section of his battery along with four squadrons of cavalry to accompany you. You should have around 700 men, two mountain howitzers and 200 wagons."

General Thayer turned from the window and continued. "Day after tomorrow I will send out additional men to assist in bringing in the supplies, and as an extra precaution against an attack. If I were you I believe I would station cavalry pickets along the various roads on your route, ah … just in case."

"Yes Sir, thank you sir. I'll prepare the men right away."

Colonel William's force, including his own 1st Kansas Colored under the command of Major Ward, 200 wagons and two artillery pieces, set out on the morning of the 17th to forage over the area west of Camden

" 'Lias, you sure this here is some kind'a honor, this here marchin' our way back th' way we just come?"

"I told you, Amos, General Thayer asked for Colonel Williams personally. He said he knew the caliber of both the Colonel and his men. That means us."

" 'Sides," spoke up One Shoe, "we gonna get to eat all the way back."

With that several of the men broke out in laughter. It was a more than pleasant prospect to the group of very hungry men of the 1st.

"I sure hope he's right," spoke up Toby. "I'm getting tired of hearing old One Shoe chompin' and grindin' up that corn with his bare teeth. He don' even … *doesn't even* bother to grind it first."

"I got's my own grinder, and I don' have to go outside to the barn nuther," stated One Shoe defiantly.

It was out of character for Elias, but he had felt depressed and dejected the past few days. He had not heard from his mother for several months, and he worried about the absence of information about his brother Cheat. He was tired and he was hungry. He looked around at the woods and occasional marshland as he recognized some of the area they had passed just a few days ago heading to Camden. The roads were still muddy, and even some of the corduroy was still visible in a few of the higher spots. The sun was getting higher in the sky and the heat and humidity, along with the weakness of hunger and fatigue, had given Elias a headache.

At the first rest period, Elias found a small puddle of water in a ditch along the side of the road. His muscles were already aching and he felt a slight amount of dizziness.

Looking out over the field, sweat pouring over his face, he knelt with one knee in the mud and bathed his face with both hands filled with the warm water. The pain throbbed and yet he could see the coolness of the woods and the green plants all around him. The plants were mostly weeds but they were healthy; healthy and strong, standing high in the morning sun.

"I wish I could be like those weeds," he said. "I wish all I had to do was build myself strong and stand high," Then he realized that the weeds were struggling as hard as he was just to remain alive. Their goal was to live and be able to survive until it came time to spread their seeds in order to keep their kind alive and thriving. Good or bad, the purpose for all things was to survive and multiply, or at least to survive.

Survival was foremost in the minds of all of them, and yet there were times when it meant keeping the unit alive, not just yourself. What causes a man to be willing to die just for an idea or a group of people, many of whom he doesn't know nor will ever meet? Perhaps the motive is in hoping someone will do that for your own people if it becomes necessary. "And yet … how am I to understand? How can I be expected to know what all this means, when I doubt that those directing this horrible effort understand it themselves?"

"You all right, Corporal?"

Elias looked up into the face of Colonel Williams. For a few minutes, without comment, Elias looked into the eyes of his leader. Did this man deserve the dedication and loyalty Elias and his men had been willing to give? Or did this man ask too much? Was he the kind of man Elias was willing to follow into the very face of death? Would he really lead Elias and the others to the freedom they so desperately fought for? Yes! Yes, he would! Elias was certain now. He recognized the determination and dedication in his Colonel's eyes.

"Corporal?" The colonel smiled and laid his hand on Elias' shoulder.

"Yes, Sir. Thank you, Sir. I believe I'm fine now. Just fine, Sir." Instead of a salute, Elias stood, grabbed the colonel's hand with both of his and shook it. "I appreciate it, Sir, very much, Sir. Thank you, thank you."

With a rather quizzical look, the colonel continued to smile. "Good, Corporal. I'm depending on you and our men."

"We'll be here, Sir. We'll be here." No more fatigue, no more headache, no more depression. "How could I be so stupid? How could I let myself think like that?" Elias muttered to himself. Then he looked down at his hands and realized that he had shook hands with his commander with mud and slimy water all over them. The colonel had never said a word nor did he pull away. "You bet, Colonel," Elias shouted. "We'll be right here."

Without turning around, the colonel waved and continued on down the road, speaking to the men as he passed.

"Jes' whut was that all 'bout?" asked Slows.

"It's all about leadership and courage, Amos. It's all about freedom and dedication."

"Yeah, well, 'long as I don' haf't know fo' sure whut you talkin' 'bout. I guess it's okay."

The rest of the day was spent following wagons alongside roads, into farm fields and barnyards. Corn was shoveled into the wagons and vegetables were gathered. Smokehouses were nearly emptied of bacon and hams when they were found. The men were warned against looting and were told to leave at least something for the country folks to subsist on. The sun disappeared and it looked like it could rain again. Thick humidity hung in the air and made the sweat run down the faces and bodies of the men. Tempers were short, but the men were too tired to even fight among themselves. The animals would trudge along with their heads down and cause the teamsters to shout and slap the reins loudly against the animal's backs.

They had come sixteen or seventeen miles along the north

Camden road and then branched out four or five miles to the north and south in search of food. With more than two-thirds of them loaded, the wagons struggled in after dark and camped for the night.

The next morning, the train began its journey back eastward. Close to an area called Cross Roads, but generally known as Poison Springs, they were met by the escort from Camden of close to 470 men, and two twelve-pounder mountain howitzers, attached to the 6th Kansas. The reinforcements, under the command of Captain Duncan of the 18th Iowa, waited along the road back to Camden for the train to pass and then fell in to become a rear guard.

Apparently, Confederate General Price's scouts had seen the foraging train leave Camden and reported to General Marmaduke whose camp was near Woodlawn. Marmaduke saw his chance to capture the train, obtain badly needed supplies and get revenge for being out-generaled at Prairie D'Anne. A Confederate skirmish line was set up between Colonel William's train and Camden along the Camden road. Then Marmaduke picked three divisions: his own, that of Cabell and Maxey, with a four-gun battery for each division, and prepared to set them against the Union train. That would cover the Federal front and right with thirty-seven hundred men and twelve pieces of artillery. Included in this force were Maxey's Choctaw Indians and the 29th Texas. The Texans had been badly beaten by the 1st Kansas Colored at Honey Springs and could hardly be contained when they learned they would have a second chance at the black Union soldiers.

Colonel Williams rode to the rear and searched for Captain Duncan. "I don't like it," he said as they rode along the side of the road next to the wagons. "I don't like it at all, and I'm sure glad you're here."

"Don't worry, Colonel," replied Duncan. "We did have a few shots taken at us on the way here, but I doubt there will be an attack of any strength. Even with some of your people dead tired, we still have over a thousand able men."

"Well, just the same, keep your eyes open and the pickets out. If there is an attack it will probably come at our rear."

Colonel Williams had hardly gotten the statement out of his mouth when he heard rifle fire toward the front of the train. He immediately raced his horse eastward toward the sounds and began to see the puffs of smoke coming from the woods, at his front and right flank.

"Pull those wagons up next to each other," he began to shout. "Form a skirmish line and push them back."

Wagons were pulled up two and three abreast as the road would allow. The 1st Kansas Colored was in the front and already setting their skirmish line. On their left, Lieutenant Utt had his 14th Kansas Cavalry formed and on their right, Lieutenant's Mitchell and Henderson had the 2nd and the 6th Cavalry ready to charge. Rebel pickets had been pushed back east about a mile after offering only token resistance.

"We've driven their pickets, Colonel," yelled one of the men with a wave of his hat.

"It's too easy," stated Colonel Williams. "They want us to follow them into a trap. Keep sharp." Turning his horse, the colonel headed toward the artillery. It was 10 o'clock when he had the 2nd Indiana battery open fire.

"We'll see if they have any of their artillery with them," he shouted to Lieutenant Walker. "Keep firing to let the wagons that are still out know they must return to the train."

Elias and his men had slowly worked their way along the road, firing occasionally when an enemy could be seen. The Confederate artillery, if there was any, did not reveal itself. Major Ward could be seen riding back and forth along the line shouting encouragement and peering into the underbrush to the south of the road.

"What happened to that eatin' part, on the way back?" asked One Shoe as he slowly moved along next to the north ditch.

"You just watch yourself so you'll be able to eat when we do reach the fort," said Elias. "I don't want any …"

Suddenly the brush to the south was alive with Rebel skirmishers. Rifle fire flooded the road and caused Union soldiers to fling themselves to the ground. The Confederate artillery opened with a deafening roar from the front and right flank of the column. The shells were being lobbed over the heads of the Confederate infantry and directly into the leading Union force. Smoke hung in the heavy air, making it almost impossible to see.

Through the noise of the battle, Elias could hear the cries of men being torn apart by shot and shell. Rifle bullets filled the air with the sound like a thousand bees. A scream came from Elias' left and he felt a tug at his ankle. A rifle bullet had taken the left side of his boot and left a mark along his leg.

Elias heard his name in a crying-like voice. Moving to his left, he stumbled across the body of Jimmy Tate. Looking up at Elias, Jimmy shuddered and died. There was a terrible hole in his chest where a shell fragment had torn its way into the boy's body. Elias froze for a second and then rushed forward gripping his rifle tightly. Off to his right he heard more screams and saw Lieutenant Henderson charge his horse into the battle.

The skirmish line had been forced to halt and then fall back several yards. The men knelt and fired at whatever targets they could find. The fire from the Rebels seemed to be increasing, and the artillery, mounted on a slight hill, were able to fire right down into the Union force.

"Hold if you can," shouted Major Ward.

Elias felt the blood running down his ankle and into his boot. There was little damage but the scrape stung like fire. Loading and shooting, Elias tried to look around and identify his men. As they were forced again to move back, Elias stumbled and fell over the body of another Union man. He was unable to see who it was, but it was the body of a black man.

"Off to the side, men," shouted Major Ward. "Lay down and try to keep out of sight until we have a decent target. Don't let them find you."

The men hugged the ground, keeping their rifles in front of them or rolling on their backs so they could load and be ready. Confederate cavalry could be seen off to the south. A mounted officer held his field glasses to his eyes searching for the Union troops. Artillery fired a searching pattern until suddenly a piece of a shell tore into the back of one of the 1st Kansas, causing him to leap into the air and twist around. The enemy caught sight of the soldier and focused their fire directly into the center of the concealed troops. Shot and bursting shell covered the area, causing those that could to seek better cover. Bodies lay strewn over the ground, some convulsing in death while others were forms so still that they almost seemed peaceful. Some of the hurt could be seen trying to treat their own wounds, while tears ran down their faces. Elias saw men crawling along the ground working their way toward the brush. The firing was still fierce but seemed to be directed over their heads. Hugging the ground, the men waited for the enemy to get close. Colonel Williams had told them to hold their fire until the Rebel skirmishers were within 100 yards. "Buck and ball," he had instructed.

"Now!" was the command. Union blue arose and fired into the Rebels as they had crossed the fields from the brush to the south. Screams and cries could be heard from both armies. Elias saw movement out of the corner of his eye and looked just in time to see Amos Porter drop his rifle and stare down at his stomach which had been opened up by a rifle ball.

"Oh, God, no," shouted Elias. Amos looked into Elias' eyes and slowly folded to the ground. One Shoe had crawled to the side of his friend and then looked at Elias and shook his head. Just then a cannon shell burst above them, scattering pieces of iron over the ground. Elias waited for the shock of a wound, but felt nothing but the earth moving beneath him. As he looked for One Shoe, he could see the big man loading and firing as deliberately as if he were at a turkey shoot.

About that time, a soldier on horseback rode into the Union midst and inquired of Colonel Williams if he could direct him to Colonel DeMorris. When immediately taken prisoner, the young Confederate cavalryman realized his mistake and Colonel Williams learned that he had, in fact, been attacked by General Price's force, part of which was led by Colonel DeMorris, with Cabell and Crawford at his front.

A Confederate flag could be seen to the south that indicated the force practically upon them was that of the 29th Texas. "See that, Tom? Our old friends from Honey Springs."

"Guess we'll jes haf't do it agin, huh, 'Lias?"

A second charge was made by the Confederate infantry and twice their flag went down, only to be picked up again and brought forward. Still after about fifteen minutes they were pushed back again. This time the effort by the 1st was more feeble due to the ranks being thinned more and more.

"You First Nigger, now buck the 29th Texas." The yell went up from the Rebel infantry as they moved on to the 1st Kansas. As the charge was made, a wild yell went up from the Texas men that could be heard well over the noise of the battle. "Now who's runnin', nigger?"

"I've got to get back to Duncan and get some help," Colonel Williams shouted to Major Ward. "You look after things here. I hope to God they hear this back at Camden."

The colonel had no sooner spoken than his horse reared and stumbled. It had been shot through the neck and lay kicking in agony on the ground.

"Here," shouted Major Ward, as he leapt from his saddle.

Colonel Williams grabbed the reins in one hand, the horse's mane in the other and was in the saddle and off to the rear. As he made his way west, he encountered several batteries that were without enough men to fire the cannons. "Spike the guns and head for the rear," he shouted and raced on.

"I'd help if I could, but we have just been attacked here, Colonel." Captain Duncan had to shout to make himself heard above the roar of the battle.

"Do what you can and be ready to form for retreat." Colonel

Williams pointed toward the woods on north. "That's the only cover we can hope to reach. We must cross that ravine."

"There's a swamp over there, too, Colonel. We'll never get the artillery through there."

"Move what you can when the time comes and spike what you can't take."

"'Lias, I'm almost dry of shot," shouted Toby. "What'll we do?"

"Check the dead and wounded," shouted back Elias. "And keep down."

"Can't keep down and load and shoot," replied Toby. "I ain't good as y'all."

Elias looked over at Toby and saw a wide grin on the boy's face. "Watch your language. You're slippin' back, Boy."

"Boy? Who you callin' a bo ...?"

A musket ball tore across Toby's chest and out the back of his left arm. Toby twisted and rolled over on his back, with an astonished look on his face. "'Lias ...'Lias, I think ... I ..."

"Lay still, Toby," called Elias, "I'm coming." Elias crawled over to Toby and gently as possible turned him on to his right side to inspect the wound. The ball had crossed his chest, entered just above the left breast and came out above his left shoulder blade. It had apparently missed the lung and had not hit a bone. Elias packed Toby's kerchief down the back of his shirt and pulled Toby's left arm over his chest. Turning Toby on to his right side, he told him to lie very still and that he would be back to get him. "Don't even move a muscle," he said. "If they see you're alive, they'll kill you sure." Elias gently patted his friend's head. "Hold on. I will be back!"

Again the 1st was called to pull back. Elias looked up to see Lieutenant Mitchell of the 2nd Cavalry galloping by, leading Lieutenant Henderson's horse with Lieutenant Henderson draped across the saddle.

Elias was sure it was after noon, and peering through the smoke and brush, he could not see as much movement by the

Union troops as he would have liked to. He was certain they had taken a real beating and that at least half of his men were either killed or wounded. During brief changes of the wind, he could see also some Confederate bodies scattered over the road and fields on either side. The Rebs had paid a price, but if he could, he would see that they paid even more.

The shelling continued, and after a third charge by the Rebel infantry, Colonel Williams ordered the men to form at the rear. Slowly, what few were left made their way to the rear of the train and could see they had been practically surrounded. Some of the men were helping wounded comrades. Others were limping or dragging themselves along from wagon to wagon, not knowing how they would make it to the woods.

"We've got to do it now!" shouted Colonel Williams, "Now!"

Chapter 27

Elias lay next to the ditch on the north side of the Camden road. As Colonel Williams moved what was left of his men toward the ravine and on to the woods, Elias had lagged behind and crawled into the ditch next to a dead mule. Elias had shoved one leg and his right arm under the carcass of the animal. Blood from the slain mule covered Elias' torn shirt, giving the appearance of a dead Union soldier having been rolled on by the animal.

It was nearing dark as Elias tried to stay perfectly motionless and not attract attention. He had lain in this position since about two-thirty or so that afternoon. He hoped he would be able to get back to Toby and get him off the battlefield and back to Camden. He had promised!

During the afternoon, Elias had heard the Confederates going over the battlefield killing the wounded black men of the 1st Kansas. Pleas for mercy could be heard followed by a gun shot and laughter. Elias had to bite his lip to keep from screaming out or rushing to try to aid his helpless comrades. Several times he heard screams, followed by a high-pitched screech. Once when he dared to look up, he could see one of Maxey's Choctaws holding a scalp high in the air.

"Where's the First Nigger now?" went up a Rebel cry.

"All cut to pieces and gone to hell by bad management," was the reply from another Reb soldier.

Dangerously close came Rebel soldiers hitching teams to wagons or just looting. It was dusk as one Confederate walked by, hesitated, and then ran his bayonet into the side of the dead mule, thinking he had stabbed Elias. It took every ounce of courage to keep from flinching or breathing until the soldier had passed. Once a Confederate lieutenant had dismounted from his horse and stood with one foot on the wagon wheel next to where Elias lay. After taking a drink from his canteen and lighting a cigar, the lieutenant remounted and trotted off down the road following a wagon of meat and vegetables.

"Hey, Buck, you wanna be free? Your time has sure come." A shot rang out followed by laughter.

"Think about this, Nigger," said a tall Confederate standing over a black wounded soldier. Taking the black man's own rifle, the Rebel drove the gun's bayonet into the wounded man's crotch. The scream was heard amid the laughter of the onlookers.

"Found me a watch," came a shout.

"Hey. Anybody see this fella's other leg? These boots is practically new."

Colonel Williams, and what was left of his command, had crossed the ravine. The cavalry performed a rear guard action, allowing the infantry to cross the swamp and get into the woods, managing to escape. Several cannon had to be spiked and left behind. Some Confederates tried to follow, but it was decided that they should take the train and leave just in case reinforcements had been sent from Camden.

Elias could hear the moans of the Union wounded as he crawled out of the ditch and tore the remainder of his blood-soaked shirt from his body. There was still just barely enough light to see. He made his way down the ditch next to road, crouching so as not to be too visible in case there were some Confederates lagging behind the main body of the army.

As Elias crawled along the ground, a hand reached out and grabbed him firmly on the arm.

"Sammy? Sammy, you go tell Mama I'm home, y'hear." The voice shook with delirium, "You tell her, now. An' tell her I'm hungry."

"Hold on, fella," said Elias. "You'll be …"

"You tell 'er, Sammy. You tell 'er I want one them fried sweet potato samwiches, you … you tell her …"

Elias recognized the young boy as Private James Erving, of Co. A. Elias started to search for the boy's canteen when the grip on his arm tightened and then relaxed. With a belch of blood and a long sigh, James was dead.

On through the horror Elias searched. He recognized the bodies of Lewis Linn of Co. D, and lying next to Lewis was Henry Wilder and Calvin Simpson.

He moved across the now darkening field to where he had left Toby. After a brief search, he located his friend and gently turned him over on his back. He heard a low moan and a cough, then a whisper. "Took yo' … *your* time."

Elias almost wept with joy. Toby was still alive. The kerchief had helped stop the blood flow, and his arm across his chest had helped close the front wound. Still the boy was weak from loss of blood and probably in shock. Toby began to shiver as Elias tried to move him to a sitting position.

"You leave 'im alone or you a dead man," came a harsh whisper from the near darkness.

"What? Who …?" Elias stared toward the sound. "I'm trying to help."

"Den maybe you kin give me a han', too." It was One Shoe.

"Tom? Is that you? Are you … how bad …?"

"Yep, guess it's me all right. Cain't tell how bad. Guess it's m' arm and m' leg."

"I'll be right there, Tom." Elias pulled the body of a dead Confederate up behind Toby and eased the boy down on the corpse. "Hold on just a minute."

Elias made his way across several dead members of the 1st, one of whom he recognized as Corporal Donaldson of Fort Scott. Several times as he brushed against a body or stumbled over one, he heard moans. Once a hand reached up and then fell as the hand's owner breathed out his last breath. It was Sergeant Gale Hamlin, Co. E.

Elias found Tom and saw that the big man had a bad wound in his left arm and another in the calf of his leg. He had lost a lot of blood but was gritting his teeth and had tried to bind up his wounds with his good right hand.

"Don' s'pose you got no water," said One Shoe. "Mighty dry for a muggy day."

"We'll find some, Tom. You just hold on." Elias tore a shirt from a dead soldier and bound up Tom's leg and arm. "You suppose you can hobble if I find you a stick to use for a crutch?" asked Elias of his big friend.

"Guess I has to. We gots to get little Toby out'n here. I thought I was gonna have t' try it on m' own, til you showed up."

Elias moved to the woods and found a small sapling that had been blown down by an artillery shell. After pulling and twisting off the upper branches, he brought it back to Tom and helped the man to his feet. He heard Tom grunt as he tried to put weight on his bad leg, but the big man managed to limp along behind Elias over to where Toby lay. Tom had stuffed his left hand down under his belt in the front of his pants. With his improvised crutch tucked under his left arm, even a small step caused a great deal of pain. "Never mind, s'gonna be okay."

Elias knelt down and placed his arms under Toby's knees and behind his back so he could lift him up. Toby sighed heavily so as not to groan as they made their way to the main road. Elias had spied a small two-wheeled cart that had been brought from a nearby farm. It had been pulled by a mule the day before the battle, but now was on its side with the dead mule still in a makeshift harness.

After a struggle, Elias managed to free the cart from the mule and put it back up on its solid two wheels. Beneath the cart was the body of Lieutenant John Topping of Co. B. One side of the hitch had been broken off and only the right side was still useable. Elias sat Toby in the cart and helped Tom to sit on the ground next to it.

"Stay here. There has to be a canteen somewhere around here."

Moving along from body to body, after almost fifteen minutes Elias returned. The commotion made One Shoe try to struggle to his feet, as he saw three figures coming toward the cart. Elias was carrying a rifle and prodding two Rebel soldiers in front of him. One of the soldiers was half carrying the other and swearing at Elias.

"Goddamn niggers, wished t' hell we'd a got y'all."

"Much more talk like that and I'll turn you over to my big friend here. He'll peel you like an onion."

"What'n tarnation y' got there, 'Lias?" asked One Shoe.

"One's got a busted arm and a couple of toes missing and the other was hanging around looting."

"Was not, damn you. I'm hurt just as bad as Chase is here. I got me a back injury. I got knocked off'n m' horse and I kin hardly walk no more." The soldier called Chase was hobbling along with his arm held in an odd position and one foot bandaged.

"And here's some water. Our cavalryman here had a full canteen."

After struggling to his feet, One Shoe took the canteen, took a large drink, coughed and took another.

"Hey there, they ain't that much there. Hold on a min …"

"That's good stuff, 'Lias," said One Shoe. "Better have a swig."

"We'll save it for later, Tom. I can smell it from here." Elias turned to the two Rebels. "All right, you grab that cart and hold it upright, while I get my friend comfortable."

"What you mean? What'r we gonna do? You can't make us …"

One Shoe swung a huge arm and back-handed the Reb across the mouth, knocking him down.

"Told ya," said Elias. "Don't make him mad. He's twice the man you are and only about half of him is working right. Now get hold of that cart and head east. If I hear one groan from that man in the cart, I'll turn Tom loose on you again."

Slowly moving down the road, Elias could hear sounds from the battlefield of men wounded and still alive. Once he had the men pulling the cart stop while he went to a man that had called out and had managed to get himself up on one elbow. Elias recognized the man as one of the 1st and was told that his name was Randell Wood from Leavenworth. Wood had been wounded in the head and was consequently blind. He had stumbled across the field, stepped in a shell hole and now couldn't walk. Elias carried him to the cart, and then the group headed on toward Camden.

They had gone less than two miles and had picked up four more stragglers from the Union force, when several shots rang out of the darkness. The two Rebs pulling the cart dropped to the ground, and one of the Union soldiers groaned and fell toward the ditch with a ball through his neck. Elias pulled Toby off the north side of the road and tried to locate Tom.

"They's either Reb pickets or they's renegades," whispered One Shoe.

"I thought I heard a couple of shots earlier before you fellas came," spoke one of the soldiers that had joined the group. "But I wasn't sure because of them other noises."

"Looks like we have to leave the road and make our way through the trees and brush," replied Elias.

"You mean try to get through that stuff in the dark?" complained the prisoner. "Hell, ya can't see three feet in front of yer face. And what about yer wounded? They can't do that. And they's snakes and …"

"Bring him over here, 'Lias," said One Shoe.

"All right, all right, never mind. Least ya could do was give me a drink from m' own canteen."

"Shut up!"

"We've no choice," stated Elias in a determined voice. "We can't be picked off like doves along the road."

They cautiously worked their way to the woods and began to move in an eastwardly direction trying to keep the road in sight. One of the men moved off toward the south and would warn the rest of the group when they were straying too far. Twice they saw several men moving along the road, and on both occasions they later heard gun fire and were certain of the fate of the men.

After several hours of very slow travel, they stopped for another rest and to check their bearings. "I can't help but think we are close enough to Camden to get back on the road," offered Elias. "We haven't heard any firing for over an hour and we have to be able to move faster. These men need medical attention."

"Foster and me will take the Rebs and go ahead of the rest of you. If there is any trouble, we'll duck into the ditch and you fellas will hear the ruckus," stated another of the soldiers.

"You can't just use us like no decoys," moaned the Confederate. "they has to be rules of war again' such ..."

"Shut up, *Boy!"* even in the darkness, the prisoner could see Tom raise his big arm ready to smash his fist into the man's face.

"I hate to have you put yourselves at risk," said Elias to the Union man, "but I see no other choice. You be careful, and thanks."

"Nuthin' to it. You just take care of your wounded."

Suddenly they could hear a faint sound coming from ahead of them: a dull thud, thud, thud, a pause and then thud, thud, thud, again and again from off in the distance, thud, thud, thud.

"What's that?" asked Elias as he shushed the rest of the men.

"That's that noise I told you about," spoke up the Union soldier. "We thought we heard somethin' earlier, but couldn't tell for sure. Now it sounds kinda like drums or sumpin'."

"That's it. It's drums from the fort," exclaimed Elias. "The wind is from the east and it's carrying the sound. Someone knows that there are men out here trying to find their way back. Let's get moving. We'll take turns carrying Toby and one of you give Tom a shoulder to lean on. We're gonna make it, men, we're gonna make it!"

"I'm afraid he's dead, Corporal." The surgeon's aide moved out of the hospital building to where Elias was standing in the pre-dawn air.

"He can't be," said Elias with a pleading voice. "He has to make it. I was certain the wound wasn't that bad. I had the bleeding stopped, and we didn't let his arm move around very much on the way back."

"Oh, no, not that one, he's in bad shape, but we may be able to save him. I mean the one with the head wound. Think you said his name was Wood?"

"Oh, yeah," said Elias. "That was Randell Wood. Gee, I'm sorry he didn't make it. We couldn't tell for sure how badly he was hurt, it was dark and all. Thanks anyway. And do what you can for Toby, he's a special little guy."

The surgeon had already treated One Shoe and was certain that he too would recover, although his army days were probably finished. He had lost quite a bit of blood, and his elbow was shattered. It was a wonder the big man was able to stand the pain of the sixteen-mile walk.

The two Confederate prisoners were turned over to the lieutenant, and Elias had been told that the noise they had heard on the way back was the 12th Kansas beating their drums all night so stragglers could find their way back in the dark. "What a bunch of guys," said Elias aloud as he walked toward his tent area.

They had made it, but at the cost of almost 200 of the 1st Kansas men. He was to learn later that some of the other men that tried to get through the swamps and woods were bitten by poisonous snakes and would be dead in a few days.

Bill and Amos were dead. George, Tom, Toby and Matthew were wounded and who knew how many others? Many killed while doing their job in a valiant manner, others butchered by Confederates while they lay wounded and helpless. Anger welled up in Elias like a bitter taste in his mouth. Only sweet revenge would satisfy his feelings now, and by God, he would have it!

"Shame on you! Shame!"

Elias looked around in the early mist trying to locate the

sound he was certain he had heard. It was his mother's voice, he was sure of it.

In his mind it came again, clear and forceful. "Is that what I spent my life teaching you, Boy?"

Her voice was strong and reproachful. "Have you forgotten what make us different from them? Are you still a man or have you turned animal, too?"

Elias fell to his knees and began to cry. She was right. Her words flowed over his mind as the tears were flowing down his cheeks. He was sobbing so hard his shoulders shook and he could hardly keep from falling over. The sounds from deep in his chest drifted over the landscape as did the first shadows of dawn.

"I'm sorry, Mama. I'm so sorry. Sorry for my friends and for the way I felt. But the loss is so great. What can I do? How can anyone be expected to deal with such horrors? The things I saw and heard, you have no idea."

"Perhaps not, but He does. He is your help when Mama can't be there. You know that."

Elias looked up just as the sun shot its orange arrows into the sky of a new day. "Thanks, Mama," said Elias out loud. "And thank You, too. I'm sorry I forgot for a few minutes. I'll try not to again."

CAMDEN, ARK., April 24, 1864
".................The conduct of all the troops under my command, officers and men, was characterized by true soldierly bearing, and in no case was a line broken except when assaulted by an overwhelming force, and then falling back only when so ordered. The gallant dead, officers and men, all evinced the most heroic spirit, and died the death of true soldiers."

Very respectfully,
J. M. WILLIAMS,
Colonel First Kansas Colored Vols., Comdg. Escort

Chapter 28

Tuesday, April 19, 1864 Camden, Arkansas

"Dammit, I know all about the trouble yesterday, is that more of it?" General Steele stood up behind his desk and glared at the orderly that was about to hand him a report just received.

"A … er … I don't know, Sir," stammered the lieutenant. "I believe it is from General Banks, Sir." The lieutenant quickly laid the paper on the general's desk and left the room.

"I knew it, goddammit, I knew it. I said this is what would happen." The general's words could be heard down the hall and in several of the adjoining offices of the headquarters building in Camden.

The report given General Steele had been delivered by a messenger who had gotten through from Louisiana with news of Kirby Smith's defeat of Union General Banks. It was near certain now that Smith and his Confederates from Shreveport could move upon Arkansas with all the Rebel troops west of the Mississippi. The only good news received at Camden the past few days was of a supply train from Pine Bluff that was to arrive on the 20th. These supplies would sustain the army there for at least a week or ten days.

Upon hearing that the Confederates were still some distance to the south, General Steele had the supply wagons unloaded and hurriedly returned to Pine Bluff to be refilled and sent back to Camden. Along with the train, the general sent 1,500 men with artillery to assure the success of the venture.

On the return trip, the Union forces under Lieutenant Colonel Francis Drake were met at Marks' Mills by Confederate Fagan and his 4,000 horsemen. The result was the capture of all wagons and nearly 1,300 Union soldiers, killed or taken prisoner.

Elias looked around to be certain he had packed everything he would be able to take. They were on their way back to Little Rock early the following morning, the 26th.

"What about me," came a small voice from the shadows?

"You'll have to come with us, Will," said Elias with frustration in his voice. "Somehow, I have to get you to Little Rock." Elias took the boy by the shoulders and stared into the dark brown eyes. "I know you've tried to stay out of the way, and you have even helped at times, but when we get up north, I'm going to find you a place and you must promise me you will stay there."

"But, Elias I can't just …"

"Will," demanded Elias, "you have to understand you can't continue to follow me around like this. Suppose I had been killed last week like Amos. What would have happened to you then?" Elias stood and then went back to packing his haversack. Elias had already spoken to the cook who had promised to put Will in one of the wagons and help get the boy back up north.

"We'll get 'im there, don' worry, 'Lias." Elias wished he could share in the cook's confidence, but realized he had little or no choice.

Toby and One Shoe had been placed in an ambulance before sunup and were at the front of the column that headed north toward Sandy Springs and Jenkins Ferry at the Saline River. For three days Elias and what was left of his men waded through water and mud. The heat and humidity would seem to cook the men during the day, and the mosquitoes and other tiny night creatures would eat at them at night. Although dog tired, sleep was of little remedy. Wagons would become mired down and had to be pulled and dug from the thirty-year-old road in order to get on to Little Rock.

Upon reaching the Saline, Elias stood with a group of other soldiers and looked at the swollen river. They had been forced to march through swamps and water on the road following Cox

Creek to the river, sometimes up to their knees, and now it looked to be impossible to go further. At least on either side of the so-called road, past the swamps, were ridges that might help to hide the long, slowly moving column of men and wagons from the eyes of the Confederates for a few more hours.

Kirby Smith had been deceived into thinking Steele remained at Camden. When he found out the Union force had left, they had almost a half day's head start. At the Ouachita, Smith's forces had few materials with which to construct their own bridge, which gave Steele an additional full day's lead to reach the Saline.

Smith made the fifty miles to the Jiles farm and Jenkins' Ferry in time to catch Steele's force preparing to cross. Here Smith would begin the assault. With a creek to his right and a swamp to his left, Steele knew that Smith would have to attack head on. During the night, log breastworks had been thrown up, and the Union troops felt confident they could hold until the pontoon bridge was erected and the main body was safely across. Building campfires had been out of the question since there was no dry wood, and the men were forced to work in the dark except when bright flashes of lightning would momentarily give them a glimpse of their work.

Early morning of the 30th found the area completely engulfed in fog and mist. Smoke from the guns of both forces added to the confusion of the Confederates who found themselves in a relatively open position. Union gunners fired from behind tree trunks and the breastworks, as the engineers proceeded to work. The sounds of the muskets and rifles seemed to be dulled by the dampness of the morning. Any movement by men on either side caused sucking sounds made by the mud and water.

At the ferry site, an India rubber pontoon bridge was constructed, and one wagon at a time was passed over the boiling muddy water. With all the difficulty, the main body was across by noon. Being at the front, Elias moved slowly northward, completely unaware of the severity of the attack. He was too far away to hear the men of the 2nd Kansas let out the war cry, *"Remember Poison Springs."* Despite the enormity of the Confederate force, the Union held, was able to destroy their bridge after completing the crossing and move on north. Suffering hundreds of casualties, the Rebels could do little but watch the Union force disappear north through the mud and into the woods.

Elias' 1st Kansas, being among the first to cross, remained at the front of the column as a deterrent against an attack from that direction. The road north of the Saline was just as bad, or maybe worse than what they had suffered the last few days, and the wagons immediately mired down again. The order was finally given to unload as many wagons as was necessary and to burn and destroy anything the enemy could use. All unnecessary baggage was to be left, and even clothing, ammunition and other supplies were thrown into the water and mud. For several miles, all along the road was burning wagons and their contents. Elias managed to sling his haversack across his shoulders and save what few possessions he still had.

On north the tired, hungry and demoralized army made its way. The scab on Elias' ankle rubbed the torn top of his boot and began to bleed again. He thought of Toby and his scars and wondered how his friend was standing the trip. He was tempted to throw away what was left of his boots, but knew it would be days or even weeks before he would have anything with which to replace them.

His mind wandered back over the last couple of summers when many of the soldiers would not have shoes. They would walk barefoot until their feet were so tough and callused that if they did get shoes, they would be more uncomfortable to wear than to go without. The men tried to save their shoes or boots for winter, but many times they would be lost during battle or along the way long before winter set in.

Wednesday, May 4, 1864   Little Rock

"That's right, Colonel," said General Steele. "Your orders are dated from the first of this month. You're to take command of the 2nd Brigade of the Frontier Division, 7th Army Corp. under General Thayer."

"Thank you, sir, I guess, but what about my 1st Kansas?" Colonel Williams stood before the general's desk with all sorts of questions suddenly racing through his mind.

"They will still be under your command, but you'll have a lot more to deal with as well."

"Yes, Sir, I'll do my best."

"I know you will or you wouldn't have this command. Now, don't get too comfortable. You are leaving Friday along with General Thayer for Fort Smith."

"But Sir, we just arrived yesterday and my men are dog tired. They are hungry and are not even fully clothed. We had to leave most of our wagons behind, and many of the men have no weapons or ammunition."

"Don't you think I am aware of that, Colonel? If you remember, I was with you. I'm tired, too, and I know what we are out of. And I'm aware if we don't do something to keep Smith south of the Arkansas River, we may never get any more supplies or have communication between here and De Vall's Bluff."

"Yes, Sir," replied Colonel Williams in a subdued tone.

"Now, Colonel," said General Steele stiffly, "if you don't mind, I have my hands full trying to secure Little Rock."

"Yes, Sir. Very good, Sir." Colonel Williams straightened, saluted and quickly left the general's office.

"The road will be much better, General, if we head north along the Arkansas to Lewisburg, then Dwight and Clarksville."

"I'm aware of that, Captain, but it will also be a longer route, and we haven't the time. We will stay south of the river; go to Perryville, through the mountains to Danville and Booneville.

It's less traveled and maybe we can attract less attention. It's going to be about 180 miles and we must make it as quickly as we can."

The wild flowers were out in abundance. Some were yellow daisy-like blossoms with dark brown centers waving in the gentle morning breeze. And there were short, single-stemmed flowers with pinkish-orange leaves toward the top that grew like a thin, airy carpet over the prairie.

Elias thought about Toby's question about wild flowers and weeds and hoped they could be counted with the flowers. He felt in his heart that what they were doing had to be right. And yet he could still see the gray-clad young Rebels racing into the fire of Union rifles. He remembered one of his men questioning, " 'Lias, now jes look at those guys. Why, them there Rebs jes keep a' comin'. They know they ain't gonna get nowhere. Ever' one of 'em's gonna die. They can't win, but they keep comin' on, and I don' understand that. Why they want to get themselves killed?"

"Why do we want to get ourselves killed?' he asked out loud.

"Huh? Who wants to git themsev's killed?"

Elias was at first startled at his own voice and then at the voice of the man walking a few feet away.

"Huh? I mean, never mind. I was just thinking about a question one of my men asked a long time ago."

"Did he?" came the question.

"Did he ask …?"

"No, did he git his sef' killed?"

"Well, yes, as a matter of fact, he did." Elias' reply was low and halting.

"Seen it lot's a' times m'sef'. Don' figure I'll ever get used to it, though."

At their next rest stop, Elias sat down by the man he had been walking next to. He couldn't help but ask, "How long have you been in the army?"

The man laughed and said, "You probably figure I been in it since the *Revalushun,* don' ya, young feller?"

"I didn't mean …"

"Dat's okay, sometimes I feel like I done been in that long, m'sef." It was hard to tell the old man's age, but Elias was certain he was considerably older than the rest of the men in the 1st. When the man removed his cap to wipe his forehead, gray curly hair could be seen mixed in abundance with the black. Although there were surprisingly few wrinkles in the man's face, there were lines around his eyes and the corners of his mouth that indicated he liked to laugh.

"Name's Ole Sam, least that's what most calls me. Full name's Samuel Jeremiah Close. I's born in N'Orleans, I's told and I do remember's livin' there for a long time."

"That means you came from the south, too," said Elias.

"I reckon I do. Don' remember living nowhere's else until 'bout twelve year ago. I lived in N'Orleans even back when Old Hickory came and run out them British. I's 'bout ten year old then, I b'leive."

"Gee," said Elias, "that would make you around 60 years old now, wouldn't it?"

"Don' rightly know, but I do know that up at Fort Leavenworth I got's my chance to be free fo' sho' and I took it." The old man got a big grin on his face as he continued his story.

"I's right there the day Genr'l Lane said he was gonna enlist up a bunch of us black folks and make 'the best damn army anyone ever did see.' I believed 'im, too, and I figure he done it, cause here we are and we doin' what we set out to."

Elias couldn't stop staring at the sparkle in Old Sam's eyes. "You know?" said Elias, "we are the wild flowers after all; there's no weeds in this army."

"Don' reckon I know what ya mean, but I do know we sposin' t' get back on the road now," said Sam as he heard the bugler.

Averaging 18 miles per day, General Thayer's forces arrived at Fort Smith on May the 16th. There had been no opposition other than from a few partisan bands roaming the woods and mountains. Only several wounded on either side was reported.

Elias did notice a striking difference as they entered the town from the south. Two Union spies had reported to Major T.J. Anderson, Assistant Adjutant-General, District of the Frontier, that Southern forces were on their way north to attack Forts Smith and Gibson. Fearing just such a move earlier, soldiers and even a few townspeople were asked to help fortify the town.

Two new forts were built, one to the south and one to the east of the town of Fort Smith, in order to command the roads from those directions. Guns were mounted so as to be able to cover any approaching enemy from the front or flank. Trees had been felled and left in place to provide not only an open field of fire, but a hindrance to advancing infantry and cavalry. It was well known that Fort Smith, being a town of mostly southern sympathizers, easily provided Confederate scouts with information as to the Union strength in troops and guns.

Due to the wet spring, the Arkansas River had been almost constantly navigable, which enabled the fort to be well stocked with supplies, a condition General Thayer was counting on. It was said that there were enough supplies for ten to twelve thousand men for six months. He was certain he would finally be able to re-arm and clothe his men, as well as feed them some regular meals for a change. He was to be proven wrong.

It was soon learned that the southern force that was expected to attack was nothing more than a heavy scouting party sent out by General Maxey to test just how far north he could set up small reconnaissance posts.

"You men will continue to be busy with the rifle pits and trenches. The people here have been at this since early spring, but there is still much to be done. You'll be given a couple of days to get settled and back on your feet, but then it's back to work."

Elias eyed the lieutenant and then turned back to his haversack. He had been issued new clothing and even a pair of new boots. He was glad to be able to throw away his old undergarments and the two pair of socks he had been nursing along.

Looking down at his torn and worn boots, Elias almost hated

to throw them away. They had been through the many difficulties he had experienced and brought him safely back. They had protected his feet as he carried Toby along the Camden road. They had allowed him to make the difficult journey north, to and through Jenkins Ferry. They had served him well and deserved more that a rubbish heap.

"Now that's really dumb," Elias said out loud. He began to giggle and then to laugh so hard he could hardly stand. "But thanks anyway," and into the trash went the ragged boots.

After a bath and a supper of ham, greens and a large potato, Elias unwrapped his book. It was a copy of *"Marmion"* by Sir Walter Scott. He had never owned a book of his own before but had the opportunity to trade a rubber ground sheet to a private in Co. K for this one. He had hidden it in his shirt on the way north and was determined not to give it up, no matter what.

"Don't make much sense t' me, some funny kind a' poetry, I reckon," said the young soldier. "I got it from a Reb lieutenant prisoner. He brung it from Virginy but was hungry enuf to gimme that there book and a rubber jacket fer some bacon and bread. Y' can have the book, but I'm keepin' the jacket."

The language was very different from what Elias had ever heard, and he didn't understand much of the poetry either. But there was one passage that he now read over and over, as he felt more alone than ever before in his life.

You can see that all is loneliness;
And silence aids – though the steep hills
Send to the lake a thousand rills;
In summer tide, so soft they weep,
The sound but lulls the ear asleep;
Your horse's hoof-tread sounds too rude,
So stilly is the solitude.

Nought living meets the eye or ear,
But well I ween the dead are near;

For though, in feudal strife, a foe
Hath laid Our Lady's chapel low,
Yet still, beneath the hallowed soil,
The peasant rests him from his toil,
And, dying, bids his bones be laid
Where erst his simple fathers prayed.

"I didn't know you were a reader."

Elias looked up and saw Dr. Harrington standing over him.

"What I meant was," said the doctor with a bit of embarrassment, "I don't doubt that you can read, but …"

"I know," replied Elias with a smile. "This doesn't look like the kind of reading material a soldier like me would have."

"I have read some of Scott, too," said the doctor. "In fact, *"Marmion"* is my second best choice. I prefer *'Waverley.'* " The doctor looked down at the place at which Elias had his finger and read the passage.

"Isn't that a bit sad for such a sunny summer day?" he asked.

"I guess it's the way I feel. I have lost just about all my friends and, in a way, it helps me remember them. Friends are hard to come by and I don't …"

"But there are new friends to be made."

"Not like the ones I had," said Elias with a sadness in his voice. "They were men I could trust with my life and depend on."

"Don't you think there are any men like that left? You know, even Sir Walter Scott has his Marmion declare that there are many good men ready to fill the gap." The doctor took the book from Elias and thumbed back toward the front of the book until he found the passage he wanted.

"Now, in good sooth," Lord Marmion cried,
"Were I in warlike wise to ride,
A better guard I would not lack
Than your stout forayers at my back;"

Elias smiled as the doctor handed him back his book. "Thanks, Doc, I guess I was letting myself get too down in the dumps."

The following days were filled with more digging of rifle pits, cutting trees and building breastworks. There were still rumors of imminent attacks, and Confederate spies were said to be watching everything and passing it on to the enemy.

"You say there is a fella named Toothman living here that they figure is a spy?" asked Elias of a fellow worker.

"Yep. I heard the lieutenant say they were pretty sure he is, but they can't prove anything."

"I know that name from somewhere," said Elias as he stopped digging and racked his brain. "Yeah, I know now, that's the name of the people at the farm up at Island Mound in Missouri, where we had our first fight. They were Rebs and I bet this guy is from the same family. I better tell the lieutenant."

"I appreciate the information, Corporal, and I'll see that it's passed on. I'm not sure we can do much, though. There are so many Southern sympathizers we can't keep track of them all, and it would be hard to keep them away from the fortifications out here in the open."

Day after day the men worked. Elias and his men were assigned to the fort south of town on the Towson Road. "Back to old *Nigger Hill,*" said one of the men. Only this time they were staying inside. Each of the two newer forts had quarters for hundreds of men, and Elias was under a solid roof for the first time in a number of months.

Early on the morning of July 27th, firing could be heard from the south. It was learned that Generals Watie and Gano were launching a series of attacks to determine the actual strength of Fort Smith. A Union force was sent out to repulse an attack south of the town at Massard Prairie and was beaten back. At that time the Rebel troops fell back as if they had had enough. Actually, it was to be an ambush if the Federals had followed, and they would have, had the heat and lack of forage not caused the animals to be in such poor condition.

For the next couple of days, the action was light due to Watie's inability to cross the swollen Arkansas River. On the 30th, Watie's son, Saladin, was sent north between the Arkansas and the Poteau rivers to fire on the fort while Watie himself attacked along the Towson road. The attack was so successful that Watie and his men were able to help themselves to the dinner the Federals had prepared prior to being attacked.

The gain was a temporary one for the Confederates, as two companies of the 1st Kansas rallied and took on the Rebels from rifle pits. Just as the Confederate battery of howitzers seemed to be gaining, two sections of the 2nd Kansas Battery brought their 10-pounder Parrot guns to bear and drove the enemy back.

One Federal artillery shell landed in the midst of enemy battery horses, killing three and wounding several more. General Douglas Cooper's personal escort raced through the fire and cut the wounded horses from their harnesses, enabling the cannons to be saved.

The shelling and skirmishing continued off and on for the next two days until the evening of August 1st, at which time the Confederates headed back south. As soon as the enemy fled, work was begun at once to clear the immediate area between the rivers in order to have a better field of fire should another attack be made.

"I have absolutely no idea what to do with them all, Captain." General Steele was replying to a question put to him by a member of his staff concerning the number of refugees pouring into Fort Smith. "There are hundreds coming in daily and we can't shelter, much less feed them all. Our men are beginning to go on short rations, and the animals are in dreadful condition. We will just have to send them on. That's all I know to do."

General Steele ordered a train of 180 wagons to take as many of the homeless as possible to Fort Scott. The train was then to be loaded with supplies and return as soon as the turn around could be made.

On the 14th, Colonel Williams and the 1st Kansas Colored were sent to Fort Gibson to help protect the Indian Territory from Confederate raiding parties.

"At least there'll be no more digging trenches for awhile," said Elias with a sigh.

"Oh, sho," came the response from Old Sam, "I wouldn't bet on it."

After arriving at Fort Gibson, Elias was approached by Sergeant Sam Wilson of Co. K.

"We need that forage badly, and Co. K is short a Corporal. Will you volunteer to go along? It will only be for a day or two, and your job will be just to help protect and assist the men of the 2nd Kansas Cavalry. They would never order you to go, but I would consider it a favor if you would fill in for us. Ya' see, I got several sick and …"

Elias was pretty sure that the favor requested probably came from higher up and was almost the same thing as an order, but with a smile and a nod, agreed to go with the foraging party.

"We appreciate it, Elias. Now if you will report to Lieutenant Sutherland and let him know you're filling in, he will let you know just when we're leaving. I believe we're going up north a few miles to a place called Flat Rock."

"I know the place," nodded Elias. "We've been through there."

"There are some fine grass lands there and it shouldn't take long to get a goodly amount of hay for the animals. Lord knows it is certainly needed."

Elias smiled, waved and started off across the fort to find the lieutenant. "Oh well, why not?"[1]

[1] See map on page 99.

Chapter 29

Friday, September 16, 1864

Captain Edgar A. Barker sat his horse and watched his haying crew cut and bundle the forage. Hay was loaded onto wagons as they slowly went from one group of cutters and tiers to the next. The men of the 1st Kansas assisted at times but generally kept watch and patrolled the perimeter of the area.

"It looks like about 200 men, Captain," reported one of the scouts sent out to check if any enemy was in the immediate area.

"All right," said Barker, sternly, "with this much advance notice, I believe we can handle ourselves. Have the bugler sound recall. We'll form up in that ravine over there for cover and see how the Rebs like fighting when they're in the open."

"How's come you got yourself a name like that?" asked Private Jesse Vaughn. His question was directed to Private James K. Polk, along with a request for a drink from Polk's canteen. The sun was hot and the water none too plentiful although several canteens were brought by each man.

"Well," replied Polk, "jes how'd you get yo' name? I suppose you was born Mr. Jesse, High-&-Mighty, Vaughn."

"Sure I was," replied Jesse. "I have you know that there was lots of Vaughns back in Missouri. In fact, we probably had some kings named Vaughn way back in our family too. I jes ain't never had a chance t'…" Gun shots! Jesse ducked and quickly looked around in all directions!

Musket fire rang out over the fields, and several men of the 2nd Kansas fell. To the south and east, Confederates could be seen running across the fields. The men in the fields had dropped their scythes and rakes, searched for their weapons and headed for cover just in time. The men of the 1st immediately began to return the enemy's fire and crouched along the edge of the hay field lining up targets in their sights.

Fifteen minutes earlier, Captain Barker had moved ahead to see for himself what kind of force he would be up against and found to his horror that instead of 200 there were more like 2,000 accompanied by artillery. Quickly returning, skirmishing all the way, Barker had his men dismount, join the others and prepare for battle.

After almost half an hour of repulsing Rebel charges, Barker determined that the Confederate Texans and Indians had them completely surrounded and they would soon be wiped out to a man. Frantically looking around,. Barker spotted what he felt was a weak spot in the Confederate line.

"To horse," came the cry from the captain as he brandished his pistol, firing in vain toward the charging Rebel force. The cavalrymen, obeying the order of their commander, raced for their animals and leaped for their saddles. In mass, the cavalry troops raced toward the charging infantry. Men sagged in their saddles and dropped to the ground as a result of the withering fire from the Rebels. Horses screamed and stumbled, throwing their riders directly into the charging forces. Union cavalrymen scrambling to their feet were shot point blank as they tried to escape.

"Stay in the ravine," yelled Lieutenant Sutherland, "and for God's sake, keep your heads down."

"Oh Lordy," cried Private Butler, "they must be a thousand of 'em."

"They's more'n we got, that for sure," answered Private Lindsy, as he crouched in the dirt.

When the first charge came, Elias dove to the bottom of the ravine just as a musket ball smashed through the head of Private Polk. Wiping the dirt from his rifle, Elias allowed his head to move just far enough above the rim of the ravine to see the Rebel charge pause to reload. Men around him were searching their ammunition pouches for additional shot. Rebels could be seen firing from the front, each flank and now from behind the ravine. Barker was right. They were surrounded and outnumbered ten to one.

Loading and firing, Co. K of the 1st showed the Indians and Texans that they were a force that was there to fight. The banners of Watie and Gano's forces fluttered in the sun as the Rebels yelled taunts over their rifle fire.

Three times the Confederates had charged the black troops that were hunkered down in the ravine, and three times they were repulsed. The Union force was taking heavy casualties even with the concealment, but the worst was yet to come.

Suddenly a large patch of earth exploded in front of them.

"They've brought up their artillery," shouted Corporal Hays. "Watch yourself …"

A piece of grape shot tore through the chest of the corporal and he toppled backwards into the bottom of the ravine. More canister and grape flew through the air and landed increasingly close to the small Union force. Elias was certain he had seen at least three or four of the mounted 2nd get through the Rebel line, but help would be too far away to save Co. K.

The artillery seemed to have the exact range and dropped their shells all along the ravine. Screams and moans could be heard up and down the thinning line of blue-clad infantry as they fought vainly to survive. The men on both sides of Elias had been seriously wounded, and several were trying to claw their way along the bottom of the ravine at his feet.

A Rebel shell landed just a few feet to Elias' right, sending a shower of dirt and several bodies into the air. Elias felt the shock of the blast and suddenly, hearing only a roar in his ears, he felt himself dropping into a deep, black hole of silence.

The sun was casting an orange blanket over the half-cut hay field as Elias opened his eyes. There was a haze to everything within his sight, and he felt as if a great weight had been placed on his chest. He lay still trying to get his senses back and remember what had happened. There was a bad odor in the air, and he could not clear his head to understand exactly where he was. He knew he had to do something to be able to breathe.

With his head still swimming he tried to move. Dirt fell into his face, and something rolled over next to his head. He was staring into a pair of dark brown, glazed-over eyes. Blood had oozed from the nostrils, and Elias jerked back from the face of Sergeant Sam Wilson. Slowly the body slid toward the bottom of the ravine, seemingly keeping its sightless eyes on Elias.

Elias lay still, as the memory of the battle came back to him. He listened for sounds of the enemy or of other of his comrades that might have survived. There was still a slight ringing in Elias' ears as he lay motionless, afraid to move for fear of attracting attention.

After several minutes of almost total silence, Elias pushed another body and what seemed like fifty pounds of dirt off of him and turned on to his stomach. He was sore and hurt all over and had a terrible headache but apparently was otherwise unharmed. Slowly he peered over the top of the embankment at a field strewn with the bodies of the men of Co. K. A number of horses lay off to the east, a bleak indication of the fate of many of the 2nd Cavalry, but the enemy was gone.

Elias sat back on his heels for a few minutes, found his rifle and canteen and took a drink of the warm water. Slowly he got to his feet, tripping over the body of Sergeant Wilson, and then slowly walked along the bottom of the ravine. It was evident that many of the men of Co. K had not only been killed or wounded, but shot at close range as they lay in the dirt.

"Over here," came a whisper. Elias looked ahead of him and saw a Union soldier push himself up on to his elbows. "They all gone?" he asked. Elias did not know the man's name, but knew he was from Co. K.

"I think so," replied Elias. "You okay?"

"Better'n these guys," came the reply. "Just got a burn along my side, anyone else alive?"

"Haven't seen anyone else yet, I just woke up myself. I guess a shell went off and knocked me out."

"They must not have noticed you. They came through here shootin' and stabbin' everyone. Poor old Ponket had fell over me and they put a bayonet into him figurin' they got me too, I guess."

"Come on," said Elias as he held out a hand to the man, "let's see about getting out of here in case they come back."

Very early the morning of the 17th, Elias made his report. "Yes, Sir, I'm afraid this is all there is of us. Anyway, all I know of. I'm not sure how many of Captain Barker's men got away, but it didn't look to me like over four or five, if that many.

"We managed to find these two horses that the Rebs didn't get and made our way back here to Fort Gibson during the night." Elias shook his head. "I didn't think I would ever see anything like that again after Poison Springs. Even Lieutenant Sutherland is dead. I still don't see how any of us got away."

"I'm pretty sure they got them a few prisoners, tho," said one of the other survivors. "I was keepin' m' head down and tryin' not even t' breath, but I did hear somebody call out that they had a live one and then drug him off. Leastwise they weren't no shootin' and so's they must'a took 'im."

"They'll learn about the train from Fort Scott, sure as hell," said Captain Benjamin G. Jones, of Co. B.

"We've got to warn them or at least send them an escort," stated Colonel Wattles. "Get Williams and tell him to be ready to leave right away."

"You one of 'em that got back okay from Flat Rock?"

Elias looked at the man on horseback and nodded.

The man hesitated, looked to his right and then to his left and said, in a low voice, "I just wanted to say that I'm sorry."

"For what," asked Elias?

"For us runnin' out on you fellas the way we did." The young cavalryman shifted uneasily in his saddle. "Ya' see, I'm one of

Barker's men and we just up and ran and well ..."

"There was nothing else you could do," said Elias quietly. "You probably would have been killed if you had stayed and that wouldn't have helped us or anyone but the Rebs."

"I ... well ... I just mean, well I just wanted to say ..."

"Never mind, I understand. I really do."

"No I gotta say it. I gotta say it out loud. We ran and I'm sorry. Maybe there was nuthin' we could 'a done, but really, we're not a runnin' bunch."

"I know that," replied Elias, as he walked over and held out his hand to the young soldier. "When we need help, I know you'll be there if there's anything you can do. I really mean that."

"You really don't have to go, Corporal. You just got back and after what you went through, you deserve a rest. All we'll be doing is just escorting the train back." Colonel Williams tried to make it sound like a routine assignment and then added, "At least I hope that's all."

"If it's all the same, Sir, I would rather go along. Nothing happened to me to cause me to be left behind, and I don't want to miss being with my men, Sir. We belong together." Colonel Williams looked at Elias, smiled, returned the salute and headed toward the officers' barracks.

The sun was at mid-morning as the men headed north to meet the supply train from Fort Scott. Colonel Williams rode toward the head of the column that consisted of his 1st Kansas Colored, the 54th U. S. Colored, the 11th U. S. Colored Infantry and one section of artillery.

"Don't look t' me like this here is just an escort for some supply train," said Old Sam. "that there man is lookin' fer a fight." The old soldier motioned toward Colonel Williams ahead in the morning light.

"I know he's worried," replied Elias. "Watie and Gano have either been too lucky or had way too much information about what we're doing."

Chapter 30

Monday, September 19, 1864 Pryor Creek

Colonel Williams sat astride his nearly exhausted horse and looked at his pocket watch. It was a little after ten o'clock in the morning. He and his men had covered a little over eighty miles in less than 48 hours. Having no baggage wagons, the men had carried their canteens and haversacks and were completely worn out.

"What did you find?" asked the Colonel of one of his scouts.

"It's Watie and Gano's men, Colonel, and a hell of a lot of 'em, uh … beggin' your pardon, Sir. And I believe they have artillery with 'em." The young officer took off his hat and wiped away the perspiration. "And … looks like they've already captured the supply train."

"Damn, we're too late." The Colonel shook his head and then sat upright. "Get the skirmishers out. We're going to do what we can to at least get back part of that train," he stated defiantly. "Move the artillery to the rear and on each flank." The Colonel turned in his saddle and motioned toward his tired infantry. "Form them in double ranks behind the skirmishers. We'll proceed from here."

Stretching out a quarter of a mile, the Union force moved ahead as the Confederate infantry opened up on the advance Union skirmishers.

Elias could hear the firing and determinedly gripped his rifle, ready and even anxious to meet the Rebels again. He could not erase the picture in his mind of the bodies of the men of Co. K lying over the battlefield at Flat Rock. Tired as he was, tired as they all were, the men of the 1st were ready for action. They were more than veterans; they were seasoned, hard-fighting soldiers. "Whatever it takes," said Elias out loud, "whatever it takes!"

Old Sam, standing next to Elias, looked over at the young corporal and grinned. "You got that right, Son."

A warm feeling crept up Elias' spine. He looked to his left to see "Honey" Carson, another of his new friends, nodding and motioning toward the Rebels with his bayonet.

The breeze had picked up and the Union colors were waving proudly. The enemy line was being tested as the main Union force firmly advanced. The enemy was within musket range when Colonel Williams ordered his men to halt. With a defiant tone, he ordered parade rest.

"We'll let them come to us," muttered the Colonel. Reinforcing his skirmishers on the front and each flank, the Colonel let his men rest awaiting the inevitable attack.

Throughout the day there was constant skirmishing. Elias and his men continued to wait in anticipation of the coming battle. Men searched their pockets for something to eat. Hard crackers were washed down with warm water. Elias chewed on a bit of dried beef that had been hidden in the bottom of a pocket. The unseasonably cool morning had turned into another warm afternoon. The collar of Elias' wool shirt chafed the back of his neck.

"What the hell are they waiting …"

"Honey" Carson had hardly gotten the words out of his mouth when the Confederate artillery opened up and the Gray infantry charged. It was 4:30 in the afternoon when Colonel Williams ordered his artillery forward. Cannons on the front and both flanks opened with shot, shell and canister as the Rebel infantry came within range. Large holes appeared in the prairie as the guns from both armies searched for the proper range.

"Watch over on the right," shouted Elias, to Old Sam. "There's a bunch trying to get through."

"I see 'em," said the old soldier as he leveled his rifle and dropped a color bearer. The flag was immediately picked up by the Confederate next to the fallen soldier only to go down for the second time as the new standard bearer was also shot.

Elias saw several of the men around him drop to the ground from wounds from enemy muskets and artillery. Elias Myers, the private with which Elias shared a first name, fell into the ditch. Then Newton Johnson and Charlie Strans went down. The smoke hung along the ground, as always, making it hard to see.

Elias searched his ammunition pouch for shot and found he was completely out. Moving to the edge of a water-filled ditch along the road, Elias stooped to take the ammo pouch from Spencer Gifford, a dead comrade. Just then an artillery shell burst at his immediate right. For an instant Elias felt himself hit hard and lifted into the air. Spinning around, Elias saw the water in the ditch rushing up toward him. Then, for Corporal Elias Mothers, the battle ended. All was quiet.

No sound, no feeling, no consciousness!

Colonel Williams' force continued the fight until dusk. Ordered to bivouac along the battle line in case of another attack, the Union forces dropped in their tracks. Many of the men didn't even try to prepare any food. Men took turns trying to stay awake in order not to be surprised by the enemy. The area was searched for wounded, and those found were treated as best they could be. Lights were hidden behind whatever could be rigged in order for the surgeon to work on the hurt and dying.

"I never saw it happen," said "Honey." "I just sort 'a come on 'im."

Sam Close knelt next to the still form of Elias.

"When things started to slow down some," "Honey" continued, "I happen to look over in the middle of the road and then's when I saw it. At first I couldn't make out just whut it was, but then I did."

"What you see, Boy?" insisted Ole Sam.

"I seen this here arm. Least that's whut I thought it was, just a arm. Then I seen this here hand barely stickin' out'n the sleeve. And th' hand didn' have no thumb."

"I'll never know how he stayed alive," said the doctor as he continued to work on Elias.

"I reckon it's cause when he lit in that there ditch, the stub of his arm dug right smack into the clay. I betcha that's whut kept 'im from bleedin' t' death."

The doctor and his aide had cleaned the stump of Elias' right arm and had trimmed away the meat and bone from below the elbow. Elias had lost a considerable amount of blood, but not as much as would have been expected. His breathing was at times shallow, but his pulse was fairly steady.

"He's lucky to be alive," continued the doctor. "I found several pieces of shell fragments in his shoulder and a small one in the right chest muscle. Now, as long as we can keep him from pneumonia I would give him at least an even chance."

"That's all this one needs," stated Sam with conviction. "That's all he ever asked fer. I heerd 'im say it several times; 'Just a chance!'"

Chapter 31

Sunday, November 6, 1864   Fort Scott

"Kind'a nice Sunday morning, huh, Elias?" the chaplain grasped Elias' left hand as Elias left the door of the church.

"Yes, Sir," he said rather haltingly, "guess it is."

The chaplain continued to greet the men as they left church and thanked them for attending. Many of the men were veterans of a number of battles, then, having been wounded and ultimately sent to the Fort Scott hospital. Elias was in hopes he might get some word about George Brothers, but knew that George would have been gone many months before Elias arrived. All Elias could learn was that a couple of the hospital workers remembered a big, one-legged colored man that had been treated and then left in early fall of '63. Elias couldn't even remember exactly where George was from. There were several things Elias had trouble remembering since his wound at Pryor Creek. Things had been hazy for several weeks, and many of the details were just now coming back to him.

He had been told that during the night after the battle, Watie and Gano had quietly moved away from Pryor Creek and headed southwest. Colonel Williams' men were too tired to give chase so they returned to Flat Rock and then to Fort Gibson.

None of the other wounded had been sent to Fort Scott, so Elias had little word about the actual outcome of the battle. Old Sam had sent him a message, by word of mouth, about young Will Taylor. Elias had left Will with a Baptist minister who put Will with a family in Little Rock. A teamster brought word to Fort Gibson that Will had run away, but was found and given to a couple that had a farm west of the town. Near as anyone knew,

Will was still there.

Elias had a letter written to his mother a few weeks after arriving at Fort Scott, but did not tell her about his wound. Elias wasn't certain how he felt about being a cripple and how he would handle his life when he returned home. He had been assured that he would be able to work and be almost as useful as he had been before the loss of his arm. Elias still wasn't convinced. He couldn't see himself as a one-armed farmer. Freedom, for Elias, would now be a little less sweet. He had told himself that his efforts were not just for himself, but for his family and other black families as well. Still, as he tried to dress himself, learn to write left-handed and decide he would have to wear boots instead of shoes with laces, he wondered how many other things he hadn't thought of would be difficult or impossible for him to accomplish.

"But just think of all the things you have ahead that you can do," he had been told several times. At least he had made up his mind about two things. First, he would not feel sorry for himself, at least not much. Second, he would make the most of whatever came his way, "regardless of how little it may be," he said to himself.

"That sounds more like still feelin' sorry for y'self, t' me." Elias suddenly heard "China Bill's" voice in his mind. Wanting to frown but forced to smile, Elias said out loud, "You just can't leave me alone, can you?"

"Who can't leave you alone?" said Tilly Brown.

"Huh?" said Elias startled at Tilly's voice. "Oh nothing, no one."

Tilly Brown was a black boy from the Indian Territory whose parents had been owned by a Cherokee family. Shortly after the war began, his family ran away, made their way north and Tilly joined the Indian Brigade. He got to be called Tilly because his young sister, due to a speech impediment, couldn't say Billy. She called him Tilly, so everyone else did so the cute little girl wouldn't feel badly.

"Who you thinkin' 'bout that couldn't leave you alone? Probably some gal back home, huh?"

"Oh sure, I had to run from all the girls back home," laughed Elias. "No, it was an old friend. Well, I guess you would call him an old friend even though I only knew him for a couple of years. He was some older than me, but a lot smarter. He was wise in the ways of people, and I learned a lot from him. Even now I sometimes remember something he said that I didn't catch on to right then."

"He gone on home?" asked Tilly.

"Yeah," said Elias, first with sadness and then back with the smile. "He retired from the army and went home."

"Maybe you kin visit him sometime," assured Tilly.

"Oh, I will. You can count on that. And we'll have lots to talk about."

"Hope you have somethin' better t' talk about than us just sittin' like we doin' " said Tilly. "I needs to git myself home and get back t' m' work." Tilly had begun to learn the blacksmith trade just before he entered the army and was anxious to get back to it. "All's I got's t' do is git used to this here wooden stump I got fer a leg and I'll be right back in binness."

Elias was impressed with the eagerness of the man. Tilly had lost his left leg shortly before Elias had lost his arm. Tilly didn't seem to look upon himself as a cripple, just a man that had to work a little harder than he used to at getting things done.

"You know, maybe I …"

"Maybe you whut?" asked Tilly.

"Oh, nothing, I believe I've made up my mind that there will be no maybe about it."

"Okay if'n I don't understand whut you're talkin' 'bout?"

"Sho nuff," said Elias with a big grin.

Elias had been given a ride in one of the wagons headed for Fort Leavenworth. It was thought at first that he would have to report in at Fort Leavenworth to be mustered out of the army, but was able to get it done just before he left Fort Scott. He would leave the train in Lawrence and hope to be home by Thanksgiving. It would be a bittersweet return to his family, but Elias had decided that he was going to be able to make the best of what he had. He had been given the chance he so desperately wanted, he had served, and now it looked like the war would soon be over and their freedom would be assured. What more could he want?

Elias had turned down a chance to ride out to the farm. He had arrived in Lawrence on Tuesday, the 22nd, three days after the deaths of Captains Macey and Welch at Timber Hills. Elias had missed that fight. He spent an hour or two looking over the changes since the burning of the town over a year ago. The Eldridge Hotel was back in business as were most of the stores up and down Massachusetts Street. There were several new establishments that had sprung up in this still rapidly growing town.

He met several people he and his mother had known and had quickly answered their questions and hurried on. He met with several stares as he walked the street, still in uniform. To his surprise, some folks almost looked down their noses at him. He felt strangely conspicuous and uncomfortable. He hadn't expected to be welcomed as a hero, but he was at least hoping for acceptance as a regular member of the community. "Maybe things haven't changed as much as I thought," Elias said to himself.

Putting the thought from his mind, he started west, wanting to get to the Wallace's place before dark. The fields showed the stubble of harvested crops as he made his way along the dirt road. Occasionally livestock could be seen up close to the farm houses. Stock was precious and was seldom out of sight by the owner. Elias was glad to be able to walk the country without having to worry about being shot at or having to run for cover.

Soon the surrounding country began to look very familiar. He wondered just how much had changed since he had been away. He was somewhat surprised when he considered that he had been gone only a little over two years. It seemed so much longer than that. He felt he had left home a boy and was returning a grown man. A man with many more experiences than someone of his age should have. He had seen many men die and had learned to grab and hold on to little pleasures that earlier had been almost ignored. The sun, as it set in the west, showed a beautiful golden orange across the sky and across the fields. *Just as it had over the field at Flat Rock.*

Elias tried to put the thought from his mind, yet he knew it would always be there. He would live with both worlds. Enjoying the new one that was ahead of him and remembering the old one that had paid the price.

The barnyard was deserted. The house and outbuildings seemed to be exactly the way he had left them. He almost expected to see the ax with its blade buried in the old stump next to the door of his mother's cabin, just the way he had left it. There were a few flowers around the cabin door that had been planted after he had gone. Some work had been done to the place, but not near as much as should have been. Elias knew that the Wallaces' two sons had joined the army, but he was pretty certain that Vern would not leave unless forced to. Perhaps Vern had not been able to keep the place up as he should have. Maybe there was a good reason

The Wallaces managed to buy the place with a house and one small shed, and then build a good-size barn. The cabin was added to the barn as a place for his mother, his brother and himself to live off by themselves.

Just then the door to their cabin opened.

"Oh, my God," came the cry from his mother as she recognized Elias. Tears flooded her eyes as she wrung her hands in her apron and half ran, half stumbled across the barnyard. "Oh, my God, it's my boy! Oh, thank you, God! Oh, thank You!"

Elias raised his good arm and the stump of his right one as his mother flew to him. "Hi Mama, it's me. I'm home. I'm home for good."

Chapter 32

"Oh, glory, glory," she cried as she took his face in both her hands. "Joy, joy!"

"You surprised to see me, Mama?"

"Surprised and so happy. What a Thanksgiving Day this will be. Oh, let me look at you." His mother stood back and looked on her boy with pride.

"I guess I do look a little different, huh, Mama?"

"Why you look just exactly the way I remember," she said, still admiring her son.

"Well, I guess I do look a little different, though." Elias moved his right arm slightly.

"Well, all I see is a boy grown into a man," said his mother as she placed her hands on her hips. "Looks like they haven't been feeding you like I would had you been home, but other than that," she paused, "other than that I guess you just look pretty good to your mother."

Placing her arm around his waist, she began to lead him to the Wallaces' house. Elias put his left arm over his mother's shoulder and smiled at the way she had almost totally ignored the fact that one arm was missing below the elbow. He felt he was probably more proud of her than she was of him.

The door to the Wallace home opened and Susan Wallace came out on the small porch. At the sight of Elias, she let out a cry of joy and called back inside.

"Oh Tom, you must come see."

Tom Wallace appeared in the door behind his wife. With a yell, he burst off the porch and rushed to embrace Elias.

"Would you look at the soldier boy," he said, as he held Elias at arm's length. "I guess I better say, look at the soldier *man.* Are you home for good or just for a short time? Golly. Let me look at you. He looks great, doesn't he, Susan?"

Elias felt his face flush at the attention. No one seemed to notice his missing arm. Maybe he was not such a freakish-looking person after all. Still, these folks were just like family. His elation was immediately dampened as Vern emerged from the house.

"Ain't no way he could go back, Dad, look at 'im. What happened to yer arm there? Guess yer all finished now, huh?"

Tom Wallace glared at his adopted son as the smiles faded from Susan and Elias' mother's faces. Some things never change. Vern was one of them.

"Don't worry, Mama, everything's going to be just fine," assured Elias after he and his mother had returned to their cabin. "I'm sorry to hear that both of the Wallace boys are missing. Maybe they are just prisoners somewhere. You know the war isn't over yet, and when it is I'm sure there will be lots of prisoners set free and get back home."

"No, Son. They know for sure that George is dead. They've had no definite word about James as yet, but haven't heard from him for almost a year."

Elias looked at his mother. "You haven't told me about Cheat, Mother. What's happened to him?"

Elias' mother raised her head and with tear in her eyes began the story of his younger brother. "For about four months after you left, he wandered about the farm all quiet and not at all like his happy little self. I thought for sure he would come out of it, but he grew more and more quiet and wouldn't play or go fishing or do any of the things he liked to do before." Elias' mother smoothed the apron over her lap. "After your first letter I thought sure he would perk up, but he didn't. He just seemed to get worse. Then the Wallaces got word about George. It was just a few days after that that Cheat left."

"What? Left …?" stammered Elias.

Mrs. Mothers arose from her chair and walked to the screen door. "He didn't even take his coat." She burst into tears. "That's the last we seen of him, Elias. I don't know what's happened to my little boy." Her sobs shook her shoulders as she buried her face in her apron.

After somewhat composing herself, she continued. "Of course, we asked all over town. Two people said they thought they saw him in town early the next day, then he was gone. No one seems to know where he has gone. Mr. Wallace asked the folks in town to keep watch, but nothing has happened."

Elias stood, walked to his mother and placed his good arm around her. Kissing the top of her head, he said, "Don't worry, Mama."

The rest of the evening was spent by Elias telling his mother of his friends and some of what happened to them and him. He told of the fun times the fellas had and how close they had grown. He told of One Shoe, Slows, young Toby and his struggle with his language, and of George, including the fact that he had lost a leg.

He told of his special kinship with China Bill, and how he almost daily remembered something Bill had tried to get Elias to understand.

"I'm going to miss them, Mama. They were the family I had while I was away from you. They took very good care of your son, Mama. They helped give me, yes, and give all of us our chance. We made a difference, Mama. Just like the boys back east are making a difference. And they will keep on making that difference until everyone is free." Elias looked into his mother's eyes. "Everyone's gonna be free, Mama, just like we are. And we are going to stay free, cause we were given that chance and we proved we deserved it."

"I'm so proud," said Elias' mother.

A couple of days later, Elias left the cabin to wander over the farm and see what changes had been made while he had been gone. Out past the barn, across a garden patch and on toward the river he walked. The sky was clear and cool as the late afternoon sun fell toward the western horizon.

As Elias crawled through a fence, his foot caught, and in falling he thrust out both arms in an attempt to catch himself. His right arm, missing the lower half, went forward digging the end of the stump in the hard-packed ground.

"Oh, damn!' cried Elias. He turned onto to his back, grasping the throbbing end of his arm with his left hand. Struggling to a sitting position, he held his arm in his lap and rocked back and forth. The pain had shot up to his shoulder and then caused his elbow to sting deep within the joint.

"You've more pain than that ahead of you, Elias."

Startled, Elias looked up toward the sound, only to be blinded by the lowering sun. In front of him was a figure on a horse or mule. All Elias could make out was a completely black image whose features were made indistinguishable by the golden-orange sun at its back. The voice was deep and resonant, with an eerie, almost echo to it.

"You've done well, Elias Mothers. You asked for a chance and did your best with what you were given. Many have sought opportunities, but few of us have been granted the satisfaction of knowing we made the most of our part in this great battle between subjugation and freedom."

"I don't understand. Do I know you? Your voice sounds sort of familiar but …"

"Oh yes, Elias. We have met. You were of great service, and I did not, nor will I ever forget what you did. You thought at the time that it was of little value, but it was just as important as the contribution of any of us."

The gentle evening breeze caused a movement about the head of the darkened figure. "Don't let the beard confuse you. It was only to allow me more time to accomplish my mission."

"Your mission, I guess I still don't … a … Mr …?"

"You may call me John, but the name is not important. I am

here to advise you that although you feel you have done your part and earned your freedom, there is still a long way to go. You are not yet free."

"But, Sir … a … John, the war is practically over and that will ensure us of our freedom."

"Not by a damn site, Elias! Don't get it into your head that it is over. It is just beginning." The voice seemed to deepen and encompass the entire countryside. Anger seemed to grow as the booming voice continued.

"You saw how you were looked upon when you entered Lawrence. You are still a black man, Elias. They will never forget that no matter where you go. You have proved little to them even though you feel you have more than done your duty."

"But here in Kansas we are free. There are no slaves. Even without the war we …"

"Is that what you felt when you were in town? Were you looked upon as an equal? Not yet. But that is your challenge, Elias. That is the rest of your work, a work that is far from over. You must overcome, Elias. The way will be difficult and you will be treated unfairly. You will have to go further and work harder to make people understand that you are just as much of a man as anyone. And you must take that challenge and become an example. You must be wiser, more trustworthy, kinder and stand taller than any man of any race."

"But," there was exasperation in Elias' voice. "How am I to do such a thing? And why should it be up to me?"

"It is up to all men to be all they can, Elias. I was a failure in most everything I did. I worked hard and got nowhere until I recognized the path God had for me. My last endeavor pained me because I did not have the multitude at my side that I expected, but that mission was triumphant and will be sung about until all are free.

"Your road will be all the more difficult because you are different. You will have to fight, and many times alone, as did we. The demands will be many, but you are aware of great black men that have overcome adversity. It will be no different for you. You have the ability and I believe you have the courage. That's why I came here."

"But I still don't know ..." The pain was still coursing up Elias' arm, and it caused him to feel a little faint and sick to his stomach. "Please, just tell me who...."

"We are proud of you Elias; Bill, Amos and I. And you are a hero to Cheat. You can do what it takes, Elias, whatever it takes!"

Elias tried to get to his knees. He let go of his aching arm and pulled himself up until he could lean on the fence. Sweat beaded on his brow and there was a ringing in his ears. "You're asking a lot," spoke Elias through clenched teeth. "and I don't even know ...."

The image was gone. Turning from side to side, Elias saw only empty space. Not a sound, not a shadow could he see. There was not a soul in sight. Where could he ... it have gone. And that voice, it was somehow familiar and yet it seemed to come from far away, like an echo in a vast cave, resounding and penetrating. Perhaps it was someone he had spoken with some time ago, someone he met while in the Army? Whoever it was seemed to know not only himself but Amos and Bill and ... and ... Cheat! How could he know? Why didn't he identify himself? Where had he gone? And why did he come? Was it just to tell him that his job was not done? To tell him that all his efforts and the loss of his arm counted for practically nothing?

"I don't want to fight any longer! I have done my job!" Elias screamed at the top of his lungs. Then again he sank to his knees. "It *is* finished! It *has* to be enough! How much ... how ... much more ...? I have given all I ..."

"I don't want to hear that," came the voice of Bill Foster in Elias' mind. "You know better."

This time Elias was sure he was just remembering what Bill had said to him in the past. There was no dark image, no eerie presence. In fact, it was a comforting feeling that came over Elias as he stood up and braced himself against the fence post. Was this just the end of the beginning? Would he have to prove himself again, perhaps over and over again? Could he do it? Was it worth it?

"You know it's worth it, Son," said Elias' mother after he had related his experience. "I have always taught you that we must do whatever it takes to make our way in an honorable and Lord lovin' way." She looked deep into Elias' eyes, "Whatever it takes!"

"Yes, Mama," said Elias. His voice was low and quiet. He felt somewhat guilty about his feelings. He had been so proud of his accomplishments and that of his friends of the 1st. Now, it appeared there was so much more to do. Was he up to it? Bill and Mama thought he was, and even John … John! Who was this person? How did he know whether Elias could or even wanted to take on the task of proving to the rest of the world that he and others like him were just as much of a man as any person of any race?

Then Elias remembered the words he had said to his mother that very afternoon before he went for his walk. *"Everyone's gonna be free, Mama, just like we are. And we are going to stay free, cause we were given that chance and we proved we deserved it."*

"Well, Mama, there's more to it now, and soon I guess I'll have to get to it," said Elias.

"What do you mean, Son?"

"Well to begin with … Cheat, Mama. I've got to find him. Like you said, Mama … whatever it takes."

"I'm comin', Little Brother!"

"What Ever It Takes!"

Epilogue

From October 1864 through October of 1865, the 1st Kansas Colored Volunteer Infantry, continued to serve by challenging the Confederates at places such as Timber Hill, Indian Territory, Joy's Ford and Clarksville, Arkansas, as well as many other encounters classed as minor skirmishes. It seems strange to classify as minor, any situation that puts men at risk of injury or death; yet the 1st, as well as many other brave commands, both Union and Confederate, did what they considered their duty to their God and their Country.

The 1st, known after December 13th, 1864, as the 79th United States Colored Troops, went from Fort Gibson to Fort Smith, to Little Rock, to Pine Bluff doing escort and garrison duty until being mustered out of the army October 1st, 1865. They were then sent to Fort Leavenworth, Kansas for final pay and discharge on October 30th, 1865.

The following is a quote from the Report of the Adjutant General of the State of Kansas, 1861-65.

"Upon referring to the reports of the campaign and battles in which this regiment was engaged, it will be evident to the reader that they neither shrank from any duty nor avoided any peril. On the contrary, it will ever be a source of gratification to the Colonel commanding to have been connected with a regiment that performed its full share of duty, and offered up, in defense of the liberties of the nation, its full share of patriotic lives, laid upon the alter of freedom for the benefit of the

present and future generations, again reunited and cemented with the blood of patriots, never to be dismembered by traitor without or foes within.

"Citizenship in a free country amply rewards the war-worn soldier, who hails with joy the advent of peace, and turns with alacrity from the 'pomp and circumstance of glorious war,' once more to engage in those more congenial pursuits incident to a time of tranquillity and peace."

C. K. Holliday
Adjutant General

THE END

OF THE BEGINNING

OTHER BOOKS BY DALE E. VAUGHN

"Buyin' the Farm"

In 1861, seventeen-year-old J.T. Morris wants his parents and himself out of the coal mines of Virginia and on to a farm in Kansas Territory, but a Pony Express conspiracy and the Civil War put danger in his way.

"His Way"

Conversations with Jesus; not bringing Him down to our level but into our level. Discovering how much fun He is to visit with and to learn with when dealing with our daily lives. What a Guy — What a God!

———— ***Coming Soon*** ————

"Black Jack — '56"

In June of 1856 northern and southern militia face off in Kansas for a three-hour fight that could be considered the real beginning of the American Civil War and showing that the fight for freedom, for many, goes back hundreds of years.

"Big Boy — Little Boy"

J. T. Morris returns to Virginia to get his family, only to find his old home deserted and a young nephew waiting for him. The Civil War has taken its toll and drags J.T. deeper into dangerous circumstances in a war that he claims "is not my fight."

"Whatever It Takes!"
The Second Step

Elias Mothers sets out in the final months of the Civil War to find his little brother Cheat. Elias discovers that his fight did little to change the way his people are treated and that heroes seem to run in the Mothers family.

Below is an excerpt from "***His Way,***" a book covering a number of conversations I have had with my friend and companion **Jesus.**

He drops around to my office quite often and we have a great time visiting and discussing many things. He is lots of fun, sometimes quite a tease, loves to laugh, always ready to listen and is a real comfort when it is needed. Believe me, He's quite a Guy.

Me, Too!

We had been sitting quietly, each with our own thoughts. It is such a joy to even be able to just sit with Him. His presence seemed to have such a comforting effect.

My thoughts were running over the events of the day and seemed to lock in on a very moving experience I had early that morning. I had been exercising, and while on the treadmill I was watching a movie whose story touched me deeply.

"I was watching ***'Gettysburg,'*** this morning," I said. "It was so real, I felt as though I was really there."

His warm, dark eyes met mine with a sadness I had never seen. "I was there," he said softly.

I stuttered, "It … it … made me cry."

"Me, too!"

"*Black Jack '56*"

by Dale E. Vaughn

In June of 1856, close to a small village near the Kansas-Missouri border, a northern abolitionist militia and a southern pro-slavery militia squared off for a three-hour battle that many consider the real beginning of that terrible conflict that became known as the American Civil War.

The free-state town of Lawrence, Kansas had been burned for the first of what would be three times, people had been killed and thousands of dollars of property had been destroyed.

People of all races and religious beliefs were ready to do whatever would be required to ensure that slavery would not contaminate their new homeland and that they would be allowed to live in peace and follow the dictates of their conscience concerning the freedom of any and all who settled the new Kansas Territory.

To some, that fight had been going on for hundreds of years, and they were determined to establish their home once and for all.

Next in the Civil War era novels by Dale E. Vaughn — available soon.

"Buyin' the Farm"

by Dale E. Vaughn

In 1861, seventeen-year-old J.T. Morris was working alongside his father in the coal mines of what would soon be West Virginia. JT, as he was called, dreamed of moving his mother, father and two sisters to a better life somewhere away from the mines and the impending war.

Having heard of the free and fertile lands of Kansas, troubling circumstances cause him to leave home a little sooner than he had planned and make his way west to hopefully realize his dream.

A conspiracy involving the Pony Express and the warring factions of "Bloody Kansas" cause JT to become involved in more than just finding a farm and new home.

Pressed into temporary service by the Union Army, getting shot at and finding himself in a dark Arkansas cave looking into the barrel of a pistol held by his would-be assassin, JT is certain that his time has finally come to ***"buy the farm."***

Another in the Civil War era novels by Dale E. Vaughn – available soon.